Star
Bridge

Book 1 of the Chatterre Trilogy

Copyright 2014 Jeanne Foguth

Acknowledgements

Many thanks to my faithful beta readers, without whom my work would have 'rogue commas' and 'renegade spelling', not to mention strange formatting anomalies. Thank you, Kensleigh, Robin, Paul, Kaj, and Debbie, I don't know what I would do without you grammar-nazis.

Thank you also to Kiara Graham for her prowess with digital design.

~o~

Cataloging in Publication Data is on file with the Library of Congress.

Books by Jeanne Foguth

Kazza's Chatterre Trilogy (Sci-Fantasy):

Star Bridge

Thunder Moon

Fire Island

Xander's Sea Purrtector Chronicles (Fantasy):

Latitudes & Catitudes

The Red Claw

Purr-a-noia

The Vi-Purrs (coming in Spring of 2016)

Contemporary Suspense/Romance:

Deadly Rumors

Fatal Attractions

Passion's Fire

*C*hapter One

Larwin dreamed of sun-drenched meadows bending in the breeze around a glistening pond. He removed his spacesuit and walked barefoot to the water's edge. Heart pounding with anticipation at the unheard of luxury of immersion in water, he paused on the shore. As he raised his foot to step into the pond, squeals of twisting metal jerked him awake. Horns shrieked. Messages screamed from the every corner of his space-fighter.

DANGER HULL BREACH

WARNING

EXCEEDING HULL SPEED LIMITATIONS

LIFE SUPPORT SYSTEMS FAILING

Larwin shook free of the cloying remnants of his dream. "What in Radzuk did you do to my ship?"

"Debris damaged the starboard thruster," GEA-4 said.

He grabbed the gyrating command-stick and re-centered it. Then, he carefully counted off the seconds. "A-thousand-1, a-thousand-2, a-thousand-3,-" A matte-black empty space in the center of his viewscreen and GEA-4's snow-white reflection were the only fixed things in the wildly whirling cockpit. Moment by moment the blackness grew in size. *I'm going to crash on whatever that is.* "A-thousand-4, a-thousand-5, a-thousand-6,-" Every fiber in his body wanted to do something, now, to bring the ship out of its spin, but the only way to recover from this type of situation took patience. "A-thousand-7, a-thousand-8, a-thousand-9,-" The circular dome of Larwin's environmental uniform fogged. Sweat burned his eyes. The space-fighter's roll began to stabilize, but the rock-solid blackness centered before him now took up more than half the viewscreen.

"Colonel Atano, you are on a collision course with a planetoid." GEA-4's voice sounded sensuous as a wet dream. "Alter course to trajectory Delta-one." He glanced to his right. Her silver-clad. petite, curvy body looked lush, where her regulation jumpsuit covered it, but her stark white synthetic epidermis looked dead. Obviously the android's designers either had been dealing with a cost issue when they had failed to add color to the plastoid covering or they had liked white. He shook his head and turned his attention back to the viewscreen. GEA'4's eerie silver eyes seemed to stare at him as her shoulder-length hair brushed back and forth across her silver-clad shoulders.

A-thousand-10, a-thousand-11, a-thousand-12. "What do you think I'm trying to do?" Larwin said through gritted teeth. He continued to count silently. At a-thousand-19, he eased back the pressure. Though the control stick moved freely, the Pterois Volitan continued to rocket toward the black orb. *If he knew what the damned prototype had done, perhaps he could correct it.* "What happened to my ship?"

"When The Shimmel exploded, debris damaged the starboard thruster."

Shimmel? His hands clenched inside his thick, black gloves at the mention of the high commander's ship being anywhere near the quadrant. Everyone knew The Shimmel had been moored in the Baleen Maintenance Facility for repairs after the pounding it had taken during the Frieberg Revolt. "Of all the infernal, malfunctioning, stupid," Larwin muttered. "If I survive I'll vaporize your designer. He or she should have spent less time on your voice and more on your prudence program."

Larwin raised a fist and looked for something to hit, but the android looked too much like a woman. Worse, all the gray surfaces within reach were covered with delicate bubble-ports, LEDs and readout boards. He had enough trouble; giving in to anger would only make his situation worse.

Assuming that anything could make it more serious.

The android's competency encoding should have had priority over the mold-makers and speech programmers.

He gripped the command-stick in a strangle-hold, wishing he'd never trusted the programmers. Wishing he could throttle them. Wishing he'd never succumbed to sleep.

"Colonel Atano, your course alteration was inadequate. Collision will occur in five point three six minutes. Five point three five minutes. Five-"

"Shut up!"

He moved the command-stick to the left. Nothing happened.

Larwin pressed the starboard thruster's activator. Nothing.

He punched it a second time. Still no response.

He hit the port thruster. An ominous rumbling sent a chill down his spine. Then the circuit light for hull pressure burst in a tiny red spurt.

The space fighter tilted left. Not good. Then, it slowly rotated around, as it dove toward the planetoid. He blinked sweat out of his eyes. Instead of featureless blackness, the viewscreen now showed jagged black mountainous ridges and uneven plains.

His suit's air supply smelled like bile.

GEA-4 ticked off seconds until impact.

Larwin turned and glared at the malfunctioning piece of scrap metal. "Some Anthropoid-Guide you are. Experimental version four be damned. If you're the latest and greatest, I'd hate to have tested your predecessors."

"...Four point zero six minutes. Four..."

The starboard thruster's red light LED burst sending tiny red shards across the control panel. The oxygen sensor's LED blew. Then like miniature fireworks discharging at the climax of a light show, the entire array erupted. Within a heartbeat, the interior filled with plastoid splinters.

At least the cockpit's ominous crimson glow had plunged into darkness. Though black didn't look much more promising than red.

"...Four point zero minutes. Three..."

Though the softness of GEA-4's voice could barely be discerned over the din of the warning sirens and the wailing of Pterois Volitan's overstressed hull, the G-series' sultry tones were all Larwin heard as pressure and blackness encompassed him. He'd never imagined dying while listening to the android count off the last hundredths of a minute to his existence.

Larwin quit fighting the inevitable. Closing his eyes, Larwin forced himself to think of his limited future. Then, he dedicated his essence to the Creator. Next, he petitioned Kues, the God of War, for a quick, painless death and an honorable reception. If Larwin had been telepathic, like his mother, he would have sent a message to her, but he wasn't, so he couldn't.

"...Point zero three minutes..."

At least he'd died on duty.

"...Point zero two minutes..."

The hull sounded like madrox claws were ripping it asunder.

"...Point zero one minutes..."

Larwin sensed a sudden decompression and knew he'd never see a meadow or swim in a lake.

Then the ship tilted sharply to port. He hung by his flight-harness and waited for the hull to collapse. Death waited a moment before the Pterois Volitan imploded.

Black oblivion engulfed him.

~0~

Nimri tilted her head back and studied the harsh face of Sacred Mountain. Her marrow-deep sense of foreboding intensified. No one in her lifetime had ever returned from the holy journey.

As the sun dipped toward the treetops, a balmy breeze fanned the perspiration from her forehead. Oblivious to the mingled scents of mint, pine and rich humus, Nimri weighed the consequences of predestination. She shook her head at the thought of the impossible task she'd been dealt. Then, rubbing the aching muscles at the back of her neck, she gazed around her high plateau garden, pausing over each patch of medicinal plants.

This may be my last look.

She knelt among the foliage, burdened by the worry that she didn't have the courage to keep the promise she'd given her great-grandfather, Rolf. Burdened by the anxiety that even if she tried, she'd fail to carry his ashes to the holy grove at Sacred Mountain's peak. Burdened by the knowledge that her best had never been good enough for Rolf while he lived and it wouldn't be good enough now.

Yet, she dare not disobey for fear he would rise as a vengeful spirit and seek retribution for the broken oath.

Since she had no mystic power, which would make it possible for her to fulfill her destiny, death by avenging spirit might be the best alternative.

She collapsed onto the fragrant ground-cover. If only she had never been born – at least not born a Tramontain, the last Tramontain in the ancient line, which made it impossible for her to avoid her hereditary duty. She sighed. How could she serve and protect her Tribe, when she couldn't even protect herself?

Nimri tried to swallow the knot of misery in her throat.

The lump didn't budge.

A pine-bough waved across the face of the sun. Even the plants, which had been her one certainty, were mocking her. She closed her eyes.

The combination funeral and induction ceremony would begin at sunset. She wished she could hold the sun in the sky, as her great-grandfather had. Her heart thudded frantically against her ribs.

She knew the healing powers of plants, but no one really valued the small bit of knowledge she had. Worse, those that remembered her great-aunt Violet, still looked at her feeble attempts to cure and asked when she would learn to myst-mend.

Even if she had learned the lost art, with her great-grandfather gone, it wouldn't be enough to save her Tribe.

Tears burned her closed eyelids. The pain of failure wracked her body. Nimri rolled into a fetal position and shuddered.

Surely, she would die before dusk.

But if she did, she doomed her Tribe.

If she didn't, they were still doomed.

Tears scalded wet trails down her cheeks and saturated the aromatic thyme.

Wind gusted against her back. Her white ceremonial robe whipped her shins like a lash. The current of air also brought distant voices.

"What are we going to do without Rolf?" a high-pitched voice asked.

If she died, now, she would only be the first of many. And she would pass on without even trying. Nimri summoned her waning strength and rose to her knees. She feebly wiped away her tears, but she couldn't rub out the throbbing pain in her chest. She crawled to a foxglove plant, plucked a leaf, and laid back down as she chewed it. Slowly, the spasms subsided.

No one else knew how to make the medicines the Tribe needed. If she died, that meager bit of knowledge would be lost.

Heart steadier, Nimri rolled onto her back and squinted past the treetops. The gloom deepened. Still, the rugged face of Sacred Mountain seemed to mock her. What were they going to do without her great-grandfather?

"Who will protect us?" A child's distant voice whined, as if reading her thoughts.

"N-ri," a woman's wind-buffeted voice answered.

Nimri's heart gave a panicked lurch. She gasped and clutched her chest. If only she could protect them. "Auuuuuuughhhhhhhhhh!" Her high-pitched keening startled birds from the surrounding trees.

"How come we need a–a–a whatever?" the child whined.

"A Keeper of the Peace," a deep voice said.

Searing pain exploded in Nimri's gut. She rolled over, landing face-first in mother-of-thyme.

"Old Rolf never even come down ta' the village, how come he was so important?"

"Seen or not, the Lost knew Rolf was watching." The bass voice sounded confident.

"For now they wait until they find out if the rumors of his illness are true." Zurgon's contralto tones were unmistakable. "Once they discover he's dead, they will attack."

"Isn't Cartwright as powerful as Rolf?" a soprano asked.

"He's stronger," a tenor said. "I don't understand why Cartwright hasn't given the Lost his blessing before now. I've been prepared for an attack since Rolf became ill."

The child wailed.

Nimri gagged.

"Don't listen to Talon," said Pearl's unmistakable singsong voice. "Fighting isn't always the way. Cartwright knows that, just as our peacekeepers always have."

"Before he left this realm, Rolf assured me that Nimri would be a worthy Keeper of the Peace," Zurgon said.

"But how can she carry the Staff of Protection and be our healer, too?" Pearl asked.

Pain wrapped Nimri in suffocating coils of knowledge that she could not kill to save them any more than she could myst-mend.

"No woman will be able to protect us from the Lost," Talon said. "Since Rolf's illness they've tested our defenses. They found my farm invincible, but what about the soft-muscled merchants? What will happen when they're tested?"

"There have only been petty paybacks when the sellers bartered defective merchandise. No one has been hurt." Nimri recognized Tansy's hesitant voice. "Some of the Lost are nice."

Talon's guffaw sounded disparaging.

The breeze died and with it, the conversation, but Nimri could still imagine shy Tansy cowering under Talon's condescending look.

"Rolf assured me Nimri would be a worthy Keeper of the Peace." She shivered at the lie. How could she protect her Tribe, when she couldn't even protect herself?

At least she could die trying to keep her vow. Nimri pushed herself upright and glared at Sacred Mountain's imposing granite face.

If she kept the vow she'd made to her great-grandfather, she had to climb that rock. Head tilted back so far that her long dark braid nearly hit the grass; Nimri stared upward at the impossibly high, smooth rock face which she had promised to climb. Bile rose in her throat. Tomorrow she would die. Tears blurred her vision.

"Rolf assured me Nimri would be a worthy Keeper of the Peace." Why had her great-grandfather demanded the vow? To test her? If by some unexpected fate, she passed the test, would she be worthy to hold the Staff of Protection? The twisted black staff, which focused power, seemed impossibly slick to hold, but Bryta, who had no more myst power than a frog, picked it up with ease.

If she failed, would death come quickly?

Did it matter?

Nimri struggled to her feet and squared her shoulders.

Behind her, a door groaned open and soft footfalls padded across the garden path. Moments later Kazza, her feline companion, rubbed against her thigh, nearly knocking her over. Nimri placed her palm on the back of his neck to steady herself. Energy seeped into her. She tickled the base of Kazza's tufted ear and the inner pain receded further.

Kazza purred deep within his massive six-hundred-pound body.

Nimri breathed in through her nose, then out through her mouth as she stroked Kazza's powerful gold, black, and white striped flanks. His tail wrapped around her waist in a companionable caress.

"You left the door open." Bryta's accusation carried across the garden.

Kazza snorted. Nimri tickled his ribs, as she turned away from the sheer rock to look at the only home she could remember. The spiral-shaped house twisted around and around the sequoia as if part of the tree.

"You could learn to close doors if you wanted to," Bryta taunted the feline from the kitchen window.

Kazza's ears flattened and his tail slapped Nimri's leg.

Bryta slammed the kitchen door, which was at the base of the series of chambers connected by stairs that spiraled upward around the massive trunk of the millennium-old sequoia at the garden's center.

Nimri gave Kazza a final caress, then trod over the dragon-grass covered path to her surrogate mother.

"They're coming." Nimri swung her knee-length black braid back over her shoulder. Bryta looked at her, as if she were a mud-covered two-year-old. Nimri looked down; green stains splotched her robe.

"More than the high council?" Bryta's pudgy hands flicked away a leaf. She looked ready to drag her into the kitchen for a bath, but the wind brought more voices. "You must learn to rectify your appearance." Bryta shook her head, at the untidiness, then touched her own silvery halo of braid as if to assure herself that at least she looked presentable. "With position comes responsibility. Not grass stains."

Nimri cocked an ear to the wind. "I hear a child's voice."

"Good." Bryta looked satisfied. "By rights, the entire Tribe should attend." She tugged at her best tunic to get it to hang just right over her wide-legged trousers.

"What will we do with so many?" Nimri looked from Bryta to her beloved garden and swallowed hard.

"Nothing. They come to escort a great man into the mystic realm, and to see you take up his staff. They did not climb up to the bluff for dinner." Bryta chucked Nimri under the chin. "Don't worry child, they'll stay by the pyre, no one will so much as sniff your basil."

Nimri looked down at her plump companion. Bryta had been her great-grandfather's housekeeper for half a century before his granddaughter's half-dead orphan had come to live with them. Perhaps Bryta had learned his mind-skills and would be better suited to replace Rolf. At least she had been able to place the staff on the pyre without it slithering out of her hands.

Bryta gave Nimri's hand a motherly pat. "They'll never get another chance to attend the last rites of a man of Rolf's standing. It'll be something they can tell their grandchildren."

As if any of them would live to see that day. Would she even be able to pick up the staff, which seemed impossibly slippery in her hands?

"No one else in our 1064-year history produced such a flood." Bryta launched into her favorite story. Nimri gritted her teeth to hold back her scream of despair. "Never before, nor since, has the river been so fierce and deadly. Nor a storm so wild." Bryta's face flushed with pleasure at the memory. She placed her fists on her ample hips and raised her triple chin, in imitation of Rolf's arrogant stance.

"I wish I could have seen Rolf raise the staff and shout out across the water," Bryta said, then she began the familiar quote, "'Any Lost who sets foot on the land of the Chosen with evil intentions will call yet another storm against their land! Next time, I will spare no one!" Bryta's eyes flashed as she copied Rolf's arrogant tones and gestures.

Nimri put her hand to her mouth in a vain attempt to hold back a laugh.

Bryta glared at her, then lapsing into her own persona, she fanned her face and relaxed her spine. "To think Pearl actually witnessed the great event." Her wistful tone stifled Nimri's mirth.

"At least you got the honor of cleaning the mud off his moccasins."

"There was that." Bryta raised her chin. "I still have it, too. All Pearl has is the memory." Her jowls jiggled with pride.

Nimri felt another bout of senseless laughter threatening. To distract herself, she grabbed a torch. "We need to get down to the funeral pyre." Nimri snapped a branch off the sprawling rosemary bush, which an ancestor had planted beside the kitchen door to bless the dwelling and protect its inhabitants. She sniffed its piney scent.

Bryta tipped her torch toward Nimri, an expectant expression on her face. Nimri took a deep, cleansing breath and prayed that for once she could work the myst-power. She snapped her fingers. A pale yellow glow ignited on the torch's tip. It flared for a brief moment, and then fizzled into a puny wisp of smoke. 'Rolf assured me Nimri would be a worthy Keeper of the Peace.' If her great-grandfather had told Zurgon the truth, she could do this. She snapped her fingers, again. This time, the flame caught and held.

Bryta smiled as the torches blazed. Head and flame high, she assumed the ceremonial gait and paced toward the steep trail, which led into the gorge. Step-step-pause, step-step-pause. Despite her age and portly build, Bryta embodied the dignity of the solemn occasion.

Nimri watched Bryta's proud posture descend over the lip of the cliff, and then looked at the secluded lodge where she'd been raised. She turned and gazed up at Sacred Mountain's peak. A huge black shadow shrouded the summit. Did the harsh, barren rock truly conceal the magic magenta of the balata grove, or were the trees merely another story only meant to entertain children? Nimri shivered.

Abruptly, the last rays of the setting sun bathed the harsh rock in blood red. Nimri gasped and fled toward the gorge trail. When she caught up with Bryta, Nimri skidded to a halt. The older woman appeared too focused on the coming ceremony to notice. Nimri adapted her longer legs to the tedious ceremonial gait. They slowly approached the waterfall, which drummed the same beat. When they came to the place where she usually dived over the precipice into deep, rock-free water, Nimri missed her step.

If she couldn't even walk to the ceremony, how could anyone expect her to shield them?

Despite her doubts, they arrived at the pyre without major incident. They turned their backs to the drumming waterfall and looked silently at Rolf. His frail hands clutched the twisted wood of the black Staff of Protection and his best robe flowed in a violet cascade over the high wooden platform, which looked like a ceremonial bed. Her great-grandfather looked more relaxed than he had in years. If she hadn't known the fabric concealed the firewood beneath the pyre, and if she hadn't confirmed his death a dozen times, she would expect his eyes to open.

If only he could arise!

Bryta jabbed her elbow into Nimri's thigh. With dignity, they turned to face the head of the valley trail. Within moments, Zurgon appeared at the head of the now-silent column. Dressed in his crimson chief's robe, and chin as high as Bryta's, he led the procession into the clearing. Slowly, they circled the ceremonial pyre three times, then shoving Bryta aside, Zurgon stepped to Nimri's left.

Nimri's jaws clenched at the subtle insult. Zurgon had always stood on Rolf's right, granting him highest Tribal status. Other Council members, attired in their flowing rainbow hues, took their places in order of rank on her right. Her spine straightened at their show of support. Flame, clad in her white baker's smock, defied tradition and slid between Nimri and Talon.

Pearl failed in her attempt to insinuate herself between Bryta and her husband. Lips thin, she settled for stepping on Bryta's foot as she took the place on Bryta's other side.

The corner of Bryta's lips twitched as she straightened her spine.

Meanwhile, the council members gave Flame furious looks, but she ignored them. Beneath the folds of her white healer's robe, Nimri touched her best friend's hand in silent thanks.

Masses of tribe members continued filing into the clearing, until every inch of land filled with farmers, millers, carpenters, weavers, blacksmiths and potters. The stragglers were forced to wade into the pond.

Torches held high, they silently watched the setting sun. As the last ray of sunlight disappeared, Zurgon took a small step forward. "We come to pay our last respects to Rolf Tramontain," he said in his most sonorous voice. The greatest Peacekeeper in the thousand-year dynasty." He stepped back in line.

"Rolf's revenge was wonderful," Pearl said to the sliver of dark sky outside the deep cleft. "When he pitted the natural forces of Chatterre against the Lost, he gave us one hundred and sixty-seven moons of harmony."

Her great-grandfather's vengeance for her parents' death had started with angry black clouds, which had formed at Rolf's command; then fire had streaked down and scorched the Lost's boats; balls of ice, big as cantaloupes had then pummeled the enemy's land. Nimri tried to hide her revulsion.

"Rolf understood the laws of Chatterre: the cycle of the seasons; the movement of the stars; the patterns within the weather," Bryta said. "He knew things he should never know, sometimes years before they occurred. He was a worthy Keeper."

"Rolf was a good and honorable man," Talon said.

The soft crackling of the torches grew loud in the ensuing silence. Nimri's skin crawled with the knowledge that they expected her to say something worthy, but she couldn't think of anything to say. A drop of sweat trickled down her spine. Then another drop fell and another, until it felt like the waterfall spattering her.

When the stillness nearly became unbearable, Pearl started the long low-pitched "Hummm." One by one, the others joined in. Soon, the sound surged, bass to high soprano, growing, expanding and building until it became strong enough to transport Rolf's myst to the Otherworld.

Step-step-pause the Tribal Council began pacing around the pyre. One by one, they thrust their torches into the kindling. The flames licked at the wood and leaped up the violet robe.

Without warning, a whoosh of flame shot skyward like lightening. It cast light and shadow across the faces and consumed the air.

"Oooohhh!" a hundred voices exclaimed. Only Pearl continued

toning, her rich alto consecrating the ascending myst-power.

As the rest of the Tribe again added their voices, the blaze consumed Rolf's body.

Nimri thought she saw the black staff aflame. If it were consumed, her fate would be averted. Her throat felt suddenly dry at the unexpected possibility of reprieve. Afraid to stare, she focused on the steps and tones of the all-night ceremony.

As the first ray of dawn appeared over the lips of the cleft, the glistening black staff lay unharmed atop a smoldering mound of ash.

Zurgon's pitch lifted, as he changed tune to the induction ceremony. The Tribe joined in with the uplifting tone. When the sound peaked, everyone looked toward her. Nimri swallowed, then leaned forward and picked up the cool, slick staff. It tried to slip from her grasp; she grabbed it with both hands and tried to hold onto the impossible stick, which looked like solid wood, but felt slick as taffy and just as flexible. Satisfied that she'd accepted her duty, the Tribe turned, as one. Left right kick, right-left-kick, all except Flame and Bryta moved toward the mouth of the valley trail.

Quark trailed at the end of the column; as he passed them, the potter paused. "I'm not good at words," he told Nimri. "But, I made Rolf this pot. I hope you find it worthy." He pressed a wheat-colored crock decorated with the Tramontain hawk into her hands, and then hurried after the Tribe. Nimri struggled to hold it and the untrustworthy staff.

With a disdainful snort, Bryta grabbed the staff of protection, wrapped it in her apron and marched back up to the house. Nimri bit her lower lip, knelt and fought back tears of shame, while she scooped ash into the crock.

"Where will you release his essence?" Flame asked, as if she hadn't just witnessed anything significant."I gave my word." Nimri looked up at the high sun-bathed peak. In the golden light, it looked magical and deadly. She must have been under a spell when she'd given her grandfather the promise. "I will scatter his ashes at the Guardian's feet."

Flame gasped. "But no one has ever returned."

Nimri swallowed, but the lump of despair in her throat refused to budge. "I know."

Chapter Two

"You would keep your word to a dead man?" Flame hissed. "A man who never had a kind word for you?" Flame glared at her. Nimri shrugged. "You'd deny your tribe protection?" Hearing the mixed shock and fear in her best friend's voice, Nimri looked toward Bryta and admired the ease with which she carried the staff. "What if the balata is only a myth?" Flame whispered expressing the doubts they'd often shared. They both looked up at Sacred Mountain's cloud-shrouded peak.

"The Chosen have Talon, Zurgon and the entire council. My great-grandfather only has me." Even if she stayed, Nimri knew she could never protect the ones who were relying on her, at least when she was gone, her tribe would no longer need to live with the delusion that she could help them. Everyone, except her, could pick up the staff of protection, but only the staff's human half could complete the magical bond. And she wasn't that person. Nimri gazed at the clouds. At least this way she would die with honor. Perhaps that's what Rolf had intended when he demanded her word.

"Talon." Flame snorted. "Hot air won't save us from Thunder Cartwright." Flame had despised Talon's loud bluster since they were toddlers.

Nimri sighed and asked, "Has anyone ever seen Cartwright?" Flame stared at her, so Nimri pushed harder at the thought she had never dare utter while Rolf lived, "Perhaps it's just a name the Lost use to terrify us with. Like the evil Yetis he supposedly lives with."

Flame shook her head and shuddered. "I know in my bones that he's real."

Wrong answer. "I must go and prepare myself." To die. Nimri gave Flame a hug. Her best friend squeezed her back, unwilling to let her go; as if she understood this might be the last time they saw each other. Tears flooded her eyes. Flame turned and fled down the valley trail.

Eyes damp, Nimri ran up the steep path to her garden. Greens seemed more vibrant and scents more intoxicating through the layer of unshed tears. Did others experience such heightened consciousness as they approached their death walk?

She sped into the house, dashed up the seven flights of curving stairs to her room and threw her flowing robe of office on her bed. Better to leave it for Bryta to immortalize than to catch her foot on its hem and fall to her death. She changed into well-worn everyday tunic and pants. The browns were faded, and there were grass stains on the knees, but they were her most comfortable clothes and after she fell, the spots she had gained while tending her garden would seem minor.

Before Nimri could lose her resolve, she headed for the old, debris-covered footpath, which her great-grandfather had sworn led to the sacred grove.

By late afternoon, Nimri hugged Sacred Mountain's treacherous granite face; she gritted her teeth and inched her moccasin-clad foot toward the next toehold on the squirrel-thin trail. Then, she dug her bleeding fingertips into the next crack and imagined the funeral crock within her backpack growing heavy with reminders of her inadequacy.

As she forced her toes into the niche and shifted her weight, a rock beneath her foot moved. She gasped. It stabilized for a moment, then dropped away. Nimri pitched sideways. Her body smacked a jagged outcropping.

Her tunic snagged.

Beneath her fingers, dirt cascaded from the widening crack. Gravity seized her with invisible tentacles and she slid toward the abyss to the chorus of ripping cloth.

Nimri screamed.

A blood coated pebble dislodged and plummeted into the chasm. A fist-sized stone broke free, hit her foot and then dove out of sight.

Waves of agony shuddered up her leg.

Desperate, blood-slick fingers scratched at the crack.

Tasting copper and blinking away tears, she pulled herself toward the safety of a slender ledge. Her vision tunneled until the hand-wide jut of rock became the only thing in her existence.

As if from a great distance, Nimri heard an odd shrill tone. It grew in shrillness and volume. The short hairs on the back of her neck quivered in response. The screeching tone gained intensity, came closer until it surrounded her.

Nimri clasped the mountain. Teeth biting her lower lip, she followed Rolf's most basic lesson and willed the rock to stabilize.

Suddenly, Kazza dashed up the emaciated lip of a path and leaped over her. Nimri screamed and closed her eyes, so she wouldn't watch him plummet to his death. He landed with a soft thud. Her scream echoed from rock to rock, but no feline cry or sounds of a fall came. She opened one eye.

Kazza sat atop a pile of loose rubble, which appeared undisturbed. A breeze ruffled the thick fur on his back. He glanced back at her, his amber eyes aglow with intelligence and mirth. The feline looked like he was having the time of his life and didn't have a clue how close he'd come to death.

When the shrill echoes of her scream subsided, Nimri raised her head and peered beyond her perch. Ahead, the trail widened, and then disappeared into a wall of haze. Though most of the mist appeared solid white, one spot shimmered magenta.

The sacred balata grove.

It had to be.

It wasn't a myth.

Elation soared through her.

Nimri scrambled toward the shrouding mist. As it enveloped her, everything chilled into a clinging white emptiness so thick that she couldn't see the end of her black braid or where the trail ended and the precipice began.

~0~

Larwin had envisioned death in victorious battle, not drifting in darkness. Yet, as he lay in the black oblivion, he accepted that his childhood metaphysics instructor had been wrong when he'd spoken of death as a bright white light place filled with wonders for warriors who had died in honorable battle.

Wrong.

Death equaled the absence of light and sound.

It was emptiness.

Blackness.

Soundlessness.

Nothingness.

Everything was gone except the stench of bile and the clamminess of his environmental suit.

Apparently, dying while testing the protocols for a new line of pilot androids and getting killed for his efforts didn't constitute an honorable death.

"All systems have malfunctioned." The android's sensual timbre conflicted with the cool oblivion.

How had the defective prototype passed into the humanoid beyond? His teeth ground as his hands searched for the restraint's release. He paused when his gloved fingers brushed the familiar controls. So, he wasn't dead. Yet. "What happened?"

"The course was not altered." GEA-4 matter-of-factly stated the obvious. Blood thundered in his ears, but Larwin willed himself to relax. "The Pterois Volitan collided with the planetoid."

"I meant, why am I still alive?"

"Dust covering the planetoid cushioned the collision, then flipped the ship upside down."

"Great," he said through clenched teeth. Planetoids were dead rock with nothing to sustain life—no water, no air, no food. Now he faced GEA-4 talking him into oblivion or worse.

Dehydration.

Asphyxiation.

Starvation.

Unless..."Were you able to transmit our coordinates after the stabilizer failed?"

"Communications were lost when the APU module ruptured," she said.

"Great time to tell me we lost auxiliary power." He found the release for the safety restraints and pulled. Nothing happened. Big surprise, with his weight suspended against the harness. Odd that the dead world retained a gravitational effect, when there was no star for it to revolve around. "How long before we crashed?"

"Seven point eight three minutes."

Like that pinpointed the location. "I was asleep then." So much had happened in such a short time. "Where was the ship located? General terms, not coordinates."

"Near the Guy-N Sector Asteroid Field."

Great, that put him at least one zone off course and smack dab in the middle of the forbidden zone. No one in his troop would risk demotion to save him. About the only traffic through Guy-N Sector were Kalamaran fuel freighters. Guerreterre's high fuel consumption should rate a favor. "Is the homing beacon still functional?" Was another ship close enough for it to matter?

"The beacon activated upon impact."

Finally, something positive. Not much, due to its short-range signal and the odds against a freighter assisting a stranded Guerreterre Shadow Warrior, but something, no matter how minuscule was better than nothing.

Suddenly, the control panel lit up with an eerie pale green glow. "What is that?"

"An ion turbulence is passing nearby." The light slowly faded. "It gave the ship a negative charge and shorted out the beacon."

"Wonderful." Was Kues testing him? "The hull is ruptured. My oxygen supply is limited. And now, we're near an atomic storm." There had to be a way to overcome these odds. "You might be able to survive, but if the radiation comes closer, I can't. Any suggestions?"

"Prior to impact, I observed a shelter point-eight-two nautical miles from this site."

He strained to disengage the restraint's coupling. "Would this shelter protect us from ionization?"

"Probabilities are high in its favor." GEA-4's calm, sensual tone assured him.

"Why didn't you say so before?" Suddenly the restraint's latch clicked. He yanked the harness aside. Gravity pitched him to the ceiling with a bone-wrenching thud. Larwin got to his feet, slipping many times before he stood on the rounded surface. "Let's run for it." He caught an emergency grip and, again, wondered why a charred planetoid would have gravity. Furthermore, how was he going to get out of the mess the worthless machine had put him in?

Still, he'd trained for worse.

Larwin crammed emergency gear inside his haversack. Next, he grabbed the largest box of rations he could find. "Can you get the hatch open?"

"I will try." The grinding sound of metal against metal accompanied her words, followed by a muffled bang.

Something streamed into the cockpit. Soot! Larwin thrust two boxes of emergency supplies at GEA-4. "Carry these to the shelter."

She gave him an abrupt nod, tossed the heavy boxes out the opening, and then pitched out his haversack. Larwin resented her strength, grace, and dexterity as she exited with the ease of a first-rate gymnast.

When Larwin emerged from the wreck, he turned on his light projector and swiveled to look at his ship, but suspended dust shrouding the crash site defied all his efforts to see more than a meter. Except for GEA-4 and a few panels of the Pterois Volitan, his world became shades of black. The site conjured up images of doom. He shook his head at the unwanted thought. "Perhaps it was the trace of sulfur in my canned oxygen," he muttered.

Larwin switched off his useless light-projector and ignored the cold knot in his gut. Next, he adjusted his oxygen mixture to the lowest percentage he could endure, yet sustain life. Then, he settled his bag on his back and refused to speculate how long his supplies would last or how far away rescuers were. Last, he turned his back on the crash-site and followed the only distinguishable thing in his matte-black world: GEA-4. Her alabaster form headed away from him at a brisk pace. Her behavior denoted a software fault. He wondered why he hadn't noticed her application discrepancies earlier.

Crossing the shifting black particles, Larwin wished he possessed the dexterity of an android. Though half his size, the android's weight doubled his and she had ten times his strength. Even more annoying, she could exist on cosmic energy. Larwin stumbled through the shifting dust, and wished he didn't need exotic things like food, water and air.

When they emerged from the dust cloud, the harsh black landscape looked no better than the shroud. If only he hadn't needed sleep. That human failing had given GEA-4 the opportunity to kill him. So what if he still lived? It was temporary. Even if the short-range distress beacon had survived ionization and someone traced him to this remote dust heap, survival seemed doubtful. Any structure, which shielded him from ionization, would also conceal his personal-locator.

Worse, he didn't have enough air to survive until help arrived.

Larwin needed a miracle.

A movement to the left caught his attention. Distant, but fast approaching, came a swirling green funnel-cloud. Another ion turbulence! What kind of tribulation was this dust heap?

No wonder the high commander classified this Sector forbidden.

Larwin hurried after GEA-4's shimmering silhouette.

Several minutes later, GEA-4 abruptly stopped then revolved in a complete circle. Her pose reminded Larwin of a ballerina he'd once known. Coryphée had been petite, too. Like GEA-4, she'd moved with grace and had light coloring. Unlike GEA-4, Coryphée had blue eyes, blond hair worn in a tight twist at her nape and a brilliant mind. She'd also had a voice that sounded like shredding metal.

"My readings indicate this shelter extends several miles below surface level. We will be safer farther down." GEA-4 turned to him. Her perfectly coiffed tresses brushed her shoulders. "This structure is not natural. It and several adjacent large, geometric areas have—"

"Are you trying to say this used to be a mine of some sort?" Larwin turned on his analyzer, which verified her assessment, but the unit seemed unable to ascertain what had been extracted. Then he turned it on himself and verified what he'd expected—his head ached because of oxygen deprivation.

Though tempted to increase the mixture, he knew such an act would be suicidal.

"A mine is a possible explanation."

Larwin gritted his teeth and wondered if he had escaped ionization and walked straight into a radiation fire. "Can your scanners pick up traces of mineral deposits that indicate what was mined?"

"No, Colonel Atano, I can not."

Gazing down at his companion, Larwin didn't feel strong, manly or in control. He didn't feel like a grown man, over six and a half feet tall. The last time he'd felt this way, he'd been three years old and had left the security of home for military school.

"Have you done a self-diagnostic program on yourself since we crashed?"

"Yes, Colonel Atano, I have."

"Were any of your systems damaged?"

"No, they were not."

Would her defective programming show faults? "Calculate our safest course of action."

"We should go deeper underground to avoid the ion field."

At least she seemed consistent. Since it appeared like the best choice, he tilted his head toward the sloping path. "Lead on."

GEA-4 guided him from darkness into deeper darkness. This demon hole seemed filled with unending piles of rubble. With every step, Larwin promised himself that if he returned to Guerreterre, he would do everything in his power to stop the manufacture of android pilots.

Perspiration filled Larwin's environmental suit until sweat saturated the air filters and each breath tortured his lungs. Beads of moisture fogged his visor and made the dark tunnel appear ominous. Worse, the deeper he trudged into the bowels of the unknown planetoid, the more wreckage he needed to climb over. No sooner had the thought flashed through his conscience than Larwin tripped over an unseen obstacle and fell into a heap of debris.

He lay there for a moment, too tired to care.

"Do you need assistance?"

"No." He forced himself upright. After regaining his balance, Larwin looked for the haversack he'd dropped. His light revealed that the pile consisted of dust-covered furniture, a small, odd wheeled vehicle and a tiny humanoid face.

His heart skipped a beat.

Larwin refocused the beam and spotlighted a remarkably life-like doll. Where had it come from? Why leave it here? Had a child discarded it or had it been ripped from her hand? The doll looked back at him with a wide-eyed expression and dirty cheeks that reminded him of Tem-Aki, his younger sister, who had always played with dirt and rocks as a child and recently graduated from the geological academy. Since she'd been suited for such a dull academic future, he'd always made snide remarks. Now, as he faced death entombed by rock. Larwin's perspiration ran cold.

Radzuk, but he missed Tem-Aki and he'd never be able to tell her how proud he was to be her brother.

Larwin bent over to pick up the toy, but the moment his glove touched the hem of the doll's tattered dress, the entire figure disintegrated into a puff of powder. His breath caught in his throat. He choked down a sob.

Swallowing hard, he picked up his haversack, turned his back on the pile and followed GEA-4, slowly at first, then with an increasing urgency. Soon, the muffled thump of his footfalls matched his pounding heart. An hour later, his boots created a new, emptier tone, as if they'd entered a large subterranean chamber. Larwin's back ached, his arms felt ready to separate from his shoulders and he could barely see past the condensation in his helmet.

"GEA-4, take a break."

She stopped as abruptly as if he'd cut her power.

Larwin fanned his light ahead and squinted at more piles of rejected humanoid possessions. In the one closest to him, antique cooking pots were topped by a deflated beach ball; none of the items colors were truly identifiable through layers of black dust.

Larwin hoped the ball's owner had met a better destiny than he anticipated for himself. He peered around the chamber, piled with every sort of household goods. He frowned and then fanned his light around the cavern. Odd that he didn't see any corpses.

Why leave everyday possessions in this cursed hole?

How much time did he have left?

GEA-4 watched him, her glittering silver eyes alert and accessing his failing body. From the top of her perfectly designed head, with its heart shaped face and full lips, down to the soles of her dainty feet, GEA-4 appeared female perfection personified. And her voltage-storage capacity provided her with enough power to last for weeks.

His teeth gritted in outrage. Larwin wouldn't have felt as annoyed if he'd been walked into the ground by a male android.

Larwin put down his haversack. Spears of pain shot like shrapnel through his shoulders. With a groan, he sat on his gear and willed himself not to think about his situation.

Chapter Three

Nimri stepped from the numbingly cold mist into a fragrant thicket of magenta leaves, which swayed in an unseen breeze. She stopped. Awe filled her as she gazed at the hallowed trees. Though the trees were merely twenty or thirty feet in height, they appeared too unsubstantial to contain their purported power. Despite that, she could feel their myst-energy crackling in the air.

Tiny, fragrant flowers formed panicles of golden ginger-scented bells. Only mature plants bloomed. She frowned. Perhaps the balata were actually shrubs, instead of trees. Despite being twisted, the trunks had smooth, silvery bark with emerald dots. As the branches swayed to some unfelt wind, her fingers itched to touch the sacred twigs. Her hand moved toward a panicle of new leaves topped by purple buds, which were unfurling into lacy magenta fronds.

Legends claimed that the Ancients had planted these trees after their deliverance from Solterre, but folklore failed to tell if the plants were put here in consecration of their deliverance or if their magic had facilitated it. Looking at such tiny trees with such exotic coloring made the millennium-old legends believable.

"Well, Kazza, shall we spread Great-great-grandfather's ashes here at the edge of the grove or at the center?" Even as she asked the question, she recalled Rolf's insistence that she take his ashes all the way to The Guardians. At the time, she'd thought her great-grandfather's unheard of request sounded like a way to gain distinction or a technique to show her how unworthy her powers were to follow in his moccasins.

Kazza's long banded tail twitched, the fur on his back rippled and his great head moved from side to side as if he seriously considered her question, but when Nimri watched his eyes, she realized a magenta frond dancing in the breeze held his attention.

Something tickled the back of her neck. She shivered and swatted at thin air. "Do you feel it, too? Maybe these trees really do have some sort of magical power."

Did Guardians still watch the magic bridge that linked the stars?

Maybe she should have considered the possibility of their existence earlier, but she had not, because she had never truly expected to reach the grove, much less imagine that she might survive to keep her vow.

The Chosen's oral history went back 1,064 years, and in every tale, a Tramontain had saved the Tribe. Before that, legend told of their race living on Solterre, a world where mighty, energy-absorbing dragons devoured sun and soil until great solar flares from the dragon-infested sun incinerated the first world, causing Solterre's citizens to seek refuge anywhere they could find it.

Nimri's ancestors had initially hidden in a tunnel. Then as they realized Solterre was doomed, her ancestors had magically energized the Star Bridge's formation. Thus, her early Tramontain ancestors and all those who had sought their protection had arrived on Chatterre.

Chills raced up and down her arms. She shivered.

Her tremors grew into a nervous snigger. The sound echoed

over the rocks and mingled with the breeze. She rubbed her gooseflesh-covered arms, grateful that no one could witness her self-doubt.

Common sense told her the tales were told to entertain children, not based on reality. Star Bridges to other worlds were as likely as dragons, complex machines and life on the tiny points of light that gleamed in the night.

Nimri straightened to her full six feet and squared her slender shoulders. She feared spreading Rolf's ashes at The Guardians' feet, which legend claimed were at the heart of the balata grove. Yet she had vowed to do just that. She'd come this far, and lived. Rolf's remains would be scattered where he'd wished. Gingerly, she pushed a sacred branch aside and maneuvered through the twisted trunks.

As the branch swung back in place, a complaint issued from deep within Kazza's chest.

"Stay there. I won't be long."

His moan intensified.

Nimri adjusted her pack and stepped into the thicket.

Kazza howled.

She glanced back through the cavorting magenta lace. Her beloved giant feline paced between the grove's edge and the sheer drop off, his fur stiff with fear. His wild kin lived high in the mighty trees at the edge of the valley, and raised their offspring in dens hollowed out of the immense trunks. He'd seemed to enjoy the climb until now. Nimri shook her head at Kazza's baffling attitude change, then she resolutely turned her back on him and headed deeper into the thick, ginger-scented tangle.

The dense twigs scratched her face. A limb hit her stomach. Perspiration trickled in rivulets down her back. It felt hotter than any mountain peak should. Nimri resolutely plodded on. Ten minutes later, her face felt afire where perspiration washed the nicks. She blotted at the injuries with her torn shirt sleeve. Abruptly, she tripped over an unseen root. She fell and hit her forehead on a flat wall of rock. The temptation to smash Rolf's urn against the impenetrable wall spiraled within her. Nimri yanked her pack forward and felt inside for the crock, yet as her fingers closed over the urn's familiar form, something stopped her.

Nimri turned to her right and shouldered aside a balata bough. A large boulder obstructed her.

Where had she gotten the idea that once she reached the grove it would be easy?

As if from a great distance, she heard Kazza mewl.

Nimri felt like crying, too. Glancing back, all she could see was an impenetrable wall of vegetation.

"Re-ow-l-l-l-l-l-l-l."

"I'm all right," she called.

He made a crying sound, which he usually reserved for danger.

"Relax!" Despite her admonition, her spine prickled with anxiety and she wished she could follow her own advice.

Suddenly, the surrealistic trees ceased their movement and everything became supernaturally quiet.

It felt like someone or something watched her. Nimri spun around, but saw no one. Still, she could sense a presence. She squinted through the still foliage until her eyes watered from the strain, her parched throat constricted and her lungs burned for air.

Kazza yowled. Her sense of doom became suffocating.

Nimri concentrated on the one tangible thing she could improve; she groped for her water bottle. Just as her fingers brushed against the flask's familiar chipped neck, she spotted a pair of golden eyes staring at her.

She froze.

The lacy leaves rippled.

Now, there were two pairs or eyes

A chill shook her.

Nimri straightened her spine and returned their unblinking intensity while she felt for her dagger.

The confrontation lasted forever, or so it seemed.

Nimri noticed that between the pairs of eyes lay darkness blacker than midnight. She thought she saw the blackness pulse and grow. Her skin turned into a mass of painful gooseflesh.

Kazza howled.

She remained locked in the intense staring challenge until her eyes felt parched. The golden eyes never blinked, never turned aside. Her own eyes became dehydrated as she stared back. Yet, she feared to flicker so much as a lash, lest the darkness devour her.

Stealthily, her fingers felt through her pack. Finally, she touched the dagger's carved bone handle. Her confidence returned as the Hawks image pressed against her palm. Quietly she removed it from her pack and raised the blade. Weapon poised to strike like a ripping talon; she eased aside a clinging bough and advanced toward the foe.

Twenty more steps.

The eyes continued their relentless stare. No matter where Nimri dodged for cover, they followed her. Yet, she knew the beings didn't move.

Had Kazza sensed these monsters lurking in the balata? Was that why he'd been afraid to accompany her?

Her fingers tightened around the dagger's familiar grip. Nimri gathered all her energy then plunged past the last bough, blade raised to slash the golden eyes.

Her foot caught on a twinning root and she fell to the rocky soil.

Nimri broke her fall with her free hand, and sprang up to attack position.

Eight strides in front of her, a life size man and a woman were carved into the side of the mountain. Shiny metal formed their all-seeing golden eyes. Nimri felt so faint that the knife dropped from her now-limp fingers.

"Guardians of the Star Bridge," she murmured. Nimri shivered and blinked, then fell to her knees, hoping they would accept her belated reverence. Her forehead touched the ground as she prostrated herself before the sainted pair.

As her oxygen starved brain analyzed the scene, she realized the ominous blackness between the male and female must be, "The Star Bridge!" She swallowed. "It exists!"

Thick sweet air settled over her like a benediction. Hoping she'd been pardoned for her ignorance, Nimri grabbed a balata bough for support and staggered upright.

Many legends involved tales about dying suns, magic gates and a new land. If the Guardians existed, how many of the other stories could be true? The balata bough she held slipped from her fingers.

The Guardians resided at the grove's most sacred spot. Intense relief filled Nimri; she could scatter Rolf's ashes and fulfill her vow. Nimri flexed her fingers, then picked up her knife and tucked it into her backpack. She took a deep breath. "There's no time like the present." She retrieved Quark's ornate ceremonial urn. Carefully, she held the side with the Tramontain Hawk out for the Guardians to see. Then closing her eyes, she envisioned the ceremony.

A soft hum formed deep in her soul. It gained strength and volume as she danced the ritual steps. Opening the canister's lid, she chanted the revered words. "Return now to the House of the Dead."

Her hands shook the urn and she released the ashes.

"Lay within the earth until violets bloom, then return to us as if new."

Her entire body quivered as the chant ended. It took a moment to realize the shaking was not from emotion, but because the mountain was shaking.

Earthquake!

A heartbeat later, a balata trunk wrenched free from the ground, whacked her spine, and knocked her into the opening.

Nimri fell down the shaft toward gigantic teeth. She screamed.

~0~

Gradually, the haze in Larwin's helmet cleared, but breathing remained torturous. Though it was tempting to increase the oxygen level, in these last hours of life, every moment became more precious than the one before. He stood quietly and stared at one portion of the chamber, which shimmered with a vague purple light. Half convinced his mind was playing tricks; he pointed his las-projector at the strange glow. It illuminated a smooth charcoal gray floor and several debris piles. The pile closest to the obscure luminescence appeared reddish instead of blackened.

Strange.

Larwin moved toward the anomaly. "GEA-4, scan this area. I want to know why it appears different."

"I am complying." The sensual voice echoed in the subterranean passage until it sounded like a brothel of risqué remarks surrounded him.

He stomped against the flat floor, hoping the thud of his boots would drown out her presence. It worked for ten minutes then from behind him, she said, "I am picking up unknown readings."

While Larwin waited for her to add more, he studied the phenomena; glad to have something besides his impending death to occupy his mind.

Dim magenta light seemed to filter past desiccated stalactites and stalagmites within the mouth of an old cave. Clearly, the water and all other moisture had evaporated when the planetoid burned. Larwin ran his glove over the surface.

Despite heavy insulation, he felt the difference between the smooth man-made wall of the mine and the grotto's natural texture, but that did not account for the glow.

"Do you detect any phosphor deposits?" Larwin asked.

"No, I do not."

Deep within the cave, a woman screamed.

Functioning on instinct, Larwin ran toward the sound. His visor fogged, obscuring his already limited vision. His left boot caught and his shoulder smashed against a stalactite. Pain shot through him as he stumbled, and then crashed face first against a wall.

Dazed, he tried to orient himself.

A moment later, he stepped back and fanned his light-projector, exposing grainy brownish rock and sinister shadows.

Perhaps he should increase the oxygen to avoid hallucinating screams. Even as he thought it, he became positive he'd actually heard one. He held his breath and listened, but the only sounds were ones he made. Larwin gasped for air; his ragged panting sounded like tiny cries. Could contaminated air induce believable illusions?

Perspiration and tears of frustration mingled. He punched the rocky wall of the dead end. His fisted black glove flashed maroon as he drew back for a second strike. He stared at his hand and trained the beam of his light on it but the plastoid appeared as shiny black as the day he'd been issued the gloves. Larwin shook his head at what an oxygen-deprived mind could imagine. No, he assured himself, the only light came from his projector. To prove it, he slowly moved his hand forward. Again, it gleamed with the odd iridescence. Larwin moved his hand left and right, then up and down, and then he peered upward.

Dapples of gently undulating light splattered from an opening high above him.

Red light.

Did the planetoid have a molten core? Larwin simultaneously felt hot and cold. He blinked hard, clearing his vision. This time, when he stared upward, he looked for an access to the strange opening. None existed. He looked down for something to climb on and saw a corpse sprawled near his right boot.

Cautiously, he knelt next to the face down form and stared at the, strange magenta confetti and odd little gold bells, which mixed with the reddish dirt covering the woman. Too bad she'd died, her lithe physique would credit a dancer. He stretched out his hand to touch her, then remembering how the doll had disintegrated, pulled back. Undecided about his next action, he sat back on his heels and studied the woman, who appeared to be at least a foot taller than GEA-4, but shorter than his own height.

Her dust-covered pants and tunic appeared remarkably well preserved. Her long hair, bound into a long, thick black braid, hung off her shoulder and onto the dirt, yet seemed to shine beneath the grime.

The lacy confetti and bells seemed alive, too. It took a moment for Larwin to realize he was looking at some sort of plant-life. A tattoo of a flower on her shoulder had been exposed when her sleeve was ripped away.

On Guerreterre, only the wealthiest owned vegetation and they kept their prizes behind the locked doors of private atriums. How odd to find leaves in this inhospitable place.

Despite her slave-like attire, the woman must have been someone of great consequence.

Why only one corpse? Were the piles of rubbish some sort of tomb offering laid outside her sleeping chamber?

Larwin panned light over her golden-hued flesh. He would have bet anything bodies dehydrated in airless atmospheres.

Bending closer, he studied the woman's strange roughly woven two-piece outfit. The fabric, a battlefield of rents and filth, had probably been brown or tan, Guerreterre's color of mourning. Panning the light lower, Larwin noted that her feet were clad in leather moccasins. One lacerated hand still grasped the remnants of a primitive urn, while the rest of the old pot lay in a starburst around her. Why did she clutch it in death?

How long had she lain in this primitive tomb?

Larwin speculated that he would join her in eternal, perfectly preserved slumber in roughly ninety hours.

Maybe less.

He could already smell his body decomposing. Radzuk, but he needed a sonic shower!

Larwin focused on the odd leaves and bells. Why were such obviously expensive, lacy, magenta leaves strewn over and around the woman? Despite her primitive slave-class attire, the foliage made her seem like someone of great importance.

GEA-4 arrived. Despite carrying all three boxes, plus his haversack, she moved with ease. His jaw tightened with the memory of his struggle to carry the gear.

Larwin got up and took a step toward the antagonizing machine.

GEA-4 stopped and stared at the woman. "The arm she lies on is broken in three places, but repairable. I detect no other major damage." GEA-4 turned aside and put down the gear.

Larwin's hands clenched as his patience snapped. "What difference does that make?"

"Probabilities indicate she will resume consciousness in seven point five nine minutes."

"You speak of her as if she's alive." Derision laced his tone. What should he have expected from an android, which didn't have enough sense to repulse space debris?

"My scanners indicate she lives."

"Impossible!" Larwin's eyes narrowed on her. Faulty scanners would explain the circumstances which contributed to the crash and why they now stood next to a corpse in the bowels of the earth. "Do your scanners indicate how? No humanoid can survive without air, water and food."

"That is correct. However, this portion of the cavern has sufficient oxygen. The woman is well nourished and has only suffered mild dehydration recently. The air's moisture is limited. Probabilities indicate water is a seasonal element. I do not detect traces of food other than your rations."

Larwin snorted. Definitely faulty scanners.

The woman groaned. Larwin jumped away from her. A small cloud of dust rose, where he'd been standing.

Once the dust settled, the tail of her braid was almost indistinguishable from the floor.

He eased back toward the woman. After a moment's hesitation, Larwin gingerly touched her. When she didn't turn to dust, like the doll, he took a good grip and turned her over. Scratches and grime crisscrossed her face. She reminded him of his little sister, partly because Tem-aki's play had usually left her a mess, but also because, beneath the grime, this woman's long, lean bone structure appeared perfect. He inhaled sharply at the astounding superiority of her beauty. He leaned back on his heels and studied her equally appealing body. Except for the contorted arm she'd landed on, her horrible clothing and her general filth, she looked flawless from head to toe.

"The bones should be repaired before she becomes alert," GEA-4 said. "Would you like me to align them?"

"Do it."

GEA-4 manipulated the arm with the typical finesse, precision and compassion of a machine. He winced.

Another groan came from the woman. Stronger this time.

"Hurry," he said. "I'll find something to use for splints and bindings." Anything seemed better than watching the brutal, but necessary remedy.

"I am conducting the repairs as punctually as possible."

Larwin grabbed his haversack, dumped out the contents and frantically searched through his belongings. He chose a sock, a belt and finally the plexiboard from his logbook. Using his las-cutter on low, Larwin molded the plastoid board into a curved form. GEA-4 yanked the sock over the woman's straightened arm for protection against chaffing, then applied the plastic for strength and supported it with a sling made from the belt.

He sat back on his heels and watched GEA-4. One part of him wanted to treat the woman, himself, but logic told him that GEA-4's probes could facilitate exact manipulations. Still, the rough handling GEA-4 provided would never qualify her as a med-tech any more than her faulty programming had met the requirements for her to be a worthy pilot.

GEA-4 finished and stepped back.

Larwin knelt near the woman's shoulder and stared at her profile, certain that he'd met her somewhere.

But how?

When?

He leaned forward, brushed aside some strands of raven hair and studied her perfectly sculpted oval face. Somehow, it reminded him of GEA-4's, yet glancing at the android's profile, he decided they were 180 degrees polar opposites. Compared to the woman, the android looked like a diminutive faded imitation.

A tan leather cord circled the woman's neck. Larwin gave it a gentle pull and discovered it secured a beaded leather amulet. This seemed familiar, too. He frowned in concentration then recalled a museum display he'd seen years before. Though temptation urged him to look inside, he restrained his curiosity and refocused on her face. When had he last seen a woman free of cosmetics? Did they all hide such exquisite natural allure under their powders and glazes?

Then she opened her eyes.

Larwin saw a flash of green, then her pupils dilated, her body went rigid and she screamed. It sounded identical to the one, which had drawn him into the cavern.

Abruptly, her body relaxed. Again, she lay limp in the dust.

"What's wrong with her?" If GEA-4 told him he'd scared the woman to death, he would pull out her speech circuit and disintegrate it.

"My sensors detected a burst of emotion. Probabilities indicate she will resume consciousness in five point nine seven minutes."

"Is that your way of saying the sight of me frightened her?"

"It is possible."

How had the rotten robot twisted the incident to make him feel as if he'd done something wrong? Worse, why would any woman swoon after a glimpse of him? He scowled. Did she fear for her life because she belonged to a terrorist band that attacked Guerreterre 's supply lines?

Larwin brushed grime from her face and wondered if she'd ever seen a man before. Then the sight of his heavily gloved hand registered and he stopped in mid-motion. If this woman came from a primitive race, as her garments indicated, seeing him in his deep-space uniform could be enough to cause a faint. On the other hand, several militant factions would use any disguise to further their goals. "GEA-4, scan the atmosphere for bio hazards and if there are none, determine if my body will tolerate it."

"Compared to Guerreterre, there is a point two less oxygen. The gravitational field is point zero one five lower."

Must the android always be so damned precise and long winded? "So you're saying it's safe to remove my environmental suit? A simple yes or no will suffice."

"Yes."

Larwin snapped a latch-pin on his helmet. "Be advised, if you're wrong, I'm disconnecting you."

"That is an illogical statement. If I am wrong, you will not survive. If you do not survive, you cannot disconnect me."

Damned logical machine. "I'll find a way." Larwin yanked off his helmet and took a breath. Dry, stagnant air would have been an improvement over his rank suit. While the expected staleness existed, an enticing, exotic aroma mixed with the dry air. The elusive scent reminded him of something sugary sweet and spicy. Perhaps cologne or perfume. He leaned close to the woman's throat and inhaled deeply but only detected the salty scent of perspiration and fear.

He frowned in concentration as he studied the strange cave. Then, he pulled off his gloves and reverently picked up a magenta leaf. He sniffed. Honey, nutmeg, cloves and ginger mixed with rich humus, an odor found in arboretums. The smell of vast wealth. The smell of power. The smell of living plants. The smell of all his dreams. Found in the bowels of a dead planet.

Mouth watering with two types of hunger, Larwin sat back on his heels and reverently twirled the leaf between his fingers.

"The female is alert."

Pretending a calm he didn't feel, Larwin turned toward the raven-haired woman. Her wide-eyed gaze fixed on GEA-4.

"She doesn't seem frightened of you." He forced his anger aside and kept his tone calm.

"That is logical." To his disgust, the woman relaxed more every time GEA-4 spoke.

"Why is that logical?"

"I am an Anthropoid-pilot-unit; not to be feared. You are a warrior, trained to conquer worlds, control galaxies and generate fear in all who oppose the Guerreterre regime."

"Damned right." The woman focused on him. He saw his

reflection mixed with panic in her darting glance and wondered how he could calm her. He forced a smile. Her eyes widened with fear. Did his rank show? Being the youngest to achieve the status of Colonel in the elite branch of Shadow Warriors had been the proudest moment of his life. Why hadn't any of his courses in the military academy dealt with how to handle a face-to-face contact?

For the first time in his life, Larwin wanted to hide the shiny black Fighting Falcon emblem. He placed his palm over the war-bird on his chest, and used his softest manner. "My name is Colonel Larwin Atano of Guerreterre's Shadow Force." He waited for her response.

She made none.

Could she be mute? Had more than her arm been damaged?

No, she could scream.

"GEA-4, place your hand on your chest and state your name." Maintaining a peaceful tone and manner seemed harder than waging war on an entire galaxy. "Now." Sustaining a smile made his face ache, but he needed this woman to show him how to survive in this hole.

"Anthropoid version 4 from Galactic Engineering's experimental pilot program."

Larwin saw a flicker of comprehension. Then, the woman tried to point at her own chest but the makeshift splint hampered her. He'd thought her eyes were already enormous, but they enlarged into bottomless black orbs as she raised her injured arm and stared at the crude cast.

He tapped the flinty matte-black thigh of his flight suit until he got her attention. Then, he pointed to her arm and made a breaking motion with his hands. Larwin grimaced to stress the point. Next, he indicated GEA-4 and pantomimed how she had set the bones. The woman gaped at him for several long moments then cautiously sat up. She pointed at herself. "Nimri Tramontain." Her finger touched her bandaged arm. She looked at GEA-4, tried smiling and when that didn't elicit a response from the robot, she spoke some more.

Her musical tones and easy smile sent chills racing up and down Larwin's spine. By the time she finished speaking, every cell in his body vibrated to her speech pattern. Not being able to interpret her was irritating, but her apparent acceptance of GEA-4 rankled more. "What did she say?"

"Probabilities indicate she expressed gratitude."

"In that case, give her your most sincere smile and nod."

"Androids are not programmed to smile."

Neither were warriors. "Try. We need this woman to show us how to survive inside this burned out husk." Larwin turned his attention back to the woman who would save him. As he looked at her, the chill at his core warmed. His lips turned up, and he gave Nimri a smile warm enough to melt a Sibertan Witch. "Also, try to analyze her language. We'll need to learn it."

Chapter Four

Mind swirling with the memory of mammoth teeth gnashing at her face; then opening her eyes and seeing fierce eyes behind a strange round window and the ghostly white image of the outlandish child, Nimri kept her lids tight shut. Even so, she could smell the strangers' unwashed scent and hear their voices. Slowly, she raised her lids and peered between her lashes. The two apparitions still persisted in this pain-ridden nightmare world.

Had the Guardians found her unworthy and thrown her into the Star Bridge? If so, were the smelly pair of unwelcome intruders in her nightmare or had she landed in theirs? Sounds came from the eerie white one, but her lips didn't move. A chill raced up and down Nimri's spine. She recalled the Guardians throwing her into the Star Bridge, intending for the fierce monster within to consume her. Had they changed their minds and transported her to some new world populated by abominable beings?

Her mouth went dry. The small silver-clad one made more strange sounds, then the big one spoke. If they were communicating with each other, she couldn't understand a syllable they said.

Was she dreaming about them?

Had the thing with huge teeth consumed her? Was she actually dead? She'd imagined death as a transition between existences, not life in a shadowy, red-tinged hole inhabited by such odd beings. Nimri shifted. An ache shot up her spine. Soon, her entire body ached, while her left arm and her chest throbbed with pain.

She probably wasn't dead.

What had the Guardians done to her? And why? Tears blurred her vision and threatened to scald rivulets down her cheeks. The large, tan-skinned one, who had stubble instead of hair, pantomimed breaking then having the white haired girl set her arm. Nimri blinked to clear her vision. Not a girl, perhaps a small woman, who looked as fragile as the fabric of her silvery one-piece suit and called herself Anthropoid. She blinked again. Colonel appeared bulky, much as she imagined a shaved Yeti would look with its bulging muscles coated in soot. He made more motions. She swallowed and wondered what he wanted to convey. Nimri placed her left palm over her right forearm, closed her eyes and looked within. Her right radius was broken in two spots and the ulna in one.

The strange, small woman had done a good job realigning the bones. Nimri wished she had the power to instantaneously heal herself. Anyone, for that matter. She opened her eyes and studied the outlandish treatment method.

While she understood that her arm had been injured, she couldn't interpret when, why or how it had been broken.

Nimri scrutinized the odd pair. She'd never dreamed of anyone remotely like them, not even in her worst nightmare, so she feared she was conscious. But if this place existed, what had happened to the monster with the huge teeth? Had they fought it to save her? Was that how she'd been hurt? The white one appeared too frail to fight a mosquito. The man looked brawny enough to fight Talon, but hardly strong enough to battle anything with the size fangs she'd seen.

Hoping for a clue, Nimri studied the strange thing covering her forearm. The leather band was the only semi-normal component. Why use the outlandish fuzzy gray thing instead of healing herbs; did it have medicinal value? She touched it with her fingertips, but couldn't detect any curative powers. She frowned. The hard, transparent cylinder resembled ice, yet it was neither cold nor damp. Like the odd pair, the items strapped to her arm left her with more questions than answers.

And she was more likely to get answers from one of them then her strange splint. Nimri took a deep breath and looked up. The male looked back at her as if she were the most important person in the world, while the female kept to the shadows and all but ignored her. Did the small, bleached woman called Anthropoid resent her because her man ignored her?

Nimri inhaled sharply and nearly choked on the stale air. He didn't break eye contact. At least the male had taken off his terrifying head covering.

Colonel twirled a balata leaf.

The balata grove! The last place she recalled being before the Guardians threw her into the Star Bridge. She bit her lip and tried to remember everything she'd heard about the meaning of the balata, and could only think of positive things. He had to be giving her a test of some sort or a sign about his peaceful intentions.

Nimri looked wildly at the stone walls and glimpsed the shadow of a swaying balata bough high up the wall. She must have broken her arm when she landed in the Star Bridge. This was not a nightmare. This was real. She'd finally understood the message he'd communicated with the leaf! Heart racing with panic, she jumped to her feet.

"Where's the entrance?" Dizziness made her stagger. The huge, repulsive male grabbed her around the waist and kept her from falling. His stench smelled even worse than his revolting head covering looked. She clamped her jaws together and tried not to gag or fight him. Until she could be certain of his motives and knew for sure if she had any more ordeals to pass, she dare not irritate him.

But, oh, how he stank.

Nimri inhaled through her mouth as she softly chanted, "I will not panic. I will not panic. There is a way out, but first I must pass whatever examination the guardians are giving me." He helped her sit down and stepped away.

Closing her eyes, she concentrated on the problem. Perhaps finding the way out was her test. If she'd gotten in, she could get out by reversing events. Maybe. It should work if the Star Bridge had not shifted and taken her to a strange new world. Nimri opened her eyes. Again, the male was standing a pace away from her twirling the balata leaf and staring at her as if he could read her thoughts. When she looked from the leaf to his face, one corner of his mouth curved up.

She wanted to trust his silent message, but that meant he'd battled the huge monster. Nimri looked behind her and saw ordinary stalactites and stalagmites. She frowned at them. She looked upward. The gray limestone wall had a square rosy hue twice her height up the wall.

If the sacred grove lived up there, she might still be on Chatterre. Heart hammering, Nimri gazed until she felt certain she could make out the color of balata leaves.

Nimri's knees quivered with relief knowing that she needed to climb upward a dozen feet. She blinked. Suddenly the color seemed too orangish for balata leaves. What if her imagination created the color or wishful thinking imagined the shapes of the shadows?

Why would she picture those plus two bizarre individuals? They had to be balata. She must be on Chatterre. She could return to her people. Nimri refused to contemplate climbing down Sacred Mountain with the encumbrance of a broken arm.

For now, getting up to the balata grove was her priority. Once there, and undistracted by the shrinking walls, she would have passed her test, which meant she should be able to myst-mend her arm. Still, she'd need to begin the long healing process, now, in order to get out. Nimri placed her left palm over the breaks while she meditated on regenerating the bone.

Colonel shifted his feet, then distracted her by tapping her shoulder. She ignored him, and focused mending thoughts on her ulna. The obnoxious man tapped harder. She hid her dislike for him before opening her eyes.

He pointed at the shaft of magenta light. "Owyat?" When she blinked, he pantomimed climbing then raised an eyebrow.

Hoping that he'd confirmed that she'd understood her test, Nimri smiled. He pointed up. She nodded. "I understand and will make the climb soon." Obviously, he expected her to heal herself much faster. That meant he knew she could do so. Lifted by hope, she renewed her efforts on the fractures.

Colonel turned to pale Anthropoid and spoke gibberish. His voice filled with emotion as it raised and lowered in volume. In addition, he expressed himself with sweeping gestures of his free hand, while the other clutched the leaf as if the balata held the answers to all questions.

Despite the fact that they appeared to be different species, the bleached woman exuded such cold resentfulness in every move she made and every word she spoke, that Nimri suspected they were mates. Nimri wished she could assure Anthropoid that jealousy was unwarranted.

Anthropoid appeared child-sized, yet she had the body of an adult. When she spoke, each syllable sounded clear and precise. Nimri felt she should be able to understand Anthropoid's words because the consonants and vowels were the same; but Anthropoid put the sounds together differently. Worse, the tiny woman's body language seemed non-existent, so it became impossible to understand her.

Strange to have a pair so opposite.

Bizarre.

Of course, the Guardians, with their all-seeing golden eyes were very strange and unnatural, too.

Colonel made a grandiose gesture, which swept from the Star Bridge entrance downward. Then he indicated her. Anthropoid said something and Colonel quickly responded.

Were they discussing her arrival or her failure to pass her test by healing herself more promptly and then climbing out?

Colonel's next hand movement made her wonder if they expected her to live here with them. Gooseflesh rippled over Nimri, as she tried to imagine never seeing the sky or her garden again.

Please, no. She couldn't live within these confining walls. Nimri worried that she'd shrink and fade like Anthropoid if she spent a millennium in the magic gateway.

Perhaps their distracting behavior comprised another part of her test, and if she continued focusing on them, she would fail. Nimri refocused her energy on knitting the bone. She had almost finished when Colonel's horrid stench enveloped her and she felt his arm wrap around her shoulders and move lower. She opened her eyes.

His encircling arm felt strong. She risked a look at the hand splayed across her belly. Either he had the oddest skin she'd ever seen, or he had the most peculiar outfit.

She shook her head to clear it. The head-covering lying on the ground caught her attention.

Colonel gestured to make a point to Anthropoid. Nimri used the opportunity and pulled free.

She leaned over, rolled the orb as she examined it. Smooth. Hard as a June bug's shell. Round, except for what appeared to be a neck opening. She squinted through the gloom to study Colonel's neck. Ha! The pieces matched, so the black muscles must be artificial. But why would a male go to such effort to make himself a suit of muscles instead of taking care of his body? Surely he didn't believe his woman would be attracted to the ugly result.

This pair was creepy.

Their discussion seemed to be at an end.

Colonel gently shifted Nimri backward and said something commanding. Anthropoid gracefully tossed a large black bag and three boxes up through the Star Bridge's entrance. Nimri's jaw dropped. She consciously snapped it shut. Could heavy lifting be woman's work? Would that explain why the male wore those ridiculous artificial muscles?

The male motioned to her and pantomimed tossing her after the boxes.

Nimri had barely survived her fall in. She stepped backward and firmly shook her head. No, there had to be a better way to get out.

Colonel gestured more emphatically. Could he be unbalanced? The last thing she needed was another broken arm. Or worse. Nimri raised her chin, shook her head and said, "No." Colonel turned to Anthropoid and spoke. A breath later, the small woman picked up Colonel and tossed him out of the Star Bridge.

Nimri's knees shook and a woozy wave washed over her as she stared at the spot where he'd vanished. A moment later, his dark silhouette appeared against the muted light at the top of the shaft. While she gazed upward, small hands firmly clamped around her waist and picked her up. Before she could protest, Anthropoid hurled her upward.

Nimri closed her eyes and screamed.

A moment later, she hit a hard, yet yielding surface that felt like a reed mat. As she tumbled forward, limbs the size of balata trunks wrapped around her. She opened her eyes and found herself staring at the base of the cursed tree that had knocked her into the pit. Her fingers itched to grasp her knife and make mincemeat of that jinxed plant.

The ground beneath her moved.

Another earthquake!

Nimri wished she'd never had such a sacrilegious thought.

She closed her eyes and rolled away from the Star Bridge. Pain shot up her injured arm, its howl radiated to every cell of her body. Nimri gasped and curled into a fetal position. Tears welled under her closed eyelids and she tasted bile.

The bindings loosened, and something heavy rolled over her.

For a terrifying moment, she expected to fall back into the portal. Instead, the ground stabilized.

Something warm covered her shoulder and Colonel's vile stench permeated the air. His deep, worried voice said something unintelligible.

Nimri bit her lip, and prayed she wouldn't throw up. Beads of perspiration gathered on her face. Interminable moments passed before the sick feeling subsided. With each passing moment, Colonel's tone sharpened. Finally, she conquered the pain and threatening nausea enough to sit upright and peek through her lashes. He was sitting on the downhill side of her, but there was no sign of the embracing branches or heavy trunk.

Colonel's distraught expression made her catch her breath. The unexpected intensity calmed Nimri. She attempted a reassuring smile.

He openly stared for an endless moment, then an answering smile spread across his lips until it seemed as if the sun had warmed the entire grove.

Mesmerized by the transformation, she gaped at him. An image of him catching her, wrapping his arms around her and protecting her from injury filtered through her mind. Is that why he'd come to her? To help her? Protect her and her tribe? Relief, warm and sweet suffused her. He leaned forward and his hand crept toward her. For a moment, Nimri thought he meant to touch her.

Instead, he rose to his feet and confirmed her earlier suspicions by removing his stiff muscle-suit. Peeling off the offensive black thing revealed a thin silvery garment nearly identical to Anthropoid's. Beneath the thin, shiny garment, his underlying muscles seemed suspiciously genuine. If they were real, Colonel was the most splendid male specimen she'd ever seen.

Why would he wear such an ugly garment if he really had strength? His pectorals rippled as if in response to her thought. Her mouth went dry. Her mind went blank.

Nimri watched him walk back to the entrance, with self-assurance worthy of Kazza. Even the way he lay on the ground and lowered his strange black garment reminded her of raw animal grace. Male magnetism.

Seconds later, Anthropoid's head appeared over the edge.

After Colonel and Anthropoid briefly conversed, the female glanced at Nimri's arm, then said, "Noitdidnot." Whatever her clipped one word answer meant, it relaxed Colonel.

Unwilling to stare in his mate's presence, Nimri placed her palm over her injured arm, focused healing thoughts on the knitting bone and willed the tissue to finish mending and the pain to subside. When the agony reduced to a dull ache, she glanced up. Colonel's fingertips caressed a shimmering leaf in a reverence for the balata grove, which she'd tried to achieve since her great grandfather had told her about it and its importance for her people. Oddly enough, Anthropoid appeared as indifferent to the legendary trees as she seemed to everything else. The impassive woman responded when Colonel said things, which ended in a higher note. Nimri deduced that he was asking questions and Anthropoid was providing answers. If she held more knowledge of the two, perhaps she'd lived here longer. Perhaps the Guardians were like tribal peacekeepers and passed their duties down at certain points.

Nimri shook her head at the odd thought. Despite Colonel's questions, it seemed unlikely that Anthropoid could be the elder, particularly when she gave the impression of being much younger.

By the time the first fracture was somewhat mended, Nimri felt certain that Colonel venerated the trees, as did her Tribe, but that was all she was sure of.

If only she could understand his words.

Where did they come from? How could it be that they didn't speak Chatterre's language? Whether Chosen or Lost, both tribes spoke the common tongue. True, the Lost sounded like they spoke through their noses, and they accused her people, the Chosen, of slurring their words, but they could communicate. Nimri massaged her forehead, willing the tender flesh to cure, instead of turn into an ugly swollen lump. Since she'd fallen into the Star Bridge, one strangeness had followed another in a dizzying array.

While Nimri became lost in thought, Colonel got something thin and flat out of one of his boxes. He handed it to her with an expectant look on his face. She took the silvery package decorated with intricate indigo markings. Nimri thanked Colonel and studied it. It felt lightweight and as smooth as his head covering; had proportions similar to the wing feather of a hawk, but this odd thing looked like no sort of feather she'd ever seen. She turned it over. It sparkled in the sun, nearly blinding her. Was it valuable? Was he giving it to her for luck? Might it be a sign of something? Could this be a sacred artifact? A remembrance of her great-grandfather? She looked at him for the answer.

He'd gotten one for himself and had torn back the silver to uncover something, which smelled like rancid food. Nimri's nose wrinkled.

He took a bite of it, chewed and motioned for her to do the same.

Surely Colonel didn't expect her to eat the filth. She shook her head and shoved it at him. Again, he pantomimed for her to eat.

Her fingers covered her mouth to hold back the threatening nausea. He picked up the object, pantomimed eating, and handed it back.

Nimri inched away from the persistent man and glared at the offensive package. If he ate such things, it was no wonder he smelled so bad.

Colonel cocked his head and studied her as if he considered her the strange one.

Nimri looked for a polite means of avoiding the nasty mess and noticed he hadn't given Anthropoid any food. Feeling compassionate and wanting Anthropoid to know she did not want her man any more than she wanted the vile fare, Nimri thrust the package at the tiny woman.

Anthropoid ignored her and stared at the sun with eyes as silvery and bright as the package.

Nimri dropped to her knees, bruised forehead flat on the earth and fought not to vomit on the Guardian's sacred shoes. When her respect was ignored, Nimri rose, laid the package on the ground in front of Anthropoid and inched backward.

After her nausea passed, she carefully got up. Pleased to discover she could stand unaided, Nimri ventured to take a step. When she didn't fall, she went to the spot where she'd left her backpack. She opened it, then found her water container and food. Turning back, she discovered Colonel directly behind her. Not knowing what else to do, she thrust a biscuit at him.

He feinted to his left, as if she were stabbing him and grasped her hand in a crushing grip. She gasped in pain and fell to her knees. The pressure eased. Colonel's eyes seemed to glitter as much as Anthropoid's as he studied her. After a moment, he opened her fingers and sniffed her flattened offering. With a contrite grin, he indicated gratitude and took a nibble. His eyes widened in appreciation. He quickly took two large bites, then licked his palm.

Colonel patted the boulder and looked expectantly at her. At least he seemed to be making an effort to be sociable. But what did he want? Sit on the rock to eat? How was she supposed to get up there when the fractures were newly repaired and still painful? Colonel uttered more gibberish, then he clamped his hands around her waist and lifted her. After gently placing her on top, he vaulted up next to her. "Thank you," Nimri said. She smiled.

He nodded.

She offered him her water container, but he gave her a skeptical look. With difficulty, she removed the top and took a drink. She offered it a second time. He took it and after sniffing the contents, took a sip. The corners of his eyes crinkled, and he took a bigger swallow. She noticed that in the sunlight, his eyes were the color of chestnuts and his rough, short, matted hair reminded her of a mixture of golden wheat stubble and brown barley hulls. Unusual color, but nice. Too bad the texture and length were such an eyesore. She felt certain she'd never seen a grown man with so little hair. Even the few elders, who had gone bald, retained a fringe, which they allowed to grow to its customary length—halfway down their backs.

None of them stank like a compost heap, either.

Nimri glanced through the balata leaves at odorless Anthropoid, who still stared at the sun. How long had the poor woman been in that terrible hole? Did she realize that the sun's light could blind? Had the sun already blinded her; was that why her eyes were silver? The Guardians stood still like that. Was Anthropoid a Guardian? Her hair was white and her skin was sallow, which denoted great age, but her body form was of a woman in her prime and she only had the size of a child. Nimri frowned at all the contradictions, then took another peek. Anthropoid wore her hair in a shoulder-length, which added to her childlike appearance … If Anthropoid stood there long enough, would her back become part of the mountain, as the golden-eyed pair had? Could that be her intention?

Chapter Five

Larwin contemplated the woman. Was Nimri the only anthropomorphic in this place? Was she even human? Despite GEA-4's claims of the woman having broken bones, he knew how appearances could deceive.

Discovering that the burned-out planetoid had a habitable interior still amazed him.

And what an interior!

If he didn't know better, he'd believe he was on the actual surface of a planet instead of several miles underground in a huge cavern. He'd give anything to know how the scientists managed to get the ceiling to look like a real sky complete with shifting clouds and moving sun.

And the breeze rustling through the leaves seemed like the most exotic thing he'd ever encountered. Of course, the distant moaning of the wind was eerie, particularly because Nimri tensed and looked toward the trees every time it whined or moaned. What did she know? Did the sound signify danger? Broken machinery? Something worse?

Unable to discover the answer, he fingered a lacy magenta leaf until its sweet/sour aroma engulfed him. What a wonderful smell. It would be worth a fortune on Guerreterre.

Again, the wind howled in the distance. Nimri turned toward the sound and shouted back, then she turned toward him, smiled and gestured that they needed to leave.

So, there was danger.

She leaped down, nimble as a gymnast. He followed her as best he could. Whoever had designed the ground had done a slipshod job. Rough seemed too kind a word for it. But he'd never complain. Larwin felt too happy to have found this place, especially after resigning himself to death by suffocation.

Maybe he was still in the cave, surrounded by piles of debris and hallucinating because of oxygen deprivation.

Maybe he lay dead.

Maybe this paradise was the afterlife.

Larwin seriously considered the possibility, but decided it was unlikely since robots shouldn't achieve immortality; and big as life, the android least likely to enter paradise stood between the two eerie carvings soaking up energy. As GEA-4 shimmered in the light, Larwin wondered if the malfunctioning hunk of scrap could actually utilize an artificial light source to recharge.

Nimri certainly had a strange home. Due to the odd leaves, Larwin had expected some sort of biosphere dwelling with attached arboretum. Only the very rich of Guerreterre could afford a tree, which they kept in a private arboretum, yet here were hundreds of beautiful trees. Maybe thousands. Being in the midst of such bounty made Larwin's mouth dry.

Due to the communication barrier, he'd hoped for more of Nimri's kind. Not two mute carvings.

Patience.

Larwin touched Nimri's uninjured arm. Instantly, her mysterious green eyes focused on him. He smiled and pointed to his chest. "Larwin." Then he pointed at her. "Nimri."

She pointed at him. "Colonel."

He shook his head. "Larwin."

She frowned at GEA-4 and he realized how she'd mixed up his title with his name. He gave her a warm smile. "Larwin."

"Le Are Win."

He smiled and nodded. Next, he pointed at the rock they had sat on and looked at her expectantly.

"Boulder," she said.

The word had a solid sound to it. He repeated the syllables. "BOWL-dar." The corner of her mouth twitched and her eyes sparkled with laughter, which made him wonder if he'd gotten it wrong, but she nodded indicating agreement.

The breeze gusted with a horrible howl.

"Kazza, I'm fine," Nimri shouted.

Nimri's voice command didn't work and the wind howled again.

She faced him and gestured awkwardly.

"What does she want?" Larwin called to GEA-4.

"Probabilities indicate she wishes us to follow her."

Good.

Clumsily, she tried to fit the pack to her back. He slipped it over his own shoulder. She accepted his help. Much better. He swung his haversack over his other shoulder.

"GEA-4, it's time to leave."

She bent to pick up the boxes.

"Leave those," he said, unwilling to drag around space rations after having real water and heavenly manna.

Several minutes later, after sliding down steep slopes, scrapping his knuckles on rocks and nearly ripping ligaments in the ankle he'd stressed in the crash, they came to the edge of the trees. Suddenly, he could see for miles. Larwin's breath caught at the sight before him. Stretching his hand forward and closing his eyes, he waited for the infinitesimal tingle associated with a holograph.

There was none. He looked at the incredible panorama and wondered about the technology. Wind gusted and the trees swayed. No one on Guerreterre had mastered the technique of adding wind to simulated scenery. This engineering was incredible.

And what a panorama! They appeared to be high on a rugged mountain.

Could the planetoid be some sort of gigantic geode? Nasty on the outside but filled with magnificence in its hollow core?

Far off in the valley, he detected the glint of reflected sunlight—most likely a river in a valley. He hadn't seen land this wild and desolate since he was three and his father had taken him camping on Callanda to catalogue the resources. When they returned, he'd been tested for future vocation and immediately accepted into the military academy.

Of course, since then, Callanda's riches had been harvested, and now it looked like most other Guerreterre holdings: barren of botanical life, heavy metals and water. Larwin swallowed, as he ignored the unpleasant thought of that world's doom.

"Warning." GEA-4 emitted a shrieking alarm. "Intruder alert."

Larwin turned as a monstrous striped something hurdled down from a house-sized rock and charged, tongue lolling and teeth bared. Reflex action and years of training leaped to his aid. Larwin went down on one knee and had las-gun in hand before he exhaled. He'd have shot the beast between its hungry, amber eyes if Nimri hadn't stepped in the way.

Did she have a death wish?

He moved to knock her aside.

She stepped forward. His arm hit vacant air and he lost his balance.

The monster leaped. Nimri did too. Nimri was protecting him. Larwin wasn't sure what he thought about that.

The enormous furry thing collided with Nimri, but didn't knock her over or shred her with its huge teeth. She laughed and hugged it. Its shoulders were as high as GEA-4's head, and its body was at least two yards long. Yet Nimri behaved with assurance and laughing disregard of the enormous, sharp teeth as the thing nuzzled her ear.

Larwin sat down hard.

She gave the monster another clumsy hug. The beast ran its muzzle from the tip of her chin to her ear and rested its neck on her shoulder. The gesture looked oddly affectionate. Could this be some sort of associate?

Surely, not.

Who but a planetary emperor could afford such a brute?

Who but a goddess of war would want such a lethal beast?

Cold sweat bathed his brow and a chill washed over him. Larwin squinted at the woman and mentally compared her to the sketches he'd seen of Kues, the God of War, but there didn't appear to be any resemblance.

The paw spanning Nimri's waist moved infinitesimally. Larwin squinted and saw six claws emerge, each one long as his entire hand. He tried to scramble to his feet, but a rock beneath his boot rolled and he landed hard on his tailbone. Pain radiated. Involuntarily, he closed his eyes. When he looked, again, no sign of the ripped flesh or the lethal weapons remained. He looked upward. The beast winked at him. "Great Radzuk, what is that thing?"

"Probabilities indicate it is a companion."

Companions were usually androids. Larwin narrowed his eyes and studied the strange thing from its tufted ears to its twitching tail. It was the oddest creature he'd ever seen—and the noisiest. He could hear gears humming. The thing must be an android that needed lubrication. Too bad he didn't have any oil; he'd lube the gears.

It was merely a machine. No wonder the woman appeared fearless. Granted it looked stranger than the wackiest Callanda contrivance he'd ever encountered.

Nimri stroked the companion's sleek gold, black, and white striped back. Watching her, yet keeping most of his attention focused on the furry thing, Larwin gingerly got to his feet. Realizing the device's true size and hearing the gear rumble even louder, his relief wavered. Androids, which were improperly cared for, could develop programming faults as well as grinding gears. In the past, before maintenance had become regulated, their own companions had killed some owners. He frowned and wondered if anyone caressed androids. Nimri tickled the thing's tufted ears and said, "Kazza, this is Larwin and Anthropoid."

The kazza made a mewling noise that didn't sound the least bit mechanical and sounded a great deal like a recording of an enormous cat. Larwin tried to recall all the information he'd ever learned about cats. He was certain he'd never heard of one so large. As he recollected, members of this species were ferocious hunters. Larwin swallowed and reminded himself that shadow warriors did not flinch in the face of any foe. Larwin's fingers tightened around his las-gun. He took a deep breath and inched his other hand toward the animal.

The kazza became silent. Watchful.

Larwin froze and glanced at Nimri. She smiled, took his hand, and placed it on top of the cat's sun-warmed furry head. Still holding his hand, she tugged it down the glossy shoulder. It was a unique sensation. Nice. Obviously, Nimri touched the cat for pleasure. The cat started rumbling, again. Pleasant vibrations caressed his fingers. Larwin stroked the animal several more times on his own and with each stroke, the low rumble grew louder and his enjoyment increased.

Larwin could have spent the remainder of the day repeating the remarkable experience, but Nimri tapped his arm. "That way is my home, but it's very hard. Why am I telling you?" She smiled and made a funny face at the kazza. "The fall must have rattled my mind. I don't need to tell them—they're magic and know all."

He wished he could understand her.

Nimri and the kazza began to walk away, then turned back and gestured for Larwin to come. He followed her toward a steep, thin trail, which was sheer rock on his right and bottomless on his left. And as barren as Guerreterre.

Soon, Larwin realized the trek down the shaft had been fun.

Hours later, when the four of them reached a small level area scattered with tufts of sparse grass. Nimri insisted on setting up camp. Before all was ready, the artificial sun sputtered out. She shared more of her wonderful food and water with him and the kazza. He could have eaten a mountain of the fabulous stuff, but didn't ask for more. Until he knew who she was and if she was some unknown goddess, it would be unwise to anger her. Besides, she was beautiful and injured.

She curled up on the rocky ground and seemed to instantly fall asleep.

His exhaustion went so deep that his bones felt weak. Larwin followed her example and lay down. The kazza's big eyes stared at him. He ordered GEA-4 to stand watch, then settled down near a clump of fragrant grass. Tentatively, he touched the fragile foliage, but instead of being soft, the texture felt wiry as twisted rope. He smiled at the leave's inherent strength.

The kazza began to rumble. Larwin rolled over and looked at it. The creature was not any sort of technology he'd ever encountered; most androids used solar, a few old fashioned ones operated on alternating current. He'd never heard of any utilizing food and water to refine power.

The few occasions Larwin closed his eyes, he felt the kazza's hungry eyes on him. Worse. the last time he'd trusted GEA-4 to guard him; he'd nearly been killed. He sat up, hoping to catch her being slack, but she remained alert. He lay back down and tried to relax, but Larwin neither slept, nor relaxed. Finally, he rolled onto his back and watched the star-filled holograph overhead, which brought back memories of his childhood, when he and his father had gone camping on primitive planets. He also kept the kazza under surveillance, even after it appeared to go into sleep-mode.

The following morning, they continued their descent. The air grew thicker and more fragrant as a dense green covering of vegetation overtook the rock. The wealth of plant life boggled his mind: some lacy, some like the softest velvet, others stiff like plastoid. The plants were worth more than the emperor's treasury.

When the path twisted around a crag, Larwin saw a tree large as a hill. Unable to believe such a thing existed, he blinked. Beyond the tree, there were hundreds more. His legs trembled so violently that he grabbed the sheer wall for support.

The botanical fortune was unprecedented.

Nimri pointed. "Sequoia." She repeated it until he realized it was her word for tree.

Dazed by his prospects for wealth and prominence, Larwin followed Nimri into the woods. Or was it a forest?

Just before dusk, they emerged from under a sequoia's boughs into a wide flat ledge, surrounded by trees on three quadrants and protected by a sheer drop-off on the other. The sudden profusion of colors seemed mind-boggling and the intermingled scents permeated his lungs with heady aroma. An unseen steady drumming sound reminded him of the kazza. The heavy rumble of machinery seemed out of place in this primordial place. He blinked and tried to make sense of his overwhelmed senses. Flowers bloomed everywhere. Tiny white ones, tall purple stalks, yellow trumpets, red ones large as platters.

He had to be dead. Only Paradise could contain such abundance.

Except for the mechanical thumping. Were they nearing the source of the planetoid's power?

Larwin would have asked, but just then, in the middle of the vibrant clearing, he saw a structure the likes of which he'd never imagined. He shaded his eyes and squinted.

It appeared to spiral up the lone tree trunk at the clearing's center. On Guerreterre, several wealthy families owned indoor gardens called arboretums. However, they kept small plants indoors away from the harmful effects of pollution and ultraviolet light. He'd never imagined a tree could utterly dwarf a house, assuming the coiling structure actually was a dwelling.

The tree trunk looked at least twenty-five yards in diameter. In the fading light, he couldn't be sure where its branches started, but the first was at least one hundred yards above ground and presided over the entire vista with regal splendor.

This was a cosmos apart from anything on Guerreterre, except for the fanciful drawings in a child's fairytale. The lowest level opened out into the garden and had smoke coming from a stone chimney. The roof looked like a huge slab of bark, and made the structure appear to be part of the tree.

Individual rooms appeared randomly positioned from ground to the first branch. Each connected by semi-enclosed stairs that hugged the titanic tree.

If someone disassembled the strange spiraling structure and laid it in a line, the house would probably be twenty yards wide and close to four hundred yards long.

Whatever architect had designed it had the strangest taste Larwin had ever seen.

And he liked it. Of course, he almost always liked unusual things.

Nimri turned off the main path and followed a curving one, which led past the sprawling patches of assorted foliage. Larwin brushed past some tiny purple flowers. A rich spicy aroma wafted around him. Nimri ignored the amazing plants as she focused on a round door near the smoking chimney. As they neared the amazing structure, Larwin realized the door was an enormous slab with concentric rings. It looked heavy, but Nimri opened it with ease. The kazza made an excited sound and bounded inside. Nimri motioned for them to enter.

The interior appeared as organic as the exterior, but what caught and held his attention was the smell of something even more delectable than the bits of food Nimri had shared.

Larwin' s mouth watered. He dropped his haversack onto the soft green cushion of a chair crafted from twining branches. Turning, his thigh brushed against a round tabletop. Like the door, the top appeared to have been crafted from a single slab with bark skirting its six-foot-diameter. Crude bowls, rocks and bits of dried plants covered the surface. He sniffed, but the delicious odor wasn't coming from anything displayed on the round surface. He peered under the slab at the base made from twisting branches, but saw no food.

Larwin straightened and looked up at the ceiling, where bundles of dry plants hung suspended on rough cord. Looking closer, he realized there were a variety of plants, with foliage as varied as what grew near the trail. There were also dried flowers of every hue.

Extraordinary. But not the source of the mouth-watering aroma.

From around the curve, a woman said, "So, you're home. Smelled the bread, did you? Well, my fine fellow, what have you done with Nimri?"

"I'm right behind him, Bryta. I hope you've made enough for guests, because I've brought company."

"Where are you going to find company on that abandoned trail, especially at this time of night?" A smiling, rosy-cheeked, white-haired woman bustled into sight. She took one look at them, stopped dead in her tracks and blanched as white as GEA-4.

Nimri quickly moved to the portly woman and gave her a big hug. Larwin heard Nimri murmur something before she stepped aside.

Without moving her lips, Bryta uttered a string of syllables. The expression in her brownish eyes reminded Larwin of the way people looked at carriers of contagious disease—something between mortal fear and horror.

Nimri grabbed Bryta's arm and pulled her forward. Nimri gave GEA-4 a mind-numbing smile. "Bryta, this is Anthropoid. She looks odd, but doesn't act ill. In fact, she's stronger than you'd believe."

The whites of Bryta's eyes expanded.

"This is Larwin," Nimri said. "I'm not certain why the Guardians materialized for me, but—"

"They what?" The woman's high-pitched tone sliced through his eardrums and ended in a thin high-pitched screech. Bryta stumbled backward until she collided with the bark wall. "They're who? From where?" Bryta gawked at GEA-4. Larwin contemplated putting in earplugs.

Nimri's smile appeared strained, but her tone remained affectionate and soft. "I saw the Star Bridge Guardians. Bryta, they are molded into the side of Sacred Mountain. I'd never imagined anything like them."

Bryta flattened against the wall, much as the carvings on the mountain had been depicted.

Nimri turned to face him and ignored Bryta's behavior, which must not be odd on this world. "They tested me and I passed." She smiled up at him. "Larwin looks exactly like one of the Guardians." He glanced from her fearless face to Bryta's eyes, which looked like burning black beads in a sea of glistening white.

"Look at his chest." Nimri recaptured his attention as she gestured to his heart. Her finger traced the outline of the Shadow Warrior's emblem on his uniform. The woman's stare switched to his chest; her mouth dropped open. Larwin wondered what Nimri was saying and if her deferential tone meant that she was pleased with him and his devotion to Kues. Or perhaps she was explaining that he'd made colonel at twenty-eight and was a member of the elite Shadow Warriors. The latter seemed more likely, since their attention focused on his insignia, but if so, how could she know? Unless she was a goddess, of course.

"See how the design resembles the Tramontain family crest? I think he's either a Guardian or they materialized him to help me." She smiled. "I think they wanted me to know he was sent to help our Tribe—that must be why he's marked."

Bryta's eyelids fluttered closed and she slid down the wall in a dead faint.

Larwin wondered what was wrong with the women of this world.

~0~

Nimri dropped to her knees and grabbed Bryta's plump wrist. She felt several erratic beats before she dropped the limp hand onto the rumpled pink apron.

Having the Guardian's gift strapped around her arm made her feel awkward as a new-hatched bird. Nimri hoped they didn't expect her to wear the ornamental tube indefinitely and wished she dared to take it off, at least while she examined Bryta.

Behind her, Anthropoid said something, which sounded negative. The small woman, who Nimri suspected was a healer, didn't sound upset. Nimri's racing heart calmed and she recalled that she'd fainted when first confronted with the reality of legends.

Obviously, Anthropoid and Larwin were accustomed to such greetings and were not worried because they considered the behavior normal.

Moments later, Nimri put her fingers against Bryta's wrist and perceived a strong, steady beat. Theory confirmed; she straightened out Bryta's legs, then got up to serve the Guardians dinner; honey-yams and black bread if her nose wasn't mistaken.

Later, after her esteemed guests were settled for the night and as moon shadows browsed the interior, Nimri returned to the main room. She placed two steaming mugs of peppermint tea on the table, then knelt next to Bryta, who was a combination of housekeeper, companion and surrogate mother. "I know you're awake. They've gone to bed. Open your eyes."

Was it a shadow, or was Bryta's jaw stiff with gritted teeth?

"I put them in Great-grandfather's bedroom."

"Rolf's room!" Bryta sat up so quickly that her forehead butted Nimri's jaw. "But all the sacred relics are there!" Nimri jerked backward, landing hard on her backside. "Oh. I forgot who they were." Bryta rubbed her temple.

Nimri massaged her throbbing chin as they silently stared at each other. A long tense moment passed. Then, Nimri got to her feet. After she helped Bryta get up, they sat down in their favorite chairs, as if this was an ordinary evening and they were discussing the usual happenings.

Yet nothing in her life felt normal or routine. It hadn't been since she'd given her Great-grandfather her promise.

Nimri's fingertip traced the leaf impression on her mug's verdant handle and tried to grasp everything that had happened in the five moon risings since Rolf's spirit had been released by fire.

Bryta took a sip of tea. "I never thought I'd see you, again." She took another quick gulp. "Was it as horrible a trip as I imagined?" Bryta asked.

Most of the hazards were something Nimri didn't want to discuss, at least not so soon or when dear Bryta was covertly staring at the stairway, as if expecting an attack. Nimri cleared her throat. "Some parts were worse, some better." She took a sip of the restorative brew. "What happened while I was fulfilling my obligation? Did you visit Lily and Tansy?"

Upon hearing her granddaughter's name, Bryta's expression softened as she nodded. "Tansy told me that after we left the marketplace last Market Day, two Lost got into a fight with Quark Dagger."

"He's such a hot head." Nimri fingered the mug Quark had designed for her and admired the way he had woven the clay into such a pleasing texture and leafy look. "What was it over this time? Glazes?" Bryta shook her head. "Design?" Again a negative shake. "What else is there for a potter to fight about?"

"A remark." Bryta took a sip of now tepid tea and settled into the cushions for a good gossip. "Tansy didn't witness the start," Bryta confided in her familiar whispery tone, which generally preceded a long recital of Tribal gossip. "She was trading some of your snakebite medicine with Otter for a pair of laying ducks."

"If I'm expected to protect the Tribe, I need to understand the problems." Nimri fingered the mug and sighed, wishing there were a better way to do so than from Bryta's seemingly endless chitchat. "I don't need an explanation of why you don't know something, I need the details you do know."

Bryta leaned forward, as if to impart juicy nuggets of scandal. "First, the Lost degraded Quark's work as inferior on every aspect. But Quark ignored them." Bryta beamed. Nimri heaved an inward groan and motioned for her to continue. "Then B-Do came by with his lunch and they began making rude comments about her."

Nimri visualized B-Do's disfigured face and understood why Quark had defended his wife from the Lost's uncouth remarks.

"Of course, he couldn't stand by while they insulted his wife," Bryta said.

"So Quark threw the first punch." Nimri wondered if both sides were trying to force her into action and test her power. Or lack thereof.

"Two to one." Bryta smiled smugly. "But Quark wiped them in the dirt. He should have burned them, like B-Do. Then they'd learn how rude remarks hurt."

Nimri's jaw dropped.

Bryta's chin came up a notch before she blinked and dropped her gaze.

Confrontation avoided Nimri's spine relaxed against the moss-filled cushion. "I wish I'd been able to myst-mend her scars." Saving B-Do's life had only given her misery and made her the butt of ridicule. She sighed. "I understand why Quark did what he did, but I'm worried about the repercussions."

"Perhaps you could talk to Thunder Cartwright. Negotiate a treaty." Bryta looked up, eyes bright with emotion. "You're the only person in our history to see the Guardians. Convince the old man that you're as powerful a foe as Rolf and make a treaty that will protect us for a lifetime."

Nimri snorted. "If I tried that, he'd squash me like a pesky mosquito." She sipped her tea. "I've never understood why he didn't attack when Great-grandfather became ill."

"Perhaps he's uncertain of you."

"It's said that he knows all that the birds see."

Bryta snorted with disdain.

"Perhaps they have held back out of respect."

Bryta jerked, nearly spilling her tea at the idea that their Tribe's worst enemy could have a decent motive for anything.

Nimri chuckled. Lost had no respect. At least not for myst power. Her great-grandfather had told her over and over that they only worshiped tangible science. Nimri frowned. Whispered gossip claimed Cartwright spoke with birds and animals. Her frown deepened. Such behavior didn't sound like someone who only worshiped science. She shook her head; many of the things Rolf had affirmed had never made sense. "They feared Rolf's power to control the heavens," Nimri uttered a belief she'd held for years, but had never dared to voice, "but I doubt if they respected him."

"Their tribe is only allowed on our side of the river on Market Day. Perhaps Cartwright doesn't know, yet." The fact that Rolf was only sick four days before he died hung unsaid. "Just because the Lost say he knows all, doesn't make it so."

It had been nine days since he'd become ill. Five since he'd died. Two since Cartwright's tribe would have brought back the news on Market Day. How many days until the first attack was mounted?

Nimri swallowed. "Not even Rolf knew everything." Bryta's eyes widened with surprise over hearing something so slanderous. "Thunder Cartwright speaks to creatures. Some say that not only birds spy for him, but animals, as well."

Bryta's eyes flicked to the shadows. "Hearsay." Bryta scoffed.

"So you say now, but you told me you've heard of his incredible skills from everyone." Bryta hitched up her chin in what would have been a defiant gesture on someone without sagging jowls. "I believe he possesses the ability." It would explain why she'd sensed her great–grandfather's hatred covering a deeper emotion. "Most days, I think I can communicate with Kazza."

"Do you truly believe we're doomed?" Bryta shakily put her mug on the table. Tea slopped. She pulled a small cloth from inside her sleeve. Her plump hand trembled as she sopped up the droplets.

Nimri cleared her throat, then voiced the idea, which had germinated when she realized the pair intended to come home with her. "Maybe the Guardians sent Larwin and Anthropoid to save us."

"That's unheard of," Bryta said. "It's your duty to protect the Tribe. No one can do it for you."

"I haven't taken up the black staff—at least not usefully. And Larwin wears the Tramontain hawk or at least something close to it. Symbols go beyond other forms of communication and are meant to establish trust." Nimri picked up a sassafras twig, worked it under the clear covering and scratched her itching arm. She wondered if her hope for help was presumptuous.

"What is that thing?"

"I'm really not certain."

"Then why wear it?"

Nimri chuckled. "Because I'm not certain." Bryta's mouth flattened. "I fell into the Star Bridge." Bryta's jaw dropped. "It was quite a long fall and I must have landed on my arm. Anyway, I got knocked out and when I came to, Anthropoid and Larwin were there. Anthropoid had realigned the bones and put this on." Nimri looked down at the annoying bandage and kept scratching. "At least I think that's what they told me."

"Haven't you mended the bones, yet?" Nimri nodded. Bryta gave her a smug look. "Well, I don't think anyone would expect you to keep wearing such an ugly thing."

"So, you don't think it's any sort of symbol?"

"When others break a bone and reset it, they tie things to it to keep it in place, until they can get to you and you can begin the mending process." Bryta gave her a penetrating look. "If you're asking me, I think the longer you keep that thing on, the more incompetent they'll consider you."

Nimri blanched, then thrust her arm toward Bryta. "Can you untie this lash?"

Bryta's pudgy fingers worked at the leather, but it didn't budge. She got up and went to the kitchen; a moment later, returning with a knife. Even the sharp blade had a difficult time getting through it, but once the lashing was gone, the other two items were a snap to remove.

Nimri sighed with relief. "Thanks." Bryta twisted a small square of saffron cloth, a sure sign something bothered her. "What are you thinking about?"

"No one on this side has ever seen Thunder Cartwright." Bryta glanced around, peering into the shadows, then leaned closer and whispered, "But years ago, I heard a description of him and this Larwin could pass."

Perhaps he had, years ago, but everyone knew that Cartwright was an old man; perhaps as old as Rolf. "What are you suggesting?" She grinned, unable to resist teasing Bryta. "That the Lost's protector is pretending to be a Guardian and is here, not to aid me, but to kill me in my sleep?" Nimri sobered and grasped Bryta's hands. "If he wanted me dead, Larwin could have killed me on the trail. Or even easier, simply left me in The Star Bridge. Instead, he and Anthropoid helped me. I'm not certain I could have made it back without them."

"Perhaps he needs you alive—he can gain control over our Tribe through you—then extract revenge or whatever he wants at his leisure."

Nimri gulped. Treachery was something Rolf would have done. Since Bryta had been his housekeeper and cook for decades, Nimri didn't know why she was so shocked that Bryta had thought of something so devious. "Bryta, you need to rest. So do I."

Bryta silently studied her for a moment, then sighed and got up. She looked ready to add a final parting remark. Instead she stomped out of the room.

Nimri was left alone with a half-drunk mug of peppermint tea and a stomachache no herbal drink could heal.

Chapter Six

A deep constant rumbling woke Larwin. It seemed close. In fact, the bed vibrated. He lay still and inhaled heavy, fragrant air. Groggily, he realized he was dreaming. With a sigh, he burrowed deeper under the cozy covers and returned to memories of his part in conquering Golterre.

Excitement permeated the barracks beneath the launch bay, where raw recruits were quartered. Some showed their tension in tone and movement, but Larwin followed the example of the ranking officers and pretended a calm he didn't feel. A steady rumbling underscored the memory. It seemed out of place. So did the strange scent of an arboretum.

He tried to roll over, but a heavy, immovable weight covered his chest. He tried to knock the immobilizing blanket aside, but his arms wouldn't move. Larwin steadied his breathing and tried to recall if he had been hurt in action, which would explain why he was strapped to a gurney.

It was difficult to think about anything except his military battles, life on Guerreterre and the things he missed most, like his sister, Tem-aki.

Suddenly, the soft blanket was whipped aside and wet

sandpaper scraped across his face. Larwin opened his eyes, but closed them when sunlight blinded him. Still, one glimpse identified his enormous assailant.

He rolled away from the cat's huge silhouette and jumped off the bed. He landed lower than expected and stumbled. Barely missing a beat, Larwin whirled to face his attacker.

The cat had sprawled on his bed. Both eyes watched him with interest. One tufted ear twitched forward. Behind the beast, GEA-4 stood silhouetted by the morning light from the window; her back to the room and her face to the sun.

Larwin remembered where he was.

The kazza studied him, while the black shaggy tip of his tail tapped out a nameless tune. Larwin squared his shoulders. The beast extended its claws and yawned wide enough to swallow the worthless android.

"GEA-4, I thought I told you to stand watch."

"I am."

"Then why is this creature here?"

"It slept here."

"It what?" Only a lifetime of military service enabled him to appear composed. Of all the malfunctioning programming he'd ever heard of; she'd allowed the carnivorous creature to sleep in his room. On the bed. With him. "That's your procedure for guarding me?"

"It is not hostile. Probabilities indicate the kazza is housebroken."

Larwin wanted to shred every circuit board in her body and reconfigure her into a sculpture. No, then he'd have her around as a visual reminder. Was any revenge adequate for forcing him to sleep with an animal, especially one that size? The creature must out-weigh him three times. One, which had teeth and claws that could probably rip the flesh from a madrox. As he watched, the cat retracted its claws, stood and lazily stretched every sinew of its body. Then it twirled its whiskers and opened its mouth, again. The cavity expanded wider and wider until every huge glinting white spear-pointed tooth was exposed. Larwin's heart fluttered.

His own mouth went dry.

He moved into a defensive stance, but feared the huge cat would be too much for him to defeat in hand-to-hand combat.

Why hadn't he slept with a weapon?

The kazza stood up and the fur on its back rippled. Then it leaped.

Larwin prepared to flip the beast.

Kazza landed next to him. Though the floor trembled, the creature totally ignored him. Instead, the cat sniffed the air, walked to the door, and opened it with the flick of a claw. A moment later, it disappeared down the outside passage.

Larwin's heart continued hammering long after the door swung shut. When the sound of padded footfalls dimmed, Larwin went to his haversack, removed his laser-cutter, then cautiously approached the door. Nothing lurked in the passage except the aroma of more mouth-watering food.

At least he thought it was food. It smelled too good to be anything else. He swallowed the welling saliva. Tempting as it was to immediately follow the scent, he paused to hunker down and inspect the door.

There were numerous round indentations in the wood. This wasn't the first time the animal had let itself out of this room.

Or into it.

Had the kazza been sent as a guard? That didn't make sense. What sort of jailer left the moment the prisoner awoke?

But, he wasn't a prisoner, was he?

A frown creased Larwin's brow. He studied the strange organic-looking chamber. The whitish-bark walls were curved instead of straight and the room's rafters were tan, bark-covered limbs, big as his thigh. The furniture was made from more branches, these were dark as night. Several overlapping golden hued mats covered the floor. Piles of ancient bound volumes massed on one of the woven mats, and more were heaped on the two chairs. Larwin gazed at the books. Which were the old fashioned sort and made from plant matter. In one corner, three towers of them reached to the rafters. Why would anyone need so many books? While they were something familiar to anyone who liked museums, as much as he did, he'd never imagined such a collection simply being strewn over a room.

How much would artifact collectors pay for this assortment?

Shelves along one wall had an odd variety of items. Larwin wasn't sure what they all were, but he recognized some of the stones because Tem-aki had collected them since she was old enough to walk. It hadn't surprised him when his little sister had been assigned to learn geology. He went to the shelves and picked up a whitish stone. While it looked pretty, it had no mineral worth. In fact, none of the collection had value, except to someone, like Tem-aki, who loved stones for their beauty as well as resource-value.

The fact that none contained precious minerals was disappointing.

Larwin took a moment to collect his thoughts and wished he didn't feel so disoriented. He massaged the bridge of his nose. His head felt as if he'd been subjected to a night of psycho training instead of sleep, but winners didn't quit just because of a headache. There were many things to do, if he was to head an invasion into this geode. "Today, we have a two-fold priority. First, we need to learn the language. Second, we need to compile a list of assets. Start by listing the botanical wealth. From what I saw, there are enough natural organisms here to buy me at least two promotions." Maybe even a governor-ship. Gooseflesh rippled at the thought. His stomach growled. "You can recharge outside, while you compile a list of the plants."

Cautiously, he peered out the door. The aromas had strengthened so much that the air seemed edible. Larwin stepped into the hallway then stopped and looked back.

Again, he studied the door's delicate perforations and recalled the creature's sinister-looking claws. The kazza was a contradiction that appeared ferocious, yet it seemed friendly and thus far, it had only consumed items his analyzer determined to be grain-based. Larwin frowned. Perhaps this geode-world did not have the combination of predator and prey found on most worlds. Larwin decided his hostess would be insulted if he appeared carrying a weapon. Feeling slightly foolish, he went back into the room and slipped the las-cutter into his haversack.

Mouth salivating more with each step he took down the endless stairs, Larwin followed the appetizing aroma to the ground floor room. He passed the table and paused, startled to see the splint lying at its center. With a shake of his head, he went on. He detoured around the spot where the older woman had tuned white as a quasar. Skin prickling, Larwin hoped the behavior wasn't some sort of alien greeting.

Larwin rounded the curve and studied the part of the room, which had previously been concealed by the curving shape of the odd chamber. A large patchwork window composed of many oddly mismatched bits reminded him of the amber Temaki collected. A wide plant-covered counter lay beneath the window and sturdy pottery laden shelves flanked it.

The enticing scent came from a black pot, which sat near the open flames of an old-fashioned hearth. Larwin picked up a crude wooden spoon and tentatively stirred the reddish, lumpy mixture. He sniffed the spoon and sipped the concoction. It was some sort of consommé, but he'd never seen any soup with green, white and orange lumps. He placed the spoon in what he hoped was the sink and decided the area was some sort of cooking zone. His stomach rumbled in agreement.

Turning his back on the savory pot, Larwin forced himself to wait until he was certain the brew was edible by humans. He studied the room. It didn't look like any sort of galley he'd ever seen. There were no cupboards, nor sleek plastoid cabinets or stainless steel counters. Here, things were either wood or glazed ceramic and placed on open shelves.

Larwin picked up a thick-bodied bluish mug and studied it. Where a leaf had been pressed into clay, the color in the imprint was deep cerulean. He placed the two-handled mug back on the lower shelf. The most disconcerting thing was the way potted plants seemed to occupy every spare nook and form a hanging ceiling.

"This room reminds me of a potting-shed exhibit I saw in the National Museum. I can't believe how primitive this race is— they use fire to cook food—at least I'm assuming its food. It tasted good," he muttered aloud. "They'll be a snap to conquer."

"The inhabitants of this abode might not be a true representation," GEA-4 said.

"Point taken."

Larwin studied the strange wall above the longest counter and wondered if the hodgepodge of yellow-toned, semi-translucent window was an expensive work of art or the product of an incompetent glassmaker. He could only see clearly through four of the fifty or so odd-shaped panes. Tem-aki would love to own it. "This is a once in a lifetime opportunity to secure my future. I can't afford to be overly confident or take chances."

"True, others could head the invasion and claim the resources."

His jaw clenched. "Not if I present a complete listing of the planet's reserves when I initially return to Guerreterre. If I have a complete list of the planet's biological and mineral resources prior to the assault, I claim it." He turned to GEA-4. "I'll also need to be familiar with the demography so I know how many troops to requisition." This discovery was big enough to net him a major promotion and a bonus liberal enough so he could live all his dreams. The enticing aroma emanating from the pot made it difficult to think. "No time like the present to start the lists."

Larwin opened the thick, round door to a view of valuable vegetation shimmering in a haze of dewy sunlight. The fortune hadn't been a dream. He inhaled deeply; the thick, earthy scent of wealth rivaled the aroma from the pot.

He squared his shoulders and vowed not to lose his focus. "Come on," Larwin said.

He stepped into the humid air. "Last night I was so tired, I didn't realize how isolated this place is. Nimri, must be very wealthy to have such a secluded, exotic home."

"Probabilities indicate this world has a low population and unlike Guerreterre, ground is inexpensive."

"Ground is always expensive." The robot stared at him with her odd, silvery eyes. Larwin paused and considered GEA-4's conclusion. While it was nearly impossible to understand how a culture could thrive without putting a premium on the ground and its resources, he had come across planets that viewed gold as worthless because there was such abundance. On Tribulck, the natives thought sand was valuable, because of its scarcity. "Okay, you may be right." The concept seemed as bizarre as this place, but the more he considered it, the more GEA-4's observation became obvious. That irritated him. So did the rhythmic thumping in the background. Turning his back on GEA-4, he studied what seemed to be a maze of paths winding through planting beds. One well-worn path formed of flat rocks led toward the drumming sound. How was he ever going to manage to categorize the wealth of this one space, let alone the entire world without the instruments in his ship? He needed access to a supercomputer.

"There is a wide assortment of chlorophyll," GEA-4 said.

Was he listening to a cadenced beat of a thousand marching feet or some sort of archaic mechanism? He hoped it was the latter. Where there was one machine, there were generally others. "I hear equipment running," he said. "Let's follow this path. We can see how advanced their machines are." His mind boggled at the thought of the technology required to create a lush world inside this burned out husk.

"I detect no machines."

"Definitely faulty scanners." Larwin rubbed his temple as he passed a patch of velvety silver-leafed plants.

The path meandered across the flat yard, past several plant beds, many of which seemed unable to contain the plants. Larwin inadvertently stepped on a purplish leaf. Mint fragrance engulfed him. He bent down and studied the pungent leaf. Who would have thought that the essence of his favorite liquor came from a plant?

As he moved toward the sound, he passed numerous shapes, colors and sizes of vegetation. Was this world truly as primitive as it seemed or were the leaves created by some unknown type of technology? He pinched a waving frond and sniffed his fingers. Again, there was an aroma, but this was not mint. He frowned as he tried to put a name to the spicy aroma.

Abruptly, the path made a turn and veered down the precipitous side of a chasm. Larwin stepped on a round rock. It moved. He stumbled and fell toward the abyss.

A hand grabbed his forearm and jerked him back to safety. Then, the artificial clouds parted and light bathed a nearby portion of the garden. GEA-4 released his arm and went to stand in the center of the beam. Larwin looked down for the rock, hoping to kick it. It moved away, its pointy tail stiff with irritation and the leathery nose held high. He gulped.

Larwin stood, knees trembling and glanced at a large, craggy boulder, wondering if it, too, was alive. Unbidden, the word tortoise came to mind and he recalled a myth about the rock-animals.

To think they existed.

The farther he went down the trail, the louder the drumming

became. Larwin wondered if it was his heart or if he was close to the machinery. He studied the rocky trail hoping for a second glimpse of the wondrous rock creature, but only dense vegetation and a smoky haze were visible in the basin. Smoke meant an old fashioned factory, yet the smoke didn't smell like burning wood or petrol products. He'd hoped for something high-tech, perhaps he was looking at the results of a mist emitter.

Larwin concentrated on his footing and followed the path downward. He rounded a boulder, ducked under the boughs of a tree and squinted through the patchy vapor. A large black rectangle lay on a narrow beach next to the path. His skin prickled as he tried to grasp why the geometric shape had been placed there. A breath of wind cleared away some of the haze. Beyond the peach colored sands glistened a secluded pool filled with turquoise water.

Breath caught in his throat as Larwin took a step backward and leaned against the boulder for support. Never, even in his wildest dreams, had he dared believe such incredible riches as an actual pool of water existed.

The path continued on, over a rustic bridge made of twisted limbs that were rough to the touch. He paused next to a clump of tall feathery plants, where the trail split: one part turned sharply toward the water; the other, more heavily traveled section, veered downhill. Several additional clumps of the plume-like plants were scattered around the pool. In fact, vegetation abounded, taking up every millimeter not occupied by rock. Knees trembling, Larwin hunkered down, until the weakness passed. Out of habit, he pretended to study the ground. Even as he gave the impression of fitness and productivity, he noticed that tiny lace-like plants grew on the boulders.

Another gust revealed the far side of the pool; a waterfall plummeted down a sheer rock wall, creating fog where moving water melded with the pool. As he stared at the incredible sight,

Nimri and the kazza emerged from the mist and swam across the turquoise water. She laughed, and then she was gone, seemingly swallowed by another bank of fog.

Larwin wondered if Planetary Sovereigns commanded enough wealth to afford such riches.

Plants, water and living stones and food worthy of the gods.

Perhaps he had died and gone to his reward.

He stood up and stepped to the edge of the pool. Heart hammering, he knelt and touched the water. It felt wet. He tasted the droplet on his finger. It tasted real. Perhaps this was not an intricate illusion, after all.

And that meant he was rich, rich, rich!

Unable to contain himself, Larwin let out a war-whoop of victory.

~0~

Nimri's morning swim was special because it was the second time in her life that she'd had the luxury of floating in sunlight. Rolf had gotten so angry the one time he caught her that she had pretended to avoid the water afterward. Today, as she climbed the trail to her garden, the sun felt wonderfully warm as her thoughts veered to the two strangers and she wondered what she was meant to learn from them.

Initially, she had resented the way they refused to communicate with her, but then, she had realized how much concentration she was using to understand their reasoning. Lack of verbal communication surely made one think and she suspected that could be their method. Perhaps, when she learned whatever they were trying to teach her, they would speak to her, which was exactly the opposite of the way her grandfather taught.

She was so lost in thought at the difference that she strayed near a yucca's spiny tip. Her dappled aqua-toned towel snagged.

When she tugged at the soft fabric; the undulating hues

reminded her of rippling water. Unbidden, she remembered her youthful nightmares and the pervasive fear that water would yank her beneath its surface and smother her in its depths. Since getting past her inexplicable childish phobia, she and Kazza had developed a ritual of starting the day by sneaking out of the house in the dark, swimming until light began to wash the sky, then sitting on a boulder and watching the sun rise over the rim of the gorge as they shivered and dried in the growing light.

The fabric ripped free, leaving a finger-long rent that reminded her of Rolf's furious expression the only time she'd let him know she'd floated in the pool. He had stood on the precipice, and raised his staff. His voice thundered as he'd ordered her away from the water. She had never understood why he had been furious. She'd expected him to be happy for her, as Larwin had been. With Rolf gone, she'd never know why he'd been angry when she confronted her fear, yet ridiculed her for crying over it. She shook her head and wondered if her grandfather was particularly difficult or she was missing something.

For months after her great-grandfather's threat, Nimri had been terrified of losing her life, but the pool's enticement was stronger than the fears it had helped her conquer. Though she'd tried to stay away from the water's lure, she couldn't. Sneaking out for a predawn swim seemed to strengthen her for the day. By the time Rolf's death was certain, she and Kazza were swimming every day before dawn.

Too bad learning to love the water was her only achievement.

Nimri looked upward to the spot where Rolf had dashed her arrogance. Anthropoid stood, still as a statue in the middle of her chamomile patch, just behind where her grandfather had been. The sunlight reflected off Anthropoid's strange eyes. Nimri winced and wondered why the odd little woman tortured herself for two or three hours every day.

A movement beneath the ginkgo caught Nimri's attention. She shaded her eyes and saw Larwin twirling a fan-shaped leaf.

Ginkgo was powerful medicine, but surely the resurrected Guardian knew that. Had she just discovered his secret for longevity? Did he contemplate the plant's memory value? Or did he suffer from ringing ears? Perhaps he was considering giving it to her for some reason. But why?

From the half-open kitchen door, Kazza mewed a plaintive reminder. Nimri pushed aside her unanswerable questions and headed for the house. She ladled minestrone into Kazza's bowl, then leaned against the counter and studied Anthropoid through the window. On the trail, Anthropoid hadn't touched a bite of food or a drop of water. Nimri wondered what terrible deed Anthropoid must have done that required her to stand still and stare into the burning rays of the sun each day. She also wondered why poor Anthropoid neither tanned nor burned.

As usual, there were no answers, just more questions.

While Kazza contentedly lapped up his fourth bowl of minestrone, Nimri filled three mugs with soup and placed them on her favorite woven tray. Then, she broke a long loaf of bread into five pieces. She gave Kazza one, left a piece for Bryta and put the rest on the tray. She went outside and placed everything on her outdoor table.

Larwin joined her before she called him. With amusement, she watched him sniff the minestrone as if it was the most delicious food imaginable, instead of an everyday breakfast.

Nimri picked up Anthropoid's portion, with the intent of taking it to her, but Larwin touched her hand and shook his head. Nimri glared at him, furious that he would deprive the poor woman of food, but his attention was on her arm. She yanked it back, flushing with the realization that she should have asked him instead of listening to Bryta. Perhaps she should put the itchy thing back on.

When she picked up the food a second time, Larwin finally took his attention from her arm and pantomimed that Anthropoid didn't eat food—that she used the sun's energy for sustenance. He acted out his message three times before Nimri accepted it.

Though she still didn't believe it. Nimri turned to look at Anthropoid and knew she'd never heard of anyone so magical. To think, the guardian could exist on sunlight.

Unbelievable to realize the poor woman wasn't doing penance, as she'd suspected, but was gaining power.

Nimri shook her head. She must have misunderstood. Yet there had been countless instances on the trail where Anthropoid's strength had been demonstrated.

Food forgotten, Nimri observed Anthropoid.

Larwin tapped her forearm. Nimri looked at him. He'd eaten his own breakfast and Anthropoid's. Larwin raised an eyebrow and pointed at her uneaten food. He's a bottomless pit, just like Kazza. No longer hungry for mortal food, Nimri pushed it and her hunk of bread at him.

Larwin drank the minestrone as if he'd been starving for the last millennium. Maybe he had.

After he finished eating, Larwin returned to her garden and stared at her rosemary. First ginkgo; now rosemary, which were both for remembering. He must be considering which herbs he needed for her, especially after pantomiming the information about Anthropoid three times.

How could she make him understand that the problem wasn't her memory, it was her disbelief at what he had told her?

Nimri closed her eyes and hoped he approved of her efforts, yet doubted he could understand any more than her great-grandfather had. Perhaps either he or Anthropoid would give up on trying to teach her how to be a protector and simply teach her the properties of some of the more exotic specimens in her garden, like guarana, which required warmth and tender care. Herbal remedies had been passed down to Nimri's great-aunt Violet, Rolf's sister, but Violet had died before passing on all her knowledge to Nimri. Bryta remembered bits and pieces of what her great-aunt Violet had used the plants for and how to process them, but not everything. Violet had revered guarana, but never explained why, before she died. Nimri had tried to determine the medical value of it and many of the other herbs, which resided in the old healer's garden, so she could better care for her tribe.

Her great-grandfather hadn't known much about botany. In fact, she'd often sensed that he disdained her efforts to learn the plants' purposes.

Nimri picked up the tray and empty bowls, then carried them to the kitchen.

Kazza was nowhere in sight, but Bryta sat at the kitchen table shelling peas into one of Quark Dagger's beautiful tan and blue crocks. The bottom of the bowl was already covered.

Nimri placed the mugs in the thyme-scented water. "Larwin explained that Anthropoid lives on the air's energy." A pea shot out of Bryta's grasp, hit the wall, then bounced over the tiled floor. "I had no idea she was such a magical creature," Nimri added, as she tried to get Bryta to understand the importance of their guests. "It's no wonder she looks odd."

The bowl crashed to the floor. Nimri jumped. Miraculously unbroken, the bowl righted itself in the center of a pool of peas, which were rolling away like ripples from a pebble tossed into water.

Bryta dropped to her knees and began collecting them. Nimri knelt to help her, but paid more attention to Bryta, who normally was fastidious about her appearance. Instead of her elegant coronet of braids, she'd left her hair loose. Worse, behind the curtain of disorderly gray and white, Bryta's complexion appeared to be colorless.

"What's wrong?" Nimri asked gently. "Do they frighten you? Or is it something else? Are you ill?"

"You frighten me," Bryta said. Nimri saw tears streaming behind her loose locks. "You were raised to protect us, but you allow unknown dangers into your – our – home."

Bryta swiveled to face her, and pushed back her hair. Spots

scarlet as cherries, wet as dew, appeared on her cheeks. The scent of peas was strong. "Rolf would never have done that. He would have, would have—"

"Killed them while they were still an unknown," Nimri said. "While they were a possible threat, but before he confirmed whether they were actually a menace or a friend." Having the courage to finally voice her opinion made Nimri feel giddy with relief. She stared at Bryta, silently daring her to disagree.

Bryta blinked and dropped her gaze to the floor. After taking several breaths, which restored some of her color, Bryta slowly nodded.

Nimri picked up a pea and studied its perfection. "Bryta, I'm not my Great-grandfather. I don't have the stomach for wholesale massacres, which I believe were rooted in the fear that our tribe might learn new ways—possibly better ways. What if we don't need to continue on as we have for the past millennium?"

"What are you trying to say?" The tip of Bryta's tongue wet her lips. "That you won't protect us?" Her voice squeaked like a mouse.

"No." Nimri wondered how to phrase her half-formed thoughts. "I'm saying I don't know if I can fulfill the duty or not, but I do know I won't kill unless there is no other choice. I must honor my first vow - the one I took when I became our Tribe's healer. The one where I swore to value all life."

"And if one of those filthy Lost kills you?" As always, Bryta's tone was hostile when she mentioned their enemy.

"Then I will have died for my beliefs and science will have proved stronger."

Bryta's blue eyes were angry. "Which science isn't." She spat on the floor. "If you die, so do we all. The Lost won't show mercy."

Nimri sighed. "I'll reconsider my opinion, but won't make any promises, because I can't believe that even the Lost are that barbaric."

"You have always been blind to other's flaws and always want to believe the best." The knuckles on Bryta's hand were white; the green ooze of smashed peas seeped between her fingers. "Do you know what Anthropoid was doing before she went outside?"

"No."

"Touching the books Rolf left in the front room. Not only that, she was looking through them. Page by page." Her fist shook. "How dare she!"

"She's magical," Nimri said. Anthropoid always seemed to have a purpose for everything she did. "Wouldn't it be wonderful if she could read the manuscripts?" A bubble of hope grew within Nimri. "So much knowledge was forfeited when we lost the ability to decipher the symbols."

Bryta snorted as she rose. She washed her hands in the basin, then swept up the peas, as if they were too worthless to even put in the compost pit. A chill swept over Nimri. "Did you say anything to Anthropoid?" Nimri asked. Bryta raised her chin. "Did you forbid her from touching the manuscripts?"

"No! I will not speak to such an abomination," Bryta shouted. She took a deep breath. "I merely observed her and told you." Bryta's expression hardened as she looked fiercely at Nimri. When Nimri glared back, instead of accepting the guilt, Bryta looked out the window at Anthropoid. "Remember, magic can be evil as well as good. Never assume the best just because she's painted herself white."

"Fine, but don't expect me to look for the worst, either."

Chapter Seven

Despite her declaration, Nimri's newfound conviction faltered when she harvested mullein leaves to make a potion for Pearl's indigestion. What if Bryta was right to be suspicious? Nimri hunkered down behind the mullein and darted a look at Anthropoid, whose head followed the beams of light, like a sunflower. Only a supernatural being could do that from dawn to midday, every day and keep a snow-white complexion. Nimri plucked a few extra leaves to dry for winter use and chided herself for doubting her convictions about her guests. Soon, the mullein plant was a chartreuse nub in a circle of black loam. Nimri sat back on her heels and stared at the barren stalk.

Beads of perspiration broke out on her forehead. Did Anthropoid perspire? She sneaked another peek, but it was just past the middle of the day and Anthropoid had left the garden. Larwin, barely visible in the forest's shadow, touched, crushed and sniffed a ginseng leaf. Nimri squinted. At least he had a sheen of sweat on his face. There were also green smudges on his hands. His skin seemed normal. But why was he inspecting her garden with such intensity? Was he looking for something to relieve stress?

If so, were his concerns about his own tension or hers? Maybe he was interested because she had given a dose to Bryta, earlier. He had yet to share a conversation with her, but she needed to know why he'd come.

Nimri's mouth flattened with the knowledge that even with Rolf dead, she still avoided confrontations. She got to her feet and brushed the dirt from her hands. Picking up her basket and squaring her shoulders, she went to find out what Larwin expected from her.

He dropped the foliage and moved in her direction. They met near her menthe patch. She opened her mouth to ask why he had come to her, then realized she didn't speak the sacred language and snapped her jaws shut. To stall for time, she stooped and picked a sprig of chocolate mint. She crushed it between her forefinger and thumb, then held it up to his nose. "Menthe." It felt stupid to name the simple plant for him.

Larwin sniffed and involuntarily smiled. "Men-th-a." He carefully enunciated each syllable.

Perhaps he wanted her to display the knowledge she'd already attained, and further test her abilities by pretending not to understand the language. Rolf had always found strange ways of testing her, too. Pantomiming as she spoke, Nimri said, "Yes. Its smell relieves headaches. Menthe stimulates the appetite." She rubbed her stomach and licked her lips. "And when made into an oil, it relieves muscle pain."

"Menthe." Larwin gave Nimri a broad smile, as he took the sprig from her and tasted it.

What if the only thought she'd shared was that mint is good to eat? Nimri smiled back, uncertain if she'd passed the test or even if he'd understood the benefits she'd just described. Larwin bent and picked a foxglove leaf. When it looked like he intended to eat it, she screamed, "No!" Nimri caught his forearm, stopping it a finger's width from his mouth. "Digitalis. Fixes bad hearts. Kills healthy people." She dramatized a heart attack.

Larwin gaped at the leaf then dropped it. His expression reminded Nimri of the horror she'd seen on Flame's face when they'd seen a snake eat a baby bunny. As Nimri wondered what to say and how to show her respect, after having been so bold, Bryta rushed out the kitchen door and frantically gestured for Nimri to come inside.

Bryta kept looking back at the empty doorway as if demons had invaded her kitchen, while smoothing her hair as if she feared someone inside would see her disheveled.

What had Kazza done this time?

Or, in light of Bryta's most recent complaints, what had their guests done that Bryta had either observed, imagined or discovered?

If Bryta kept on extolling Rolf's questionable justice and continued complaining about Larwin and Anthropoid, Nimri didn't know what she would do. Nimri acknowledged Bryta with a jaunty wave, and hoped Larwin didn't see her hand tremble. Then, she turned to Larwin and gestured that he should not to eat any more plants until she returned. Judging by his look of horror at the idea, her warning was unnecessary.

As soon as Nimri came close enough, Bryta grabbed her upper arm, hauled her behind a quince bush, leaned close and whispered, "I went upstairs and saw that sick white one looking at Rolf's sacred books! Again!" Nimri's jaw clenched. "I didn't know what to do, so came to get you." Nimri opened her mouth to tell Bryta to stop complaining and let Anthropoid do whatever she wished. But Bryta rushed on to add, "And as I passed the front window, I saw Zurgon coming up the path."

"The Chief Elder is coming here?" Nimri was horrified to hear her own voice turn shrill. "To me? Why?"

Wringing her hands in distress, Bryta stepped around the shrub and sneaked a glance at the front door. Her expression looked like she expected a Yeti to attack her at any moment, but it was doubtful if Zurgon would demand anything more than tea from

Bryta.

Nimri knew she wouldn't be so lucky.

Bryta ducked back behind the quince. Her trembling hands twisted her cleaning smock into a wad. "It has to be about the Lost." She sneaked another quick peek around the quince. "He must be coming to get you so you will perform your duty."

She'd reached the same conclusion. Nimri forced herself to straighten her spine and square her shoulders. Given the ability, she would have done anything for her people, but realistically, she was only capable of being their healer. No matter what Zurgon wanted, he and the Tribe were bound to be disappointed. Even if she'd been able to control the weather, she knew she'd never be able to indiscriminately murder in the name of peace.

Larwin sniffed a sprig of lavender. Though edible, he didn't taste it. Could it be that he didn't know the values of the herbs, or had he been testing her, earlier?

In the distance, there was a purposeful knock on the door.

"He's here." Bryta whimpered. "What will you do?" Bryta's white knuckled hands knotted the fabric of her cleaning smock and her sobbing increased.

"Is Anthropoid damaging the books?"

"No," Bryta said. "Looking at them, but who knows what a person as odd as she is will do."

"Fine," Nimri said. "Then Zurgon is my most pressing problem." She softly added, "He's only a man." A powerful man, who could turn her life into a misery, but he was still only a man. He'll understand I'm only a woman—not a shaman to keep the peace. The thought sounded feeble, but with no other option, Nimri lifted her chin and entered the kitchen.

As Nimri entered the back door, she paused and closed her eyes to adjust from the bright midday light. When she opened them, Zurgon was seated at the table, sipping a mug of tea, and looking at her as if weighing her worth. He had become the highest-ranking member of the Chosen Tribe when Rolf died, and obviously believed he no longer needed to wait on anyone's stoop.

Nimri's stomach and heart leapt in fright. She wasn't sure, but she thought her entire body jumped before she came to a dead stop. "Zurgon. I thought I heard someone knock." She squinted in the dim room, hoping to judge his attitude by his expression, but his face became as blank as his eyes had been alert.

Nimri felt Bryta behind her wringing her apron into a lump. Somehow the knowledge helped Nimri find a kernel of calmness to center herself on.

Zurgon put down the mug and rose to his feet. "Nimri, I have come to offer my condolences to you for your loss. Rolf's passing is terrible for the Tribe, but it's particularly hard for you." He lifted a thin, blue-veined hand and offered her a seat at her own table.

"Thank you." Nimri took the seat facing him and focused on the serene kernel of courage amidst the flurry of butterflies in her stomach. With every breath, her nerve seemed to shrink and spawn a dozen more butterflies.

Zurgon sat down as if wet noodles held his skeleton together. Nimri suspected his arthritis was acting up, but didn't mention it. Zurgon and Rolf were alike in many ways. Years ago, she'd learned it was better to allow them to direct the conversation and pretend they were right.

His pale green stare made her back prickle. Nimri wished she dared to look away. It would be easier to study his beaded amulet, his snow-white hair or even scrutinize the pattern of wrinkles at the corners of his eyes.

But when faced with an unknown or an enemy, she'd been taught to keep her attention on their eyes.

Bryta shoved a mug of tea in front of Nimri. When the brew slopped over the edge, Zurgon frowned at Bryta. Bryta quickly cleaned up the mess with the skirt of her rumpled smock. Zurgon's scowl deepened, Bryta sprinted out of the room as if pursued by a swarm of bees. The corner of Zurgon's lips twitched. "Bryta has acted like an overwrought yard-bird since she was a child." Zurgon laughed softly.

Nimri felt a surge of loathing for the man, who found intimidation rewarding, but she refused to be baited into a childish display of temper. Instead, she took a sip of tea. Raising her chin, she forced herself to remain as aloof as the Chief Elder. "You didn't journey all this way to discuss Bryta's personality, did you?"

"No, I came to remind you that the Tribe needs you."

"I know, bu—"

"The Lost push harder each day. They desire our land for they have destroyed their own in their greed for digging up worthless minerals." Zurgon's fist hit the table. It took all Nimri's control not to jump or flinch. "As Rolf's heir and protector of our land, you must quell them. You must take up the staff and be seen protecting the village."

Nimri swallowed. How did he know she hadn't been able to touch it? It was a question she dare not ask, for it would reveal too much. "How do we know they've ruined their land?" Zurgon gave her an exasperated look. "From Sacred Mountain, I could see the entire valley. Their side may lack trees, but it didn't look ravaged. The fields looked tended."

"Lies. Rumors spread by the heathen Lost. How dare you repeat them?"

"I could see their land from Sacred Mountain." Nimri rose, placed her hands flat on either side of her unwanted tea and leaned across the table toward her uninvited guest. "If they truly are a threat, I will do everything in my power to save our people from them, but I need to know they are a genuine menace." Screaming in his face would never solve anything or quench her doubts. She took a deep breath. "Zurgon, I wish to cross the river to see their way of life for myself." He didn't believe the truth of what she had seen with her own eyes. "Since you are so determined to believe the worst, I think you should come with me."

"Never!" He surged to his feet and matched her stance. Their faces were a hand's breadth apart; Nimri could smell garlic on his breath as he enunciated each syllable. "And neither will you. Those savages will kill you."

"Will they?" Nimri wished she wasn't half convinced he was right. Wished she could ignore the nagging doubt. "How can you expect me to have the power to protect the entire Tribe if you don't even believe I can look after myself?" Despite his words of confidence to the Tribe, as they had come to the pyre, he didn't seem to value her any more than Rolf had. "Answer me. Don't you think I can protect myself?" Zurgon blinked in surprise. "I survived the pilgrimage to the Star Bridge. Surely, I can survive crossing the river." Nimri felt a fleeting moment of victory as emotions of shock and wonder scrolled across his face.

He asked, "Would you have me break the law?" She shook her head. "Would you break it, yourself?" She didn't know how to respond, so simply stared at him. Again, his fist hit the table. Tea sloshed on the hickory slab. "You may not cross the river except by swimming or a boat. If you leave and the Lost don't kill you when you get to their shore, you will be considered one of them and will only be allowed to return to our sacred soil on Market Days."

"I know the law."

"Is that what you want?" Zurgon straightened and his expression became confused. "To become one with the enemy?"

"No, but I'm not ready to pick up Rolf's staff, either." Nimri wet her lips and tried honesty. "I don't have the power to weld it."

She didn't know what she'd expected his reaction to her

admission to be. Zurgon stared past her, as if she'd become invisible.

A shadow moved across the floor.

Nimri turned and saw Larwin standing in the doorway. She smiled encouragingly and gestured for him to join them. Larwin's attention never left Zurgon, as he came and stood next to her.

Zurgon's vigilance never faltered either.

"Who is this man?" Zurgon asked.

He has not the look of the Lost, nor is he of the Chosen. I know each member of our Tribe."

"He is from the balata," Nimri said.

As her meaning sank in, Zurgon's throat-ball bobbed, the whites of his eyes expanded and his feet shifted until the backs of his knees pushed the chair rearward. Wood on tile whined. "The balata is home to our sacred guardians," he whispered. It looked as if Zurgon might drop to the floor and prostrate himself before Larwin, as if he was the most junior member of the tribe.

She'd never expected to see any Elder unnerved, much less the Chief Elder.

Nimri was tempted to look to her left and see what Larwin thought of Zurgon, but suddenly the Elder's attention switched from Larwin to her. He now looked at her as if she was as magical as Larwin. Surely the Elder didn't think she had raised the Guardian!

"From the balata..." Zurgon's voice cracked like an adolescent's, as he repeated the thought. His tongue darted out to moisten his lips.

Nimri turned to Larwin. He watched Zurgon as if he'd either never seen another man or was ready to commit murder. She gulped, desperate to quell the hostilities. "Larwin, this is Zurgon, our Chief Elder." Larwin's chestnut brown gaze never faltered, but his posture did seem to relax at her calm tone and the primary etiquette of greeting.

"Why do you call him Larwin?" Zurgon faltered.

"Because it's what he insists on being called, though he initially introduced himself as Colonel."

Zurgon cleared his throat. "Why does he not speak for himself?"

"He simply doesn't." Nimri shrugged as if the question wasn't one that plagued her. "Maybe he chooses not to or maybe not speaking is a test or maybe our language and customs are new to him or maybe -"

"Chatterre has but one language."

"Yes, Chatterre only has one, but what of Solterre?"

"Surely you don't believe he's from the first world." A shudder rippled Zurgon's tan and brown tunic and revealed how emaciated his legs were underneath the layers of cloth.

"I don't know what I believe." Too weak to stand, Nimri sat down and held her mug as if the residual warmth would save her. "Rolf said that on the first world many countries were populated and each country had its own language and traditions." Larwin moved to stand behind her chair.

"Fairytales," Zurgon said.

"Touch a balata leaf and fairytales seem possible." Nimri hoped Zurgon had chamomile tea. Judging by the way his slacks were vibrating, he could use something to calm his nerves. Nimri had previously thought knocking knees were a euphemism.

Zurgon clenched his hands and straightened his back. "Some are, Child of Tramontain." His tone turned sarcastic. "Why have you raised the Lou Wren from the old tales to help us?"

Hadn't he heard a word she'd said? She paused, stared at Zurgon and ran his pronunciation over in her mind. "Until you said something, I'd forgotten the tale about the Lou Wren of the Ancients; Lou Wren, the Son of Light." Heat crept up the back of her neck.

"Why have you raised him for us?"

She had not raised Larwin; he'd raised himself. "Perhaps he or Anthropoid know the answer to that, but they aren't saying."

"Anthropoid?" Zurgon sat down hard enough to rattle his bones. He mouthed Anthropoid's name several times, reminding Nimri of a beached fish. "Throp Anthrus..." He swallowed. "Not Throp Anthrus the prophetess?" His voice cracked. "Have you raised her, too?"

The man must be losing his mind. It happened to some of the older ones and Zurgon was well into his eighties, so dementia could be a possibility.

"Is that why you avoid me?" Zurgon hissed. "Because the danger is so great?"

Nimri held her mug between both hands and wondered what she should say. What if he was correct? What if she was the obtuse one? Why had the Guardians materialized to help her?

If the danger were so great, it might explain why The Guardians chose not to speak to her. They may well believe revealing the truth would frighten her too much or that she was too ignorant to handle it.

~0~

After the strange visit from Zurgon, the rattle-bones, Larwin returned to his bedchamber. GEA-4 was scanning the ancient manuscripts, which were stacked in the corner. Ignoring her, he went to the window and watched the elderly man march away. What an odd encounter that had been. Were all the men on this world in their fifties? Was the skinny old guy the only male?

Larwin scratched his head and wondered if Nimri and Bryta had swooned over him because they'd never seen a man in his prime before. He didn't like the idea of the old woman having such thoughts, but he had to admit that he wouldn't mind Nimri having them—assuming her physical makeup proved nontoxic to his, of course.

Larwin pushed his non-productive thoughts aside and turned to GEA-4. The book she held had an illustration of a combustion engine. What a surprise! The most complex thing he'd seen since arriving were a pair of crude scissors so despite the fantastic images of a paradise, he had begun wondering if the inhabitants knew anything about mechanics. Yet, combustion engines were light years away from the technology he'd seen, so far. He looked up at the pristine blue sky and frowned. Their technology must have advanced on an entirely different level for them to create this geode-world.

"GEA-4, have you gathered any useful data on this place?"

"Yes, Colonel Atano, I have." She flipped the page.

"What are your conclusions?"

"Your inquiry is not specific." Another page turned.

Larwin waited, getting hotter and angrier by the moment, he silently willed the infernal android to behave properly.

GEA-4 continued scanning pages at a rate of one per second.

"Have you figured out a pattern to their speech or any specific words?" Larwin said through clenched jaws.

"No, I have not."

He sighed. "Nimri took her cast off. Did you notice?"

"Yes."

"Have you had a chance to scan her arm?" Breaks like that usually took months to recover from, when treated in the field.

"No sign of the injuries remain."

His jaw dropped. He'd give anything to have some alien DNA like that. But he couldn't dwell on such an innocuous issue. "Have you been able to determine where the power station is?"

"There is none except the sun."

Nothing except the what? He closed his eyes and saw red. He counted to twenty-five, then continued on to fifty. "You and your faulty scanners!" Larwin barely managed to control his irritation and knew he should have continued to a hundred. "We're in the bowels of a planetoid. There is no sun." Perhaps he should have counted to a thousand. "They merely have the technology to make it appear so ... what other information or misinformation do you have?"

"Probabilities indicate this planet's diameter is eight-thousand-four-hundred-twenty-six point-three miles. Its distance from the sun is ninety-three-point-two-nine-nine million miles. It rotates on a magnetic axis, thus its core is molten metal with a high probability of iron mixed with gold. Each day is twenty-six-point-seven-three-nine-two Guerreterre hours. Each day the planet tips one-point-two-six miles to my left." Right on schedule, she flipped a page.

Larwin's hand clenched at the thought of strangling the sinewy metal neck. Not that GEA-4 would notice...

She began to turn a page, but paused. "Probabilities indicate the tunnel is an undiscovered wormhole."

A current of electricity surged from his mind to his toes. Could she possibly be right?

No!

Larwin put his fists on his hips and glared at GEA-4's perfectly shaped ear. "All known wormholes exist near black holes."

GEA-4 closed the book and picked up one with the picture of an ocean liner on its cover. Did this planetoid have a hidden sea, too? It made sense, since the river he'd seen from the mountain had to deposit its water somewhere.

Instead of opening the cover, she pivoted to face him. "Yes, Colonel Atano, all known inter-space conduits are located within black holes." Larwin realized she was agreeing with his point and found that even more confusing than her continual misstatements. "However, that does not mean wormholes cannot be found elsewhere."

"Assuming that's true, where are we?"

"Your inquiry is not specific."

"Can you scan the stars and plot our astrological position?" He was using the same tone he'd heard Nimri and Zurgon use, but at that time, he'd focused on grasping her words. Now, hearing in his own voice and understanding the language, he comprehended that the aliens had been quarreling.

Had he been the source of their discussion? If so, was their discord over his discovery of their hidden world or the fact he was living with two females? Larwin didn't know their cultural standards; so found the question impossible to answer. For certain the old man didn't trust him and refused to stay in the same house with him.

So, where did Zurgon live? Larwin looked around the chamber. Everything in it indicated the owner of the room was male, probably a mature one, judging by the clothing in the chests. Larwin narrowed his eyes and studied the thick, twisted black staff in the corner. It was the sort of thing someone who was either in poor heath or somehow disabled would use, if they lived in a primitive culture such as this. Could Nimri have put him in the old man's room? Was this a matriarchal society, which gave her the power to throw the old man out of his home? Was that the crux of the discord he had just witnessed?

"My programming only covered known star systems," GEA-4 said.

He blinked in confusion at the abrupt change of topic. Then her meaning sank in: they had gone through a wormhole and were lost in an unknown quadrant of space. Cold, chilblain-raising air moved over Larwin. If correct, that meant he might be stranded here for eternity. Ripples of alternating hot and cold rushed over him. He sat on the edge of the bed wondering if GEA-4 had purposely used such a calm tone while giving him the devastating news.

"Everything I worked for—lost. My family—lost." He'd never see Tem-aki again. Larwin put his face in his hands and focused on breathing. Living. While there was life, there was hope. By the time he looked up, GEA-4 was halfway through the ocean liner book. "Did you realize you were ruining my future when you destroyed my ship?"

A page flipped. "Your inquiry lacks adequate information."

"It wasn't a question. I was making a statement." Larwin's throat ached with the strain of swallowing unshed tears. "You ruined my life. I'm stuck on this forsaken planet; destined to spend the rest of my life surrounded by treasure I can't profit by and I'm forced to live with a beautiful alien, whose flesh burns me when I touch it."

The sheer power of his loss made him feel as if he had been disintegrated by a photon torpedo. "Here, I'm no one and probably as poisonous to them as they must be to me." He stood up and paced the room. "On Guerreterre, I had rank. If I brought back this bounty, I would have become a Lord."

"My scanners don't show a heat differential for Nimri or alien DNA," GEA-4 said matter-of-factly, as she turned a page.

"Of course they don't." Faulty scanners had to be the cause of all his problems. "Why do I keep asking you? I'll use my analyzer." Once it proved the android wrong, he could theorize her celestial calculations were correct.

Chapter Eight

After Zurgon left, Nimri returned to her garden and resumed picking chocolate menthe. Being in the garden had always calmed and helped her think. The minty smell helped, too. Thanks to Zurgon, she had a lot to ponder.

Bryta appeared around the corner of the house; part of her smock hung in an uneven wad; she gripped the other part as if it was a lifeline. Bryta's irrational worry had begun when Rolf became ill, then day by day her absurd behavior and nervousness had increased. One evening, she'd confided that she feared Rolf would never recover. Day by day her panic had grown. Nimri's qualms had intensified, too. On the final day of his illness, Bryta had wailed over her uncertain future. Nimri assured her that she had a home and position for as long as she wanted it, but her offer had not calmed Bryta. Nimri had hoped Bryta would improve after her great-grandfather's ashes were laid in the balata.

Now, Nimri wondered if her surrogate mother intuitively sensed impending doom, if Bryta sincerely missed Rolf or if she had more complaints about their guests. Judging from the white-knuckled grip Bryta had on her rumpled saffron apron, her sallow complexion coupled with the thin lips, and the tentative gait, Nimri knew she should prepare for an earful about something.

Before Bryta had a chance to say whatever was on her mind, Nimri gave her a sunny smile and said, "Zurgon told me Pearl's muscles were sore. I need menthe to make an ointment." Nimri sighed. "Pearl always seems to be the first to fall ill, then within a week, everyone is sick."

Bryta's lips thinned and her eyes shifted as she fought a mental war over desire to say whatever she had come outside to say and the need to discredit Pearl, who had been her bitter rival since they were children. She opened then closed her mouth several times, the way fish did and almost looked comical. Then, Bryta's eyes sparked with a familiar fire; she let go of her apron, straightened and thrust out her bosom. Nimri bit the inside of her lips to hold back the bubbling relief of laughter and prepared to hear Bryta condemn Pearl for having attracted the man she'd once favored, but now feared.

"That's because she is the worst gossip in the tribe," Bryta said. "And she always refuses to stay away from others when she's ill." Bryta had never had a nice thing to say about Pearl in the twenty years that Nimri had known her. "She'd sooner spread her gossip and infect everyone. She thinks rules don't matter because of Zurgon's status."

"Who? Pearl?" Nimri hoped her expression appeared genuinely perplexed. She and Flame often joked about Bryta's jealousy over Pearl, who had become Head Woman when she bonded with Zurgon. Worse, Pearl always knew the latest news first, whereas they heard it last because their home was halfway up the mountainside and it was rare for them to have visitors, so they usually found out the news on market day. Ever since Nimri had known her, Bryta had alternated between being Pearl's sworn rival and her best friend. But whether friend or foe, she'd always viewed Pearl as her only true competition.

Bryta's face flushed. "Of course, Pearl. Who else is such an infernal gossip and always such a know it all? What's worse, she gets away with spreading lies along with her germs."

Bryta had just described herself, as well as Pearl. Nimri barely managed to contain the threatening chuckle. Certain that her smile would give her away, she kept her head down and acted as if choosing menthe leaves absorbed all her attention. "Pearl does, doesn't she?" She muttered after the inclination to laugh abated.

Bryta snorted and mumbled something under her breath.

"You're right," Nimri still didn't trust herself enough to stop picking or look up. "I'll probably need enough ointment for everyone." Nimri sat back on her heels and took a deep breath. She darted a look up at Bryta's fiery red cheeks. "You can help harvest." She resumed her chore.

For a moment, she thought Bryta would continue venting, but Bryta stooped over and yanked leaves off the plants as if they were weeds.

Nimri's eyes began watering as mint permeated the air. Her sinuses purged and she swallowed a thick lump of mucus. Abruptly it seemed like the aroma intensified tenfold. Nimri hoped the ointment would work as well on Pearl as the main ingredient had on her.

"Well, I see I'll have plenty to carry to Market tomorrow." Bryta grumbled. "What's worse, I'll have extra barter to carry back, if I'm expected to cook for two more."

Complaining about the additional food they needed to satisfy Larwin's appetite seemed to cheer Bryta, but for once, Nimri found validity in her surrogate mother's grumbling. Bryta wasn't getting any younger and it was a steep climb back to their home. Worse, Larwin could out-eat Kazza and they hadn't gone to market the previous week, due to Rolf's failing health, so they needed ten times as much.

"Don't worry about the load," Nimri said. "I'm going with you."

"You. But you hate the chaos of Market Day. I thought—"

Nimri shrugged. "Going is my responsibility since I was the one who invited our guests to stay, which is why we need extra supplies. Plus, I need to see firsthand how the Lost are acting...I need them to see me, too." And even more, I need a plan.

An hour later, Nimri felt no closer to a solution than she had been when she realized that she had to do something about the Lost, but she had enough leaves to make cold syrup for the entire valley. In addition, she had collected the ingredients to make all the other medicines, which the people continually needed. Nimri picked up her basket and went into the kitchen to process the remedies she would take to Market.

Like it or not, competent or not, having accepted the staff or not, she was the Keeper of the Peace. Zurgon wouldn't allow her to shirk her duty, neither would anyone else, especially not the enemy.

Nimri added a handful of twigs to the banked embers on the kitchen hearth and blew softly. A tiny white thread of smoke rose. She blew again and a flame appeared. Soon, the fire was going well, so she began stirring a mixture of herbs to combat the effects of congestion.

Bryta came in, sat down at the table and without a word started sorting menthe leaves. The next time Nimri looked back, Bryta stood on tiptoe atop the table as she hung a bundle of celery seed heads from the rafters.

As the eye-watering mixture approached boiling point, Larwin come around the curve from the main sitting room. His posture reminded her of Kazza's stalking technique, and she admired the coordinated way he moved. Forgetting to stir, she marveled at the sheer masculine charisma Larwin exuded.

She turned her attention back to the pot when Anthropoid emerged next to him. The woman acted more devoted than any wife Nimri had ever seen.

When she glanced back, again, Larwin watched over Bryta's

shoulder, as she sorted bay leaves.

A hot droplet spattered her hand. Nimri took a branch and shoved the embers back, then stirred to cool the mixture.

Unable to help herself, she again glanced at the other three.

Hands quivering and eyes focused on her task, as if ignoring them would make them go away, Bryta grated camphor twigs. She gave a loud sniff. Experience had taught Nimri that the chore was impossible to do indoors.

Just as Nimri opened her mouth with the intention of suggesting she go outside, Bryta shrieked, threw down the shredder and surged to her feet. The chair toppled over backward, nearly hitting Larwin.

Larwin grabbed Bryta's right shoulder and kept her from falling. Bryta screamed louder.

Nimri stared at them, wondering what was wrong with Bryta this time. Then, she noticed that Larwin had an odd little black box in his hand and was moving it over Bryta's torso. While he touched the box, it wasn't touching Bryta. Nimri couldn't understand why Bryta screamed so loud since it clearly didn't hurt Larwin.

Torn between the necessity of stirring the medicine for those who would eventually need it and helping Bryta, who obviously thought she was in immediate distress, left Nimri helpless to do anything but watch.

Bryta turned to Nimri, her expression panicked, but Nimri couldn't see any problem other than the camphor on the table. Anthropoid stood still, staring at Bryta. Larwin seemed to be helping her or offering her the black box, which appeared slightly larger and lumpier than the silver package, which had contained rancid food.

"Is that box grounds for your fuss?" Nimri asked. Bryta ignored her. With her free hand, Nimri gestured for Bryta to stop. Bryta gave her a look of pure fury.

Nimri realized that somehow, since Rolf's death, their roles had switched. Perhaps she had grown up when she'd faced her worst fear and kept her vow. Had her great-grandfather foreseen that the hardship of the mountain would help her grow up?

Larwin continued moving the dark box over Bryta. He frowned and brought it closer to his face. Then, he hit it.

Good. He'd punished the thing for whatever it had done to Bryta.

As his palm smacked it, again, Bryta eluded Larwin's grasp. When the table separated them, Bryta warily watched the box and Larwin's apparent frustration with it.

"This can't be right," he muttered in his unintelligible language. "Perhaps this one's flesh is cooler." He slapped the offending thing, again. "Perhaps there are two separate breeds, they simply appear similar," Larwin muttered.

"Probabilities indicate they share the same heredity," Anthropoid said.

With no real problem in sight, Nimri turned so she could continue stirring, yet see if Bryta had any serious problem; Bryta clutched the back of the chair Nimri had sat in when she dealt with Zurgon. Her plump fingers bit into the wood, while her attention focused on the disobedient black thing.

Nimri squinted at the odd object. As she watched, a small flat square section turned from black to white then small black symbols appeared. Since she was halfway across the room she couldn't be certain, but the squiggles seemed like the symbols in the old books.

Her jaw sagged.

Was it possible they understood the symbols?

Did Anthropoid look through the old books and know the lessons?

The idea seemed incredible. Yet it made sense, since the

books were said to have come from the old world, along with her ancestors, who had fled to save their lives.

To think that after all these centuries, someone might unlock the secret of the symbols! Nimri stared at Anthropoid in wonder, then recalled the theory she'd had about the woman being an ancient guardian and Bryta's continual complaints about her interest in the books. Anthropoid and the manuscripts must be the same age. Of course Anthropoid would be able to understand them. Of course, she would be white as a moonflower, if she were over a millennium old. Nimri couldn't believe she'd been so ignorant.

Nimri swallowed. Would Anthropoid share the knowledge?

Searing droplets of ointment splattered Nimri's wrist. She quickly turned back to the pot and agitated the brew.

Larwin turned toward Nimri and extended the hand holding the box. Nimri tried to see the odd square part, but like the rest of the thing, it was black.

Had the color change and symbols been her imagination?

Except for stirring, Nimri stood perfectly still as Larwin held the box a hand's breadth away from her torso and moved it in a zigzag pattern. She felt a vague tingle and didn't know why Bryta had been so upset by the experience.

Just as the screen changed, Larwin held it close so she couldn't see. Nimri bit her lip and wondered how to ask him for a peek. A Guardian had the right to withhold information; still, she had her duty, too, and status as the Tribe's peacekeeper. If he or Anthropoid could teach her how to understand the symbols, it could help her immensely.

Larwin hissed and smacked the box with his palm. "Maybe my analyzer was damaged in the crash." With that incomprehensible statement, he stomped out of the room.

Anthropoid followed him.

Nimri watched them leave. Her eyes stung from more than mint and camphor.

Bryta kept the table between herself and their guests, then edged toward Nimri's side. Bryta's right hand gripped her favorite cast-metal pan in a white-knuckled grip behind her ample back. Obviously, Bryta had intended to use it on Larwin if he hurt her. The image of fearful Bryta trying to protect the Keeper of the Peace with a skillet struck her as heartwarming even though it seemed ridiculous.

Nimri didn't know whether to laugh or cry.

The following dawn, Nimri quietly hummed to herself while she packed her market basket with small, sealed crockery jars filled with assorted medicines. She cushioned them with bundles of culinary herbs and poultice leaves to keep the jars from knocking against each other and chipping.

She didn't know Larwin had crept up behind her until he said, "Good."

Nimri whirled around so fast that she almost upset the basket. It took her a moment to realize his attention was focused on the window's most translucent pane. It took another minute to comprehend that he'd spoken a word from her language. Granted, it was only one word, but good was a fine place to start. Did this mean he would actually speak to her? And, what was good? The view? The weather? The way she was packing the cures?

Had she passed some sort of test?

Nimri's knees felt weak and her heart thudded harder than when she'd nearly fallen to her death, yet he remained oblivious to her and silently stared out the window as if all that interested him was the approaching sunrise.

He had said "good," hadn't he? It hadn't been her imagination, had it?

She felt certain he'd spoken to her. Nimri prayed that his change of conduct meant she had passed whatever tests he'd been giving her.

Had the box been part of his test?

Dawn's first rays bathed Larwin's face in a rainbow of light. Nimri swallowed and hoped he hadn't noticed her addled reaction, hoped she sounded calm. Hoped she hadn't been mistaken about him speaking to her. "You're right it is beautiful."

"Yes, beautiful." He gave her a smile that made her heart skip a beat. Then he pointed to her basket. "You go?"

They were actually having a conversation. She hadn't felt this wonderful since…since…never.

"Yes, today is Market Day." He raised an eyebrow, a sure sign that he wanted her to demonstrate what she meant, but now that she had him talking, she didn't want to go back to children's games. Nimri put her hands up in frustration. "I can't explain it." She spoke slowly, syllable by syllable. "Would you like to come? Everyone both Chosen and Lost will be there." Her words poured out faster. "Unless they are ill, of course, but no one has sent for me, so they must be fine." He stared at her. "Everyone should be there." Nimri realized she must have been prattling on, as her great-grandfather had always complained of. She snapped her mouth shut and waited respectfully.

Larwin frowned and appeared to consider her offer for an agonizingly long time. "Yes, I come." He gave a decisive nod.

Nimri couldn't contain her delight. If he'd been a friend, she would have hugged him, but he was a guardian, so she gave him her best smile. Then she realized he couldn't possibly go anywhere in his outlandish silvery garment. "But you can't wear those clothes." He frowned at her. He looked bigger than her great-grandfather, but his tunics might work. "Come, you can wear Rolf's things, but if your mate wants to come, I don't know how I can hide her magical origins. You do want to go incognito, don't you?" Larwin gave her a bewildered look. She was chattering, again.

"I go." He looked at the stairway and smiled, as if expecting Anthropoid to appear, petite as a child and posture perfect, as

Pearl. Nimri waited for his woman to pass them as she went out the back door to greet the morning light. But she didn't come. Heat rose up Nimri's neck, as Larwin continued to stare at the steps. He was used to Anthropoid's looks and must think his mate looked beautiful. He couldn't possibly know how eerie Anthropoid seemed to her and her tribe.

Nimri wet her lips. "Maybe she should come, then the Lost might fear my power." Nimri grimaced and wished she had merely opened the invitation to his mate without adding the last bit.

Larwin frowned and looked down at his clothes. Then he turned to her and fingered her sky-blue tunic. When he looked her in the eye, she could tell that he understood how different he would look and the need for him to blend in as much as he could.

"More likely, they would either try to kill you or kidnap you," Nimri confided. Larwin gave her an indecipherable look. "The Lost, not my tribe." She hastened to add. Nimri decided she'd better drop the subject of the enemy, since it was impossible to be certain that Larwin and Anthropoid knew that the original refugees from the doomed world had split into adversarial tribes. Rolf had even hinted that other clans had splintered away from the initial group shortly after they had escaped certain death on Solterre. If they had been living in that cave for over a millennium, with only a rare supplicate making a pilgrimage to their summit, they might be trying to learn as much from her as she was from them. Nimri quickly pushed the unsettling thought aside. "Let's get you dressed properly."

When they entered Rolf's bedroom, Anthropoid stood on the far side of the room, looking at a book. Amazingly, it had no pictures. The certainty that Anthropoid could understand the symbols intensified. Nimri wished she dared to ask the Guardian to teach her what the squiggles meant, but embarrassment prevented her from admitting that the knowledge had been lost.

As soon as Larwin saw Anthropoid, he switched to their intimate speech. "The language program works, and I can understand some of what Nimri says, but it's inadequate for serious conversation. Can you finish the program today?"

Obviously, they didn't want her to understand, Nimri busied herself with finding Larwin something to wear. She squinted at Rolf's favorite burgundy tunic, but the shoulders were so narrow that she'd have to rip off the sleeves for Larwin; even then, he would probably feel like a sausage. She dug deeper into the chest.

"Colonel Atano, your inquiry is inadequate," Anthropoid said.

"Figures," Larwin said. "I think Nimri intends to take me to an emporium. Surely there will be more aliens and opportunity to study them."

Anthropoid turned a page. "My solar cells need to recharge."

Nimri looked up from the clothing her great grandfather had accumulated over recent years and squinted at Larwin, until all she saw was a black silhouette against the window. Larwin looked considerably larger than Rolf. Maybe this wasn't such a good idea.

Then she remembered that bones shrank with age. She also knew her great-grandfather kept everything.

Nimri shut Rolf's newest chest and dug into his oldest clothing-box. Near the bottom, she found a tunic, which had once been white, but now appeared ivory. She shook it out and held it up. It might fit. Next, she chose a navy pair of britches, which looked like they had never been worn. A glance at Larwin's boot-clad feet left her guessing at what size foot-wear he would need, but she felt certain that Rolf's moccasin would never fit. She chose a sturdy pair of woven sword-leaf sandals, as a compromise.

Nimri handed the clothing to Larwin. He tossed them onto the closest stack of books. Then he did something to the shirt he wore. The silvery fabric opened to reveal solid muscles, skin and some tantalizing hair.

Cheeks flaming, Nimri dashed out the door before more was exposed.

When Larwin came downstairs alone, Nimri noticed that while there was ample room in the shirt's body, it was four fingers too narrow on each shoulder and the sleeves, which were supposed to come to the wrists, only came to Larwin's elbows.

The pants fit, but should have been two fingers longer.

At least the sandals fit.

Before she lost her nerve, she took a step closer, grabbed a lace holding on the sleeve and pulled. When it didn't budge, she yanked harder. The lace came out slowly, then faster. Finally, the sleeve slipped down. She thought she heard Larwin give a soft sigh of relief. My, but he gave off a lot of heat. She fought the urge to fan herself as she quickly unfastened the other sleeve. Nimri felt flushed by the time it lay on the floor. Thankfully she didn't need to find a cloak to fit Larwin since the warm weather held. Perhaps the heat hadn't been from her own disobedient thoughts, but from the gentle breeze coming in the open door.

Nimri stepped back to survey her work. The outfit would pass, as long as Larwin stayed inconspicuous.

She chewed her lower lip and studied his short hair. There was no camouflage for that. She'd simply have to think of an explanation. Perhaps if she came up with a good enough one, others would cut their hair. As she pondered the problem, Bryta entered with the basket full of embroidered hand towels that she intended to barter. Upon seeing Larwin dressed in normal clothing, she stopped and gave Nimri a confused look.

"He's coming with us," Nimri said.

Bryta's mouth transformed into a tiny o, but she didn't make a sound. Nimri quickly went into the kitchen to get her own basket.

Larwin insisted on carrying everything, but even that gallantry didn't win Bryta's respect. Nose high, she strutted down the gorge path, as if she was the Head Woman and they were her followers. Though Nimri rolled her eyes to Sacred Mountain, she found secret pleasure walking with Larwin, who continued to take delight in everything new. She told herself that his child-like appreciation helped her see things in a new way.

As they passed Rolf's funeral pyre, Kazza playfully chased several chrome yellow butterflies off a tuft of vibrant orange nasturtium, Nimri laughed. "Whenever he does that, I pretend he's protecting us from roving Yetis."

"Yetis!" Bryta stopped as if struck and swiveled to look back at them. "You think the horrid Lost are hiding in the shrubbery with their vile pets?" Her gaze darted to the encroaching forest. "Yetis eat flesh, you know."

"Bryta, I was joking." Nimri and Larwin edged past her and continued on, side by side down the lush forest trail and entered the richly scented shadows under the sequoia boughs. As the branches swayed overhead, sunlight appeared to dance over the ferns, moss and dirt path. Nimri would have been content if they never reached the settlement.

"Yetis are not a joking matter," Bryta said.

Nimri glanced back. Bryta was still looking sharply at each shadow.

"Yet-ease?" Larwin asked. Bryta's head swiveled toward them, then her plump legs pelted down the earth track. She trotted past them and continued to pick up speed, her tunic flapping and her intricate braids falling.

Nimri put her hand to her mouth to hold back her laugh. She reminded herself that Yetis were not funny. "Huge, ugly creatures," Nimri said, with an involuntary shudder. "Horrible."

"Ah, like madrox."

"Whatever you say." Nimri doubted if anything could be as awful and frightening as a Yeti.

A butterfly landed on the tip of Kazza's nose. He went very still, except for his crossing eyes. When he hunkered down to study a thick patch of moss, Bryta, now running faster than Nimri would ever have believed her capable of moving, disappeared behind a dense clump of tree ferns.

Larwin pointed to a thick clump of chartreuse moss. Nimri told him everything she could remember about it, while he moved his odd black box over it.

With Bryta gone, the peaceful seclusion of the trail wrapped around them. As they ambled downward, Nimri identified various plants for Larwin, then added anything she could think of that related to the specimen. He leaned close, as if he didn't want to miss a single syllable. Had anyone ever paid such close attention to her? She didn't think so, but knew that she would treasure the memory of this day for many seasons to come.

After they climbed out of the last shallow, fern-filled ravine, Nimri heard the unmistakable sound of Market Day—shrieks of laughter, squawks of geese, the crow of a rooster, all underscored by the murmur of dozens of conversations. Kazza's ears perked forward, his nose rose to sniff the air, then he sprinted away.

With their destination so close, Nimri's pace slowed and she tried, again, to think of an explanation for a grown man having a shorn head.

Larwin slowed his pace to match hers. His back straightened and he kept glancing at the impenetrable shrubbery to their left, which stood twice his height. Obviously, he sensed that the village lay down the slope behind the dense leaves. Nimri wondered if he dreaded the next moments as much as she did.

They rounded the base of the last sequoia and the path led straight down the gentle grade to the village's center.

Larwin stopped stock-still and surveyed the scene, eyes wide, as if he'd never seen a trade center.

Nimri tried to see the scene the way he saw it, but everything looked normal to her. Breeze's ducks were squawking in a woven cane pen, plus she had a large basket of eggs to exchange. Quark Dagger's display of pottery looked like a beautiful rainbow of earthen tones. Flame didn't have any fried pies, but she did have black bread. Kazza already was happily munching a loaf under the display table.

Nimri's mouth watered. Lest her stomach growl, she looked at the waterfront where a bark-clad boat was docking. One man tied up the craft while four more burly Lost disembarked. Something seemed off-kilter about them, but she couldn't quite figure out what felt wrong. Nimri gave her head a tiny shake. The Lost were peculiar in general. They always appeared ragged and unkempt with their uneven haircuts and their wrap-around fringed tunics that were pieced together with odd bits of leather, instead of woven fabrics. For some reason, these five seemed particularly ominous, even though they moved around the various tables, joking and bartering, like everyone else. Frowning hard, she tried to figure out why they had caught her attention, but still, only the vague sense of unease came to mind.

Only the Lost's rougher men came to Market Day and these were typical. One had a black mustache that hung down each side of his mouth and looked like black drool trying to stretch itself to his chest. Another had unusual hair, neither brown, nor red, but a dirty mixture of the colors. Half of them had beards, which bushed from their chins like unkempt briar patches. The last one looked clean, but he had such long fringes on his tunic that it reminded her of the shredded camphor from the evening before.

Nimri wondered if they really were as vulgar and dirty as they appeared.

The worrying group split up. Two bearded ones made a beeline toward Quark's table. Nimri abruptly realized what was strange about the group—none of them carried a basket or bag. Worse, all were armed with vicious hunting knives.

Had they come to fight with Quark?

Her stomach clenched and her mouth felt dry. She didn't know if she should turn around and run home so that she could stay out of the anticipated fight or hurry toward Quark's table and try to head off the coming conflict.

At least the knives were not drawn. Still, her stomach tightened. For the first time, she wished she had brought Rolf's staff, even though it was useless in her hands. They wouldn't know she could barely hold onto the slippery thing or that she couldn't weld it.

The one with the longest fringes started chatting with Tansy, Bryta's granddaughter, who dimpled and smiled up at him through her thick lashes. Nimri looked around the crowded tables to see if Bryta had noticed Tansy's antics. When Nimri didn't see her, she gave a tiny sigh of thanksgiving and prayed that she wouldn't hear that her granddaughter had treated the enemy pleasantly. If Bryta caught wind of it, she'd complain about it for a hundred seasons, and use it as a reason why they should totally ban the Lost from their side of the river.

If the Lost would bring their women to market, there would be fewer problems.

If the Chosen didn't have the banishment law, they could build boats and cross the river themselves, then they might not feel so invaded.

Larwin took a step toward the market, then walked faster, as if he was eager to barter.

Nimri hurried to catch up.

As they approached the bakery display, Kazza came out from under the table and grabbed another long loaf of his favorite braided bread. Flame, who looked particularly lovely, tickled his ears and crooned to him as he sprawled back in his shady spot. Kazza's expression of bliss almost looked comical.

"Flame, you spoil him." Her best friend laughed. "You look wonderful," Nimri said. "There's something different about you. A radiance. Are you with child?"

They both laughed and hugged each other.

"Aren't you nice," Flame said. "Can't I look radiant unless I'm—" Flame stopped and gave Larwin, who had begun moving the odd box across her, a startled look. "Who is he? What's he doing?"

"Try to stand still," Nimri advised. "He did the same thing to Bryta, and me. There was only the slightest tingling. Sort of like the way Kazza's whiskers tickle."

Flame stared at Larwin, through narrowed eyes. Nimri thought she heard the box hum, then realized Kazza was purring.

"His name is Larwin," Nimri said, using a calm tone. "He's a traveler, who is staying with us."

Flame blinked in surprise. "Traveler? We haven't had one of them since we were small." Larwin gently gripped Flame's arm to hold her still. Her mouth flattened for a moment, then she ignored the box. "Remember the old Lost woman who was almost too frail to walk? She was so nice."

They'd been in a forest glade picking berries when they'd heard someone singing. "Yes. She had that odd shawl." Nimri's eyes misted. She gulped. "I think I saw her bones on the Sacred Trail." Nimri tried to swallow the sudden lump in her throat.

Larwin finished with the box and glared at it. For once he didn't hit it. But his expression looked like he wanted to. Assuming a box could misbehave, Nimri suspected it was still being disobedient.

Nimri glanced to where she'd last seen the Lost. They were admiring one of Quark's beautiful emerald green milk pictures. It didn't look like they intended to fight—yet.

"Would he like to eat one?" Flame whispered.

Nimri looked back and saw Larwin moving the box over the

bakery goods. "Sure. I have your burn ointment." Nimri bent to get it out of the basket at Larwin's feet.

"Thanks," Flame said, with a self-depreciating laugh. "I'm the clumsiest—"

Someone screamed as if the world was ending.

Nimri's heart froze. She looked from the Lost, who appeared equally startled, to the docks, where the scream had come from.

Sunlight blinded her. She shaded her eyes. Tansy was beating someone's chest. Long fringes of his tunic whipped around her flailing hands. The man grabbed her forearms and tried to shove her into the bark boat. She screamed a second time.

Nimri ran to help Tansy. Within an instant, she heard Kazza behind her.

"No!" Tansy shrieked.

"Get in," the man said. He half picked Tansy up, and dangled her feet over the dinghy.

Tansy shrieked. Her arms and legs flailed the air as she tried to beat off her attacker.

Nimri ran onto the dock; grabbed the kidnapper and half –spun him around. The fringes on his sleeves whipped against her hand. "Let her go!"

"No."

Tansy kicked his thigh. He grunted. Nimri yanked his arm. Kazza growled.

The Lost jerked and looked at Kazza. Tansy wrenched free of his grasp. The floating dock tipped. Tansy yelped. The man lunged after her. Nimri yanked him back.

Tansy somersaulted backward off the dock.

She screamed. Her head hit the dinghy's side with a terrible thud, ending her shriek.

"Tansy!" The Lost roared like an enraged beast and pushed

Nimri toward the water.

Nimri kneed him in the groin as hard as she could, then kneed him in the jaw and knocked him down.

Kazza leaped on the moaning man and sat on his chest. Muzzle to nose, he seemed to dare the man to get up.

Nimri ran to help Tansy, but didn't see her. She stopped and looked around. Larwin, who had followed her, was fighting two of the men who had come with the kidnapper. The other two, had their long bladed knives drawn, as they closed in on him from the rear.

For a moment, she didn't know if she should help Larwin or Tansy. Then, Larwin kicked one of the Lost in the jaw. The man tumbled backward. Larwin did something to the other's arm and sent him flying headfirst at the gathering crowd.

Nimri didn't need to see more; she jumped into the water next to the spot where she'd last seen Tansy. The water was deeper and dirtier than it looked. She bent double, dove into the murky depths and frantically grabbed at shadows.

She surfaced for a breath. Kazza still held the kidnapper, but his attention was on Larwin, who now had three of his attackers down and was fighting the last one. Amazing.

Nimri dove, again, but this time, she closed her eyes and tried to sense Tansy's presence. Then, she extended her right arm and felt…hair.

Then a head.

Nimri grabbed Tansy's limp form and thrust her upward to the light. As they broke the surface between the boat and the dock, she wondered how she would get Tansy back onto the land without getting them bogged in the bank's sucking mud. Larwin's head and shoulders appeared over the dock's edge. He reached down, grabbed Tansy under her armpits and plucked her from the water as easily as if she were a baby.

Nimri heaved herself up. She landed on the rough wood with a sodden splat. Larwin laid Tansy on the dock, as if she were dead. Kazza got off the Lost and took a step toward the adolescent.

The fringe-tunic man struggled to get up. For a moment, Nimri thought he still meant to kidnap Tansy. Whatever he intended, three of his companions grabbed him and hauled him toward their boat. The trio was so covered with dirt and trickles of blood that they looked like they'd been used to till a field. One bearded man's cheek was turning dark with a bruise and he held his head at an odd angle. The three Lost leaned on each other for support and kept a wary eye on Larwin as they edged past him and made a beeline to their dinghy.

The droopy mustache groaned loudly as he stepped down into the boat. The one with the bruised face collapsed in the bow as if moving two strides further was equivalent to a week's worth of toil. The auburn haired one fumbled with the ropes, while the other two winced and moaned as they set the oars in their grooves. The one with the long black mustache tried to lift his oar to push the boat away from the dock.

Before the mustache found the strength to push away, the last one dragged himself through the crowd that lined the bank five deep and got into the boat.

Finally certain that the danger was past, Nimri turned her attention to Tansy. One good look at her wan complexion, motionless chest and the blood trickling across her forehead made Nimri taste bile.

Larwin touched Tansy's throat in gentle petting movement.

Nimri felt rooted in place, yet a part of her noticed that Larwin looked fresh as when they'd started to Market. How could he fight so many of the Lost and not have a scratch? But his spotless tunic wasn't her most pressing problem.

Nimri crawled to Tansy. For the first time, she had a good look at the girl's pale heart-shaped face. A large liver-colored goose egg on her temple oozed blood and looked serious. Nimri touched Tansy's wrist. There wasn't a pulse.

Oh, no! What could she tell Bryta? Lily? Sandor? She'd known something bad was going to happen with that group when she realized they didn't have market baskets. She should have stopped them before it was too late. Tansy's death was her fault.

Sobs clogged Nimri's throat.

Larwin, kneeling on the opposite side of Tansy, got out his odd box and moved it over Tansy's chest.

"We're doomed—betrayed by our own Keeper of the Peace," someone in the crowd said.

Nimri clamped her teeth together and tried to ignore the truth her tribe had seen. Larwin continued dishonoring the dead with his nasty box. When he touched Tansy's wound with the horrid thing, her fist clenched with the urge to slap the box into the water.

But no one had the right to attack a Guardian. The crowd shifted ominously, as if wondering why their protector would allow a stranger to desecrate the dead.

Unable to speak, Nimri turned her attention to the Lost. They were the ones who had caused this horror.

The dinghy was two lengths into the river. Well out of range for any pathetic retribution she could dispense.

When Nimri turned back, Larwin had his palms flat on Tansy's chest. Suddenly he pushed down for all his worth. Tansy's corpse quivered.

Desecration!

The crowd murmured in horror. "Why doesn't the healer help Tansy?" someone asked.

"Tansy is dead. I heard her head crack like a melon, when it hit the wharf. See how Nimri mourns? No one can raise the dead."

Larwin put all his weight against Tansy's chest again, then lifted his hands, only to push again.

Dismay transfixed Nimri.

Kazza moved behind Larwin and placed his paw on Larwin's shoulder.

Suddenly, water spouted from Tansy's mouth.

The crowd gasped.

Nimri's jaw dropped.

Then, Larwin did the most outrageous thing yet—he pinched Tansy's nose with one hand, tilted her head back and grabbed her jaw with his other hand. Then, he clamped his mouth to hers. Next, he blew his breath into Tansy. Tansy's chest rose. Stupefied by shock, Nimri stared motionless, unable to say or do anything.

Breeze, near the front of the crowd, sank to the ground in a dead faint at the outrage she was witnessing.

Larwin placed his hands on Tansy's chest and pushed his breath out of her chest.

Then he blew in, again.

Nimri felt dizzy.

Somewhere in the distance, she heard Kazza purring. Had everyone and everything gone loco and decided to have inappropriate reactions to death?

The light dimmed. Somehow, Nimri knew that she was on the verge of passing out. She put her head down so she couldn't see, but she could still hear.

"Then what is that stranger doing to her?"

"Odd looking fellow. Perhaps he's drying her body for the pyre."

"Looks more like he's capturing her myst energy."

"He did come with Nimri."

Someone coughed.

"He's the one who taught those four a lesson. 'Bout time

someone did that."

Many murmured, but no one dared step closer.

The blackness seemed to spin. Close by, someone groaned. If Tansy hadn't been dead, Nimri would have thought it sounded like her.

The crowd gasped and murmured Tansy's name. Nimri thought she heard someone say Tansy was alive.

Suddenly, she felt Kazza's rough tongue lick her cheek from chin to forehead. The blackness cleared. Larwin's fingers were at the base of Tansy's jaw and Tansy's eyes were open.

Sacrilege!

Tansy moved.

Larwin removed his hand.

Tansy's eyes closed, and then she struggled to sit upright. The effort apparently was too much, too soon and she lay back down.

Nimri thought she was hallucinating. Half the people in the crowd sank to their knees and silently stared at the dock. Just as Nimri decided she was dreaming, she heard a distant scream.

Looking uphill, she saw Bryta running down the slope as if her apron had caught fire. Bryta barreled through the crowd as if they were chickens. Then, seeing Tansy dead on the dock, she stopped, bent over and gasped for breath.

Nimri tried to find the energy to get up.

Larwin sat Tansy up. Somehow, Tansy's head turned and she winced with pain.

Nimri hoped this was some horrible dream, but knew it wasn't.

Bryta took a deep breath and straightened. She stared at Tansy, who squinted back at her, pain in her unmatched pupils. Bryta's face turned livid. "Ancients preserve Pearl for telling me Tansy was dead!" Bryta moved to Nimri's side, knelt and touched Tansy's hand.

Tansy's slim fingers wrapped around her grandmother's plump ones. Nimri felt lightheaded. She closed her eyes and fought to analyze the impossible.

Nimri leaned close to Bryta's ear. "She was dead. Larwin returned her to us." But for how long? The head injury looked bad.

Bryta stiffened and gaped at Larwin.

A murmur of sound swelled to a riotous din of conversation.

Bryta turned to Nimri and spoke directly into her ear. "But no healer is strong enough to—"

"Yet, he did," Nimri said. She turned to Larwin. "Thank you. Bless the Ancients who sent you."

How inadequate her words sounded.

Nimri leaned across Tansy and gave Larwin a clumsy, one-armed hug. To her surprise and delight, he kissed her forehead.

"She needs bed," Larwin said.

Nimri sat back on her heels and wondered what exactly he had in mind.

Larwin scooped Tansy into his arms and stood up. He gave Nimri an expectant look.

"Come." Nimri scrambled to her feet. "I will show you where she lives."

She led him off the dock. The crowd parted to let them pass. Quark Dagger watched Larwin as if he worshiped the ground he walked on. Flame's expression held awe and admiration. Other eyes held terror, as they looked at Larwin. Several dropped to their knees and touched their foreheads to the ground in reverence

Nimri glanced back and saw Bryta walking close enough to touch Larwin. She had a mixture of love and anxiety in her expression, but all her attention was on Tansy.

If nothing else, the incident had changed Bryta's outlook toward their guests. Perhaps she wouldn't hear any more complaints about Larwin and Anthropoid.

Though Lily and Sandor's home was at the upper reaches of the village, Larwin didn't get winded carrying Tansy there.

Without pausing to knock, Nimri opened the door then stepped aside to let Larwin and Bryta pass.

Bryta hastily arranged some yellow cushions on the tile. Larwin gently laid Tansy on them.

Nimri stopped the crowd, which had followed them and ordered them to stay outside. They peered into Lily's main room from the doorway and every convenient window.

"Tansy, what is all the commotion ab—" Lily appeared in the doorway to the solarium, stopped and stared at the unexpected sight of the entire tribe looking intently into her house.

"A filthy Lost tried to kidnap Tansy," Bryta told her daughter. "He killed her in the attempt."

"No," Tansy murmured. Lily's eyes widened. She looked past her mother to her daughter's unfocused hazel eyes. "That's not –"Tansy winced as she groped for words.

Lily gasped at the ugly, dark welt on Tansy's forehead and rushed to kneel next to her. "That happened? Did the vile creatures beat you?"

"I'm fine," Tansy said in a faltering tone. "My head…hurts."

Nimri shook herself and looked at the crowd. "Would one of you please go get my medicine basket? I left it at Flame's." Breeze turned and hurried away, but two long-legged youths quickly passed her as they raced each other for the honor of helping the healer.

Nimri got down on her knees between Lily and Bryta and took their hands. "Tansy was dead." Nimri glanced at Larwin and wet her lips. "I don't know how, but Larwin's breath brought her back to us."

Lily scrambled around her mother, bowed low to Larwin and kissed his foot. Larwin's eyes widened, he grabbed Nimri's arm and silently asked her to explain Lily's action. Nimri smiled and gave his hand a comforting pat. Larwin relaxed his grip.

"Oh, so he breathed his own myst into her, instead of steal hers," someone said.

"Of course he did," a woman said. "You're a fool if you believe Nimri would do anything to anyone or harm our tribe."

Movement caught Nimri's attention. Reed held her medicine basket in front of his chest, like a prize as he sprinted toward the house. Nimri was glad she'd packed the medicine with care. He stopped at the door, then thrust the basket forward with a flourish. Nimri thanked the boy, as she grasped the handle. Reed had the audacity to wink before he melted back into the crowd.

Nimri chose a silvery mullein leaf and laid it over Tansy's right temple. Gently, she placed her palm over the leaf and focused on drawing out the pain, as she willed the damaged flesh to heal. Tansy closed her eyes and sighed with relief.

Lily knelt next to the cushions and held Tansy's hand.

Bryta stood back, hand to her mouth. Her tears ran in rivers down her plump ashen cheeks.

Nimri continued to draw out the pain until she sensed that Tansy had gone to sleep.

Nimri removed the leaf. The swelling had subsided and the cut had closed. Relief poured through her.

Larwin's spine straightened and his odd box appeared in his hand. When she got an empty crock and mixed preparations of chamomile, ginseng and Echinacea, he leaned forward and moved the strange thing above the reduced bump, then he tickled the mullein leaf with it. After Nimri adjusted the mixture to her great aunt Violet's specifications, she handed the small tan urn to Lily. "Two drops in a mug of water when she wakes, then more as the sun wakes and again as it sleeps. It will dull

Tansy's headache and ward off lung congestion." She hoped. "Tansy should be fine after seven sun risings, but I'll come to make sure next Market Day." Nimri handed her several more mullein leaves. "Keep these over the lump for two more risings. Three if her eyes still don't focus."

Lily quickly kissed Nimri's cheek, then cradled the medicine to her chest and gave her a silent look of thanks.

Nimri nodded to Lily and turned her attention to Bryta. "Bryta, will you be staying here or coming with me?"

Bryta gave her a look that made her wonder if she'd been insane to ask.

Not knowing what else to do, Nimri touched Larwin's arm and nodded toward the open doorway that framed the silent crowd. For the first time, Larwin seemed to realize they had an audience.

Lily accompanied them to the door. As Larwin went out, the crowd parted to allow Larwin passage. When Nimri moved to follow, Lily pulled her aside, leaned close and whispered, "The last time Mama looked this upset, she cleaned my house from top to bottom and I couldn't find anything for a moon cycle." Lily gave Nimri a pleading look. "If you could, would you please find need of her, soon?"

Nimri smiled and nodded. She and Lily hugged then she hurried after Larwin. Several people were touching the hem of his tunic with reverence. He glared at them with thinly veiled hostility.

Nimri frowned in confusion over the guardian's apparent aversion to the attention.

Chapter Nine

That night Nimri lay on her back, quilt tucked under her chin and stared out her bedroom window at the indigo sky. Was Tansy the reason Larwin had come? Was there something particular about Tansy or was the fact that he'd been there to save her life simply a coincidence? Until he'd saved Bryta's granddaughter, she'd assumed he'd come to instruct her. But that morning, he'd spoken for the first time, then before midday, he'd saved Tansy in his first display of power over death.

And on the walk home, Larwin hadn't said a word.

If he'd come to save Tansy, did the girl have some special purpose? Was there any significance to the fact that he'd fought the Lost and breathed life into the Chosen? Nimri's thoughts and confusion whirled faster than the bats circling the garden for moths. Was the morning's display about Tansy or was she simply chosen because she was Chosen?

Nimri closed her eyes and acknowledged that there were no answers for some questions.

Had he saved Tansy because she was barely past being a child? Because she was turning into a beautiful woman?

Nimri rolled to her left and kicked at the clinging linens. A moment later, she turned to her right, closed her eyes and tried to sleep, but all she saw was the image of Larwin's mouth touching Tansy's cold wet lips. Lest she lose control and let out the threatening sob, Nimri fisted her hands in her colorful patchwork quilt and brought it to her own mouth.

Again, she rotated to her other side. Moonlight highlighted a ruby square of the quilt. "This piece is from the tail of your father's betrothal shirt," Great Aunt Violet had told her as she sewed the square into the memory blanket. "He was a good man. Don't let anyone say otherwise."

She sat up and looked at the squares. When the shaft of moonlight moved across the bed, she touched the soft blue piece from her mother's tunic, then the dark green from her own favorite nightshirt, finally, the light came to rest on the dark square from the pants she'd worn the day she met Flame.

Thank goodness for Flame, who stood by her, no matter if it meant listening to her lament her inability to learn Rolf's lessons, holding her hand at the pyre or collecting the barter and distributing the medicine, which Nimri had not had time to do because Larwin was in such a hurry to leave the village.

Nimri decided she'd think of a way to show Flame how much her support meant.

The bedroom door opened and Kazza padded in. Nimri thought she saw his whiskers twirling, but decided it was a trick of the light. When he got closer, he moved through a shaft of moonlight. He really did look pleased. Nimri wondered if he'd found a forgotten loaf of bread somewhere.

Nimri moved to the left side of her bed as Kazza claimed the right. He settled in, stretched and purred. Nimri hugged her quilt, soaked up the heat of her life-long friend and felt secure. The last thought she had before she went to sleep was that it would soon snow.

"Nimri, wake." The tender baritone voice seemed to sing instead of speak.

"What? Where?" Nimri sat up in a moonlit forest glade.

"We don't have time for foolish questions," the unseen man said.

"Who are you?"

In silent response to her question, an area under the boughs of a blue pine shimmered with clear white light. The image gained clarity around the gentle eyes, but the rest remained indistinct.

"Is this better?" he asked.

"Where am I? Did I die?"

"No." He chuckled. "Your body lies sleeping in your bed. We have little time, and you have much to learn. Events have rushed the point of confrontation forward."

"What are you talking about?" A cold sweat bathed her back.

"Larwin has come. Trouble will follow."

Nimri tried to understand the logic. "Because he thrashed the Lost and saved Tansy?"

He growled a curse. "Lost are only an irritating illusion to give the appearance of an enemy." The glow suffused with red, then cleared. "There is a real threat. You must harness your power and take up the Staff of Protection."

"I can't," Nimri said. "I have no power other than a minor skill at healing. I thought that's why the Ancients sent Larwin and Anthropoid to me."

"Carved stone did not send him." The tone sounded mocking, the light turned orange. "He sent himself, but he cannot save you. He is strong in body but too weak in power to do more than aid you." The glow changed to pastel colors reminiscent of a rainbow. "Does he please you?"

Nimri frowned at the odd question. "Yes, but he belongs to Anthropoid."

"That is not so. The one you call Anthropoid and he calls GEA-4 is not mortal, only made to look so—think of her as a doll that walks and talks. She does belong to him, but not him to her." The glow turned yellow. "You are attracted to him." The tone warmed with amusement. "And he to you. He fears this."

Nimri didn't know what to think. Without a doubt, this was the oddest dream she'd ever had. Still, she had to ask, "Is he mortal or only made to look so?"

"His ancestors were from Solterre. They escaped to another world." The light pulsated in a multi-colored pattern. "Larwin's destiny is to be your cherished partner—assuming you both survive." The light dimmed. "If you keep shirking from your destiny, everything on Chatterre will die in the confrontation."

"Confrontation?" Nimri echoed. "You mean the Lost will attack?"

"No!" The word vibrated like thunder. Then, in a tone of restrained frustration, he added, "Their threat is no more than that of an annoying insect."

The glow pulsed like a heartbeat. Its center altered and Nimri saw a distant, panoramic view of her valley. It reminded her of the view from Sacred Mountain, but in this image, the valley was burning. Worse, a huge metallic gold object in the sky, which, periodically emitted bursts of blue lightening. Nimri felt an inexplicable terror when she looked at the twisted thing.

"This is what Chatterre will become if you don't learn to harness your abilities," the baritone said. "You, Kazza and Larwin will die." He paused. "Everyone, Chosen, Lost and all the other lost tribes will die. Plants will wither. The earth and air will be poisoned. The river will cease to flow. And then, Chatterre will become like Solterre."

The image crumbled into a black cinder, then disappeared.

Nimri gasped. "I want to help, but I can't."

"By believing it is hopeless, you make it so."

"Tell me how—what to do."

"Believe in your power and abilities. Act with confidence. Look within for the answers," he said. "This will remind you." The glimmer compressed into a tiny bright light, and floated toward her. It settled on her palm. When the luminescence faded, a tiny, radiant pinecone bud lay in her hand. The light of the bud diminished until the only light came from the moonlight through the boughs of the pine.

Slowly, everything turned black.

"Come back!"

From a great distance the man said, "Follow your destiny. If you do so, the Chosen and the Lost will be joined to live in harmony. This is the future you can give or withhold."

"I can't do this alone."

"Then all will die," the man said. "When the cone is mature, your power will be too and you will know how best to use it."

Nimri awoke with a gasp. She sat bolt upright and threw her quilt aside with such force that she knocked both it and Kazza off the bed. He hit the floor with a soft thud. Mustering his dignity, Kazza got to his feet, gave Nimri an indignant look, then he stalked to the door and disappeared down the hallway.

Heart thudding, as it had after the path fell away beneath her, Nimri gasped for breath, while hot tears seared trails down her cheeks. She bent over and put her hands to her face.

Tears on her left cheek sizzled, her palm felt blistered and she smelled flesh burning. Nimri jumped out of bed and wildly looked around. Tangled linens grabbed at her ankles. The fitful moon filled the room with moving shadows, adding to the nightmare feeling.

Nimri thrust her left hand into a feeble beam of light. The bud of a cone lay on her blistered palm. She shivered as she stared at it, wondering if this was still part of the dream. While she watched, her flesh healed. Panting for breath, she clutched the cone to her heart. She stood there, heart racing for a long time. Eventually, her sweat-soaked nightgown chilled and she began to shiver. One handed, she removed her amulet bag and put the small cone inside. As she closed the pouch, it gave off a feeble glow. Nimri blinked. Then looked harder, but this time her amulet appeared as it always had.

She crawled back in bed, more than half convinced that she was still dreaming. Nimri put the cord around her neck, tucked the pouch under her nightgown and held it next to her heart.

~0~

When Larwin awoke, a heavy weight on his chest made breathing difficult. He saw red through his closed eyelids and heard a jumble of riotous sound in his mind.

Mind-meld.

Larwin tried to clear his mind of thought and open himself to GEA-4's subliminal language lesson. When the data transfer ended, GEA-4 took her hands away from his temples, but Larwin realized he still felt weight on his chest and in addition, he heard a heavy motor running.

He opened his eyes and looked straight into the cat's enormous amber eyes. The animal's ears perked forward. Worse, the weight on his lungs was the huge paw, which spanned half his chest.

"Kind daybreak, Larwin," GEA-4 said. "I completed the analysis of this language. During your sleep, I taught you, but the books were old, patterns and words may have changed." She laid a hand on the beast's head and drew it along the cat's back, as Larwin had seen Nimri do. "The kazza seems fascinated with the subliminal technique."

The purring intensified until the entire bed vibrated. Larwin was certain that Kazza winked at him and smiled. Without the lethal claws in sight, he relaxed and looked at the animal. For the first time, he studied the cat without thinking of it as a predator. Larwin wet his lips and addressed the animal in the soft tone Nimri used when she spoke to it. "You are fascinated with the teaching technique, are you?" The cat yawned and stretched. "At least you didn't gut me with your claws."

GEA-4 moved to the window and gazed into the first rays of

sunlight.

Larwin addressed her back. "He's a cat. Cats are nocturnal. I think he's here because you are awake and he likes your company. Don't ask me why." Kazza leaned forward, his whiskers grazed Larwin's ear. He felt the urge to laugh. Instead, he gave the cat a playful shove and continued addressing GEA-4. "Cats are pets. My people keep pets for status; aliens have them for a variety of reasons, protection, food or the acquisition of it and companionship being primary. Despite the fact that this animal meets both qualifications, he is worthless because he's too large and he consumes too many provisions."

Kazza's ears flattened, then he leaped off the bed, leaving an aftershock like an earthquake.

Larwin was surprised the bed frame didn't disintegrate or that the floor withstood the cat's landing. Kazza's tail twitched as he swished out the door. Larwin blinked and wondered what had possessed him to remember so much information about cats, much less articulate it. He rubbed his temple and decided it must have been a side effect of GEA-4's mind-meld.

By the time he got up, dressed and descended the stairs, his headache had dissipated.

Nothing simmered near the fire. Larwin's stomach clenched with disappointment. He glanced out the amber window; GEA-4 stood in a pool of sunlight near the center of the garden. He wished he wasn't so dependent on food or the people of this world to show him what was edible. But he couldn't exist on solar radiation and he wasn't certain what was toxic in the garden.

Movement caught his attention. He peered out the transparent section of the window. Nimri slashed at the ground with a long-handled stick.

Why?

Larwin turned to go outside then spotted the basket of wonderful black bread that Nimri's red-haired friend had given them. He took a long, thin loaf and munched as he ambled out. He chose a dry grassy spot, and sat down to watch Nimri.

What was she doing?

Now that he was closer, he could see that a flat object had been fastened to the end of the stick that Nimri sliced the dirt with. Odd. Then, she cut the roots of one of the plants, reached down and yanked it out of the ground. Larwin choked on the bread.

Sacrilege.

No, he told himself. You need to be open-minded. He sat for a moment, trying to think of why anyone would kill a perfectly good plant, then recalled when he'd tried to taste the digitalis leaf and she'd pantomimed that eating it meant death because it tore out a person's heart, so they died in agony. Unheard of as it was, killing some plants might be a good thing.

Nimri finished the area she was assaulting, straightened and stretched her back. Though it was cool, sweat beaded her brow and the puffs under her eyes made her look exhausted. He smiled and waved. She laid down her stick and walked toward him.

"I wish you would choose to speak to me," she said quietly, as she settled near him. "The few words of greeting are nice, but I wish you'd tell me why you chose to come—to be here." Red colored her cheeks and she looked down. "Did you come to return Tansy's myst to her?" She stole a quick peek at him. "Have you come to help me?" Larwin stared at her. She took a deep breath, sat up straight and turned to him. "Is the future good or terrible, as my dreams predict?"

He shrugged, reluctant to test the subliminal program after having given such an impromptu chat to the cat.

"Am I too weak to know?" Nimri sighed, closed her eyes and turned her face to the sun. "I wish I had your healing power," she said. "You never told me you were such a powerful healer that you could raise the dead. You're the most powerful myst-mender I've ever seen, yet my dreams tell me you can't save our world, but I can and must."

"I am not myst-mender," Larwin said. He wondered if she'd gotten this notion from the rudimentary resuscitation and decided that if she had, the planet was even more backward than he'd realized. "I am a Shadow Pilot—a Warrior." Since GEA-4 hadn't given him a translation, he added the last in his own tongue.

Nimri turned to him, surprise and delight in her glowing green eyes. "You saved Tansy's life. She was dead, yet you breathed your essence into her and brought her back. Only a powerful mystic can do that. Until yesterday, I thought GEA-4 was the myst-mender, but then I guess anyone can repair simple bones." She patted her broken arm.

"GEA-4 is not myst-mender. She is Pilot."

"Are pilot and warrior special types of healers?"

Larwin felt frustrated at the language gaps. "Pilots and warriors only know basic healing skills—things needed in battle to survive." He frowned in concentration. "True healers go to cellular level to cancel pain and disease." He smiled, pleased that he'd found the Chatterren words to accurately describe what he wanted to say.

Nimri stared at him. "I know you just told me something very important. I wish I understood you."

Larwin noticed that tears welled in Nimri's eyes. His own eyes felt damp, too. He hoped he didn't cry. Warriors never cried.

"I guess that's why you haven't spoken to me before—I'm too ignorant to understand. I thought I was a good healer, but I can't even understand your methods of healing," Nimri said.

Nimri looked down at her broken arm, then squinted at GEA-4, who was recharging on the other side of the garden.

"GEA-4 only reset the bone, and secured it," Larwin said. "That is the duty of battleship medic."

"Your use of the language is strange." She blushed. "And I don't understand what a battleship is." A tear teetered at the corner of her eye. If she moved so much as a lash, he feared she'd start crying uncontrollably. He bit the insides of his cheeks and wondered how he could make her feel better. "And even if she's only a doll, I don't understand why your GEA-4 worships the sun, either. Unless it is because you are the Son of Light and it is her duty," Nimri said.

Larwin had never had such a confusing conversation or such conflicting emotions.

"GEA-4 is not worshiping sun, she is recharging her systems." Seeing her look of confusion, he mumbled, "She is sopping the sun."

Nimri's jaw sagged as she turned to GEA-4 and stared. A moment later, she blinked and clamped her mouth closed. When she turned back to him, she looked as radiant as if she'd swallowed daylight. Then, to Larwin's astonishment, Nimri sprang to her feet and mimicked GEA-4's centered stance—her feet a foot apart with hands at the sides. She took a deep breath, then exhaled, lifted her chin and with eyes wide open, looked at the sun.

Larwin jumped to his feet. "What are you doing? Your cellular structure is humanoid, not android." He unconsciously slipped into Guerreterre. "You'll burn your eyes and end up blind."

"I'm gaining power." Nimri's lips barely moved, and she held her position. "I'm recharging my systems."

"You are not an android." He realized she couldn't understand and paused to think of the Chatterre words. "Why do you need collect sun energy?"

"You were sitting in the sun. Weren't you gaining power?"

"I sit here because sun dried mist," Larwin said.

She smiled. Her lashes trembled. A tear fell and rolled over her cheekbone. More tears welled. Her facial muscles tensed and he suspected that for some unknown, self-destructive reason she was fighting the need to close her eyes. "I'm never going to figure out how to capture myst in time to save us, am I?" As she spoke, more tears rushed downward.

Larwin fought the urge to grab her and shield her beautiful eyes. "Would you please try explain what you talk about and why you think you need save us?"

"When I was little, Bryta told me stories about our old world." A tiny cloud passed overhead, giving her a temporary respite. With relief, Larwin watched the delicate muscles relax. He wished the sky were totally overcast. "Our old world burned when demon dragons attacked the sun," Nimri said. "Bryta believed that the sun exploded, sending flames across the sky —some scorched our world."

"It is only story," Larwin said. But a vaguely familiar one. "My mother tell me twin story before I turn three and move into military academy."

"You lost your family early, too? I'm sorry."

He stared at her. All children's abilities were tested at age three and then they were sent to whatever school matched their talents.

"My mother, father and brother died at the Lost's hands when I was two." Nimri sniffed. "Bryta is as close to a mother as I can remember, but Great-grandfather was constantly furious with her for telling me fairytales. He always claimed that scientists killed the Old World with the energy and chemicals they created in their laboratories."

"You confuse," Larwin said. "Do you stare at sun because of fairytales?"

Nimri gave a decisive nod.

"Do you expect sun explode?" Surely she couldn't be that uneducated. Or maybe she could. When she didn't respond, he tried another tactic. "Why you speak of dead world?"

"This is the New World. There are no dragons here." The cloud moved, and again, the sun seared her eyes. He involuntarily flinched as her skin tightened. Nimri tilted her chin a bit higher, so that the sun could do its worst. "No dragons, but the Lost are across the river."

He'd heard the term before, but still couldn't figure out what a Lost was. All he knew was that it was something or someone bad. "If you say."

"At first," Nimri said, "I thought that you were sent to me to quell the Lost, but if the dream was right, I must do more than that." He wished she wouldn't speak so fast or slur the syllables together. "I now know you are a myst-mender. A superb myst-mender, of course, what you call a warrior. I wish I understood that term better, I guess it means you're one of the most powerful doctors. Yes, that must be it, since you can breathe life into the dead and return lost myst. Amazing. Even Rolf, powerful as he was, couldn't raise the dead—"

"I warrior not myst-mender. Warrior is warrior." Larwin ground his teeth and cursed the incomplete language program. "The girl have water inside." He thumped his chest. "I take water out, put air in."

"Tansy was dead. Her heart did not beat."

"There life. Air need. I give air, not life." At least that's all he'd thought he'd done. What if Nimri could be right? If he hadn't helped the girl, she would have died. The thought was unexpected; one he'd never experienced or anticipated. He suddenly felt light and full of excitement, as if he'd been part of a team, which annihilated an enemy battle cruiser. "Warrior take life, this is first I give." And it had felt good, maybe even better than dispensing death.

"Your breath gave life; your breath is life," Nimri said.

"My breath not life." Didn't the woman listen? "That illogical as thought humans and androids both gain power from sun."

"But didn't you say the sun took away the myst?" Nimri made a sweeping gesture that encompassed the garden. She ended with her hand pointing at GEA-4. "And that she is gaining power?" He nodded. Nimri smiled. "Surely taking back the power from the sun is the secret."

Unable to deter Nimri short of physically restraining her, Larwin's hands fisted. "Oh, for the love of Radzuk." GEA-4 must have flubbed up the mind meld. "Fine," he continued venting in Guerreterre, "Copy GEA-4. Stare at the sun and tell yourself that you are recharging circuits you don't have because you aren't an android. Burn out your eyes and blind yourself. That's exactly what you need." Larwin turned and stomped away. With each step, he told himself that when Nimri blinded or killed herself in her foolish stunt, he didn't care.

He told himself that he wasn't willing to stand there and watch because he was busy making his lists of resources. He'd get right to his work, after he found something to eat.

Larwin rummaged through the market baskets looking for another loaf of the fabulous bread; instead, he found some dark purple knobby berries tied in a stained piece of fabric. He picked one up between thumb and forefinger and tentatively sniffed it. It reminded him of Tiberian Tinglish. His mouth watered. His stomach growled. He took a tiny nibble. It tasted as wonderful as it smelled. Though he felt like popping the whole thing into his mouth, he waited a few minutes to see if he experienced any ill effects. When none came, he took another small bite, then another and another. An explosion of sweetly tart flavor radiated through his mouth with every nibble. He wouldn't have thought it was possible, but the fruit was better than the stew.

He delved into the basket and carefully extracted the lumpy bundle of fabric. He untied the knot, his mouth salivating at the sight of the dark purple heap. He popped another into his mouth. Everything seemed right with the world—until he glanced out the window and saw Nimri with her face raised to the sun. "Oh, for the love of Radzuk!" He'd hoped she'd cease her stupidity when he left, but all she'd done was close her eyes.

For a moment, he felt tempted to go back outside and tell Nimri she must stop the foolishness. Then, he asked himself why he should care. Aliens weren't important. If Nimri personified the typical native, conquering this planet would be a cinch.

He popped another fat, juicy berry into his mouth.

He would be richer than his wildest dreams.

Chapter Ten

Nimri forced herself to gather myst long past the time she thought her face would drip away like wax from a burned down candle. Long past the time she would turn to dust from dehydration. Long past the time she thought her eyes would either burn to a crisp or fulfill Larwin's prophecy of blinding herself. Shade covered her face. Though she knew another cloud provided the relief, this time, the colors didn't return.

Distracted by the change, she realized how feeble she felt and acknowledged that she probably had failed at this, just as she had at every other type of myst exercise in her past.

Her eyelids felt like fire and she understood why GEA-4's had burned away. Her throat muscles worked, but no saliva came. If she had succeeded, she should sense strength instead of weakness.

She had to quit before she collapsed. Nimri sank to her knees and bent to the ground. Even the soft grass felt harsh against her tender skin.

A memory of the Guardian's yellow stare flashed in her mind. GEA-4 must intend to become one of them and be well on her way to that goal if others didn't even view her as human. Would she have such eyes once she gained power?

Nimri shuddered.

If she had to blind herself to serve her people, she would do that, too. She might already have accomplished that goal.

Though the grass was green, the only color Nimri saw was red. Her head felt feverish. Dizzy, too. Crawling along the grassy path, Nimri made her way to the aloe patch. She fingered the fat, spine-tipped plants until she found a sap-filled leaf, which felt right for picking. Nimri squeezed the pulp into her right hand then she rubbed her hands together. As soon as the gel covered both palms, she gently messaged the aloe into her burning flesh.

Sucking in her breath and biting her lower lip, she smeared some on her eyelids. The combined pleasure and pain seemed almost unbearable.

Heal, she thought.

Nimri heard a sound to her right and turned her head. Sunlight touched her cheek and the resulting pain seared so bad that for a moment, Nimri couldn't breathe.

Heal! She commanded her body. The pain eased to a sting.

When she could open her eyes without feeling stabbing pain throughout her entire head, Nimri realized GEA-4 had returned to her other pastime—admiring plants. GEA-4's face still appeared as white as a bleached bone. Nimri could feel fire in every pore. Without looking, she knew her own flesh looked boiled and that no matter how hard she tried, she'd failed to absorb the power she needed to fulfill her destiny – again.

Larwin had been correct; she did not have Anthropoid's capacity and probably never would.

Despair washed over her in a hot tide. Tears flowed in stinging streams down her cheeks.

Hearing movement at the garden's edge, she sensed Larwin striding up from the gorge, Kazza close on his heels. Squinting to clear the blurred image, she saw that both of them were damp. Obviously they'd been swimming.

When Larwin glanced her way, a sudden look of revulsion marred his expression. Nimri could almost hear him think, "failure" when he looked at her. He abruptly turned his back to her and took two uncompromising steps. Then, as Nimri tried to hold in a sob, he stopped.

She thought the feeling building inside her would explode if he didn't hurry up and leave.

Larwin turned toward her and moved in her direction.

Nimri tried to swallow the boulder in her throat and appear indifferent to her burning, tear-bathed flesh.

Larwin hunkered down in front of her. "Nimri," he said softly, "you past being child. Do not crying."

Unable to speak, she glared at him.

"On my world we discipline mind and body when we three. I never seeing adult uncontrolled." The tone held a hint of rebuke.

"You aren't on your world," she said, her tone strangled by the unreleased sob. "You're on mine. You can go home to your world. I haven't got another home, so I must save this one."

He blinked twice. "I hope you right. I hope I go back." He frowned and looked her up and down as if measuring her value. "Why you certain this world die? And you think save it you?"

How could he not know? Was this a test? "A vision," she said, hoping truth was the answer he wanted.

"More like heat prostration and sun blindness." The foreign words and tone held amusement. He hunkered down next to her. Larwin broke into a mixture of his and her language. "What is power you speak? Is atomic? Hydro?" She shrugged. He chewed on his lower lip, his expression serious. "How you fight? My world need this." He patted the ground. She frowned. "How you, alone, save or protect all?"

So, he was testing her. "Myst Power is something that passes down through my mother's line." There, now he knew that she'd learned her genealogy.

"Explain, please."

"It controls nature." He nodded. Nimri gained courage and went on, "My great-grandfather, my mother's grandfather, protected us from the Lost for years, simply by the threat of annihilating them."

When Larwin appeared genuinely perplexed and started muttering to himself in the sacred language, "How? With germ warfare?" Nimri wondered what she'd left out. "Mutations at the microscopic level make that dangerous." As he mumbled, he shook his head in perplexity. Nimri wished she could vanish, so she didn't have to witness how disappointed he was in her. "My world give up disease-make centuries ago." Even when he spoke her language, it still felt as if he didn't speak it, yet on some level, she understood his bizarre assessment.

"A disease would have taken too long." She tried to think of a way to explain properly. "When Great-grandfather's temper flared, he wanted revenge and retaliation immediately, not in a week or a month." She'd always felt he was wrong for never allowing anyone to explain their mistakes. Did the Ancients know how many punishments she'd endured simply because Rolf didn't take the time to understand what had motivated her errors?

Larwin motioned for her to explain. His look of total concentration seemed encouraging. She hadn't failed his test—yet. Nimri worried her lower lip and tried to decide how to explain Rolf's egotistical behavior favorably.

"When Grandfather lost his temper, a bolt of lightning would split trees—that's why he was forced to live so far from everyone." Nimri grimaced and wondered why she'd admitted the last. Larwin raised a questioning brow. "He used to lose his temper a lot." Her face felt so hot, she didn't know if she was blushing or not. This was good; he couldn't tell how much she'd hated Rolf's temper.

A tiny smile toyed with the corner of his lips. "This planet has outer space weaponry?"

"I don't understand when you mix in the spirit words."

"Never mind." He rubbed his temple and sighed. "We get back to that. Did bolt make hole in ground?"

She nodded. "Sometimes it would fell a tree." Knowing he hung on her every word, Nimri felt better. "Mostly, it vaporized whomever he was angry with." Larwin didn't seem appalled by her great-grandfather's lack of control. In fact, she sensed he, like Bryta and her tribe, was impressed. Nimri swallowed and told him the story Bryta loved to share. "The most talked about time was when great-grandfather was enraged with the Lost tribe for kidnapping my mother, father, brother and me. Great-grandfather called all the powers of the heavens together. Day became night. Rain came down like water from the falls. The river rose and its waters covered the other side. Most of the Lost drowned." So had her family. Thank the Ancients for her burned face, which should hide her true feelings. She'd despised her great-grandfather for his temper. Never wanted to be like him. Her dream had said, she'd made it impossible for herself to learn to handle the power; perhaps her negativity toward her great-grandfather and his methods caused most of the feelings.

"Hydropower." Larwin's right fist hit his left palm with a resounding crack. He looked pleased. "Primitive use, but hydro. Natural storm. Temporary dam. Do you people expect you control weather?"

Nimri nodded, appalled that she seemed to have passed his test by telling the story that made her uncomfortable every time she heard it. Yet relieved. Much as she hated the idea of learning to use her power, because it could kill, she knew her dream had been a forewarning and that all would be lost if she didn't get past her aversion. "You mentioned how children can discipline their minds. Could you teach me?" She held her breath and hoped she hadn't overstepped her bounds. Hoped he wouldn't think less of her than he already must after her failure with the sun.

"Sure." He laughed. "Do I do." Larwin smoothly sat down and assumed an odd, cross-legged pose by resting each foot on the opposing thigh. When Nimri tried the position, pain worse than her sunburn radiated over her lower extremities. She gritted her teeth and tried to appear as unaffected as Larwin.

Larwin's smile of approval made the agony worthwhile.

Next, he leaned forward, and gently positioned her hands over her knees, palms upward.

Nimri felt certain she could feel every segment of her backbone and some body parts she'd previously been unaware of. She swallowed and tried to ignore the fact that even her eyelashes hurt

"Relax," he said.

How, she wondered?

"Breathe. Like this. Helps close eyes…Yes, that correct. Now, take deep breathe…yes, that correct. Now, slow let breathe out." Her eyes opened. He demonstrated. She tried to copy him. "Yes, you good. Now try clear mind of think."

"Great-grandfather always told me never to simply try to do something. He said to either do it or don't try." She closed her eyes and did her best to simply breath.

Time passed, each minute longer than the one before as Larwin showed her how to relax and control her breathing. Why hadn't her great-grandfather ever taught her that mindless peace was the place to begin her training?

Eventually, Nimri realized she had been listening to a deep, soothing hum for several moments. The sound came from Larwin and while it seemed reminiscent of the chants Rolf had used to invoke myst, the sound differed, more constant, less melodious. Tentatively, Nimri tried to copy Larwin.

Her first attempt grated her ears. She pressed her burned lips together and listened to the tone. It was the same note they had used at the pyre for sending the myst beyond. This time, her note sounded correct. Nimri tried to hold it as Larwin did. But he hummed long after she'd gasped for air. Still, she felt much better and her burn had even cooled.

Why hadn't Rolf instructed her about humming's healing properties? Why hadn't he told her a lot of things?

Nimri focused inward, trying to find her inner core of peace. Unbidden, she wondered why she could see Larwin's shimmering form in her mind's eye. Pausing, she realized that while her thoughts were within, she seemed outside herself.

How very strange.

Her inner eye saw Larwin give her a tender look, instead of the somewhat wary one she'd become accustomed to. Slowly, almost imperceptibly, he leaned forward from his waist. Nimri suspected such a position would be physically impossible in real life.

As if to synchronize with her vision, the humming sounded closer and warmer. Nimri tired to imitate the slightly changed frequency. She imagined Larwin leaning so close that his breath brushed her cheek. She visualized him lovingly kissing her temple.

He stopped humming and his lips…

Nimri jerked as she opened her eyes. Larwin's face was only a finger's breadth away. She gasped. "What was that for?"

"Luck." His tone sounded strangled.

"I was having luck more luck than I've ever had—you distracted me."

"Well, excuse me." Larwin's mouth flattened and his jaw didn't move as he said, "Since I'm a distraction, I'll leave you in peace." With the grace of a butterfly, he rose to his feet. He then stalked off like an enraged Lost.

Fresh tears made stinging trails down Nimri's cheeks as she watched him leave.

How dare she speak to a Guardian like that!

Why did she always say the wrong thing?

When would she learn to be grateful when she got what she wished for?

Taking a ragged breath, Nimri tried regaining the harmony, but she only managed to hold in sobs, which felt as if they were tearing her apart cell by cell.

She lunged to her feet and stomped unsteadily toward the pool trail. If nothing else, she could take a soothing swim. Perhaps she'd drown, like Tansy and…No she didn't want to think about that.

Nimri rounded a tree and caught sight of the pool below. She stopped and stared at the figure wading through its azure depths. Her breath caught in her throat. He dove into the water and stroked across the width of the pool. She'd never known a man who moved so well or seemed so desirable. Though she knew it was an invasion of Larwin's privacy, she couldn't leave the wondrous view.

High overhead, a bird screamed. Nimri looked up. A goshawk lazily circled over the waterfall, searching for a breeze to climb. As a child, Bryta had told her its piercing scream called the wind.

Larwin rolled over on his back and floated in the azure water.

Nimri shook herself back to reality. "I must learn to control my mind." Since she couldn't control her thoughts when Larwin lay naked on the sun-warmed water, she turned and went back up the path.

Chapter Eleven

The luxury of immersing himself in the deep, wide pool nearly overwhelmed Larwin. Heart hammering, he waded into its sensual silky depths. Bending down, he stroked the iridescent surface with his fingers, and held his breath at the wonder of being up to his waist in the most valuable commodity on Guerreterre. How wonderful it felt against his skin. How different from what he'd expected; cold by his feet, but sun-warmed at the top. Who would have thought that water would have layers of temperature?

He lay facedown on the water. Luxury beyond imagination.

When he ran out of air, he turned onto his back and allowed the water to hold him. Had the Planetary Emperor ever experienced such an indulgence? Larwin lived his dreams until he became cold. Reluctantly, he moved back to shore and stood up.

Abruptly, a tremendous force swept him off his feet. He somersaulted backward into the pool in a great splash. A moment later, he scrambled upright and came face to face with Kazza's merry eyes.

Larwin took the heel of his hand and splashed water into the huge cat's face. Kazza returned the dousing in full measure. They splashed each other in a mad war of droplets, then the cat dove beneath the surface and disappeared as mysteriously as it had appeared.

Tired from the exercise, yet warmed by the activity and unwilling to leave the extravagant setting, Larwin waded to a smooth sun-baked boulder, which was big as the barrack's dinning table. He lay on his back. Despite occasional gusts of sharp, cold spray from the thundering falls, the sun's heat soon allowed the residual tautness in his muscles to relax. His spine seemed to melt against the solid warmth of the rock and become one with it.

Wind gusted, sending a sheet of frigid water over him. He licked a droplet from his lip. Who on Guerreterre had ever imagined this sort of opulence?

A soft, stealthy noise alerted him. Slowly turning his head, he peeked through his lashes. A nearby bush trembled. Larwin told himself it was only the wind. Then he saw glowing eyes.

His heart made a mad leap. One amber orb winked.

Kazza.

As he recognized the cat, it burst from the glossy leaves and leaped onto Larwin's rock.

Larwin sat up so quickly he saw flashes of white light.

Kazza touched him with the tip of his twitching tail. The cat faced Larwin, one tufted ear drooping and an expression of sheer delight shining from every fang. Larwin imagined the cat took glee in stalking him. As droplets beaded on Kazza's heavy wet coat, Larwin laughed and tickled the closest ear. Kazza's purr reverberated over the thunder of the waterfall until the boulder trembled with happiness.

"You like this, do you?"

Kazza leaned against Larwin's left hand.

"Thank Radzuk you aren't a fighter. I'd need twice as many

infantry divisions to take over this planet if you knew how to use your teeth and claws." Larwin continued tickling Kazza behind his ear. "Conquering this planet will require infantry. There's no way to use our traditional outer space approach from a wormhole."

Kazza's purr deepened. The cat leaned over to him and rubbed his muzzle against Larwin's jaw.

To Larwin's consternation it felt nice.

The cat sprawled onto its belly. Still stroking the sleek, damp fur, Larwin settled on his side, facing Kazza. Who would have thought touching an animal's fur could be so relaxing?

"Despite the handicap of not being able to use our shadow fighters, this planet is going to be a snap to defeat. Primitive and magic-oriented as the inhabitants are, the inconvenience of the wormhole shouldn't matter."

As it had done so many times, a bird screamed as it circled overhead. And, as always, Larwin looked up.

"At least it won't as long as the wormhole is stable." Larwin frowned. "I have to verify that soon."

Kazza nuzzled his ear. The whiskers tickled his neck and the purring seemed to vibrate down to his toes.

"Don't worry fella, you're a pet worthy of a planetary emperor, which I'll be if I play my cards right. I'll keep you as a status symbol."

The tail beat the rock like it was a drum.

"Nimri might be worth keeping, too," Larwin said. "It's harder to make plans about her. She's got looks, personality and status here, but once this planet comes under Guerreterre's cloak, she could turn into a liability."

Unexpectedly, Kazza tore away, leaped off the rock and did a belly flop in the middle of the pool. At the same time as the big cat disappeared beneath the surface, a sheet of frigid water sloshed over Larwin. He shook his head; droplets arced away like solar flares.

Larwin wondered why he always spoke his mind so freely to the cat. Gooseflesh rose on his arms. Larwin rubbed them and realized he was cold. He got to his feet then made his way across the rock-strewn sand to the clothes he'd left hanging on a branch.

~0~

Nimri fell across her bed and buried her burning face against the cool cotton of her headrest. Instead of feeling the expected comfort, all her miseries and failures welled within her until her broiling skin felt stretched by the enormity of her inadequacy. Even the fabric turned hot with radiating power, yet she knew she had failed to absorb any, which she could change into myst-energy, as GEA-4 did.

She fisted her hands, and hit the headrest, wishing the goose down could absorb her frustration as easily as it did heat. She threw another punch—this to strike away the duty to her tribe. "How can I help them, when I can't even help myself?" Another jab. "Why does fate keep playing such cruel jokes?" One more blow. "Why did I have to be born a Tramontain?" Thump. "Why do I always fail?"

She raised her fist for another strike, but stopped in mid-swing when she heard movement behind her.

Why did Kazza have to be so snoopy and stick his whiskers into everything? With the intention of physically throwing him out of her room, Nimri leaped to her feet, swiveled, and came face to face with GEA-4. "What are you doing here?"

"Colonel Atano ordered me to seek. I am seeking." GEA-4 picked up Nimri's favorite fairytale book. The golden dragon on the cover twinkled as it passed through a stream of sunlight.

As always, the petite woman was unemotional, which made Nimri feel even worse about her own lack of control. And just what was she looking for in a fairytale book? Or had GEA-4 vaguely said she was seeking because she didn't want to tell her what Larwin wanted?

"Must everything you and Larwin say be so obscure?"

"Your inquiry is inadequate."

Nimri cleared her throat and fought the urge to wipe away her tears. "Why are you here?"

"Larwin commanded me to evaluate this planet's culture and the best way to conquer it. He wishes to formulate a method which is nondestructive to the assets."

Nimri knew she'd just been told something important, and wished she understood. She licked her lips and tried to smile. "His way of assisting me is odd."

GEA-4 ignored her and paged through the book. Nimri watched, fascinated to finally observe the conduct, which had upset Bryta. Since GEA-4 took care with the pages, Nimri saw no reason for the fuss. A page turned with the same speedy rate as the others had. "Do you do everything he tells you?"

"No, I do not."

"You don't?" She couldn't stop her squeak of surprise. "Why not?"

"I only perform tasks defined by my basic programming."

Another elusive answer. "And those are?" Nimri wiped away her tears and perched on the edge of her bed.

"Protect and preserve." GEA-4 turned to a black and white drawing of a flying dragon. "There are five hundred and thirty-six articles covering conduct."

"Five hundred and thirty-six?" Hand to chest, Nimri held her heart in place. Five hundred and thirty-six! She'd never be ready. Never be able to fulfill her duty. "Great-grandfather once told me that books contained power and knowledge, but the keys to unlock the wisdom were lost during the hardships of the first generations. Even without the keys, they are sacred."

"That is illogical. The ones I've scanned have neither religious significance nor locks."

Nimri tingled from head to toe, but had to be certain she'd understood what had just been said. "Can you decipher the marks?"

The cold silver eyes seemed to hold recrimination. "Yes, I can."

"I should have realized. You're a Guardian, of course you retain the old knowledge." The implications were so staggering Nimri gripped her quilt for support. "Is that why you came—to teach me the old ways?"

"Your inquiry is not complete." GEA-4 turned a page.

"GEA-4, can you teach me to scan the manuscripts?"

Everything in her future hinged on the answer. Nimri couldn't even swallow as her fingers dug into the quilt and she waited for the answer.

A page turned. "Yes, I can."

Breath whooshed out of Nimri. "How soon? Will it take long? I can't believe I'll be able to understand them."

GEA-4 turned to the next page. Then the next. Nimri wondered whether she had misunderstood. She forced herself to breathe as Larwin had taught her. She told herself to be patient. GEA-4 flipped to the last page. A moment later, the book snapped shut.

Afraid to blink, Nimri watched GEA-4 return the book to the precise spot where she'd gotten it. Then, without a word of explanation or even a comforting smile, GEA-4 raised her slender white hands and came toward her.

Before Nimri understood her intent, GEA-4's thumbs clamped over her ears and her index fingers connected with her temples providing an inescapable trap.

A deluge of thoughts and pictures flooded Nimri's mind. Panic exploded within Nimri's chest as she tried to understand the wild jumble. For a second, the pressure over her temples slacked. Nimri felt her vertebrae sag, but before she could fall back against the mattress, the force holding her head returned along with a confusing tumult of unexplainable words, symbols and pictures.

Gooseflesh rushed over Nimri as a high-pitched, disembodied tone resonated within her mind.

Suddenly, Nimri started putting words to symbols and her chill transformed into a kernel of hope. If pain were necessary to understand the sacred writing, she would gladly sever an arm. Nimri mentally embraced the discomfort and its tentacles uncoiled.

A wealth of understanding poured into her mind.

When the stream of knowledge ended, Nimri slipped off her bed, knelt on the floor and touched her forehead to GEA-4's silvery footwear.

Inexplicable as always, the female Guardian moved away.

By the time Nimri sat up, GEA-4 held the semi-polished pink rock Nimri had found the day she'd met Flame. As their friendship had grown, the stone had become a symbol of friendship and trust. "Rose quartz." For a moment Nimri wondered who had spoken and where the name had come from. Her jaw dropped, when she realized it was her own voice. Moreover, she now had scientific data for several things. "Please, keep the rock as a token of my appreciation."

GEA-4 replaced it and picked up the egg-shaped piece of jade, which Bryta had given her to commemorate her thirteenth birthday. "I have no use for such a decoration." She put it down in the precise place it had been, then picked up the huge crystal skull, which her aunt had given her. Though she spent more time examining that, she discarded it, in the same way she had her other mementos.

Nimri looked away in shame then realized nothing in her room seemed the same. While things still retained their sentimental value, nothing held a sense of mystery, because she now knew the mineral content and forces of nature it took to create each item. Wide-eyed, she looked at her room as if for the first time.

Her gaze settled on a book lying next to her bed: Scientific Explanations for Mysticism by Lorwerth Sandram. She understood the words. She grabbed the volume with trembling hand and opened it, not to look at the exotic pictures, but to scan the words.

Her euphoria waned as she realized the writer boldly condemned everything she held sacred and called it fraud. She snapped it shut and glared at the cover. Until now, this had been her favorite book. Nimri couldn't count the number of blissful hours she'd spent looking at the beautiful illustrations.

Tears stung her eyes and she wished she'd never asked GEA-4 to give her the keys to wisdom. "GEA-4. Do you realize that according to the ancients, myst wasn't true power?" Her palm slapped the cover. "This, this, this—person—says it's an illusion."

She had no response.

Nimri glanced up. GEA-4 studied a piece of amber with meticulous attention.

Perhaps the Guardian was mute with rage over the heresy.

Sighing, Nimri reopened the book and paged through it. Her stomach tightened with every caption she read. Act by act, Sandram analyzed various manifestations of Mysticism and showed a scientific truth for how people had been tricked. If she believed the writer, then the Lost were right. "If I accept this, there is no myst power…that means—" Unable to articulate the horror, Nimri shook the offending book at the Guardian.

"My programming indicates that if there is belief in a thing, it becomes so." GEA-4 took the volume and paged through it.

Nimri tried not to fidget as she waited for GEA-4's assessment. At page forty-six she felt a lump in her throat. When seventy-three turned, the obstruction grew larger. "I've always been told I had power but I could never learn to use it." She swallowed hard. "No wonder." Despite her resolve, her lower lip quivered. "It doesn't exist."

GEA-4 turned to page ninety-seven. "There must first be belief to make anything."

Was the Guardian testing her?

She swallowed her unshed tears. "Are you suggesting that I don't believe in myself?" If she'd been any less sunburned, she felt certain she'd be blushing. "You may be right. Isn't it absurd? Everyone, except me, believes it." She hung her head. Then, the truth hit her like a landslide. "GEA-4. That's it." Nimri placed her palm on the silvery sleeve. "Will you help me?"

"Your request does not compute."

"Will you help me create an illusion?" Nimri's heart pounded so loud she couldn't hear the waterfall.

"Probabilities indicate scientists will understand the illusion."

"There aren't any here. Scientists, that is." While the Lost valued science, even if they didn't have anyone who knew the old ways. At least Nimri had never heard of such a person.

"Your request is incomplete."

"Sandram explains how a miracle is performed." Nimri grabbed the book out of GEA-4's hands and flipped to page eighty-five, then thrust it back and tapped the pertinent paragraph. "Will you help me create one? It could help us avoid a fight and save lives. Will you help?"

"Yes, I will. Saving allies is a prime directive."

Nimri felt lightheaded. "First, we need to make you look more natural—more human."

Chapter Twelve

After the sun reached its zenith, Larwin searched for GEA-4 in the garden; then he expanded his exploration to the surrounding woodlands. Shortly after entering the pine-scented shade, he stepped off the path to analyze a plant he hadn't seen before. When he finished, he spotted yet another interesting specimen deeper in the shade. Whistling merrily to himself, he catalogued all the pertinent information. Then, he turned back to the path, but couldn't see it. Confident of his navigational skills, he walked to where it should be.

Instead of a path, he found a moss-covered log.

After spending hours walking in circles, he finally stumbled across a hash mark he'd made the day Nimri had showed him the way to the settlement. Larwin stepped onto the isolated mountain trail then looked left and right, as he determined which way led to Nimri's clearing. Though his impression had been that town was down and Nimri's was up, the fern-strewn area seemed flat.

He turned right and jogged along the narrow path, which had seemed much wider the day before. After several minutes of jogging, he spotted some chrome-yellow butterflies lingering over a muddy spot. Hunkering down, he found footprints from where Kazza had chased one into the forest.

He was going the wrong way.

Pivoting as he surged to his feet, Larwin retraced the steps he'd just taken. Within a hundred yards, his lungs burned and sweat stung his eyes. Gnats swirled around him in an annoying cloud. Then, he inhaled one through his mouth. He coughed long and hard, before he got it out.

Another gnat landed in his eye. Try as he might, he couldn't dislodge it.

Grimly, he hiked up the trail, swatting at the pesky bugs. Strange that he hadn't noticed the things before.

Finally, as the setting sun painted the clouds mauve, he arrived at the edge of Nimri's clearing. The insects mysteriously departed. His gaze moved over the clearing. How beautiful it looked at every time of day. It would almost be a shame to harvest the enzymes and transport them to Guerreterre.

Almost.

But not completely. Billions would stay alive on Guerreterre because of this garden and the thousands of other areas on this planet like it. While only a handful of primitives from this world would miss the greenery.

And best of all, if he handled everything correctly, his future prestige and wealth would be secure enough to put him in the top two percent of the population. He'd be wealthy enough to build his own arboretum and have his own tree. The thought of such a fabulous future coming from the ashes of his crash brought forth a chuckle.

Larwin spotted GEA-4 bending over a low-growing velvety clump of grayish foliage. "How is the inventory progressing?"

"On schedule."

"Great. I wish I could say the same for my analysis of troops needed for the invasion."

"Why are troops needed?"

"Radzuk! Your programmer really muddled fragments." Larwin counted to fifty. "Takeovers begin with an invasion. It's been that way for a millennium."

"The method wastes resources." GEA-4 moved to a plant with burgundy flowers and stared at its tiny, dainty leaves. "You commanded me to find a procedure, which minimized the loss of life and resources."

Larwin wished androids were programmed to carry on normal conversations. "How would you do that?"

"As Nimri plans—by using a peaceful demonstration of strength."

He blinked. "Surely she doesn't think that will fend off a squad of Shadow Warriors."

"She is unaware of Guerreterre and its forces."

"Explain."

"Nimri's foe is the Lost tribe."

Ah, so the Lost were another tribe. Larwin recalled the bullies he'd fought. They must be from the Lost. Big deal, they were just a bunch of unwashed clumsy bullies, their only weapons were pathetic knives, which a kindergartener could take away, and then go on to win a fistfight against them. "What is the crux of their disagreement?"

"Nimri has not said. She indicated that the two tribes have only been able to co-exist on this planet due to the river's limitations. However, I am unclear how water is capable of retaining peace."

He grunted. "Does this planet have a magnetic pole?"

"Affirmative."

After his day in the forest, he'd decided compasses would be an excellent idea for ground troops. "Anything else you can tell me about this world or their culture?"

"The altercation between the two tribes is a millennium old. This makes me hypothesize that the original source of the difference between the Tribes is long forgotten and the altercation has become a way of life."

"And that's why she thinks she can conquer them with a peaceful demonstration?" A good thrashing was the way to deal with habitual bullies, like the four that had attacked him. Larwin couldn't believe anyone would give credence to "peaceful methods." But if his unit didn't have to engage in a planetary battle, it would be possible to salvage more plants. And that meant he would be even richer. Perhaps he needed to research this concept of peaceful takeover. "Do you think her plan will succeed?"

"Probabilities are high in its favor."

His heart lurched. "Great Radzuk. How many are involved?" His tone was devoid of its previous sarcasm.

"Nimri, a Lost and myself."

Larwin massaged his right temple and wondered if he could be going insane. Two aliens and one android certainly couldn't achieve better results than an invasion by four divisions. Unless…"So, she's working with a mole." Larwin shook his head, surprised he hadn't thought of the strategy earlier. "Clever." Historically, this had worked on more than one occasion, but since he'd entered the academy, there hadn't been any coups of that type. His instructors had theorized the change was due to so many secret allies having their own agendas, making such scenarios futile.

"Nimri's only moles destroy root crops." GEA-4 pointed to an elongated pile, which zigzagged across a planting bed. Larwin squinted at the dirt and frowned. Before he could question her meaning, the android added, "The Lost will be used due to consistent behavior patterns. Thus, Nimri's demonstration will be a spontaneous reaction to an unspecified future event."

"When is this event scheduled to happen or is that unspecified, also?"

"She hopes for the forthcoming Market Day." GEA-4 moved to a tiny plant with fat yellowish leaves.

"And that is?"

"Market Day is every eight days."

"And you believe there's a better than average chance of success?"

"Yes, I do."

"Interesting. If she has such influence over the people, it should be worth my while to observe her plan in action." Larwin's entire body tingled with previously unforeseen possibilities. "GEA-4, have you noticed any evidence of roads? My assessment is the invasion will need to be done either on foot or by sky."

"There are only footpaths."

Larwin's hands clenched at the android's denseness. Despite further interrogation the worthless android didn't have the answers he wanted. When he later met Nimri, and tried to casually engage her in conversation about takeover tactics, she acted confused by his question and it became obvious that she wouldn't tell him her strategy.

Thus, Larwin formulated his own surveillance plan.

During the next five days, he got up at dawn and made sure he passed in view of Nimri's bedroom window as he walked into the shadows of the sequoia. Then, he stealthily ducked behind the first trunk, slipped off his shiny flight suit, and climbed to a high branch, from which he watched Nimri and GEA-4's activity. Even though he used his audio-visual viewer to increase perception, their activities appeared boringly typical: the two of them picked leaves and flowers, brewed combinations of plants and put them in quaint jugs, cooked, cleaned and enjoyed the tiresome activities so much that they sang from dusk to dawn. At least, Larwin determined their activity appeared normal instead of primitive war preparations.

For all he knew, Nimri knew of his takeover plans and this method could be her way of stalling for time as she brewed some sort of potion. He scratched an ant bite. What had the infernal insects consumed before he'd begun his investigation? And what were bugs doing a hundred or so feet up a tree?

He swatted a fly. He knew GEA-4 had scrambled programming, which caused her to misinterpret information. In disgust, Larwin concluded his own avarice and desire to protect all the botanicals might have contributed to his misunderstanding. He petitioned Kues, the God of War, praying that he hadn't been suckered by the android, again, and that his faith would be rewarded with riches and plunder. He looked forward to returning to Guerreterre, where all insects had died off centuries ago.

The day before Market Day, Larwin lay on his stomach, watching GEA-4 recharge. He never wanted to see another branch or spend the day in another tree, no matter how exotic tree climbing had seemed prior to the discovery that bugs considered him a tasty meal. After having spent days lying on the broad branch, spying on Nimri to discover her military plan, he felt no closer to finding out her strategy than he'd been when GEA-4 mentioned it. He felt like a giant bug-bitten fool for having listened to the dysfunctional machine. When the sun reached its zenith, GEA-4 finished recharging. As if on cue, Nimri came out of the house holding a large crock of dark brown goop. Nimri swabbed some of the goop on GEA-4's forearm. Larwin's interest perked. What reason could anyone have to put food or medication on an android? He increased the viewer's magnification.

He keyed up the audio. Though broken, their conversation centered on Sir Keram or maybe they were saying Serk ram. Who was Sandram and what problematic detail were they talking about? Was he the mole? Or was 'Sandr am' some sort of jam. Larwin's mouth watered at the memory of jam on white bread. Of course, if they were conversing about a 'serk ram', it could have to do with sheep. Strange that he hadn't seen any evidence of those oddities on this world.

Nimri swabbed more goop on GEA-4. Gradually, the android's skin tanned. Whoops of delight erupted over his audio unit. Larwin yanked off his audio-visual unit, cast it aside and massaged his aching ears. For a horrible moment, he feared the high volume had done permanent damage to his hearing, then a bird twittered and he heaved a sigh of relief.

Since he couldn't believe they'd spent days brewing dye, he climbed down the tree to get his headpiece. The high-pitched shrieks of laughter emitting from it made it easy to find in the underbrush. As he picked it up, Larwin turned down the volume then put it on. "Watch me skip." The voice was unknown.

"You're too perfect for a kid," Nimri said. "Be sloppier." Larwin rubbed his temple and wondered what he'd missed.

Instead of climbing back up the tree to see, he put on his flight suit, sat next to the tree trunk and dreamed of the day he would join Guerreterre's elite. Kazza found him leaning against the bark as he imagined his riches. The great cat nuzzled him, but Larwin didn't feel like playing. Abruptly his fantasy darkened with the thought that after the planet's resources were harvested, he could never sit under this tree again.

Larwin lunged to his feet and went to find out what Nimri and GEA-4 were up to. Though he couldn't find the annoying android, he found Nimri seated in the ginkgo's shade, doing something with fabric. It took Larwin over an hour of casual peeks to realize he was witnessing old-fashioned hand sewing.

He went to bed early and fell asleep before GEA-4 arrived. The following morning, for the first time since he'd arrived on Chatterre, Larwin woke alone. As he dressed, he kept having the feeling he'd forgotten something.

Loneliness was a new feeling and an unpleasant one. Larwin rejected it as he stomped down the steps. When he entered the main room, he heard Nimri chuckle and say, "Remember a child moves a bit randomly—yes, like that."

Larwin paused to listen, then hearing someone approach ducked back out of sight behind a potted plant. He peered through the green and white striped leaves. GEA-4 skipped into the room, swinging an empty basket and humming a vaguely familiar melody. At least, he thought it was GEA-4. He blinked twice. The individual was the correct size, but she wore a blue tunic similar to Nimri's, her skin was tan and her hair was as blue-black as space.

The aberration twirled like a ballerina and skipped back into the kitchen area.

Androids did not skip or hum.

Larwin shook his head then slipped out the front door and hastened around the outside of the house to the kitchen window. He positioned himself behind a prickly shrub and peeked through one of the more transparent amber panes. Nimri sat at the table sipping something steaming from her blue mug while the odd girl cavorted around the kitchen.

As the stranger twirled and posed, he saw a flash of silver beneath the shaggy bangs. "How do I look?" It was a high-pitched voice, not GEA-4's sultry tones.

"You look perfect," Nimri said. "Do you remember everything?"

"Yes, I do." Hearing the sensual inflection, Larwin's skin crawled with the confirmation that this indeed was GEA-4.

"Speak with your hands and always use the squeaky tone when others are around." Nimri shook her finger, as if she was chiding a real child. "You're supposed to be a human child, not a midget seductress."

This was the plan that he'd spent so many uncomfortable days trying to fathom? Larwin staggered backward. This was insane. Ridiculous. Weird. Something sharp prodded his spine. Or else he was simply taking what he was seeing at face value and overlooking the real plan.

GEA-4 slapped her forehead in a disconcertingly human manner. "Sorry." GEA-4 executed some dance steps and hummed a song in an eerie imitation of a true child.

The pain in his spine intensified. Larwin grabbed his back and touched a nose and silky fur.

"Much better." Nimri clapped. "This is going to work. I just know it." She got up from the table, moved to the counter, just the other side of the patchwork window and rinsed out her mug.

Was Nimri's crazy plan a sign of dementia? What if he and his strategy instructors were the unbalanced ones?

And why hadn't someone told him the blasted android could change her voice on command? Larwin thought of all the hours of torment he'd endured during the weeks they'd been secluded in outer space, isolated from all but high-priority communication, as step by step he'd tested all phases of the machine. While he'd been accustomed to the solitude, the android's sensual voice had triggered an involuntary response in his dreams. He could think of several days when her sultry tones had haunted his wake up calls. He could have avoided so much frustration if he'd known the voice circuits were adjustable.

Of course, doing so could have voided the analysis. Thank Kues those tests had become irrelevant. Larwin rubbed his temples and shook his head. Kazza purred.

Larwin sighed. He dropped his hand and stroked the cat's head. Inside the kitchen, Nimri packed her basket with small pots and several bunches of leaves. GEA-4 loaded a smaller basket with flowers.

He ducked behind the prickly bush when they headed toward the door. GEA-4 cavorted past his hiding spot. Nimri laughed. Larwin peered through the leaves and watched them disappear down the path that led to the pool. Kazza leaned against his shoulder and purred loudly. "Well, fella, it looks like Nimri intends to go through with her crazy scheme. It might work, too." Anything as insane as staining an android then reprogramming it to act like a kid had to have some sort of crazy potential and be an example of what his tactics teacher had meant when he'd said, 'Some unexpected phenomena work by the sheer fact that they are ridiculous and audacious.' Larwin gave Kazza's head a final pat. "I'm going to follow and observe. How about you?"

The huge cat appeared to twirl his whiskers. Larwin interpreted the response as collaborative agreement. When Kazza confidently moved toward the path, his feeling that the cat understood him intensified.

Larwin and Kazza shadowed Nimri and GEA-4 to the last ridge before the river. The breeze shifted. Larwin heard squawks and snatches of conversation. Abruptly, he recognized Nimri and GEA-4's murmuring voices.

Though he couldn't understand what they said, it sounded as if they were on the other side of the large clump of ferns. Much too close. Kazza sat down. His head inclined toward the voices. His ears pointed forward, the furry tufts trembling in the breeze. Larwin grinned and caressed the cat's broad, striped back. Kazza winked at him then refocused his attention on the discussion. Larwin peered through the dense foliage, straining to hear their conversation.

The sun beat down. Perspiration trickled down Larwin's back. The shady patch just a few feet further down the trail would provide a better view of the next section of the trail. But as he took a step toward the sanctuary, Kazza's tail whacked him across the back of the knees. It was all Larwin could do to remain upright or hold back a startled shout. He gritted his teeth and glared at the cat.

Kazza winked and looked upward. Larwin glanced at the spot that held the cat's attention. GEA-4 stood silhouetted atop the ridge. If he'd moved into the shade, her sensors would have picked him up. Worse, Nimri would probably have noticed him and wondered why he was tailing her.

Larwin started counting to one hundred. At fifty-eight, Kazza nudged him toward the shade. Larwin surveyed the path from his new vantage point; moving earlier would definitely have exposed him. He wiped his forehead. The cat actually understood more than he'd given the creature credit for. But then cats were supposed to be predators. It stood to reason that the beast would understand the concept of stalking prey.

Kazza ducked into a gigantic fern clump at his left. The tip of his tail seemed to beckon. He took three steps forward before he realized he was following the direction of a cat. While Kazza was a very intelligent creature, it was not wise to simply follow without reason.

A moment later, Kazza's head reappeared, a huge red flower draped rakishly over his right eye. Larwin stared at the silly spectacle, then despite logic, Larwin felt himself drawn toward the intelligent amber pools. Involuntarily, he took a step forward. Then he took another step.

Fifty paces into the underbrush, Kazza stopped at the base of a mighty tree. This sequoia was at least twenty percent bigger than any Larwin had encountered previously in the amazing and confusing woodlands. As if in a trance he strapped cleats on his boots and gloves and began scaling the mighty trunk. Several feet up the trunk, Kazza's body brushed his right hip.

Larwin paused to catch his breath. How had the cleats gotten into his backpack? Moreover, when had he gone back into the house to get his backpack? He frowned, at the discrepancies between his memory and the reality of his situation.

Kazza padded past as easily as if he was strolling on flat land. It took a second to comprehend that the cat's long, lethal claws were ideal climbing equipment.

The compulsion to follow Kazza seemed overwhelming.

Several minutes later, Larwin crawled onto the lowest branch of the tree. Though precipitously rounded near the edge, the limb had at least six feet of flattish upper surface, which made it markedly bigger than the tree overlooking Nimri's yard. The great cat ambled far out on the branch then sprawled across a smaller fan-shaped limb, which acted like a hammock. Larwin wet his lips. He'd always used the main trunk as a backrest, never venturing out on the limb. Tail twitching, the cat watched something below. About thirty feet of rugged bark separated them. Larwin's fingers dug into the trunk's rough surface as he evaluated the situation. Many parts of his basic training had been much worse than walking thirty feet across a wide, flat expanse, but none of his training had contended with such a high, uneven surface. And all exercise courses had catch nets. This one only had ferns, which provided doubtful protection against a fall.

He hadn't come this far to be ruled by fear.

Larwin squared his shoulders, lifted his chin and let go of the trunk, then went to see what had captured the cat's attention. Where the huge limb formed a Y, Larwin took a breather and peered downward. The town's market area spread in front of him. A pen of geese sent up a ruckus as a bearded man in a frayed coat jabbed a stick through the wooden slats. Nine crude boats were tied up to the dock. "Swear to Kues, you can read my mind. This spot is perfect."

Larwin pulled his audio-visual unit out of his backpack. As he tuned in the visual, he tried not to wonder when he'd packed everything that he needed for this reconnaissance. And he tried not to ponder when he'd gone back to get the pack that he distinctly recalled leaving in his room.

The market day scene appeared boringly typical and peaceful, but something didn't feel the same as it had when Nimri had taken him.

Nimri moved around the square, smiling politely at everyone. She didn't appear to have a care in the world other than trading her little pots and bunches of leaves for unidentifiable items. Odd that she didn't hug others, as she had the red haired woman.

She didn't laugh out loud, either.

In fact, everyone seemed to be conducting his or her business without the joy he'd previously witnessed. Was this normal or had the mood altered after the girl had fallen into the water?

After watching Nimri quietly move around several more tables, Larwin decided that GEA-4 must be some sort of key to Nimri's plan, so he searched for the android. He spotted her as she grabbed an odd purplish thing from one table, then took a big bite. Who had ever heard of oval purple food or an android eating? As a rough-looking group approached her, the android threw down the thing and started twirling around like a demented idiot had programmed her.

What chemical contaminant had been in that thing?

Larwin adjusted the audio reception. Remnants of at least ten different conversations mingled. He narrowed the reception to focus on the group of men, which looked like the ones he'd fought with. "Would you take five eggs for the red?" the man with the droopy mustache asked as he pointed to a rectangular object.

"Six," the woman countered.

The man shrugged. "How about the blue?" With a desultory move, he pointed at a more ovate item.

The conversation seemed dull as the scene, but Larwin could sense undercurrents of veiled emotion, which could flare like a flame, if a spark were struck. "This is the strangest strategy I've ever heard of," Larwin said, "but I hope it works." Kazza's fur rippled. "You have no idea how many worlds Guerreterre has taken over. I never minded the bloodshed and death before—." He grimaced, then softly added, "This time the enemy has a face." Unwilling to admit more of his weakness, even if it was only to an animal, Larwin focused his attention on the rustic market. He disliked the idea of harming an enemy he'd come to know. Larwin cleared his throat. "A non-violent takeover method...what an amazing idea."

Kazza pricked his ears toward Larwin and purred.

Larwin placed his audio-visual unit on the limb and stroked the cat.

~0~

Nimri ran her index finger over a beautiful green-glazed soup tureen. Quark Dagger smiled as her fingertip traced the intricate indentions of the fern leaf he'd embossed into the clay, then used as his inspiration for the vessel's flowing shape. Though she admired both the beauty and function of Quark's design, most of her attention stayed on GEA-4.

Nearby, one of the Lost, who had a scraggly mustache, haggled over the price of eggs with Breeze. Though Breeze was making a joke out of the barter, Quark's body language tensed as he glared at her tightfisted customer and watched his every move to be certain the stale-smelling stingy man didn't pinch anything.

"Quark," Nimri said softly, "I want this, figure out what you want for it." He'd given her so many fine pieces that even an exorbitant amount for the tureen would be fine. He grunted, but his attention didn't stray from the Lost's hands. "You're busy, wrap it up for me when you have time." She placed it on the table, and gave the intricate design a final caress.

Abruptly, a hand closed on Nimri's upper arm. The Lost on her mind, she spun to confront her attacker. Lily leaped backward in surprise. Nimri put her hand to her thundering heart. "You startled me."

Lily's wide smile didn't reach her eyes. "I'm glad to see you, as well."

Nimri hugged her. Lily felt as stiff as cured wood. Was her underlying tension due to her mother's presence or worry over Tansy? "Let me guess, you came to beg me to convince Bryta to come home."

"Yes," she said without pause to think. Then she colored. "No." Lily sighed and looked down. Her hands twisted her apron into an unidentifiable wad. Why hadn't she ever noticed that Bryta and Lily shared the same nervous gesture? "I'm worried about Tansy." Lily's voice quivered with unshed tears. "Would you please come look at her?"

Not now. Nimri clasped Lily's cold hands between her own and turned so that she could watch GEA-4, while she determined what might be wrong with Tansy. "What upsets you about her?"

GEA-4 kicked dirt on a Lost's boots.

"All she does is lie in bed." Lily twisted her apron. "Both eyes adjust to light correctly, but she acts sicker—weaker—now than when you – the Guardian – brought her back." Lily pulled a hand from Nimri's grip and put trembling fingers over her mouth.

"Does she complain about anything in particular? Poor vision? Aches?"

"No." Lily looked ready to break down and bawl like a baby. "She has hardly spoken a word since the Guardian brought her home."

The Lost laughed at GEA-4 then moved away from her. Nimri considered Lily's obvious worry and frowned. Information always seemed to arrive at the worst times. "Does her perspiration smell odd?"

"No. Her body appears healed but she acts near death. She barely speaks or shows an interest in anything. She spends the entire day staring out the window." Again, Lily stifled a sob. "Her room overlooks the river." A tear ran down her cheek.

Nimri wondered if Lily could actually be close to nervous exhaustion or if she simply wanted attention. Perhaps the girl stayed in her room to avoid her grandmother. Since she hadn't sent a message for help prior to Market Day, she suspected the second or third option. With that judgment, Nimri smiled and patted Lily's hand. "Tell me all about it." As Lily opened her mouth to do just that, Nimri turned most of her attention on GEA-4's efforts to antagonize the Lost, but the man only seemed amused by her annoying, childish antics.

"It's as if the river has taken hold of her mind." Lily whined. "Tansy doesn't eat. She doesn't speak. She just lies in bed staring at the river. Nimri, I'm afraid." Lily's tone cracked. "So afraid." Her words rang with true fear.

"Let's go look at her."

Side by side, they angled across the market. As they neared GEA-4, Nimri tried to signal her to hold off. Instead, GEA-4 moved toward a burly Lost, who had the yellowed remains of a badly bruised face and a swollen nose; labeling him one of the ruffians Larwin had dealt with. The man looked like he was itching for a rematch.

GEA-4 could set their plan in motion after she checked on Tansy, now and save the many in a few minutes.

Praying that GEA-4 saw her leaving, Nimri headed up the path.

A glob of putrid brown juice landed two paces in front of Lily. Instead of stepping forward, she teetered backward. Nimri caught her arm, preventing her from falling. Once Lily regained her balance, she turned toward the man with the broken nose. Her eyes narrowed and she glared at him, but instead of speaking to him directly, Lily hissed at Nimri. "That filthy Lost needs to be punished. They all need to be taught a lesson." Lily put her fisted hands on her hips, in a vengeful image of her mother. "I wish Rolf had killed them all." She stopped and turned to Nimri, hands still on her hips.

Nimri heaved a mental sigh. How could she salvage her plan and the present situation without resorting to the violence, which never really seemed to solve any problems? "Lily, no harm was done."

Lily's mouth flattened.

GEA-4 cut in front of the rude man. Ignoring him, she did a dance step. The man grabbed GEA-4's shoulder and spun her around. "Get out of my way, brat," he shouted.

GEA-4 shook free of his grip, then keeping just out of his reach, she continued her squeaky song and dance. The man's blotched face turned red, which caused the healing bruises to appear a sickly orange. Scabs and a tiny brown rivulet at the corner of his mouth became visible underneath his beard stubble.

"What are you going to do about him?" Lily jabbed her thumb toward the uncouth man.

"Teach him a lesson."

"When?"

GEA-4 stuck her tongue out at the man.

"Soon."

Lily snorted. "It's been eight moon risings since they tried to kidnap my Tansy. Rolf would not have let the sunset on that outrage. How much longer is soon?"

The man's hands clinched into fists. "Instead of thinking about revenge, you should be encouraging Tansy to get out of bed," Nimri said. "Unused, muscles became useless. Lack of physical activity and pampering warp a mind more th—"

The Lost lunged at GEA-4 as she twirled around on tiptoe. He grabbed her shoulder and shoved her aside. The android did a perfect imitation of a child falling as she landed with a splat in the dust.

"How dare you suggest—" Lily was cut off by a blood-curdling scream from GEA-4. Though Nimri had been anticipating it, the shrill cry chilled her blood. It brought instant silence to the market, as everyone turned to see what had happened.

GEA-4 curled into a piteous pile and raised her arms as if she expected the bully to beat her. Though it looked natural, it had taken five days to teach the Guardian how to behave convincingly.

"I didn't push you that hard, you obnoxious little whiner!" The man's voice echoed over the staring crowd.

Lily's white fingers covered her mouth and she edged backward.

Nimri shook herself into action and stepped between the man and GEA-4. "What's going on? Why did you attack that child?"

Brown, beady eyes glared at her from beneath wild, saffron brows. "Attack? I didn't attack the—"

"He pushed me!" GEA-4's high pitch made Nimri's teeth ache. "He hurt me! Protect me!" GEA-4 surged to her feet, then in a fluid motion; she threw herself at Nimri, buried her face in Nimri's stomach and seemed to wilt as she cried.

Some in the crowd murmured. Nimri patted The Guardian's rigid back and hoped no one had noticed how coordinated she'd been. It was amazing how difficult clumsiness was to teach.

"Protect you from what?" The man's rage seemed solid as GEA-4's dusty back, which he was glaring at. "Yourself?"

"Quiet, both of you!" Nimri stroked GEA-4's wispy black hair in the soothing manner they had worked out as a signal. GEA-4's crying subsided. The man's mouth compressed to a thin white line. "Thank you," Nimri said as the man's mouth formed a thin angry line. GEA-4 sank to the ground and huddled into a rumpled ball of misery.

The crowd formed a loose circle around the three of them. There were over one-hundred-people, but they were so quiet that Nimri heard flies buzzing. She took a deep breath. The air smelled of perspiration, fresh bread, stagnant water and dank poultry. The normal aromas of Market Day, yet somehow today the air seemed spiced with expectation.

She exhaled then addressed the crowd. "This time we're lucky. No one has been hurt."

Keeping her eyes averted from the crowd, GEA-4 whined in pitiful protest. Nimri bit the inside of her mouth so she wouldn't smile with pride at how well The Guardian was playing her part.

"On our side of the river, we teach children to respect adults— we spank them," the Lost said. His look dared her to disagree.

"When I was a child," Nimri said, "spankings didn't teach me anything." The man glared at her. "Would you hit her if she was able to defend herself?" Nimri used her softest tone and perused his bloodshot eyes. He didn't flinch or look away. An unseen man made an insolent comment about Nimri but she didn't allow her gaze to waver from the bruised face of the angry Lost.

Some in the crowd, primarily male voices, whispered in favor of the Lost's views on proper behavior for children. Females disagreed. As the conversation welled, she continued to stare-down the man.

"Find your backbone," Quark called, "and teach the filthy oaf a lesson." Agreement boiled from the crowd.

"Quarrel, teach them both how to respect others," a gravely voice shouted. The Lost's eyes narrowed on her forehead.

"Quarrel -Quarrel -Quarrel." More and more voices of the Lost joined the mantra.

"She doesn't have the Staff of Protection. Without it, she's powerless," an unknown voice called.

Quark began to chant 'Nimri'. Soon others joined his mantra. The voices got more raucous. Nimri knew she had to do something before her plan ended in a brawl.

"Apologize to her for hitting her," Nimri said.

"I did not hit her!" Bits of putrid saliva showered the bridge of Nimri's nose. "She's faking pain."

"Is she?"

"Children need to be taught respect," Talon said.

"You want him hitting your Fern?" Breeze asked.

Nimri pretended a calm she didn't feel and turned to GEA-4. "Stand up, child." Sniffing and wiping her eyes on her sleeve, she obeyed. Nimri knelt in front of GEA-4 and gently ran her hands over GEA-4's rock-hard body. She wondered if Guardians split like trees. "No bones are fractured."

Nimri stood up, and placed herself between GEA-4 and the Lost. "Would you have treated me so rudely?"

"If you had shown me no respect?" A wave of foul breath washed over her. "Yes, I would." He thrust out his chin.

"You weren't teaching her respect," Nimri said. "You were teaching her to fear you."

"You want to take her place?" He gave her a lewd smile. "I'll be glad to teach you. You might enjoy a spanking."

Most of the crowd gasped. A few men laughed.

Nimri smiled, focused on her role and ignored the rancid-tobacco-laced halitosis. "Thank you for the kind offer. However, I think it would be more interesting for you to attempt to continue your instructions of the child."

The man blinked in surprise then gave her a wide smile. One of his yellowed teeth was broken. "Gladly." He raised his hand and stepped forward. GEA-4 grabbed the back of Nimri's tunic, shrieked and cringed in terror.

Nimri held up her right palm. "Before you begin, I will give her a small amount of my power…I'm sure you won't mind, Quarrel."

The man's bravado faltered for a moment, but Nimri doubted if anyone else noticed. He gave a curt nod.

Nimri turned, placed her hands on GEA-4, as GEA-4 had to her in mind-meld and silently begged the Guardians to help the plan work, then she stepped back and signaled for the man to carry on.

Quarrel grabbed GEA-4, turned her over his knee, raised his hand a notch, then smiled as he let it descend on GEA-4's posterior. The impact made a loud whack. He groaned, but GEA-4's banshee wail drowned him out. He looked up and glared at Nimri as if to say, 'You're next.' Then, his mouth flattened into a grim line, he looked back at squirming GEA-4 and he raised his hand, again.

This time, as his blow descended, GEA-4 twisted and grabbed his wrist. The sickening sound of torn cartilage preceded the man's airborne summersault.

A woman snickered. Others gasped as the bully sailed several feet into the air. Quarrel landed hard on his back.

After a long moment of silence, he lurched to his feet, his right forearm at an odd angle. He kicked her flower filled basket out of his way and charged at GEA-4.

GEA-4 shivered with apparent fear. A look of triumph glistened in his eyes. A hand's breadth before he grabbed her, she took a step to her right, moved her foot and tripped him. Quarrel landed flat on his face.

A woman laughed. A man snorted. Others taunted Quarrel.

He rose, covered with dust and fury.

Still displaying cowardly actions, GEA-4 danced out of his way.

He sidled close, raised his left fist and punched.

Using his own weight and force, GEA-4 grabbed his arm and sent Quarrel in a high arc over the crowd. As the man sailed past the distant tree line, Nimri thought she saw Larwin and Kazza sitting on a bough.

With a bone-jarring thud, Quarrel landed in Talon's pigsty. He remained immobile in the deep mud.

Several people stared slack jawed at him. Others gaped at GEA-4, who was retrieving her scattered flowers and putting the bruised petals in her basket.

A goose honked.

Water sloshed against the dock.

Flies buzzed, but no one spoke.

Nimri fought the urge to rush to the man and access his injuries. Everyone followed her lead, standing still as rocks until two men elbowed their way through the crowd, climbed over the woven-wood fence and knelt next to Quarrel.

Hands folded in front of her, Nimri tried to appear unconcerned as she watched the tableau. Had her solution to avoid death actually caused one?

"He's alive, isn't he?" GEA-4 asked. Nimri heaved a sigh of relief when she heard the previously arranged phrase, which told Nimri the man's injuries were not life threatening.

"Yes," Nimri said. Relief tasted sweet. "He lost his wind. With no water in the way, it will return." She hoped.

Nimri cleared her throat and raised her voice even more as she addressed the redheaded Lost helping Quarrel. "Take him back to your shore. If he ever raises his hand to another child of the Chosen, I will give that child enough of my power to kill." She swallowed and squared her shoulders. "Make sure he understands that."

The redhead scowled at her. "I thought your power was to heal."

"To heal and to protect." Nimri looked at the river, then turned back to the man. "Cartwright supposedly has similar power. Since you'll probably be taking your friend to him for healing, tell Cartwright I'm considering giving every member of my Tribe myst power. Tell him that if I do, bullies wouldn't know until it is too late." To her relief, her tone sounded confident.

Once the three Lost were in their boat and the two conscious ones were rowing across the river, the people began to speak. Before anyone could ask her questions, Nimri grabbed Lily's arm and shoved her toward her house.

Chapter Thirteen

Larwin turned off his viewer, walked the twenty steps back to the massive trunk, without noticing the height and leaned against the rough bark. He twirled some long green needles between his fingers as he digested the scene he'd just witnessed. How would a primitive culture grasp the ridiculous incident? And how could she avoid a fight with such a bold-faced lie?

The strong scent of pine smelled like prosperity.

Kazza looked at him expectantly.

Gradually, understanding came. "I knew she was smart," Larwin said in his native tongue. The big cat's ears slanted forward. "I just didn't realized how smart. If the other side doesn't force the issue and is dumb enough to believe what they saw, her peaceful takeover might actually work." Kazza's tufted ears bobbed side to side as he batted at a shiny black beetle. "This knowledge would be worth a fortune to The Supreme High Commander." Larwin felt light-headed at the possibilities. "Winning a war without loss of commodities or life. And base it all on one whopping lie. Brilliant. Simply brilliant to understand that the IQ of the commoner is so low that they'll believe one person can have magic power and share it with others." He shook his head at the locals' childish belief. "To think, a takeover without the cost of war for either armaments or loss of assets."

He whistled a soft, toneless tune, then climbed down from the limb.

~0~

Though it was still morning, Flame was the fifth person to visit. Even when Rolf lay dying, they hadn't had so much company. Nimri glanced at the counter, where the bribes lay bathed in rainbow rays from the window. Flame's brimming basket of assorted loaves of bread dominated the other offerings. Shame over her lie suffocated Nimri, like swamp-slime.

Flame sighed contentedly, took a sip of tea, then leaned back in the woven-willow chair. "I expected you to be excited or at least relieved now that you've mastered your power." She formed a triangle with her long, tapered fingers. "Instead, I sense increased anxiety."

Only her best friend could read her so clearly. Nimri held her breath, waiting to hear what excuse her best friend would give for wanting myst power bestowed upon her. She glanced at the rack of bacon Talon had offered in exchange for the power, the basket of eggs Breeze had given her, and the intricately woven basket the Mordoc twins had presented her. The back of Nimri's neck heated with the memory of the lies she'd told each of them. The offerings lay, untouched. And now, Flame twirled a long lock of her fiery-toned hair around her finger, as she worked up to asking for power.

Flame settled into the chair, the same way she always did when anticipating a long gossip. "Some are worried that the Lost will fear your power so much that they will stop coming to Market. They'd rather have barter than peace." She rolled her gaze upward, as if to say, 'Can you believe how they act?'

"Are people ever satisfied?"

Flame shrugged.

"I wish I could have gauged Cartwright's reaction."

"Do you think he even exists?" Flame absently played with her hair. She leaned forward in a conspiratorial manner. "I don't know anyone who has ever seen him, do you?"

"What do you think?" Nimri couldn't allow herself to be lulled into the illusion of normalcy.

"So many speak of him that he must exist, but I can't believe all the stories about him. I always thought that the tales of him living in rock and mating with Yetis were exaggerations, but..." Flame raised one of her shoulders in an exaggerated half-shrug.

Nimri knew what her best friend meant. "The stories of Great-grandfather's revenge are fantastic, but they are true."

Flame straightened abruptly, all casualness gone. "How can you know for certain?"

Nimri tried to smile, instead her eyes blurred, at the memory of the view she would never forget. "I saw the evidence from the cliff near the balata grove. Imagine how bad it must have been, if I could see the difference between their land and ours after so many years." How awful her grandfather's rage must have been. How dreadful that he attacked everyone, instead of pinpointing the guilty.

"I need to get home and make dinner." Instead of moving, Flame sipped her tea.

Now it was coming. Nimri braced herself for the plea and her throat swelled in anticipation of the lie she would be forced to tell about why she had chosen not to impart her power to others – yet.

"What do you think about Tansy?" Flame asked.

Nimri blinked. "She slept when I looked in on her, but looked healthy." She frowned. Since Bryta hasn't come home, maybe it really was something more serious than a casual glance could

see. "I thought Lily was exaggerating and Bryta was staying away because Larwin made her nervous."

"Sometimes Lily does stretch a story, but not this time." Flame picked up her mug and took a sip, as if needing fortification from the brew. "I go to see Tansy every day." Her voice sounded as if her words were blocked. Flame swallowed. "I think she's dying."

Panic rose like a swarm of flies. "But Larwin gave her the breath of life."

Flame looked out the window. Nimri followed her gaze and saw Kazza approaching, followed by Larwin. Flame blinked back tears and quickly said, "I think the river claimed her mind when she breathed it—your Larwin may have given her his myst, but it wasn't strong enough to overcome the water's hold."

The door swung open. Larwin and Kazza surged into the room. Suddenly, it didn't seem like the room contained enough air for everyone.

Flame scrambled to her feet, almost upsetting her chair. "I must get home. I'm late." She dumped the bread from her basket onto the table and holding the handle in a death-grip, sidled toward the door. "I'll bring more bread tomorrow." Her voice receded.

Larwin and Nimri looked at each other. Kazza looked at the heap of bread, then batted at the largest loaf of black bread. As it rolled off the table, he caught it in midair.

Nimri glanced from Kazza to Larwin to the open door. Unwilling to tell Larwin the devastating news, Nimri grabbed her harvesting basket and scooted after Flame.

Once in the garden, Nimri went to her lavender patch and gathered buds, then she collected rosemary. Slowly, the soothing scents worked their magic.

Clearly, Larwin terrified Flame. Apparently while his breath could bring back life, it still wasn't strong enough to counteract the river's curse. But that, alone, didn't make sense and didn't

explain why Flame hadn't made the request that everyone else had.

As Nimri's fingertip traced a daisy-like bud, an even more horrible scenario gelled in her mind. What if Flame believed Tansy lay dying of an overdose of power? A chill washed over her as she looked for flaws in the second possibility and found none. It would explain why Flame hadn't asked for myst power —it was the last thing she'd want if she thought it meant death.

What if others adopted the view? What if the Lost learned of her tribe's vulnerability?

Her hand fisted. Tansy had to live. She felt like rushing down to the village and seeing the girl with her own eyes, but since she hadn't been summoned, could not do so. Nimri stared at the oozing pulp in her palm and wondered if Larwin knew about Tansy's inability to cope with his cure.

As if responding to her thoughts, the kitchen door opened and Larwin, followed by Kazza came out. Each had a braided loaf and they appeared to enjoy each other's company. They went to the ginkgo's dappled shade, sprawled on the mossy grass and ate.

Nimri had never felt so alone.

Later, Larwin dug a hole in a vacant planting bed nearby. Kazza sat next to him and together, they studied every scoop of soil.

Nimri, knowing she needed his assurance about Tansy, moved to a nearby clump of lavender and tried to bolster her courage with its heady aroma.

The breeze shifted. Larwin sniffed and straightened. "That has odd smell. What for?"

"The soul." She plucked a sprig and held it toward him. "I'll place it in bowls. A small amount of lavender will make an entire room smell of summer memories." Lavender was a versatile herb. Its fragrance got varying responses depending on the person's particular need. She hoped it could bolster Tansy's ability to contain myst and would reduce the water's claim.

"Today feel cooler."

Nimri, grateful for the safe subject, nodded. "In two moon cycles we will have snow."

Larwin turned and looked at Sacred Mountain's summit. "What happen to trail?"

"The upper reaches become impassable." As if they were ever truly adequate. Surely he knew that.

"For how extensive?"

Perhaps he hadn't been awake for the past millennium or maybe he'd simply stayed inside the Star Bridge. "Some years it never melts."

"So, if I to leave, it must soon."

"Leave?" Her tone hit a high note. "I thought you'd stay with me. Make this your home."

"I stay long than sine qua non. May not able leave. May back. Hope soon."

Nimri tried to swallow but couldn't. "I, I will miss you."

"Will you?" He gave her a searching look.

She remembered that GEA-4 could see a person's life force from thirty feet away, could hear sounds better than Kazza. Nimri tried to smile so he wouldn't realize how much she'd been relying on him to somehow take Rolf's place as Keeper of the Peace.

She held a lavender leaf to her nose and inhaled deeply. "What was it like?" she asked. "Spending the last millennium in the mountain?" He frowned at her then shrugged away her question. She tried again, "You could stay here." The lump in her throat nearly asphyxiated her.

"I back. Bring invasion forces."

He was returning with gifts. Her heart leaped, then she remembered what time meant to him. "When? In another thousand years when one of my descendants needs help?"

Unshed tears stung her eyes. She blinked. "I thought you were here to become my cherished partner. That my children would be yours." Seeing the shocked look register in his eyes, her face burned.

Slowly, he smiled. "I back soon—you lifetime. I bring squadron medical analyzer. If pass medical, you couple me. Rule at side."

"Rule?" She frowned, wondering what he meant. Was a squa-run-med-ick-all-ann like a dowry? Had he just proposed?

"I bring industrialists. Show ways commerce." He gave a decisive nod.

"You think these things are needed?"

"For Guerreterre, yes."

She'd often heard him speak of grrrr-tear, but still hadn't figured out if he was speaking about felines fighting over cantaloupe or it was someone's name.

He'd said he'd return in her lifetime. Nimri tried to focus on that and figured she'd eventually discover what all these wonderful gifts were.

Larwin and GEA-4 departed at dawn the following day. Nimri stared at the spot where she'd lost sight of them long after the shadows deepened. As bees collected pollen and dawn scented the air with promise, she started picking dill and anise seeds to season mid-winter foods.

Finally, she forced herself indoors, and laid the herbs on the kitchen counter. Instead of processing them, she stared out the window at Sacred Mountain. She watched the exposed granite so intently that she imagined she could see Larwin and GEA-4 on the trail. She didn't notice Flame until her friend tiptoed up behind her and tickled her in the ribs.

When Nimri jumped, a meow of delight came from under the table. Chair legs scraped the flagstone as Kazza emerged. His whiskers quivered as he sniffed the rich smell of pumpernickel.

Flame chuckled as she placed the basket on the center of the table. Kazza sat, eyes shut, leaning closer to the heavenly lure with every passing moment. "Kazza, you're forgetting your manners." He straightened and half-opened one eye. "You forgot to greet me." Flame smiled.

Two amber eyes opened wide. Kazza bounded upright. Purring, he balanced on his rear paws; without leaning on Flame for support, he nuzzled her ear. Flame laughed and chose a large loaf of Kazza's favorite black bread as well as a pumpernickel one. He accepted the loaves with dignity and a twirl of his whiskers.

Purring loud enough to shake the rafters, he sprawled back under the table; Kazza chewed on the black bread, and held down the pumpernickel under a massive paw, as if he expected it to escape.

Nimri hugged Flame, then placed a steaming pot of mint tea on the oak table. While Flame slid into a chair, Nimri added two mugs of swirling blue glaze, a pot of honey and a platter of oatmeal-nut cookies.

"I made a potpourri for Tansy." Nimri sat down and poured the steaming tea. "Would you take it to her? I'd go myself, but..." Words failed her.

Flame kept her gaze downcast. "Some speculate that the infusion of magic saved her body, but her spirit had already died." Flame took a quick sip of tea.

It was just as she'd feared. "And?"

"They see Tansy waste away more each day and some whisper that too much power is crippling her." Flame's lips twisted into a disapproving smile. "Of course, some, like Talon boast that no amount of power is too much for them to handle." She looked over her shoulder, then turned back to Nimri and leaned forward. "They haven't seen the other girl," she whispered. Nimri frowned in confusion. "The one who got so much power that she could throw more than her weight over the crowd." Flame took a long swallow of tea to fortify herself and dropped her gaze to the floor. "Some whisper that she died. Pearl thinks we should refuse an infusion of myst. She says that mere mortals are too weak to survive it." Flame looked up; her pupils were so dilated that her irises appeared black. "Nimri, soon the Lost will hear, then Cartwright will know."

Nimri nodded. "I'd hoped to avoid becoming a sanctimonious protector."

"Like Rolf."

"You understand."

Flame shrugged. "You've never liked being the one in charge. And I know how you've dreaded having to take up the staff of protection." She grinned. "You have always preferred allowing people to deal with their own problems."

"True." Since Flame was her friend, she was always the last to hear Pearl's dire predictions. Now that she'd heard the gossip, that meant everyone, including the Lost already knew.

So much for her plan.

"Once Cartwright suspects we're vulnerable, he'll have his people test you." Hearing Flame utter Cartwright's name in a normal voice, instead of the typical whisper, Nimri blinked. A tear tumbled down Flame's cheek. "Oh, Nimri, I don't want to see another man hurt like that." More tears sparkled in Flame's expressive leaf-green eyes. "Tell me I'm foolish to worry."

"I wish I knew if that old one still lived." Nimri tried to stall for time, as she weighed her options for dealing with her problems without Larwin and GEA-4's help. "Great-grandfather despised Cartwright so much that Bryta and I couldn't utter his name without fear of lightening striking us dead." How long would they be away getting their gifts? A year? Ten? More than a day without Larwin and GEA-4 was too long. "I've always believed our tribe's hatred was because Great-grandfather viewed Cartwright as the one person whose ability rivaled his."

"Few people like a worthy competitor."

"Perhaps that was part of it, but the way my grandfather despised Cartwright seemed to go beyond that." Nimri shook her head over the strength of her grandfather's animosity. "A few times I wondered if Great-grandfather's loathing for confrontations and his decision to save some of the Lost was the reason he chose not to instruct me in some intricacies. Later, I realized he didn't train me because I didn't have—" Nimri choked and coughed. Covering her mouth with her hand, she held in the admission about her own failings. And the theory that perhaps her great grandfather hadn't killed the entire enemy tribe because his power had limits, despite his posturing about being all-powerful. Nimri noisily cleared her throat.

Flame glanced around to make certain no one had come in. "My mother told me Cartwright curbed the river's rising and saved lives...Lost lives." Flame's whispered words were startling as a shout. "We fear what we perceive to be more powerful."

Certain that her best friend had read her mind, Nimri took a sip of tea, hoping her movements looked casual and unconcerned. "If Cartwright is as powerful as Great-grandfather, he probably knows he can squish me like a bug." It felt liberating to voice her fear.

"His power may have withered with age."

Nimri fingered the mug's blue swirl. "Great-grandfather's power grew—his ashes of death were strong enough to bring Larwin to aid and teach me." A chill washed down her spine. She looked at the amber window and imagined them struggling up the barely visible mountain face to get things they needed because they'd misjudged her ability.

Flame brightened. "Then Larwin can deal with Pearl and her rumors."

"Larwin left at first light."

"Oh." Flame's face blanched. She gripped her tea mug, as if it was a helping hand. After a pause, she asked, "Couldn't you find the girl? Show our people that she lives?"

"She went with Larwin."

Flame looked up, sharply. "Why?" Her tone was shrill with fear. "Did she need him to help her control the power?"

"She left with him because it was her choice." Nimri tried to sound as casual as possible.

Color began to return to Flame's complexion. "Well, if he felt he could leave, that must mean our tribe is safe despite Pearl and her gossip."

Nimri hadn't thought of Larwin's departure in that light. "Perhaps for now." She stole a glance at the window. "He said he'd return. I had the impression he disapproved of our way of life. He intends to bring back some...things." Nimri moved the mug back and forth until a wet oval of condensation expanded on the table's golden surface.

Flame frowned. "Weapons?" Nimri shrugged. "What didn't he like?"

Nimri sighed. "I'm not exactly sure."

"You must have a guess."

"I don't know what to think," Nimri admitted. Flame was truly her friend, and she deserved the truth. "All I can think about is Pearl and wonder if her tales will bring us ruin."

"You're beginning to sound like Bryta." Flame chuckled. "Yesterday, she told me she wished Zurgon would send Pearl across the river."

Nimri gave a half-hearted laugh. "With the competition gone, Bryta might stand a chance of finally getting Zurgon for her cherished partner. About time, don't you think? She's wanted to be head woman for over fifty winters."

"Since before her cherished partner died in that fire?"

"Probably," Nimri said. She leaned closer to confess. "From a few comments she's made, I have the feeling that Bryta has desired Zurgon since she was a child." Though she'd never understood Bryta's fixation with high-handed men.

"So that's why she hates Pearl."

"Partly. I think she likes the thought of being head woman, too." A mischievous grin dimpled Nimri's cheeks. "If Pearl did cross the river, her constant meddling might focus attention away from us."

Flame shook her head. "Naw, annoying as she can be, I think Zurgon would miss her. Worse, I think Cartwright would feed her to his Yetis. She grimaced. "I wouldn't wish that on anyone."

Gooseflesh rippled over Nimri. "Yetis." She rubbed her arms. "I hope I never see one."

"Me too." Flame shuddered. "Do you really think they exist?"

Nimri didn't know what she thought. "If Cartwright exists, perhaps they do, as well." A chill washed over her. "I hope we never know." But in her heart, she already knew that her nemesis and his evil beasts existed. As the deception she and GEA-4 had carried out fell into a shambles, it would only be a matter of time until a Yeti lunged at her out of the night's darkest shadows. She could imagine its fetid breath and the pain as it ripped out her throat, spilling her life's blood and the hopes of her Tribe.

She gulped tea and wished Rolf had lived forever.

Chapter Fourteen

Larwin's boot caught on a rock. Arms flailing, he stumbled, and instinctively threw his body away from the precipice's deadly drop. His shoulder connected with the sheer wall to his left and his sleeve snagged on a granite spine. Fabric ripped, as the knife-sharp shard dug into his biceps. Pain radiated out from the wound. Decades of training gave him the ability to control his reaction and save himself from stepping back too quickly.

"Radzuk."

Carefully, he eased his upper arm away from the rocky spike. Blood oozed at an alarming rate, but fortunately, it didn't pump in bursts. He dug into his haversack and extracted his med-kit. Ripping open a metallic envelope, he pulled out a sterile cleansing pad. The antiseptic stung. Then, he grabbed the tube of bonding agent, applied it, pinched his torn skin together and counted to twenty-five.

Perspiration stung his eyes and it felt like his arm was on fire. He looked at GEA-4, who had made no effort to aid him. Her profile blended in with the rock wall as she stopped and surveyed the panorama of the valley. Larwin's teeth clenched. "Get that brown gunk off."

"Why?" Her alien voice whined. "I appear more human."

"You are not supposed to look human. You aren't supposed to act indifferent, either. You're supposed to protect."

"Then why was I given this form?"

"It's functional," Larwin said.

GEA-4 scanned the distant valley floor.

Larwin tried to breathe so he could conserve oxygen.

"There is no reason to make this journey," GEA-4 said.

"Gibberish."

"The odds of rescue are 123,893 to one. Furthermore, there is minimal chance the Pterois Volitan will have any functional equipment. Even if some useful devices escaped damage during the crash, it is probable that the planetoid's high ion levels will interfere with any transmission. Staying here is a one-hundred-percent survivable solution."

His fingers dug into the rock wall and Larwin wished it were her neck cables. "For whom?" He turned toward the infernal machine just as an icy gust of wind swooped downward. Rather than be blown off the wafer-thin path, he pressed his body against the rough rock wall, but to his disgust, the annoying android maintained her casual pose on the edge of nothingness.

"Your inquiry is inadequate."

Though his teeth clenched with the temptation to give the wind some help, he knew a warrior could never win when he allowed emotion to rule his thoughts and actions. He took a deep breath then patiently explained, "Guerreterre's resources have been gone for over two centuries. Everyone would have starved decades ago, if we hadn't conquered primitive planets like Callanda and commandeered their resources." He refused to remember Callanda as it had been when he was three and his father had taken him there. Now, Callanda's resources were nearly depleted and if another world weren't found, soon all of

Guerreterre would suffer. That was enough reason to go back to the Pterois Volitan and try his best to alert his commander, lousy odds or not.

Of course, the lure of wealth and status made the choice irresistible.

"True." Except for her hair, which swirled in a stringy cloud, GEA-4 stood unaffected by the erratic blustering wind. "It is illogical to expect a rescue ship."

"We must find a way to send the High Command a message and let them know there's more at stake than my life and the data from your trial run," Larwin explained. "This planet can grow enough food to feed millions. As soon as we manage to notify the High Command, we need to figure out a way to get agricultural equipment through the wormhole." Of course, if the wormhole was not stable he was probably trapped here for the rest of his life. He frowned as he realized the thought was not completely upsetting.

"This world is in balance. Probabilities indicate that bringing in Guerreterre equipment would destroy the ecological equilibrium and eventually turn this world into another Guerreterre or Callanda."

"And if I don't bring this world to Guerreterre, my family and colleagues could starve." Larwin stamped his chilled feet and tried to ignore the burning pain in his arm.

"Bring them here." GEA-4 gestured toward the lush valley.

"Impossible. I don't know where most of them are."

GEA-4 turned to him. "Nimri knows where everyone is."

"Yeah. The whole ignorant population is right in that valley."

Her head cocked to one side. She'd developed the annoying anomaly when Nimri had dyed her skin and hair. "I do not have data pertaining to Guerreterre families," GEA-4 said. Who would have thought that her singsong kid's voice could grate on nerves as badly as her seductive tones? "I have only had

Chosen families to observe. Why is your family so different, that you do not know where they are? Do you suspect they've moved since we left on our trial-run?"

An icy blast hit Larwin in the face. This one held stinging droplets of water. He suspected that GEA-4's understanding was restricted to her initial programming and any knowledge gained since the Pterois Volitan had left on the training mission two months before. His ill-fated flight hadn't provided the android with any understanding of the planet, which she was intended to serve. "On Guerreterre, sexual bonds are temporary. My parents were rare because they had two children together."

"That is not a real family."

"Your interpretation is flawed. There are vast social differences between a primarily agricultural society, such as the one which inhabits that valley," Larwin gestured toward it, "And a system as vast as Guerreterre's, which spans two galaxies. That means the person's job is more important than any non-related personal involvements and they could be assigned anywhere within the realm."

She tilted her head to the other side. He gritted his teeth. "Many must work off-homeworld." He nodded. "Then, why is food for that planet so important?"

"Supply lines." How was he expected to explain such simple concepts to an android with faulty scanners? And why was he even trying? Since he wasn't sure he understood the differences or why Guerreterre's ways were better than Chatterre's, Larwin changed the subject. "I should be grateful you ruined the Pterois Volitan by running into debris. Otherwise, I'd never have discovered this bounty."

"There was no debris."

He stared at her wondering who her programmer had been. "You said that debris damaged the engines and they didn't fail on their own."

"Correct."

Larwin closed his eyes, took a calming breath and vowed that if it was humanly possible to return to Guerreterre, after he secured his future by advising the High Command of this planet, he'd find the programmer and either murder him/her or give them a kiss.

He massaged the area around his aching shoulder and wished he had fast-healing alien DNA, like Nimri and the other girl. "We'll never get to the peak standing here." Nimble as a ballerina, GEA-4 pivoted and headed up the treacherous, ribbonlike trail as if it was a wide boulevard. Larwin pinched the bridge of his nose. Conversing with the annoying android had given him a headache that threatened to turn into a migraine if he continued trying to make sense of her corrupted data files. Larwin sighed and cautiously followed her as he vowed that he'd make sure GEA-4 had a complete diagnostic overhaul as soon as he had the chance, but for the moment, his primary goal was to find a place to camp before the sun set.

Late the following afternoon, Larwin and GEA-4 arrived at the balata grove. Long shadows gave it such an air of mystery that Larwin finally understand why Nimri thought the silver and purple trees were magical. He smiled at the possibilities for using the primitive belief to his advantage.

Though his lungs burned for more air, his shoulder stung and his muscles felt like pulp, Larwin's thoughts kept remembering the individuals and Kazza he had met in the past days and often, he found his thoughts wandering to how they would be affected when progress came to their planet. He shook his head and told himself that he had been on Chatterre's surface too long if he was thinking of them as individuals instead of an enemy to be conquered, If or when he succeeded in getting through to the High Command. His instructors had always taught them never to get emotionally involved with aliens, but Larwin had never met anyone outside the empire before now. Before he could rest or have second thoughts, he donned his environmental-suit and keyed on the oxygen. Inhaling deeply, he immediately felt revived.

It was amazing what oxygen could do.

He attached his sidearm and his light-projector, then got a length of primitive rope out of his haversack. He fastened the rope to a well-rooted balata and climbed down into the cave.

GEA-4 followed.

~0~

Nimri dreamed that jagged teeth were gnashing at her and that gigantic earthen lips were opening wide to swallow her alive. She spun around and fled from the gaping jaws rising from the ground. Glancing over her shoulder, she glimpsed glistening teeth gnash at her, but a moment later she ran into the balata grove and safety. Panting for breath, she scrambled behind one of the sacred trees and sank to the ground. Her lungs burned from the effort and heart hammering, she leaned against a silvery truck and listened for sounds of pursuit, but all she could hear was her own harsh breathing. She clamped her mouth shut and whipped sideways, instead of getting a glimpse of the earth demon, the movement sent her rolling. She scrambled upright, fearing the horrible jaws had ripped into the sacred tree, but they were nowhere in sight. Exhausted, she got to her knees, holding onto a tree trunk for support. Beneath her fingers, the life-force pulsed with vigor and strength, then the tree undulated upward, wrenching its roots from the rocky soil and shaking off its leaves from its branches. Nimri fell backward, too terrified to move. The balata molded into a huge serpent. Writhing upward, it ripped its last root free from the ground and soared skyward, expanding in length and thickness until it dwarfed the central trunk of her sequoia-home. Within moments, the sky was filled with menace.

She closed her eyes and tried to think, but a roar from above took her breath away. Looking at the source, she saw glowing red eyes and bared fangs rushing toward her from the sky

Nimri screamed and sat bolt upright.

Skin clammy with perspiration, Nimri fought the constricting coils until she realized her linens were suffocating her.

Just then the door, swung open.

Nightmare or reality?

Nimri's heart thudded and she gazed wide-eyed as the door arced into the moon's beam. She didn't know what she'd expected, but it wasn't Kazza.

The big cat looked pleased about something as he ambled into the room. Ignoring her mood and the sodden linens, he vaulted onto the bed. Somehow the constricting sheet released as he landed.

Intent on escape Nimri jumped out of her bed, then realized how irrational she was acting, so instead of bolting out the open door, she closed it, then began pacing back and forth in her shadowed room. Out of the corner of her eye, she noticed Kazza's inquisitive expression. She took several deep breaths. How could dreams hold such terror even after waking? She patted her hot face with icy hands, then stroked his head.

Kazza purred.

Adrenaline still racing through her veins, she walked to the window, placed her hands on the sill and leaned out and stared at Sacred Mountain, as if a balata really would rear up out of the earth and transform from mystical shield to attacker. The vivid memory of her nightmare persisted with such strength that she began to shiver violently.

Kazza mewed as if her fear terrified him.

Rubbing the gooseflesh covering her upper arms, she turned her back on the mountain. "Sorry, Kazza. I had a bad dream." He meowed with doubt. "It's okay. Really." Pushing herself to move, she located a dry quilt in her linen chest, wrapped it around her shoulders, then feeling suddenly drained, she sat on her bed. Kazza's purr intensified as Nimri lay down. Since he weighed more than four times as much as she did, the tilting mattress made her roll into him, as she had for all of her remembered life. His presence calmed her so much that she slept.

Her new dream began in shades of black under an inky sky, but this time, she wasn't frightened because Kazza stood by her, purring contentedly. They stood in the mouth of the unpleasantly cold cave that overlooked a black landscape. His luminous eyes roved the charcoal-colored sky, pausing on certain tiny white lights, which glimmered in the distance. How handsome Kazza looked when he glowed! Much better than the stars. She raised her hand to stroke his gleaming fur and noticed her hand was shining, too.

What an odd dream.

"We approach the tunnel entrance," GEA-4 said, from a distance.

Nimri turned back toward the bowels of the cave, where GEA-4's voice had come from.

"Scan the area," Larwin said.

Nimri frowned and squinted at the darkest point of the cave, which was where the voices seemed to have come from. Rocks started glowing, then a round, bobbing whitish-yellow luminescence appeared. Nimri squinted past the glare until she could make out GEA-4 and something else. It took her a moment to recognize Larwin, who was again dressed in the foul-smelling black muscle suit and big round head covering that he had been wearing when she first saw him.

"There is an odd energy reading," GEA-4 reported. "Also, an ion turbulence is six point nine-two miles distant at eighteen degrees."

"Is it approaching?"

"No it is not."

"Does the other energy have poisonous properties?"

"No, Colonel Atano, it does not."

"Plot a course to the Pterois Volitan," Larwin said.

Nimri waved and smiled at them, happy to be reunited. GEA-4 was quiet for a moment, then she walked within a hands-breadth of her and Kazza as if they were invisible. When Larwin also ignored her, a lump of tears formed in her throat. Kazza mewed. "You're right. It's only a dream." She swallowed her hurt, turned and followed Larwin onto the desolate land.

Tail swishing in a gossamer arc, Kazza accompanied her across the black, shifting surface of the midnight land. The farther Nimri went across the bleak ground, the more tiny specks of light she noticed above and the more real the terrain seemed. There were also odd brownish things floating high overhead she paused and squinted at them, until she realized rough chunks of rock hung suspended in the strange sky.

What a peculiar place this was. Nimri sighed. Thankfully, it only seemed odd, not threatening. She sniffed the air, but there was no scent, nor could she feel the ground beneath her feet or Kazza's fur against her fingertips, so it had to be a dream, yet something seemed different about this dream. While it felt unique, it looked more bizarre and boring, and colder than any dream she'd ever had. Worse, Nimri kept feeling that somehow, this bland world actually existed. Could this be a long distance mind-meld from Larwin, letting her know he was safe and that he would soon return? If so, that would mean this lifeless black place was where he lived. "Oh, Larwin, is this your world? How awful." Nimri looked over the total devastation and wondered how someone who loved plants so much could exist in such a horrible place for a day, let alone a millennium. Perhaps he loved plants simply because he'd been without them for so long. Heart heavy with sadness for his past, she hurried across the colorless ground until she caught up with them.

Boring black time passed as they tromped across the shifting ground. GEA-4 led Larwin to a spot that looked like everything else in the dead land, but she pointed to the place as if it held the keys to all knowledge. Larwin and GEA-4 bent down and began to scoop away the grime with their hands. Kazza sat down and divided his attention between watching them and craning his neck to look at the dark sky. One chunk of floating rock appeared to be so close that its jagged contours were visible.

After a few moments of digging, the edge of something silvery was revealed.

"Why in Vilecom was the hatch left open?" Larwin demanded, as he kicked the dirt. "Dust has filtered into everything."

"You were the last to leave." Leave? If this truly existed, Larwin had the strangest home imaginable.

Larwin kicked the ground and cursed. Nimri looked away from his anger and admired Kazza's gentle radiance. The great cat looked handsome as he posed nose high; a typical posture, when he found something interesting to watch. But what could he find so fascinating among the distant specks of light and floating rock? Kazza's hair slowly rose along his spine.

Gooseflesh rose on Nimri's arms.

A moment later, GEA-4 mirrored Kazza's action.

Nimri looked in the direction that held their attention. Nothing. She looked back at Larwin, who was still scooping handfuls of dust out of his home.

Nimri frowned and looked at the sky, again. One point of light changed from a white speck to an elongated tawny shape, which seemed to undulate like the balata tree had in her nightmare. A chill washed over her. Nimri told herself that this was only a dream and tried to control her breathing as she watched the light approach. When it got larger and closer, she imagined she saw a golden dragon from her favorite childhood fairytale coming toward her.

She hadn't dreamed of golden dragons since she was ten. This one didn't look as fierce as the one from her nightmare.

"Intruder alert!" GEA-4 said.

"What intruder?"

"A madrox."

"Great Radzuk!" Larwin bounded to his feet and grabbed a lumpish thing from his belt.

Larwin put the thing against the clear dome surrounding his head. A moment later, he hooked it back at his waist and moved back toward the cave as fast as he could walk over the shifting ground.

Nimri blinked in surprise when GEA-4 went with Larwin.

Kazza slapped Nimri's leg with his tail, as if he was trying to get her to move.

"Let's get back to the tunnel," Larwin said. "The beast should be too large to follow us there."

Nimri followed them, her mind occupied with figuring out what she was supposed to learn from this strange dream or whatever it might be. Frequently, she stopped and turned back to gaze at the magnificent dragon.

The slower she walked, the more agitated Kazza became.

GEA-4 and Larwin had disappeared down the tunnel by the time Nimri and Kazza arrived at the cave's mouth. Despite Kazza's upset, Nimri stopped and watched the dragon. Its intense golden glow seemed to soak in all other light as it descended from the sky like a glimmering mountain.

A huge puff of black soot billowed as the first of ten clawed feet set down...Two. Three. Four.

Kazza frantically butted Nimri in the stomach.

"What's wrong?" She tried to pet him, but he pushed her toward the dark tunnel.

The fifth foot landed and sank deep into the surface. The billowing soot seemed to dissolve around each enormous leg. The area beneath its belly glowed like a hot ember on a hearth.

Believing she was witnessing a bizarre dream, Nimri pushed Kazza away. "It looks like a horrible mythical beast from my childhood storybook. I always thought they were beautiful, but never thought I'd actually see one, even if it is only in a dream." Though the one in her favorite book seemed less menacing, this one seemed larger and more powerful.

As the sixth foot sank into the dust. The dragon seemed to propel itself toward them. A wave of fetid heat rolled over Nimri.

Kazza spun around and hissed at the beast. At the same time, he bumped against her leg and shivered. Then he turned and ran into the cave, where Larwin had disappeared.

A tongue, resembling cerulean lightening crackled toward Nimri, but stopped a hands-breadth from her stomach. Every fiber in her body tingled with sharp stings of pain. She'd never felt such intense heat or pain in a dream.

This was not a dream!

As the tongue retracted, the beast growled. Step by thundering step, it came closer.

Nimri turned and ran for her life.

The dragon roared and lunged into the shaft's mouth. Its tongue flashed toward her, again.

Nimri's scream welled from the bottom of her feet, up her spine and her hair shuddered with the strength of her fear. She ran faster than ever before.

The tunnel, behind her, glowed and her back pricked with perspiration. She tried to tell herself that the light was good because it illuminated the piles of debris.

The stench of rotting eggs made her throat burn. Things had been much better when this place was senseless and boring.

Blue lightening continued crackling, with a rhythmic regularity. Nimri kept running across the unyielding surface, leaping rubbish and fighting for each burning breath as she looked for sanctuary.

She caught up with Kazza, and passed him.

Odd.

Kazza was much fleeter than she was and he could see in darkness.

Nimri slowed and matched her pace to Kazza's energy conserving one.

The ground shook as the dragon let out a furious bellow. A pile of debris to Nimri's right shifted and fell.

Though she tried to leap over it, her left moccasin got caught in the dusty avalanche. Frantically, she fought for freedom.

Kazza stopped and waited for her, his whiskers trembling.

She wondered if he was amused by her clumsiness or fearful of the beast.

The dragon's thundering escalated, but it didn't get closer. Nimri dared to hope that the tunnel had gotten too narrow to accommodate its great size.

Once she ceased her frantic pulling, she slipped her foot out of her shoe, then pulled the moccasin free of the rubble.

Rounding a barely discernible curve, she saw two light-orbs, a familiar silhouette centered in each.

Nimri and Kazza quickly caught up with Larwin and GEA-4. As they passed them, Nimri realized that Larwin moved much faster when he wore Chatterren attire.

The awful black muscle-suit presented another prickle of validity for the nagging hypothesis that she wasn't dreaming.

A flash of iridescent blue and a bellow seemed to encompass the dragon's fury over its escaping prey.

Dust and bits of rock fell from the cavern's walls and ceiling. As the enraged sound echoed up and down the shaft, the avalanche increased. Dust obscured Nimri's vision.

The Dragon's fury escalated to the point that Nimri's head pounded with its rage. She felt horrible for leaving GEA-4 and

Larwin behind, but she knew the sound would cripple her if she stayed. She put all her energy into escaping.

She and Kazza ran into a huge chamber. From there, Kazza led her to an ancient cave. Arriving at the end, she recognized the place where she'd fallen into the Star Bridge.

Clumsily, she grabbed the thin white rope and climbed into the moonlit balata grove. Half expecting to find gnashing teeth or a guardian tree turned serpent, she held her breath and peered into the shadows. Finally, realizing that she'd escaped the danger, Nimri collapsed into a sobbing heap. Despite the occasional trembling of the earth, as if the mountain was in pain, she cried herself to sleep.

Nimri woke with a scream and sat upright.

Kazza fell off the bed, but landed on his feet. His fur stood up straight and he stared at her with huge dilated pupils.

She tore free of the clinging quilt, jumped out of bed and ran up two fights of stairs until she got to Rolf/Larwin's bedroom. Without knocking, she burst into the room and dashed to the window. Fingernails digging into the sill, she stared at Sacred Mountain's summit, as she'd seen GEA-4 do countless times.

A golden glow and a thin column of smoke rose from the Star Bridge's location.

It was real! That was why GEA-4 always watched the mountain! That was why they'd returned to their home! Nimri shivered so hard that she sank to her knees, forehead on the sill, she realized Larwin and GEA-4 had to face the beast alone. Hot tears of shame scalded her cheeks. She was the protector. She should have stayed with them.

When there were no more tears left and her eyes focused, Nimri found herself looking at the spine of a book titled, Cosmic Phenomenon. A compulsion to read it overwhelmed her. After pulling it from the pile, she flipped it open, only to be confronted by a picture of the monster. She dropped the book. When nothing happened, she gingerly picked it back up and studied the photo with the words madrox also known as Ghilwehlen's dragon written under it. Next to the photo was written: *Madrox: mad-rocks n. genius of dragoun celestial 1. Mythical monster usually depicted as a molten gold serpent with wings, and claws. Its azure tongue resembles lightening. 2. These beasts have been known to inhabit the volcanic cores of some of the active Versuvian volcanoes. 3. Scientists claim these creatures can also live in solar flares.

Breath rasping, Nimri raced back to her bedroom and began dressing.

"Golden dragons exist," she told Kazza, who was still pacing wild-eyed around the chamber. He acted distraught, as if he hadn't gotten over being pitched out of bed. "They really burned the first world and it followed me here. We're doomed!"

Kazza's growl sounded part agreement, part objection.

"I can't fight this alone. I need Zurgon. If he won't help, I'll go to Cartwright." The very thought of asking her enemy for assistance made her feel faint, but aside from Zurgon, Cartwright was the only one who might have enough power to save them. Assuming Cartwright truly did exist and lived up to the stories told of him. Nimri swallowed, but the taste of bile remained.

Zurgon, the overbearing elder, and Cartwright, their worst enemy, had become her only hope. What had her life come to?

Clutching Cosmic Phenomenon to her chest, Nimri ran out. Kazza followed, his fur still trembling.

Nimri jogged all the way to Zurgon's house and pounded on the door.

Pearl screamed for quiet.

Nimri pounded some more and begged them to open the door. Kazza ducked into the shadows of some shrubbery when footfalls pounded down the stairs.

A moment later, the door burst open to reveal Pearl's

disheveled hair and rumpled nightgown. "Nimri! My stars. What's the matter?" Pearl squinted and looked past Nimri. "The God of Light isn't with you. I'd hoped to meet him." Abruptly, she glanced down at her garment. Her pudgy hands smoothed at the wrinkles. A lock of graying hair fell across her eye.

"He left," Nimri said. "Is Zurgon awake? I need him."

From the darkness behind Pearl, Zurgon crossly said, "Now, I am." Nimri caught a glimpse of his shadowed silhouette.

"Zurgon, I need your help." She pushed past Pearl and thrust her open book at him. "I saw this thing." She tapped the picture with her finger. "It's coming to destroy our world."

He strained to see the illustration, then, as Pearl lit a candle, Zurgon gave Nimri a befuddled look. "Where is it?"

"At the Star Bridge. Larwin is there, but it may have already killed him." Nimri shifted her weight from foot to foot.

Zurgon stared at the likeness and massaged the muscles at the back of his neck. He cleared his throat. "You are the Keeper of the Peace. You fight it. It's your job."

"I have no power." Nimri sobbed. "The girl wasn't a girl, she was GEA-4—Anthropoid, Larwin's companion. We pretended I had power to trick the Lost so they would leave us in peace." Though Nimri had thought she'd already shed all her tears, twin trails gushed down her cheeks.

"Instead of dreaming up hoaxes, you need to put your efforts into harnessing your power." Zurgon snapped the book shut. "The deception served its purpose, though."

"I have no power." Nimri switched her appeal to Pearl. "Maybe I'm just a mere mortal, too."

"Stop denying your heritage," Zurgon said. "Rolf once told me that you had more power than he possessed, yet you buried it behind a mountain of self-doubt. If Ghilly-dragons truly exist aside from the likeness in the book, and it truly has gotten past the guardians, you must use your power to defeat it."

He wasn't going to lift a finger to help her. Nimri tried to swallow her rising panic, but she couldn't. "Maybe the Lost have weapons we could use." She verbalized her last, desperate hope.

Zurgon glared at her then chose to ignore the remark. "According to legend, these creatures live high above the clouds. Lost arrows don't fly as high as a Tramontain can." He narrowed his eyes at her. "As you can. Arrows are useless," he concluded with a snort.

"Maybe we all can use myst." Pearl seemed to glow at the possibility she'd just voiced. "My mother told me Golden Dragons spawned in volcanoes and lived in lava until they grew too large. She said the adults lived in the core of the sun."

"The book said that the beasts had been known to inhabit some of the active Versuvian volcanoes," Nimri said. Pearl's head bobbed like a chicken. "And GEA-4 lived on the sun's power."

"Legend says that an overpopulation of the Goldens depleted the sun and it exploded," Pearl said.

"Our ancestors viewed the creatures as a nuisance." Zurgon gave his wife a withering look.

"A nuisance?" Pearl gaped at her husband. "That's what you call the demon creatures that killed our original world?"

Zurgon's glare hardened. "Your mother's tales were worthless stories told to entertain a child." His chin thrust out and Pearl frowned back. "History tells me that the beasts couldn't differentiate between a reactor core and a volcano. Do you understand what I'm telling you? There are no reactors nor volcanoes on this world."

Nimri ran her dry tongue over her lips. "I don't know what those things are, but I saw this one—it wanted my life-energy."

"You had a bad dream." Zurgon patted her shoulder. Nimri resented being treated like a silly child. Judging by Pearl's tight-lipped expression, she did, as well. "The Star Bridge was closed a millennium ago. No one can get through."

How did he know? Hearsay? Why was hearsay good when he wanted it so, but not when it inconveniently disputed his beliefs?

"Did anyone go back to check?" Nimri demanded. "Believe me, The Star Bridge is open. Larwin and GEA-4 entered through it from the Old World."

"Go home." Zurgon gave an elaborate yawn meant to intimidate more than show fatigue. "Go to bed. This time, don't dream."

Pearl edged in front of Zurgon, her rigid back to her husband. "Generations ago, my mother's family lived near the Versuvian volcanoes. She used to tell me a story called a Golden Dragon. Have you heard it?"

Nimri shook her head and despite the tension felt a hint of pleasure when she noticed Zurgon's mouth tighten. For the first time in her life, Nimri decided she might enjoy one of Pearl's interminable tales.

"An injured dragon returned to the lava core where it was born, but it was too large to enter and replenish its powers. It went into a fit of rage and began to tear the land."

"How did it get hurt?" Nimri asked.

Pearl ignored her question and started whirling around the foyer, hands and feet slashing at the shadows, as she imitated the hurt beast. "Its jaws and claws ripped great gouges." Pearl knocked a feather-wreath from the wall. As feathers splattered over the floor, she stopped, blushed and turned to Nimri. "My mother never said, but I always thought it was trying to enlarge the core, so it could get in."

Zurgon grabbed Pearl, immobilizing her arms before she could start slashing, again. "Pearl, we don't need your mother's fairytales. The Star Bridge is not open. Nimri had a bad dream."

Pearl twisted in his grip and looked ready to kick him in the shin. "Fairytales are based on historical fact, just like your stories. You can't condemn my mother's when you accept your own family legends." She placed her hands against Zurgon's chest, and gave a push. "Either be quiet and listen or go back to bed."

After giving her a withering look, Zurgon turned on his heel, stomped into the adjoining sitting room and sat on a chair, which was shrouded in shadows.

"As I was saying," Pearl said, "the dragon was destroying the land. The volcano was on a small island in the middle of a great ocean. When the dragon returned to its home or nest or whatever the volcano was." She gestured helplessly, as if confused.

"How big was the dragon?" Nimri asked.

"Bigger than any living creature. Longer than the river is wide." Pearl's glance darted to the seating area. "Let me tell the story before my husband grinds his teeth to dust." Nimri nodded. Pearl took a deep breath and began, "On the island lived a young man named Zeb. He came home and saw the beast ripping and blistering the ground." Pearl again acted out the dragon's movements, but this time, her gestures weren't as violent. "His home was gone. Vanished, along with his wife. The destruction was so bad, he wasn't sure where his home had even stood. Zeb vowed to kill the dragon, or die trying."

Nimri couldn't stand the sudden silence. "Did he succeed?"

Pearl grinned. "Zeb had grown up on the island, he had watched young dragons all his life because it was a favorite spawning place. He knew they avoided water. As he watched this dragon rampage, he noticed it never went near the shore. I don't know how he came up with his plan, but he found a way to turn on irrigation valves to spray it." She winked.

Nimri blinked. "What are irrigation valves?"

"Hollowed canes that move liquids to far away places," Zurgon growled from the shadows.

Pearl nodded and smiled. "Zeb sprayed the beast, and it is said the dragon's bellow was heard on all the islands of Solterre. In its haste to flee the irrigation, the dragon fell from the volcano's side and landed on its back with its head in the ocean."

"And?" Nimri demanded. "What happened then?"

"Why, it died of course. The water killed it."

Zurgon got up and stalked back into the foyer's light. "It's an interesting fairytale, but Nimri doesn't need to think about this. She needs a good dreamless sleep."

"It isn't a fairytale," Pearl said. "Zeb was one of my ancestors. His story has been handed down generation to generation." She gave Nimri a superior look. "Spray it with water."

"Pearl!" Zurgon said.

Pearl gave Nimri another meaningful look then, head high, she retreated up the stairway.

"You'll have to forgive my wife, she loves fairytales."

Nimri raised a brow. "Don't you believe her?"

"No. Phelim Chasen, the Chosen's founder was my ancestor." Zurgon straightened his spine and raised his chin. "I know myst emitters repelled the beasts. You are our myst emitter."

"So, it's all up to me." Nimri felt as if the entire weight of the world was balanced on her spine. And she couldn't hold the load. There had to be help somewhere. "Dracon Lamhfada took several written records with him to the other side of the river. Do you think those books still exist? Do you think they'd have any helpful knowledge?"

"It's possible, but it makes no difference. Even if you understand the symbols, as you suggest, you can't go there. You know the law."

"Surely, an exception can be made," Nimri said.

"The law was made to make people think before making a rash decision."

"I'd be trying to save everyone."

Zurgon gave her a withering look. He really believed her panic was spawned by a dream, but if it had only been a dream, why could she see smoke, when she awoke? She glanced toward the summit, but it was shrouded by trees. "Whoever crosses the river will never be allowed to walk on Chosen soil, again. The reason for the crossing matters not."

Nimri's hand clenched. "Why must the Lost have more freedom?" Zurgon stared at her as if she'd lost her mind. "What if I could find a way to satisfy the law?" Nimri asked, even though she knew that if that was possible, it would have been done centuries ago.

He smiled at her question as if she was an amusing baby. "In a millennium, no one who crossed has managed to return without swimming or by boat. If you believe you can find a way to return by another means, then go." His expression hardened. "However, if you go, I'll see to it that you're considered to be a Lost one. You will be allowed on this side of the river on Market Day. Only on Market Day. Is that clear?"

Unable to speak, Nimri nodded.

Pearl's voice drifted out of the stairway. "Why don't you send a message to Thunder Cartwright? Have him come here."

Nimri sighed. "He's probably too old to travel and there isn't enough time. And don't tell me that it was only a dream." She glared at Zurgon. "Yes, I saw the beast in a dream, but it wasn't the normal kind of dream, it was the sort that-"Her voice trailed off, as she acknowledged her inability to explain the difference.

Zurgon snorted and began to walk away.

In total rejection, she turned. Feet dragging, she moved toward the door. As she let herself out, she saw Zurgon striding toward the stairs.

Once outside, Nimri stared into the darkness and wondered if there was any hope.

Feeling the heaviness of failure in every step, she trudged toward the upland trail. As she approached the crossing, she heard furtive footfalls.

After the emotional bruising she'd taken from Zurgon, Nimri didn't want to speak to anyone else. She ducked behind a tall clump of ferns, then squinted through the darkness to see who else was up at this time of night.

The fern's shadows danced over her, making the approaching person look like one of the Lost. The man's posture seemed dejected as he tramped down the trail, heading toward the dock. As he passed within a forearm's length of her hiding place, she recognized the long fringes on the coat of Tansy's would-be abductor. Nimri stepped into the pathway and demanded, "What are you doing here? It's not Market Day."

The man jerked. His movements indicated an internal war between running and staying. Staying won.

"I needed information," he said, belligerently.

"You're coming from Lily and Sandor's home. Did you try to abduct Tansy, again?"

Hands fisted at his sides, he took a step toward her. It was all Nimri could do not to sink back into hiding. "I did not take her against her will."

The liar. "I saw you. I heard her scream. You tried to force her into your boat." He was one Lost she'd always remember and distrust

"I did not use force."

"She fought you. You pushed her off the dock. You nearly killed her." Nimri felt her hands fist and almost wished he'd punch her, so she'd have an excuse to claw his face.

He shook his head. "She fell." Just as the moon peeked from behind a cloud, his hostile attitude seemed to melt and his face twisted with regret. "We love each other." His tone and expression sounded sincere. Nimri blinked. "I would never hurt her."

Nimri hoped he couldn't see her shock and confusion. "She loves you? How? When?" Did Lily or Bryta know?

"We can only see each other on Market Day," he continued. "We've wanted to become cherished partners for months, but the law makes it impossible for me to stay on this side." His eyes looked misty and his tone sounded like frustration mixed with despair. After having just left Zurgon, Nimri identified with him. "We decided the only way we could be together was for her to come with me." He straightened his back and looked her straight in the eye. "And that's what we were doing." He dropped his gaze to the ground and his shoulders sagged.

Nimri thought he might actually start crying and wondered if this was some crazy story to cover a worse truth. "So tonight, you crept over in the darkness to—what?"

"To find out the truth. Since the accident, all I've heard are rumors." He cleared his throat. "One says she died when she fell into the water." Nimri nodded. "The other says that though she died, the powerful fighter breathed his life into her." His voice cracked with pain.

"That's true."

"I haven't been able to sleep, eat..." His voice cracked with emotion. Nimri started to believe his story. "I was so afraid that I'd lost her."

"You risked your life simply to see Tansy?"

He nodded. "Are you going to tell the Elders?" he asked with resignation.

A cloud crossed the moon. Insane though his version was, Nimri felt certain he had told her the truth as he saw it. He was also providing her with an opportunity to secretly cross the river. "I will not mention this to the Elders if you do something for me."

He tensed. "What?"

"I must talk with Cartwright. Take me across the river and show me where to find him."

"Cartwright?" Fear tinged his tone.

"If you take me, I'll speak to Tansy. If she confirms your story and wants to be with you, I will do everything in my power to help." Nimri held out her hand. "Agreed?"

After the briefest hesitation, the man thrust out his hand and clasped her wrist, in the time-honored Chosen signal of an unbreakable contract. Nimri didn't know if she was excited at her daring, was fearful of the outcome of her adventure or if embarking with a Lost was the stupidest thing she'd ever considered.

Chapter Fifteen

The madrox slammed its tail into a pile of debris. Glowing red dust boiled past the crevice where Larwin had taken cover. His only option was the safety of the old cave, which provided air and food, plus had the benefit of being too small for the beast to enter. He hoped. Carefully, he plotted his course to reach the cave's mouth and prayed to Kues that the beast would turn its attention elsewhere.

The madrox bellowed in rage, then its eerie, iridescent tongue crackled forth like demonic blue lightening.

The chamber groaned. Dust showered down from the high domed ceiling. Within a moment, Larwin couldn't see through the haze. He hoped the beast couldn't see, either. Knowing that this was probably the best chance he'd get, Larwin sprinted from his sanctuary, counting his strides. At fourteen, he slowed, put out his hands and felt for the wall.

The madrox roared so close and loud that Larwin's head rang from the sound. The beast sensed movement. Hopefully the dust blinded it, too. Larwin hurried toward what he prayed would provide safety.

Four paces later, he tripped over something and sprawled face-first onto the hard dusty rock floor.

He tried to hop back up, but something heavy trapped his foot.

The earth shuddered.

Larwin moved his hands to his boot and felt for the obstruction. Rough, unyielding contours were detectable through his thick gloves. Again, the floor vibrated, as the beast took another lumbering step forward. The thing imprisoning his boot seemed cone-shaped and smooth, yet the larger end felt rough and gouged by a jagged crevice. He remembered having seen a fallen stalactite inside the cave.

He'd made it.

Maybe.

The madrox's tongue slashed above him, attracting the dust as if it was magnetized. When the tongue receded, the view cleared. Mere yards from him, the madrox's fiery red eye peered into the opening. Larwin lay petrified, half-hidden behind the ensnaring stalactite; not even daring to breathe. Then, the madrox moved back. Its blue tongue shot forward, mere feet over him. When it retracted, the membrane was purple with dust. The beast snorted. It tilted its head until one eye again filled the opening. Larwin stared back.

Breathing at a standstill, Larwin infinitesimally twisted his ankle. He felt the pressure from the stalactite slacken.

The madrox screamed. Again, blue lightning flashed over him. Incredible heat radiated through his suit as the forked tongue hovered mere centimeters above him.

Larwin didn't know which of the beast's senses was stronger, but he suspected movement dominated, so though his lungs cried for oxygen, he didn't breathe or blink until the tongue receded.

The dragon made a rumbling sound. This time, the unblinking crimson orb remained focused on Larwin, but it made no effort to attack. Was it delaying until he made a mistake like blinking?

The sweat in his suit accumulated until Larwin worried he might drown before the predator's contest ended. His body needed air so badly that he worried he would either collapse and be eaten after an involuntary gasp. Slowly, carefully, he drew a minuscule bit of air into his starved lungs. It was enough to fend off blacking out, but not for much else. With a killer like that watching, blacking out would be the last thing he would ever do.

After many infinitesimal breaths and what seemed like forever, the beast turned away. This time, Larwin remained still as the stalactite, which partially protected him. For the first time in an hour, he dared to hope that he would reach safety.

The beast whirled and turned back to the crevasse. Its eye lingered at the opening for what felt like eternity, then it made a snorting sound and moved across the doomed chamber. As it got farther away, Larwin realized the cave opening was smaller than one of the beast's eyes. He suspected that if it had been larger, the beast would have been able so see exactly where to test with its tongue.

He waited, continuing to take tiny breaths. He'd seen how quickly the beast could spin and snap and sensed that was one of the predator's tricks.

When the beast reached the far side of the cavern, its scaly tail still curved against the nearby wall and the top of its head grazed the doomed ceiling. It began to circle around the outer wall. Was it trying to find the way out? Larwin prayed to Kues for deliverance. The tip of an opalescent wing scraped past the cave. How had the monster squeezed through the narrow tunnel? Was it as trapped as he was?

Once the scaly tail swept past the aperture, Larwin quickly freed his boot, staggered to his feet and hobbled toward the rope.

The madrox roared. The ground shook as it tried to spin around in the too-tight chamber.

The walls around Larwin glowed red and the back of his spacesuit heated. Larwin sprinted in an uneven gait to the rope and climbed as fast as his arms could propel him to the safety of the pretty trees.

The azure tongue snapped beneath him and an inferno of heat surged upward. The rope blazed, sending flames with the scorching heat. Larwin threw himself onto the mossy ground at the feet of the stone statues. For a moment, fire blazed in the mouth between the statues, then it fell back into the cave.

Larwin yanked off his helmet and squinted at the opening, certain that the beast couldn't burrow through rock, but fearful that he was wrong.

The madrox roared.

Dust billowed from the opening and coated the magenta leaves with black soot. In one spot, Larwin thought he saw a tiny tendril of smoke rise, but when he leaned close for a better look, he only saw the ashen remains of his rope.

He wiped sweat from his eyes and leaned back against the sculptures.

The earth trembled. GEA-4 stared at the opening. Where had she been when the madrox had him pinned down? Off singing silly ditties? "Since the cave is too narrow for the madrox, it is trying to bore through." The shaking increased. Boughs whipped, as if in a stiff wind. Assuming it continues at its present rate, it should succeed in three days."

Wonderful news. "Madrox are attracted by energy emissions," Larwin fumed. "They stalk ships with faulty warp drives. Why did it chase us?"

"I monitored unfamiliar energy readings in the main tunnel."

"From the madrox?"

"No. At times, the energy split into two random units, both of which moved down the tunnel as if fleeing from the beast."

"Perhaps the energy was from the wormhole."

"It is a possibility." GEA-4 picked a wilted leaf and studied it. "Or perhaps it followed the Pterois Volitan."

Larwin snorted. "The Pterois Volitan didn't come down the wormhole and it didn't have warp capacity."

"Perhaps the animal followed the plutonera."

"The what?"

"Plutonera."

He snorted. "My ship didn't use that."

"Correct."

Coldness washed over him. "Was the debris you ran into an old plutonera canister? Is that why you think the beast followed us?" The sweat in Larwin's suit seemed to form ice crystals.

"As per Article 123—"

Larwin tore at the suit's bindings. "What does Article 123 have to do with anything?

"The Schimmel was carrying plutonera when it blew up."

"Schimmel?" Larwin went very still. What was the android talking about? It occurred to him that he'd made several assumptions about the events, which had ruined his ship and landed him atop a mountain with the most magnificent view he'd ever see. "I think you'd better tell me exactly what happened while I was sleeping and begin with telling me if you're talking about the high commander's ship."

"This Schimmel was a Quergi freighter. At 18:42 I monitored a distress call from it," GEA-4 said. "The ship was immobilized and loosing life-support. There were five crew still alive."

The dragon bellowed, and the ground trembled, but it didn't sound quite as close and less dust billowed from the cave's mouth.

He nodded. "The Quergi are allies." Larwin stepped out of his environmental suit. The night breeze hit his saturated jumpsuit with the promise of a severe winter. He shivered, but was more concerned with understanding what GEA-4 was trying to report. "123 makes sense. Continue with your report."

"Thirty-six point ten minutes later, I rendezvoused with the freighter. I was in the process of coupling our ships to save the crew when the Schimmel exploded."

So that was how she'd gotten so far off course and they had crashed in the forbidden territories. Why hadn't she said so earlier? He frowned and looked at her. "You told me our engine was damaged by debris."

"That is the factor that shattered it and impaired steering."

"Are you telling me you failed to scan the area?"

"No, I am not," she said. He was afraid that was what she would say. "I completed all inspections prior to docking. The madrox had bored through the hull and was in the freighter's hold consuming the cargo. Probabilities indicated it would remain there while I rescued the crew."

"Let me guess. The cargo was plutonera and the beast hiccuped." He closed his eyes, envisioning the situation. "Of course, the freighter disintegrated and you didn't complete the rescue, because there was no one left to rescue." He sighed as he opened his eyes. GEA-4 inclined her head. Why did worst-case scenarios always happen to him? Larwin rubbed his temples. "Would I also be correct in presuming the Pterois Volitan got bathed in plutonera residue?"

"Yes."

`Madrox were known to act like Prudian bloodhounds when it came to plutonera. The tension in his temples increased. "I assume that the beast followed us here." And the debris, which had damaged his ship, was part of the Schimmel. Everything made sense. Her scanners were fine; they were the victims of fate.

"Yes, Colonel Atano, that is correct."

"Can you tell me why it bypassed my ship and chased me

down the tunnel?"

"No, I can not."

"Not even a theory?"

"Only the two odd energy readings."

The ground shook as the beast bellowed. A small trickle of pebbles rained down on Larwin. There was only one way to deal with a cosmic dragon. "GEA-4, scan this area for a water source."

He clenched and unclenched his hands while he waited for her conclusion. "My search did not encounter anything but moisture in the vegetation," she said.

That's what he'd feared. He tried to keep his tone calm. "Will it rain prior to your estimate of when the madrox breaks through?"

"I am not programmed to predict weather, but logically, it is doubtful."

"Does the atmosphere here have enough vapor to deter a madrox?" He was perspiring so much, it might.

"The moisture level at this altitude would irritate the madrox. Should it be provoked, I predict it would respond with brute force."

"Great. Anything else?"

"This one is unpredictable. Madrox normally like hot, high-energy destinations."

"Yeah, like Kalamar's volcanic moon." Vilecom was a molten ball, which had the notoriety of being a place one could always spot madrox. Larwin shivered. "Scan the planet's surface for water sources."

"I did. I can't detect any closer than the valley."

Larwin sighed. Amazing how inconvenient a madrox could be when he didn't have his space ship. Any other time he'd encountered one; he'd simply detoured around the beast and zipped away. How could he find an expedient way to alleviate the problem in this primitive place? "Why is it so determined to get at us?" GEA-4 tilted her head and looked at him. "You said it was boring through solid rock. Why would it do that for days?" He frowned as he studied surrounding rocks and trees. The creature's fixation on him didn't make sense, especially when a layer of plutonera must linger on his ship. "Scan for whatever a madrox would consider food or shelter."

There was a long pause, as GEA-4 turned in a complete circle. "There is no lava or radiation within my scanner range. However, it is possible that volcanic activity or heavy metal deposits exist outside my range."

Without food or heat sources, the beast should leave. What reason could a madrox possibly have for pursuing a human and a machine down the tunnel? None, yet it still persisted. "It should go away." Larwin settled between the legs of the larger stone guardian, which gave him some protection from the chilling breeze and prepared to wait.

Through the remaining night, the madrox continued its uncharacteristic assault.

As a gentle breeze heralded dawn's promise, Larwin chewed a Vitameal bar and grimaced at the foul flavor. He looked at the package and was surprised to discover it was omelet flavor. Until he'd eaten on this planet, he'd thought omelets were his favorite food. He hacked his way through the branches and sat in the spot where he'd first seen Kazza. Looking into the distance, he contemplated what the madrox would do once it broke through. For certain, it wouldn't follow the feline's pattern and turn into a friendly companion. Sunrise broke over the distant ridge, bathing the land in magical light.

GEA-4 joined him. "The madrox is still on my predicted timetable. We have time to reach the valley floor, where there is adequate water for protection."

He stared at the scene and wondered what attracted the beast. It couldn't be the wealth of plants. And he doubted if it was after any residual plutonera that might be on his suit. If it had been that, the beast would be digging up the planetoid's dusty surface to get at the Pterois Volitan.

With the madrox blocking his way, there was no possibility of reaching the Pterois Volitan and calling for backup. Even if he could reach the planetoid, the brute would consume whatever energy attracted it and melt all botanicals before support from Guerreterre could reach the planetoid's remote coordinates. He sighed. Even if help could arrive, his commander would never allocate water away from the home world.

In less than three days, the beast would break through.

Larwin dusted off his uniform and marched toward the trail, which he'd just spent two days climbing.

If it broke through, the creature would ruin everything for him. Even if it didn't break through, chances were that he could never go home. Clumsy and destructive as madrox were one of them could destroy billions in resources simply by exhaling toxic fumes. Being abandoned here was not a bad fate and he had already lived longer than he expected.

The ground shook causing several small rocks to clatter downhill and leap over the precipice. The magenta branches swished as if in an unseen wind. The intense heat madrox radiated would probably dehydrate plant life, even before it actually broke through the wormhole. Worse, it could desiccate him like the doll he'd found in the tunnel.

Larwin shuddered at the memory. He looked over his shoulder. A crimson puff of smoke rose from the mouth of the cave. Once the beast broke through, the only sure safety was near water. And there wasn't a drop on the darned mountain.

Purposefully, he began to move down the hand-wide ledge that Nimri euphemistically called a footpath. Veiled as her home was by the high humidity from the falls, they should be safe, at least for a while.

It would be nice to see Nimri again, too.

~0~

Nimri stumbled over an unseen rock. She fell toward Chase, who was a pace ahead on the narrow, winding path, but caught hold of a towering boulder to her right and the bough of a spiny bush to her left. While she fought to regain her balance, Chase continued upward at a steady, determined pace. Nimri massaged her aching ankle and watched the resolute set of her guide's shoulders. She shook her head at her puzzling escort's back. Was he too wrapped up in his fears of Cartwright and his Yetis to notice that she'd injured her ankle? Did his disregard stem from her disbelief that he, a Lost, claimed to love Tansy?

Assuming Tansy had actually shared his feelings, after the terror she'd suffered, it was highly doubtful that she still retained any tender sentiments. Did he realize that?

If he'd spoken the truth, so many things made sense. It might even mean that Larwin's breath of life could cure all but a broken heart.

But, if Chase had made up the story that Tansy loved him, he could be leading her into more danger than Cartwright and his Yetis. Assuming they existed. She'd never find out while she hung onto a boulder and healed her ankle.

Her half-healed left ankle protested, but Nimri got to her feet and hurried after Chase. Soon, the narrow path twisted upward, snaking along the vertical face of the rocky mountain. Strange how both Cartwright and Rolf had chosen such isolated spots. Or perhaps the Lost lived high on the rocky bluff to avoid future floods. Maybe the path would seem more walker-friendly if clouds didn't blanket the moon. As it was, starlight provided the only illumination on their perilous trek.

Perspiration stung her eyes by the time she caught up with her unhappy guide. She wished Chase would stop long enough for her to totally ease the sprain.

Or at least slow down.

As she thought that, he abruptly halted. Nimri nearly bumped into him. Chase stared ahead, transfixed. She peered around him. Two tawny eyes glimmered in the dense shadows. Did Yeti eyes shine yellow in the dark? Chase lurched backward. The eyes looked huge enough to belong to such a horrible creature. Nimri sidestepped, landing on her sore ankle. Her right knee connected with rough rock. Gasping at the sharp pain, she blinked. When she looked, again, the watcher was gone.

Gooseflesh broke over her as it did when she plunged in ice-laden water.

Not knowing if she would need to flee or not, she waited, all senses alert. Predators often moved in packs, and she was in no condition to walk, let alone run through the night over unfamiliar territory. Nimri grabbed her knee with her left hand and her ankle with the right then sent binding thoughts to the ligaments and healing thoughts to the torn flesh.

Chase, cowered behind her, his back protected by the craggy wall and his other side by the trunk of a twisted tree. He raised his arm and pointed, finger shaking, up the trail at a patch of desolate blackness. It lay just past where she'd seen the shining eyes. "Cartwright's." His trembling hand dropped. Chase's throat-ball worked up and down several times. His complexion appeared white in the darkness. Just then, vermilion rays of moonlight broke through the clouds, illuminating the jagged terrain they'd just come up.

Nimri looked from Chase to her destination. Hut-size boulders faced each other across the thin trail. Beyond them lay impenetrable blackness.

Involuntarily, she shivered.

No wonder Cartwright never came to market. Old men and impassible trails were incompatible. Eerie as the trail to his home appeared, it was no wonder Chase feared to venture there at night. She inhaled. The myst power was so strong that even she could feel it. With that understanding came the certainty that she was being watched.

Nimri shivered.

Chase turned and scrambled down the path as if the winds of misery were whipping at his heels.

Unwilling to sever her last link with humanity, no matter how surly, Nimri called after him, "Where are you going?"

"Home."

"But—"

Chase stopped and partially turned. "I did what you asked."

"You still need to show me Cartwright's home."

"It's the only one." Chase edged a step downward.

"Why does Cartwright live so far from everyone?"

"If his Yetis don't kill you, you'll have to ask him." He gulped. "I hope you survive long enough to keep your part of our bargain." With that, Chase sprinted out of sight.

Yetis! Cartwright actually lived with Yetis? It wasn't a story concocted by the traders to frighten them? Did the creatures have big yellow eyes?

The feeling of being watched intensified.

Swallowing her fear, Nimri took a step up the footpath. She sensed movement behind her and heard sniffing.

I am not afraid.

A bass growl from her left made the silent thought a whispered mantra. "I am not afraid," she whispered, loud as a falling leaf. "I am not afraid. I am not afraid..." She repeated the mantra a dozen times for every unsteady step.

A cantaloupe-sized rock slowly rolled past. Nimri stepped out of its way, then hoping she sounded more assured that she felt, asked, "Cartwright, is that you?" Her voice sounded as alone and afraid as she felt. "I am Nimri Tramontain. I've come a long way to speak with you."

Silence.

She ran her tongue over her lips and wondered if she should go on, wait for dawn or—what?

Abruptly, a man stepped from between two huge boulders bordering the path. He stood arms akimbo. At that moment, the moon's sinking red orb moved behind the boulders, silhouetting him. Had he timed his appearance? Moved the moon to make the event appear more dramatic?

The short hairs at Nimri's nape stood on end and tried to uproot her braid. Then she realized the silhouette looked familiar.

Larwin!

How had he gotten here? Why was he here? Had he disguised himself as a Guardian to check out her and her defenses, as Bryta had imagined? A breeze gusted, chilling the sweat enveloping her body. Nimri shivered as she remembered Bryta's intensity. 'No one on this side has ever seen Thunder Cartwright, but years ago, I heard a description of him and this Larwin could pass.'

"Gunda, Carn, go home." Not Larwin's voice.

"I am not afraid. I am not afraid..." She resumed her murmured mantra.

Movement to her right.

Movement to her left.

Huge hairy things, half a head taller than her and three times wider emerged from the shadows on either side of her. They came toward her, knuckles of too-long arms dragging in the dirt. They had to be the Yetis Nimri stared straight ahead, afraid to blink. One shuffled close and started snuffling. Air currents tickled her neck.

"...not afraid. I am not afraid. I am not..."

Coarse fur brushed her forearm.

Nimri locked her knees and kept whispering her incantation.

A large heavy body bumped her other hip, knocking her against the sniffer's bristly side. The hairy beast grunted. Nimri fought to hold back her scream.

Instead of attacking and ripping her to bits, the beasts ambled toward the silhouette. Bigger than the man, they hunched over, their knobby knuckles swinging just above the dusty path. The man didn't move as the creatures lumbered past and brushed against him.

After the creatures receded into the shadows behind the left boulder, Nimri was alone with the shadow-shrouded man and crimson moonlight.

Despite the athletic appearance of the man's outline, it had to be Cartwright. Who else could order Yetis to leave, then ignore them as they passed?

"Cartwright, I apologize for disturbing you in the middle of the night, but times are desperate." Good, her voice only sounded a bit breathless. Hopefully, he'd think she was merely winded from her climb.

"We'll speak inside. Come." He turned, took two steps and disappeared into the blackness.

Inside what? Nimri squinted into the dense shadows. She took a deep, cleansing breath and forced herself to take one big, confident-looking step. The ninth step brought her to the huge boulder. Eight more and she passed it. A candle flickered in the all-encompassing darkness. Nimri straightened her back and blindly walked toward it. As she entered the gloom she was able to distinguish dark shades of gray from pure black; Cartwright, veiled in shadows, stood near a cleft in a mammoth stone and motioned for her to come. Head high, she limped forward.

Cartwright made a gesture; a large slab of rock swung outward. The opening revealed a candlelit room, which bore no resemblance to a cave.

Her steps faltered; she stared, mesmerized.

Cartwright tilted his head, apparently studying her reaction.

Must the man always stand with light at his back?

Warm air fanned her neck and a Yeti snuffled. Nimri sprinted into the room and dodged behind a wide stone table so fast that the candle flickered out. Heart pounding, she listened to the darkness and tried to sense danger.

With a soft tread, Cartwright entered. There was some shuffling, then the door grated shut and all escape was blocked.

Something scraped. Nimri smelled the faint scent of rotting eggs, then light blossomed in Cartwright's hand. He relit the candle. A black, hairy, Yeti was a pace away from her.

While Cartwright lit other candles, Nimri watched the beast raise its horrible, hairy arm.

Nimri stood still as a corpse. The Yeti snuffled and opened its jaws. A drop of saliva clung to a pointed tooth. Nimri's mouth went dry. The beast was worse than anything she'd ever imagined.

She hoped her death would be quick and painless.

The Yeti covered its eyes and grimaced in an oddly childish way. Then the ungainly creature ambled away from her.

Whop-whop-whop. Nimri jerked her head to the right. A handsome, dark-haired man plumped large earth-tone cushions in the corner of the room. The browns, tans and gray made the room seem stark and masculine, just like the man who was ignoring her.

She glanced around looking for Cartwright, but concluded that he must have gone through one of the two dark archways.

The other Yeti huddled next to the man with the long black, feather-laced hair. Kazza would never have sought protection from Bryta. That left the possibility that Thunder Cartwright was nothing like what she'd expected.

Nimri blinked away the silly thought and swallowed as she took in her first impressions of her enemy's home, which seemed much more durable and solid than the wooden structures she was accustomed to.

The man threw down the thick tan cushion, then turned to face her. Despite the fact that she was certain that she didn't know him, a shiver of recognition went through her. His unlaced leather vest revealed his bare chest and an ancient amulet, with a pattern oddly similar to the one worked into the leather of her bag.

She touched her concealed amulet, then her hand lingered at her throat.

The man's vivid green eyes took in her movement. He smiled. She dropped her hand to her side and tried not to wring her tunic as Bryta did her apron.

Why did he seem so familiar?

He appeared to be her age, perhaps a year or two older. He was certainly as physically fit as Larwin. Could a master practitioner of myst hold off aging?

No, if that could have been done, her great-grandfather would have done so. This couldn't be Cartwright.

A bright purple feather fluttered against his glossy black hair. She glanced upward, certain he was the housekeeper. The man stared at her as if he'd never seen a woman in the room. Since his master, Cartwright, actually lived with Yetis, it was likely that no other woman had ventured here.

He smiled at her.

Her skin prickled with the feeling that she knew him from somewhere. Nimri gave her head a tiny shake and decided the sensation was because his body reminded her of Larwin. Still, there was something terribly familiar in his emerald eyes and sculpted cheekbones.

"Have we met before?" Nimri asked.

The corner of his mouth twitched as he gave a slight nod.

The Yeti cowering next to him rose and circled a small brown woven rug. With a groan, the other Yeti emerged from under the table.

Nimri gulped. The man's smile widened. "Gunda, Carn, go back to bed." It was the voice from the path. The ugly beasts left. Nimri breathed a sigh of relief, then the man gave her his undivided attention, as he settled onto the cushions. "Why are you here?"

"To see Cartwright."

He grinned and made a gesture that said, "You've found me."

Nimri's mind turned to mush. She picked up a pretty blue polished pebble from a stone table and focused on it instead of his mesmerizing gaze. "You are Cartwright?" He nodded. "I expected someone older." She rubbed the pebble between her fingertips and felt her tension begin to ease.

He grinned. "What is so urgent that you're willing to defy tribal law?" He raised a brow. "If it's Rolf's death, I've known he was dying since he first took ill." His casual tone could have been reserved for any topic. "Surely you didn't come all this way to borrow my worry stone?"

She put the pretty rock back on the table and looked down at his burnished stone floor. "Do you ever have visions? See things that will be, if nothing is done to alter the outcome?" She raised her head and looked into his face. He looked comfortable, as he reclined on the cushions. Apparently Thunder Cartwright was more used to having strange women drop by in the middle of the night than Zurgon.

"What if I did?" He gave her a devastating smile.

"Then you can better understand what I'm going to share with you."

"Did your vision concern the unjustness of Rolf's rage?"

"Coming danger." Nimri swallowed. "Have you ever heard of Ghilly Dragons or Golden Dragons?"

"All children have." Cartwright patted the ginger-toned cushion next to him. She moved a step toward him before she realized her legs were moving. "Why don't we talk about something more pertinent than ancient history? The rift between our Tribes comes to mind." His smile was devastating to her peace of mind.

She'd imagined that Cartwright would despise her; instead he actually seemed happy to have her arrive unannounced in the middle of the night. Unbidden one of Rolf's favorite sayings popped into her mind, 'Keep your friends close, but your enemy closer.' She held her position and stared at the man who was too handsome and friendly.

"I'd be interested in talking about changing several Chosen Laws," he said.

"So would I." The table's edge pressed against her thigh. "But first we need to protect everyone from a worse foe. A Ghilly Dragon is breaking through the Star Bridge."

"You came to talk to me about a child's story?" He chuckled.

Men! "I saw it," Nimri said. "I was there." She took a step toward him. "It almost killed me. When I came back to my body, I saw smoke rising from the balata grove."

Cartwright stiffened, then sat up and nodded. "I saw the smoke rising crimson in the dusk."

Nimri didn't know what to think. Hadn't he understood the significance? "Will you help me save this world?"

His eyes glinted. "For a price."

Her hands clenched at the typical Lost reaction. She swallowed past the lump of fear. "Name it." No matter what he asked, she'd pay it, because if they didn't succeed, there would be no future. And if they succeeded, the value of saving their world was worth anything he could ask.

Cartwright studied her, as if trying to read her mind. "You'll find out what I want after we defeat the dragon." He settled back and again patted the cushion.

"I'd like to know now."

"If you look within yourself, you will know my price."

She sank down to her knees, but stayed away from the cushions. "Cartwright, I give you my word that I will do whatever you ask, no matter what." She licked her lips. "Please tell-"

He cut her off. "You can begin our alliance by calling me Thunder."

"Fine, Thunder." She took a step toward the door and freedom. "For now, I must leave, so I can get home before I'm missed."

He moved as swift as Kazza and grabbed her upper arms. "Until this matter is settled, you stay here. If we fail, it won't matter how sullied you get by living on the wrong side of the river. If we succeed, I'll know you won't go back on your word."

Her heart skipped a beat. What had she agreed to that he felt it necessary to hold her hostage? Wildly, she looked around the room, hoping to find an escape. Instead, she saw a crystal skull that was nearly identical to her own. Her eyes fastened on it, and her racing heart calmed. She tore her gaze from the empty eyes, to his vibrant green gaze. "I have never deceived anyone," Nimri said. "If it's within my power, I will do whatever you ask."

He dropped his grip, but stayed close—too close. "Oh, I guarantee it's within your power."

She felt the truth of his words. Knew that without him all would be lost, that even any changes in the laws would be nothing compared to complete annihilation of their world.

"Than it's settled, I shall stay here." She took a backward step and held out her hand. They clasped wrists to seal the bargain. Nimri told herself it was the only thing to do, but wondered if she'd also sealed her fate. "Now, will you tell me what I've agreed to?"

A smile played around the corners of his lips as he shook his head.

Chapter Sixteen

Sunset's final rays painted Nimri's garden in golden hues, which highlighted the encroaching colors of autumn. But as Larwin emerged from the mountain path, he was more absorbed with analyzing the clearing's humidity and running calculations on his analyzer than appreciating the beauty of the garden or its spicy aroma. He studied the small screen's result: seventy percent moisture. He frowned as he tried to recall every scrap of information he'd ever heard about madrox's destructive habits. At the academy, he'd been taught to avoid the fiery things. It had been simple as a pilot. It wasn't so simple without a ship that could fold time and space.

The air's condensation content might be enough to offer protection from the madrox.

Unless dampness enraged the beast beyond all sensibility, as GEA-4 had direly predicted. Larwin looked up, at the spreading branches of a sequoia, which hid Sacred Mountain's summit and considered the heat-loving creature which wanted something badly enough to dig through cold stone. What if the beast was already psychotic? Would vapor of any density offer protection? Unpredictable as this madrox seemed, would sinking to the bottom of the river be enough of a buffer?

Larwin turned and studied the house, looking for Nimri, dreading to tell her what he'd found out.

"The house is deserted," GEA-4 said.

"Good, I can put off seeing fear in Nimri's eyes." He preferred facing the madrox alone, to telling her. He squinted at the building, which had come to represent home, and gauged which window would afford him the best view of the mountain's summit.

The chamber he'd occupied probably had the optimum vantage point, since it was highest, but her bedroom should have the potential for an outlook and it was quicker to get to. It would be difficult to enter her private domain, see her possessions and breathe her fresh scent. Thank Kues she wasn't home. Adrenaline and desire could make a lethal combination, especially if Nimri and her bed were accessible.

Again, Larwin squinted at the windows, debating between best long-term surveillance position and closest. Before he could act on his theory, he heard movement deep in the forest's shadows racing toward him. Larwin grabbed his las-gun. Kazza erupted from the forest and bounded toward him, happy as if he had been gone a year. A moment before impact, Larwin dropped his weapon. Kazza skidded to a halt, stood on his hind legs, then wrapped Larwin in what could best be called a tender embrace.

Larwin laughed and returned the exuberant greeting. "Missed me, huh?" A wet, rough tongue nearly tore off his ear. "Hey, cut that out." His big friend nuzzled his neck and purred louder than a jumbo turbo. He chuckled. "Your whiskers tickle." Larwin gave Kazza a hard hug. "I missed you, too." He was rewarded with a second lick. Gentler, this time. "Buddy, I think your tongue is made of sandpaper." He clasped the cat tight. "Don't skin me."

Kazza eased back on his haunches, but kept his paws on Larwin's shoulders. He stared into Larwin's eyes. Unable to blink, Larwin returned the intent look until nothing but the cat's glowing amber gaze existed. Then, fearful thoughts centering on misty images of madrox poured into his mind. Larwin staggered a step backward. The deluge quit. "Why do I suddenly think you're telepathic?"

Kazza leaned forward and nuzzled his ear.

He swallowed. The possibility that animals could possess psychic powers was more than he could deal with at that point. "Are you hungry?" Larwin asked, willing to deal with a basic like food. "Do you want me to see if there is bread in the house?"

Kazza gently nuzzled his ear, then padded toward the house.

Larwin decided to go up to Nimri's room while she was still gone, and confirm his analysis about the sight line from her room. As he suspected, treetops hid some of the view. So, he climbed up to his own room. He put on his audio-visual viewer and studied the peak, which he'd previously taken for granted. The odd trees marking the cave's entrance were more black than maroon and bursts of smoky exhalations spiraled up from their midst.

As he'd feared, the demented creature was still there, determined to break through the wormhole. At least this one seemed to be an eccentric renegade. Since madrox normally moved in packs, a loner was good luck; Larwin told himself that he should be grateful for small favors.

But he wasn't. He slumped onto his bed, hands massaging his temples. He had two choices: he could either pretend things were right or tell Nimri the truth.

His mother had always said honesty was the best choice.

And if he chose the truth, he could comfort her right here. He patted the bed. Hopefully their body chemistry would be compatible enough to survive coupling. It was the only positive among a thousand negatives.

Unfortunately, even that single optimistic outcome would eventually end in death.

He'd cheated Kues when he'd survived the crash. And he'd cheated the war god a second time when he'd found Nimri face down in the weird wormhole. Perhaps destiny intended them to be together. To join.

Larwin went back down the winding stairs to the kitchen, nibbled on some bread, and waited for Nimri to come home. Though he stayed up until the morning star rose, she never returned.

Larwin finally trudged back up the long winding stairs and went to bed.

He dreamed that madrox teeth gnashed into Tem-aki. She vanished in a cloud of dust. After his sister disintegrated, the puff of particles swirled and churned, then amalgamated into the ash-covered planet where he'd crashed. He stared at the slowing revolving sphere's dark surface, then the soot shimmered shades of red and gold. He blinked. When he looked, again, hundreds of madrox covered the planetoid's surface. Their satanic red eyes glared at him. Sweat drenched his spine. Larwin woke to Kazza's rough, wet tongue rasping his cheek and a damp nose purring into his ear.

The next minute, Kazza's chin was on Larwin's chest and his big amber eyes were staring straight at him. Into him. Into his soul. Into his mind. Larwin relived the madrox chasing him and GEA-4 down the strange tunnel, but this time, he saw himself, GEA-4 and a quivering image of Nimri fleeing alongside.

Odd.

Larwin looked down and saw glimmering paws racing over the desolate grime. A shiver went from the top of his head to the tip of his tail. He was Kazza.

The tunnel scene dissolved and it was suddenly morning. He was high up a tree that had a wonderful view of Sacred Mountain's summit. Many of the lovely purple trees were blackened ruins and smoke rose from the cave in a steady, malevolent column. His sharp cat's hearing picked up sounds of the madrox's fury as it battled through solid stone.

The image switched to his bedroom and centered on the

twisted black stick, which leaned in the corner, near the pile of books. Larwin stared at the ebony wood, trying to figure out its significance; suddenly, the stick glowed so bright that the light in the room seemed to darken.

He blinked. Abruptly, it was the dead of night. He was outdoors standing shoulder deep in reeds and knee deep in water as he watched Nimri clamber into a bobbing boat with someone he couldn't quite identify. Larwin squinted, but the light from the red crescent moon wasn't enough, even for his feline eyes to determine who the person was, other than the fact it was a man.

Before Larwin had a chance to savor the jealousy that bloomed within him, he was soundlessly swimming through the dark, silky water. Next, clammy fur plastered against his flanks, Larwin stretched out on top of a house-sized rock and peered through at a lighted window-like opening in a huge hollowed-out rock. Candlelight from a dozen tapers flickered within. Abruptly, another flame flared, then another and another, as it had when Nimri lit candles at night and made the room an intimate retreat. He squinted and saw a man's hands cupping the fire. Once the tapers burned, the stranger lounged on top of a cinnamon colored cushion and smiled at someone who was just out of sight.

Larwin's teeth clenched. The handsome man wore robust muscles and little else. He shifted to his left, wanting to see whom the stranger's companion was, but afraid that he already knew. Nimri leaned against a nearby table, unable to take her eyes off the nearly naked man.

No!

Larwin's stomach clenched. He tried to force unwilling legs to leap through the too-small window.

Abruptly, the image vanished into blackness. Again, his vision congealed into the black stick. Larwin's hands itched with a strong compulsion to touch it. As he reached for it, he jerked out of the odd dream.

Kazza's intelligent gaze studied him.

"You are telepathic, aren't you." It wasn't a question. Every fiber in his body knew the great cat was more than he appeared. He also knew for a fact that as soon as he'd left, Nimri had gone with the half-naked, handsome man. Was the gorgeous guy her lover? Husband? Betrothed?

Bile rose in Larwin's throat.

In all the time they'd spent together, the subject of her life before he'd arrived had never arisen, so he'd assumed Nimri would be his for the choosing, if and when he was ready. She'd reinforced his belief when she'd mentioned that she wanted him for her cherished partner, and he'd made the stupid conjecture that she meant lover. Now, he knew that his assumption painted him for the fool he obviously was.

Kazza purred so hard that the bed shook.

"GEA-4 mentioning strange energy readings, while we in cave," Larwin said. Kazza licked him from Adam's apple to hairline. If he understood cat communication, the answer was yes. "I wish I knew if that was you and Nimri." If licking was the feline's standard response for yes, and he kept guessing correctly, he'd never need a razor. "How did you cloak yourselves?" Too many more yes's and he'd need his dermis replaced. "Tell you what, I'll accept a wink or purring for yes and you can swat me— lightly, mind you, no claws, for no."

Kazza gave him exaggerated wink, leaped off the bed and went to the door. He flicked out a claw, whipped the door open, and gave Larwin an expectant look.

If this didn't beat all.

When he didn't jump out of bed, Kazza sat on his rear haunches and glared at him. "I'm coming. Let me get dressed."

Larwin put on his clothing, half expecting the image to shift, so he would know this was all part of a crazy dream.

Instead, something twirled to the floor. He ignored it and

continued dressing, but Kazza came over and sniffed the odd purple splotch. Then, the feline batted at it, sniffed some more, sat down and gave Larwin an expectant look.

Larwin hunkered down and studied the strange thing. It took a moment before he finally recognized it as a winged seedpod from the balata grove.

As soon as he'd identified it, he felt an urge to plant it.

He'd never planted anything in his life.

Larwin looked from Kazza's big paws to the fragile pod. "You want me to place this in the ground?" Though he'd spoken in his native tongue, the feline purred and gave an exaggerated wink. A feeling of euphoria flooded his mind. "Do you think Nimri will like it?" Another wink. The happiness intensified, as did Kazza's rumble.

Larwin picked up the fragile pod and held it as if it was the most valuable thing he'd ever touched. And it was, because it would be the only thing he'd ever done to try and preserve a botanical specimen.

He took a step toward the door, but Kazza blocked his way, his amber gaze centered on the crude black stick leaning in the corner. Wondering at the feline's odd behavior, Larwin grabbed the twisted stick and brought it with him. Though it looked slick standing in the corner, it fit his hand like a glove.

Kazza preceded him to the middle of the garden. In the spot, between the menthe and lavender, the cat dug a small hole. Rich, relaxing aromas rolled over Larwin as he held the purplish wing in his palm. Then, as Kazza sat back on his haunches, Larwin laid the seed in the depression and drizzled fine black dirt over it. A songbird trilled a blessing.

Larwin sat back on his heels, feeling as if he'd done something wonderful. Even better than conquering a world. He looked at Kazza, who was twirling his whiskers in delight.

"Okay, we planted the victory tree. Now how do we win?"

Kazza surged to his paws and headed for the village path, which GEA-4 was already descending. Larwin rose. For a moment, he was torn between following the cat and staying next to the sweet earth, where he could protect the fragile seed. But the best way he could shield it was catching up with GEA-4 and getting her to help him figure out a way to defeat the demented dragon. Using the stick as a walking aid, Larwin hurried toward the path.

~0~

She could feel warm, moist puffs of air against her left hand. A glance downward revealed a barely concealed Yeti in the head-high ferns, saliva dripping from its incisors. Before the drop hit the moss-covered ground, the creature leaped at her from the undergrowth. Nimri screamed and jumped into a warm golden pool of honey. The sweetness engulfed her in a slimy embrace, which seemed to suck the life out of her.

Nimri's eyes snapped open.

The dawn's rays coming through an odd opening next to her bed nearly blinded her. She closed her eyes, then squeezed. Still, the glimpse was enough to see a Yeti holding her braid. She gasped a breath of thick, sugary air, and told herself she'd imagined the beast.

Another peek confirmed that her nightmare had merged with reality. Worse, she was in a whitish cavern where fractures let in light and the domed ceiling looked far too heavy to stay suspended overhead.

Scrunching her eyes closed, Nimri assured herself that she didn't feel any tugs on her hair. Didn't smell crushed rosemary mixed with an exotic, sour-sweet honey-like aroma. Nothing but her imagination was snuffling at her ear. She wasn't strangling on a scream. And drool wasn't running down her neck.

In the distance, something grunted. A man laughed.

Memory of the previous night returned. She'd spent the night in Cartwright's home. The blubbering beast was his pet and supposedly harmless. Nothing that looked like that could be safe, no matter what he said. Just as Thunder Cartwright didn't seem at all like what he was supposed to be. He should have been old and manly as mold; instead, like Larwin, he looked like masculinity personified.

Remembering the way his chest muscles had rippled under his unlaced vest made her breath catch. Since meeting Larwin, she'd often felt hot twinges move across her flesh. Though the intensity of the heat was less with Cartwright, the sense that she had always known him was strong. Could the sense of acquaintance be caused by all the stories she'd heard of him?

Nimri bit the insides of her cheeks. She'd heard countless tales of Lou Wren, the Son of Light, and Throp Anthrus the prophetess, too. While she'd felt a bone-deep awareness of Larwin, she'd never experienced this odd sense of association with him.

And why should someone who was so opposite of how she'd imagined him seem familiar?

A bird warbled. To her relief, the Yeti ambled out the largest crevice without tearing a bite out of her throat.

Nimri leapt out of bed and tried to smooth the wrinkles out of her grass-stained tunic.

If the dragon hadn't been in the Star Bridge and she didn't need to save this planet, she would sneak out the narrow window and try to get back across the river before she was missed.

But times were desperate and if Cartwright didn't help her, Chatterre with its beautiful valley and bisecting river would cease to exist. So, it wouldn't matter that she'd crossed the river and was now banned, except on Market Day. If the planet turned into a cinder, it wouldn't matter that she couldn't even go to her garden for the plants she needed to make medicine for her tribe.

Nothing mattered except dealing with the Ghilly dragon. If they could defeat that, she would have time to worry about salves and potions.

And she'd given her word that she'd stay here until he was ready to tell her what he truly wanted.

Giving up on looking presentable, Nimri crept to the largest fissure in the wall and peered at the main room where she'd had her first good look at the enemy.

Except for the cushions, table and other typical things found in a home, the room was empty.

In the distance, a man chuckled and a beast whined. Nimri swallowed hard, then went in search of Cartwright. She saw him in the sun-filled center of an unexpectedly lush garden. He was seated on a squared off grayish rock next to a large slab of tan stone, one Yeti squatted on his left side the other beast perched on another seating rock. A third rock sat empty.

Nimri stopped in the main room's shadows and watched the odd trio. All three were eating something reddish orange. Juice oozed through the Yeti's fists and matted their dark fur as blood saturated predator's coats. A gust of air buffeted the raised hair on her arms and brought the exotic, sour-sweet honey aroma of her dream. She shivered.

The intimacy between man and beasts reminded her of the bond she had with Kazza. As she grappled with that thought, Cartwright glanced at the spot where she stood. His smile widened to reveal perfect white teeth.

"Good morning," he said. "After getting to bed so late, I thought you'd sleep in." She was amazed that she had relaxed enough to sleep at all.

He motioned for her to join him. She lifted her chin and squared her shoulders, then entered the sun-drenched garden, which seemed to have been cut into the side of a rocky cliff. Though the Yeti closest to her made a lip-smacking sound, she tried to ignore it. Cartwright smiled and motioned for her to sit on the flat-topped rock across from him. There was no way she was going to eat shoulder to shoulder with a Yeti. She glanced at the beast. "I prefer to stand." He laughed, much as she'd been tempted to do, when Larwin first met Kazza.

Nimri took a deep breath and moved around the hairy creature. She focused on the lush foliage that filled the walled garden and recognized several herbal shrubs that she kept in her own yard.

Uncomfortable with her back turned to the other three: she looked over her shoulder and caught Cartwright's speculative gaze on her. "I never sleep in."

Cartwright's chuckle was a rich, familiar sound that made her think of security, sadness and yummy raspberry pie.

The shrubbery swayed in the wind and revealed a solid stone wall enclosing the garden.

The Yeti next to Cartwright looked up at her, its muzzle black with juice. Obviously, Cartwright didn't get many guests. No surprise, since he lived with killer beasts.

Again, he motioned her to sit down. Nimri shook her head.

"Maybe some things do change," he said.

A shiver of recognition coursed down her spine. "Do you have people watching me?"

"People?" He barked a short laugh and shook his head.

Perhaps the tales that he communicated with birds and that they spied for him were true. If so, it could explain why he seemed to know so much about her. But it didn't account for why he seemed so familiar. Nimri pretended to study a yellow swallowtail as it circled the buddleia bush's deep purple spikes. While she loved butterflies, the shrub's main attraction was its distance from her captor.

Or should she think of Cartwright as her host?

To her horror, the standing Yeti lumbered over to her and raked her hair with a soggy juice-saturated paw. The exotic, sour-sweet aroma intensified until it seemed overpowering. Nimri stood still as death and prayed the beast wouldn't yank her braid hard enough to break her neck.

Cartwright glanced up. "Gunda, stop." He chuckled. "She's trying to groom you. I guess it's her mothering instinct."

She swallowed the suffocating fear, but a large lump remained firmly lodged in her throat. "Gunda is a female?" Nimri tried to look at the shaggy dark beast without moving her head.

"You've never been close to a Yeti, have you?"

"I've never even seen one at any distance." Or ever wanted to. "I have a pet feline, he's at least six–hundred-pounds and has teeth and claws that could shred me to pieces, but I feel safe with him."

"Why wouldn't you feel safe with Kazza?" The casual intimacy of his tone made her throat dry. "He's protected you since birth."

How long had he had his creatures been watching her? Rolf hadn't even been gone for a full moon-cycle. The in-depth fact of how long she'd had Kazza wouldn't have been something, which should have interested him as he tried to gather information about his new foe.

Cartwright, unaware of her astonishment, focused on dividing a bumpy, russet-colored fruit into crescents. He smiled and handed her a juicy crimson crescent. "Try a pange. It's from my own tree." He gestured toward the distant corner of his garden.

"You know about Kazza." Nimri stared at him, uncertain whether she was more shocked over his detailed knowledge about her life or her own sense of having known him forever.

Cartwright gave her an odd look, but instead of responding simply held out the fruit. Nimri took it.

He looked at the sandstone, which covered the ground. "It would be easier if this planet had large masses of fresh water."

"What do you mean?" Nimri sniffed the pange, which was unlike anything she'd ever imagined.

"Solterre had fresh water oceans. This planet's oceans are saline."

She nearly dropped the fruit. "There are oceans?" Why hadn't her great-grandfather mentioned them?

"You don't remember?" Cartwright looked genuinely surprised. He blinked. "After we defeat the beast, we'll get Kazza to come with us on a tour of Chatterre. In the meantime, the only body of fresh water which might be large enough to kill a Ghilly is the river, so despite the fact that it may endanger our tribes, our own valley is where we'll need to make our stand."

"Because of the lack of salt in its waters?" Cartwright nodded. She hoped her confusion and skepticism didn't show.

His gaze focused on her; his expression turned thoughtful. "Did Rolf teach you anything useful? Take you anywhere?"

She wished he hadn't asked. She wished she could lie. Nimri pretended to concentrate on tasting the pange.

The silence lengthened. A swallowtail butterfly landed on the Yeti's sticky nose. Oblivious of the fluttering yellow and black wings, the Yeti continued to fondle her hair. Streaks of reddish grit stained her tunic.

"Well?" Cartwright asked.

"Great-grandfather was too feeble to travel." Cartwright smirked. Nimri rushed on to add, "But he and my great aunt taught me about herbs. He taught me everything I was capable of learning."

His harsh laugh startled the Yeti and swallowtail. "He knew nothing of herbs value." Nimri bit her lower lip to hold back comment about that truth. "Rolf was a selfish, lazy, egotistical tyrant and he was afraid of competition." His brilliant green eyes studied her. "I'd be surprised if he taught you anything of real value."

Could he be correct? What if her incompetence wasn't due to her own lack?

"He wanted the tribes divided so that his position was assured. That's why he started the rumors about the Lost." Cartwright's tone was filled with disdain.

Much as his assessment coincided with her own suspicions, Nimri couldn't voice her agreement to the enemy. "I don't want to discuss my great-grandfather."

He gazed at her for a moment then gave an abrupt nod. "At least he taught you how to spirit travel...actually, that's more than I expected."

Nimri glanced at the soft red sandstone. "I don't know how I did that." She raised her head and locked gazes with him. Familiarity, hot as fresh cooked bread, rippled through her.

The Yeti grabbed the pange crescent out of her hand, stuffed it into its mouth and ambled back toward Cartwright.

"Dealing with a dragon will require both of us, but I don't know if you'll be able to learn everything you need to know in time," he said.

"So you don't think we have a chance." Would it be her fault for being so stupid or her grandfather's for not teaching her?

"I didn't say that, but we both need to be able to control our auras and each accomplish one part of the plan. I can't both create a storm and lure—"

"Like Rolf did?"

His mouth flattened with anger. The intimate feeling which had permeated the clearing vanished.

Still, she felt drawn to him. Nimri settled onto the sun-warmed rock. "You can do that? Control storms? Kill—"

"My plan isn't to exterminate humans." Cartwright's look was sharp as his tone. "We need to bait the beast to a remote area —preferably far downstream, but before the ocean mixes its brine with the water."

"How could we do that?"

"You said you saw the beast in a vision."

The way Cartwright changed subjects was disconcerting. Nimri took a section of pange from the pile before him and nibbled. Strange sweetly acidic flavor burst across her tongue.

"Didn't the Ghilly's ability to pursue you strike you as odd?" His knowing green gaze seemed to hold the secrets of the universe.

Suddenly she understood.

"It could sense my power." She'd spirit traveled! "I actually used myst!" Then the reality of the threat hit her. "That's what attracted the dragon. It sensed me." It was her fault that their world was in danger.

He nodded. "Zurgon is correct up to a point; Ghilly Dragons do feed off atomic, radiation, and electrical power. But they love auras as much as Kazza loves pumpernickel. If you learn to control yours and are willing to be the bait, we'll have a chance to defeat it." Cartwright frowned. "Where is Kazza?"

Again, he'd managed to unsettle her with his unexpected knowledge. "I don't know. He comes and goes."

Cartwright waved his hand as if everyone knew her cat's odd habits personally. "He'll be here when we need him." His expression grew pensive. "Pearl's story is true, too, but she didn't tell all of it."

"Zurgon didn't want her to tell me any of it." Nimri licked the honey-sweet juice from her fingers. "What didn't she tell me?"

"Her ancestor won the first round, when the dragon fell into the ocean." Cartwright's expression darkened. "But its death wail attracted others."

Nimri hoped she had misunderstood his insinuation that if they killed this one, a whole flock of the horrible creatures would follow. "Are you saying we have two problems? First we have to get the Ghilly wet with river water; second, we either need to make sure it doesn't contact others, or fill the Star Bridge with water?"

"None of this is simple," he said. "You saw how massive the

beast is. Did you notice its heat?"

Nimri started to shake her head, then remembered the searing heat from the creature's tongue. "Hot enough to vaporize water and melt rock." She swallowed. "It'll take a lot of water to annihilate it."

Cartwright nodded and stood up. "So, now you understand how difficult it will be to actually get the beast wet." The seated Yeti lumbered to its paws and moved behind him like an awkward shadow. He stretched. Well-toned muscles rippled as he paced between the buddleia bush's deep purple spikes and the smooth gold trunk of a twisting firespike tree.

"We don't know how far away its kin are," he added, "or how long it would take for them to get here." He frowned. "After all this time, we don't even have records of how dragons communicate."

One monster offered enough intimidation. A pair or more equaled terror beyond imagination. By comparison, the shuffling Yeti seemed friendly as a kitten. Nimri sighed. "You aren't very encouraging."

Cartwright stopped so suddenly the Yeti bumped into him. "Because of the death of one, their kind destroyed our ancestors' entire planet. Would you be optimistic?" He put his hands on his lean hips. The pose accentuated his wide shoulders and perfect physique. Her mouth went dry. "Being realistic gives us an edge. We won't underestimate the problem." His tone was hard as his muscles. His body reminded her of Larwin. "What's wrong? Having second thoughts?"

She shook her head.

He mimicked the movement and the feathers, which were bound to his hair fluttered. If only Larwin's hair would grow. If only Cartwright didn't seem so familiar. If only the warm friendly sensation that she knew Cartwright quit gnawing at the edges of her awareness.

"Yes, I'm having second thoughts," she admitted, "But probably not what you think. Cartwright—"

"I told you, call me Thunder."

"Thunder seems so informal." So personal. More like a private name reserved for loved ones. "You deserve respect."

"Respect?" He laughed. "From you? That'd be original." Her skin prickled at the intimacy of his tone and the long-standing relationship it implied. His expression sobered. "You really don't remember, do you?" She didn't know what to say. He shrugged. "Never mind, you will."

Was that a threat or a promise? Nimri swallowed. "I'm not sure if I want to." She popped another pange crescent into her mouth before she could say something she'd regret.

He grinned. "I was a good memory." His lips twisted into an impish grin. "At least I was most of the time."

Nimri choked on the pange. After recovering her breath, she still didn't know what to think about his confident statement. In defense, she changed the subject. "Larwin is—was confident like you."

For once Thunder Cartwright looked confused. "Larwin? A boyfriend?" Eyes gleaming, he leaned across the table.

Nimri gulped. Odd that he knew nothing of Larwin. If she'd been in Cartwright's place and had his watchers, she would have known. "A Guardian who materialized when I was in the Star Bridge." She nibbled another slice of fruit. "He and GEA-4 returned to the Old World. That's why I spirit traveled – to make certain they got home safely." The memory of their desolate home and the fact that her aura might have lead the dragon down on them all brought a lump to her throat. She put down the half-eaten fruit.

Thunder's fingers wrapped around her hand. He pulled her to her feet and urged her toward a large bench-size sitting rock, tucked next to the far side of the buddleia. He straddled it and tugged her toward him. Nimri wobbled, nearly falling into his lap. A flush burned her skin as she tried to regain her equilibrium. He jerked her, again. This time, she landed next to him, thighs touching. He turned toward her, both hands enfolding hers. "You have to tell me everything."

Her neck burned hotter. "You're a stranger." At least he should be, though the way she felt with him seemed more like she'd found a piece of herself that had been lost for a long, long, long time.

"Only because you have forgotten me. Do you trust me?"

No. She didn't even have faith in herself or her memory, if she'd forgotten him. Assuming she'd ever really known him and he wasn't playing mind games. That had to be it. Rolf had loved mind games and keeping her off-balance, too.

He cupped her cheeks between his hands until their gazes locked. Warmth and something nameless spread through her. Despite the fact that she'd been raised to believe he was her enemy, she trusted him. The revelation made her blink. Thunder Cartwright seemed to read her thoughts and a look of relief softened his features. An instant later, he engulfed her in a hug.

Nimri surprised herself by hugging him back.

She thought she heard him whisper something about missing her, but how could you miss someone you never knew? Still, despite her certainty that he was playing with her common sense, she felt like she'd been unknowingly yearning for him, too. Oh, he was good at misinformation, maybe even better than her great-grandfather.

Did his arms feel familiar because Thunder Cartwright reminded her so much of Larwin? Or did she and Thunder Cartwright truly have a past and if so, did her feelings for Larwin stem from some forgotten passion for Thunder? The spinning thoughts gave her a headache.

"Are you ready?" His affectionate expression unsettled her as much as the way his arms felt so right.

Was she ready? "For what?" A bee buzzed past her right ear and butterflies danced among the deep purple blooms.

"To spirit travel to the balata."

No, she wasn't ready. She shook her head and pushed free of his embrace. But she knew they had to go. She'd have to fake it. Nimri twisted to face him and assumed the hatha position Larwin had taught her.

Cartwright raised an eyebrow, then shifted until he mirrored her stance. Their knees touched lightly. "Interesting. It's more comfortable than it looks."

He leaned forward. With his index finger, he traced a pattern in her right palm.

He repeated the star design in the left.

A wispy memory rippled on the fringes of her consciousness and Nimri felt something unidentifiable, yet sacred seep through her body. She glanced at Thunder Cartwright's knowing green eyes.

He smiled then engulfed her hands in his larger ones. Strange how he and Larwin could touch her and make her feel safe.

"Power is magnified when you're in contact with living soil, other mystics and healthy plants," Thunder said softly.

Nimri tried not to think how hot her hand was getting. "Larwin taught me to sit this way and to hum."

"Do you miss him?" The gentle tone invited honesty and confidences.

"Yes." He tilted his head into a wondering pose. Nimri swallowed. If Thunder Cartwright wanted the sort of unsaid promise that she suspected, it wouldn't do to let him know about the depth of her feelings for another man; even if the other man lived on a dead world and had lived in the time when fairytales were true. Nimri smiled and added, "Other than Flame, he's the only friend I've ever had."

"Why?" He seemed genuinely surprised.

"Because it's true." Nimri focused on a tiger swallowtail instead of his expressive gaze. "Rolf's home is a long walk from everyone else. Great-grandfather and Bryta were the only people I ever saw. When I was nine, Bryta let me go to Market with her. That's where I met Flame. Other children avoided me. I think they feared me because of my great-grandfather." Nimri stole a quick glance at Thunder Cartwright.

His nod of agreement was slow and thoughtful. "Even adults fear our power."

"Is that why you live far from your tribe?"

"Perhaps it is partially the reason. Most fear the Yetis more than me." Thunder gave a tiny shrug.

The gesture was the same one Nimri used to dismiss ridiculous concepts. It felt odd, yet endearing to see someone else do it.

Cartwright smiled. "Shall we begin?"

Nimri nodded.

"I want to journey to the Star Bridge and see if the monster is still there," he said gently. "Close your eyes." Nimri nodded, feeling as if the movement was in slow motion. He began a low, warm monologue about the Star Bridge.

Could Thunder be hypnotizing her with his touch and words? Did it matter? Gradually, his words and tone blended with the buzz of the bees, the warmth of the sunshine and the dampness of the stone they sat on. His voice told her when to breathe in; when to breathe out. Which muscles to tighten; which to relax.

Colors swirled around her. Impressions of shapes slowly formed then gradually faded to white. Except for her warm right hand, her skin cooled as it had when she'd stepped into the fog shrouding Sacred Mountain's peak.

Abruptly, the cool white vanished. "You may open your eyes, now." Thunder's soft tone was almost like a thought. She was high up, looking down. The sun warmed her back as she floated. Distance dwarfed mighty trees into shrubs. Majestic mountains appeared as hillocks. Buildings were no bigger than pebbles. The river was but a silvery ribbon.

This must be how birds viewed the world.

When another feathery fog shrouded Nimri in cold mist, she basked in the gentle touch. Flying was wonderful. Nimri gasped. People couldn't fly. Abruptly, she began falling, but the hand holding her arrested the momentum.

"Relax," Thunder said, "I have you."

Nimri closed her eyes and breathed a sigh of relief. His hand, warm and secure, caressed her fingers. His thumb circled her palm. She squeezed back.

When she opened her eyes the next time, they were hovering over the balata grove. Only it looked different from the last time she'd been here. The trunks of several trees were twisted, while the leaves closest to the entrance were dry and withered. All over, branches had been torn from trunks and more trees had been uprooted. While some of the damage had been done during the earthquake, the majority was new. Had there been another upheaval?

They descended toward the cave's mouth, where a thin, wispy column of bluish-gray smoke rose into the thin air.

Moments before they touched ground, there was an ear splitting roar.

The hairs on the back of her neck stood on end.

The ground heaved.

A boulder the size of a room dislodged from the peak. It tumbled toward them gouging soil and ripping up more rocks until it formed a tide of dirt and rock. Thunder yanked her upward. The rockslide flowed past the entrance of the Star Bridge, over the place where they had been, smashed into a balata and tore it up by the roots, as if it was a weak weed. The avalanche continued on; it tore up more trees as it roared through the sacred grove then it crashed through to the precipice. It seemed to pause for a heartbeat, then the flood of rock and trees shot over the edge. The mass hung for a moment before it plummeted out of sight.

Thunder's dazed expression would have been comical if Nimri didn't suspect she looked the same way. She squeezed his fingers for confidence. He shook his head, as if waking from a bad dream and kissed her forehead. "It's there."

She nodded. Strange that when Thunder kissed her, she felt comforted, but Larwin's touch made her flesh tingle with excitement. "So, now, we go somewhere safer."

He shook his head and pulled her earthward. "Now we try to judge how much time we have." They landed on the mutilated ground. Thunder dropped her hand and went toward the cave's entrance, where he grabbed a scorched vine. "Wish me luck." Before she could respond, he descended out of sight.

Was Larwin still alive? Was he trapped in the cave? Still defending them from the beast? Nimri snatched the vine and followed Thunder.

Smoky air swirled around her ankles. As she slid lower, the acrid stench invaded her nostrils. Then, her eyes burned. She blinked, but the sting only intensified.

By the time her feet touched the ground, she had to squint through the fog and tears. She thought she saw a man's silhouette. Thunder or Larwin? In the distance, something big moved. Fingertips lightly touching the unseen wall, she felt her way toward the figure.

The enormous thing stirred again then a terrible scraping sound indicated faster movement, as if something huge hurtled toward her in the blinding haze.

She couldn't turn and run. Thunder and Larwin were there. She had to help them but as she moved forward, her moccasin caught on something unseen and she tripped into the wall.

The stone beneath her fingertips smoothed. With the flatness came residual heat and aching flesh. She leaned toward the wall and squinted through the dust. The granite looked like some of Quark's glazes—melted then solidified. And it felt sticky yet slick. Every nerve in her body screamed for her to run away. She clenched her teeth and rejected the fear by focusing on her hand.

Her fingertips looked raw, as if she'd burned them, yet the heat wasn't high enough to sear. Nimri frowned and tried to concentrate. Some plant sap contained chemicals that burned. The ghilly's saliva must be like that.

Keeping away from the wall, Nimri went to the figure, which was surrounded by a reddish gold haze and hunkered down beside a broken stalactite.

Nimri's skin crawled with the knowledge that the beast was near and knew where they were.

As she tiptoed toward Thunder, she held her breath and stared at the luminescence surrounding him. The closer she got, the brighter the red became. Beyond the man, dust and haze seemed to change shape and congeal into a form. Gooseflesh raged up and down her limbs.

Abruptly, Thunder stood, grabbed her hand and tugged her back the way they'd come.

A booming bellow numbed her, yet he pulled her onward.

Blue lightening eclipsed the warm light.

"Let's get out of here!" Thunder shouted as he yanked her after him.

The blue was closer.

She ran for her life.

The dark swirling fumes brightened with a harsh, azure light. He pulled her behind a stalagmite. Though her shoulder ached from the way he'd wrenched it, she welcomed the rocky shield.

"What's that thing?" Thunder asked, as the blue lightening stopped short of them.

"Its tongue."

Something crashed. Iridescent bits of green exploded through the swirling orange cloud. Crumbs of rock hit Nimri's shin.

The tongue retracted.

Thunder's hand tightened and he pulled her toward safety, but the azure beam shot toward them again. This time, bits of the stalagmite they had just been behind exploded.

The dragon roared.

"We're trapped!" Nimri said.

The beast roared. Rocks rained down as the searing heat crackled closer. Nimri closed her eyes and screamed.

Thunder hugged her tight and shouted into her ear, "Wake... Now!"

Her body felt like it was exploding, yet incongruously, she felt intact.

Something buzzed by her ear. With mingled memories of the Yeti and dragon, she flinched. When the buzzing came no closer, she opened her eyes. Thunder's concerned expression was the first thing she saw. Behind him, the buddleia bush teamed with bees and butterflies.

They were alive.

Her hand felt numb. When she glanced at it, she realized she was holding onto Thunder with a white-knuckled grip. Nimri loosened her grasp and flexed her fingers. Then, she massaged the ache in her shoulder. He gave her a lopsided smile.

"Sorry," she said. "Is your hand all right?"

He raised his hand and wiggled the fingers. Then he picked up her hand and kissed her knuckles. "Yes."

"How can we fight something like that?" she whispered.

"We'll find a way."

Nimri thought Thunder sounded more confident then he looked. "I don't know why, but I believe you." She had to. Failure meant death, not only for her, but also for everyone and everything she held dear.

Thunder reached toward her, but instead of caressing her cheek, fingered a loose strand of hair.

Did he want to kiss her? Her heart picked up a beat. No, even if she now thought of him as Thunder instead of the faceless villain Thunder Cartwright, he was still her enemy.

The idea of kissing him in the way of cherished partners felt wrong, but she would do it if necessary. She would do anything to save everyone and everything that she held dear.

He placed the strand behind her ear, but his attention centered on something behind her. When she started to turn and look, he asked, "Was it my imagination, or did the dragon eat stone?"

Nimri blinked. Where had that question come from? "I thought the stalactite broke. I didn't realize the thing ate it."

Thunder grinned and shook his head. "The walls looked like they'd been brushed with acid. I believe they were dissolving where the tongue had touched them, but I'm not certain if a dragon actually consumes rock."

She touched her aching fingers, amazed that the real flesh showed no sign of trauma.

Could things eat dissolved rock? Digest with acid? "I guess anything could be possible if something like that exists."

"If the monster's bimolecular system is acid based," Thunder said, "a few tons of alkali might weaken it."

She tried not to show her confusion over what he'd just said. The only thing she'd understood was that Thunder wanted to figure out a way to weaken the dragon. She wanted to stop it. Kill it. She massaged her temples; amazed that such hatred and fear could drive her, and worried that she'd become as vicious as Rolf. "Why don't I think there is a simple solution?"

Thunder laughed and tickled her under the chin, but his real interest remained somewhere behind her.

She turned, expecting to find the hair-loving Yeti behind her. The sticky-fingered thing was nowhere in sight. A tiny movement farther away caught her attention. She studied the strange flutter of wiegelia branches, then noticed a break in the stone wall beyond them. Amber eyes peered at her through the foliage. Behind them was a man's broad outline.

She knew that silhouette. Larwin was alive. The beast hadn't killed him.

Nimri scrambled to her feet and ran to greet him. Halfway there, she saw Larwin's cold, furious expression. She stumbled. When his expression didn't soften she realized that she'd attracted the dragon and it had kept him from his home. Her step faltered, then Nimri noticed that Kazza and GEA-4 were with him. She altered course to Kazza and hugged him. His purr soothed some of the rejection she'd seen in Larwin's face.

Guilty tears stung her eyes. She buried her face in Kazza's fur and held him tight. If she'd known the dangers, she would never have spirit traveled to Larwin's world. Coolness rippled over her. It was just as well that Larwin wasn't as happy to see her as she'd been to see him. If she knew he cared the same way she did, it would become much more difficult to honor her word to Thunder. And that was a promise she must keep.

Mustering her dignity, Nimri straightened and smiled at Larwin. "You're back."

Jaws clamped so tight that a muscle jumped in his cheek, Larwin gave a curt nod. She looked him over. He'd picked up the Staff of Protection and held it as if he never intended to let go. Anyone willing and able to hold the staff claimed its power and became the Keeper of the Peace. Despite the personal rejection in his gaze, her heart leaped with happiness for her Tribe and Larwin's obvious willingness to fight for them.

She should never have doubted his ability. Doubted him.

"You must be GEA-4," Thunder said from behind her, "and Larwin." He thrust out his arm.

Larwin grasped Thunder's forearm in the proper greeting and nodded, but seemed more like he was testing Thunder's strength than giving him a polite greeting. Nimri moved to the side, so she could study Larwin's face. Even now, his mouth was flat with anger. Her only solace was that he was glaring at Thunder, not her.

"I'm afraid you have me at a disadvantage." Larwin's voice was deadly calm. "My guide never mentioned your name."

"Thunder Cartwright." Thunder paused for a moment and glanced at her. "Friends, like Nimri, call me Thunder." Thunder smiled at her, then looked back at Larwin. His demeanor was as welcoming as Larwin's was hostile. "She spoke of you."

Larwin shrugged, as if to say that Thunder was so insignificant that she hadn't mentioned him.

Nimri laid her hand on Larwin's arm. "I thought the dragon had killed you."

He jerked and stared at her. "You know about the madrox?" Larwin demanded in surprise. "How?"

Nimri paused. Madrox must be his word for dragon. Would she ever understand him completely? And why was he still testing her when their world was in such peril? Did the answer have something to do with the cause of his anger?

She shrugged. Larwin was here. He was powerful enough to carry the staff all this distance without collapsing from exhaustion. Everything would be fine.

Larwin's hand closed over hers. Despite the aloofness of his look and touch, a tingle went from her fingertips to her toes before he brushed her hand aside.

"I've never seen one behave the way this one does," Larwin said.

"Dragons are familiar to you?" Thunder gestured for them to sit on the seating rocks. "They were a problem on the first world, but most of the information has been lost over the years." He gave Larwin several sections of fruit, but seemed to know intuitively that GEA-4 existed on the sun's magic.

Larwin plunked down on the stone bench. "There are no madrox near Guerreterre, which is located in Alif Sector. Madrox are mainly sighted in the Guy-N Sector." Larwin popped a wedge into his mouth. "The planetoid I crashed on is on the outskirts of Guy-N." A buddleia branch caressed his shoulder.

Nimri sat down on the far end of the bench and let Larwin's gibberish wash over her. Thunder sat on the stone he'd occupied when she first came into the strange garden, but instead of facing the table, he twisted to face them. If she had to choose between the two men, she'd put aside her feelings and chose the one she'd given her word to; just as she'd scaled the face of Sacred Mountain, to keep her word to another man she'd given a vow to. She stifled a sigh and promised herself that if she survived this, she'd never make another vow as long as she lived.

"But you know how to deal with them," Thunder said.

"They're rare." Larwin focused on Thunder, who was acting the perfect host, and appeared relaxed. "I've seen two others, but they were harmless." Larwin unconsciously took her hand and caressed her fingers. "Most of what I know, I overheard from captains of Kalamar's eepyllihg tankers." He gave a slight shrug. "They tend to take the attitude that the Dragons are a nuisance." Larwin frowned. "The one in the wormhole seems to be a destructive loner."

Nimri's gaze darted to GEA-4, but she watched the insects feed, as if nothing else mattered.

Kazza rubbed against Thunder's thigh. He tickled him behind the ears, with a familiarity that suggested he'd done it countless times before. Nimri looked away rather than allow Thunder to read her confusion. Why did her enemy seem so familiar and act like such an important part of her past? Did Kazza actually know him, or was the apparent closeness simply part of Thunder's reputed bond with animals?

Larwin turned toward her, then stiffened and dropped her hand. He looked past her. His pupils dilated. Nimri peeked over her shoulder. A Yeti blinked at her from behind the buddleia bush. Kazza made a guttural sound, then he bounded toward the Yeti. The Yeti hurdled the bush. Nimri leaped out of the way in one direction, Larwin went the other.

Kazza and the Yeti collided in a vigorous crush, which toppled them to the sandstone paving in a heaving, whining fray. They rolled over and over making a horrendous uproar. Larwin pointed at them, with a small gray thing in his hand. He looked ridiculous as his arm moved with every movement the animals made.

Thunder ate a section of fruit and acted like the interchange between a cat and a Yeti was a normal event instead of a life and death struggle. Nimri bit her nails and wondered what to do. Then, the Yeti bit Kazza's neck. He yowled.

Thunder laughed. "Cut it out, guys."

The wrestling match stopped. Kazza rolled over and winked at Thunder before he got up. The hairy beast cooed like a dove.

Nimri became even more confused.

Thunder focused on Larwin, who was slipping the gray thing under his tunic. "Have you ever known of anyone killing a dragon?"

Larwin imitated Thunder's attitude of ignoring the Yeti. "Conventional weapons don't work against them—instead of harming the beasts, proton blasts invigorate them."

Nimri sprinted to Kazza. Keeping a wary eye on the hovering Yeti, she ran her fingertips over his neck, searching for the injury. Kazza purred and appeared to wink at the beast. There didn't seem to be any wound. Nimri hid her confusion and resumed her seat near Larwin. "Do you think Pearl might be right about water killing them?" she asked.

Larwin shrugged. "I would have flooded the tunnel if any was available."

"It's our best bet, but we can't afford to ignore any possibilities," Thunder said. "What about using alkali against it?"

"Hypothetically, that is a possibility," GEA-4 said.

Thunder clapped GEA-4 on the back. "We need to pool our knowledge. Surely, we can come up with a solution."

If they didn't, it wouldn't matter if she didn't want to choose between the two men, she would be dead.

"I think we should look for a way to block the Star Bridge, as Larwin wanted, instead of wait for it to break through," Nimri said. Through her unshed tears, Thunder and Larwin both looked determined as they looked toward the barely discernible peak. GEA-4 leaned closer to a buddleia bloom, as if it held the answer to fighting dragons.

"Impossible," Larwin said.

Yes, it certainly was.

"So, we must begin immediately." Thunder stood up. He looked at Larwin. "Do you know how to make a throwing machine?"

Chapter Seventeen

Larwin followed Nimri's handsome friend through a cleft between two massive stones that formed the entrance to a large hollow chamber. The space reminded him of the huge underground amphitheater-like space at the end of the long debris-filled tunnel. But while the tunnel had been filled with soot-covered piles of debris; this room held sturdy stone tables. Some were empty, but most held strange metal, stone and wood things, grouped by basic shape and assembled in military precision. Primitive, but tidy. More oddities hung from pegs on the walls. Larwin shrugged the strap for his haversack off his shoulder and left it next to the doorway. Thunder handed him a long, thin, jagged piece of metal, which had sturdy pieces of branch lashed to each end. Like the other bits and pieces in the chamber, it was barely discernible as a tool.

Thunder made a sweeping gesture with his arm. "My shop." His tone held pride. "We need to start on the catapult." Thunder went to a relatively uncluttered table, where he grabbed a chunk of bark-like stuff, then proceeded to draw on it with the tip of a blackened stick. Larwin watched over his shoulder. "There was picture of one in my mother's favorite book. I think it was something like this." With an economy of movement,

Thunder completed the crude sketch.

"Do you have the book?"

"It was lost in the river." A look of anger darted over Thunder's expression. Just as quickly, he rose and moved toward a pile of squared wood. "Can you grab that end?" Thunder picked up one end of a long, straight piece of waist-thick wood. Larwin lifted the other end and stifled a groan. Either he had the heavy side, or Nimri's friend was stronger than he'd suspected. "I need it there, on the sawhorses." With a tilt of his head, Thunder indicated that they needed to lay the log on top of two matching triangular hunks of wood, which bore close resemblance to massive, elongated wedges.

It landed with a solid thud.

Feathers in his hair fluttered from a tiny whoosh of wind. Thunder didn't appear to notice how heavy the piece was or that the odd adornments gave him an effeminate look. Much to Larwin's disgust, they were the only sissy things about the man.

"The sawhorses are wide enough that we could each work on a limb." Thunder gave Larwin a speculative look, as if baiting him to say that he didn't want to hoist a second piece.

Instead, Larwin grabbed another end. Once the pieces lay side by side on the sawhorses, Thunder carefully measured the length with a slender vine and marked the bark, so that both pieces were marked the same length.

"Can you use a saw?"

Larwin shrugged. In another silent challenge, Thunder plucked the long jagged metal strip from the pegs. Carefully, he moved to the opposite side of the logs and passed one of the branch-handles to Larwin. "Since we're in a hurry, we can save time if we cut these with one movement."

Larwin gripped his handle the way Thunder did and tried to match the man movement for movement. Pointy end down, they moved it back and forth across the two beams.

Slowly, a thin trench began to form beneath the metal points and brown crumbles collected under each log. This ridiculous contest to see which man was better was going to take forever.

Something thumped the wall. Larwin jerked and looked to see what caused the sound. Sharp points bit into his tunic and thigh, instead of wood. The small rent in the fabric was bigger than the dent in the thick log. With a curse, Larwin hefted the device and studied its jagged teeth. "This will take forever."

"Not forever, but maybe longer than we have." Thunder rubbed his temple. "You didn't have to do this; I can get a carpenter."

Right, like he would step aside and let lover-boy get all the credit if the weapon succeeded. Nimri already looked at the man as if she couldn't stop thinking about him. Of course, he'd known that the moment he'd seen the two of them seated on the stone bench and staring at each other as if nothing else in the world existed. Larwin's teeth clenched. Kues, but the longhaired, feather-wearing freak was fast when it came to seduction. But then, judging by their level of intimacy, their relationship might not be new. Perhaps it was simply something she never bothered to tell him about.

Larwin flexed the saw blade. It emitted a high, whining warble. Thunder looked at him, as if he was demented.

Larwin slammed down the tool. With a barely audible sigh, Thunder chose a one-handled saw from the wall. Larwin held up his hand. "I'll cut them. You go find some other aspect of the project to work on."

He stomped to his haversack and dug into it. Out of the corner of his eye, he saw Thunder shake his head as he went across the workshop and hoisted a smaller block onto the stone table. So, he thinks he's won, does he? Larwin opened his haversack. Pretty boy could do things his primitive way, but as he'd pointed out, this was a matter of life and death; not who was the better guy for Nimri.

There was another loud thump. "Gunda come," Thunder said.

Larwin applied a quick antiseptic spray to his thigh, then he reached under his tunic and removed his laser-cutter from the pant's pouch. As the hairy ape-like creature ambled into the chamber, Larwin adjusted the setting to plastoid, aimed at the wood across the room and fired. Thin red light zipped through the wood. With a flick of his wrist, the ends of both logs thudded to the floor.

The creature squealed. Thunder's mouth dropped open.

For the first time since he'd seen Nimri affectionately touching the handsome stranger, Larwin felt superior to him. Trying to appear casual, he turned to his rival. "My way is quicker than yours."

Blood had spurted over Thunder's bare chest. A knife-like tool lay where he had dropped it. As if his injury didn't matter, Thunder applied pressure to his wounded wrist. He didn't take his attention off of Larwin's palm-sized las-cutter while he walked to the severed beams. Thunder knelt reverently and ran a finger along the two-inch deep gouge in the workshop's stone wall. The thin, bloody trail simultaneously pleased and repelled Larwin.

"Such power," Thunder said.

"Yeah. Too bad its energy only nourishes madrox." He looked pointedly at the wrist Thunder had injured. If the guy died, it would be him and Nimri against the madrox. Larwin glanced at the doorway. "GEA-4 is a decent field medic and I've got a fully stocked med-kit."

Thunder waved his hand dismissively. Larwin squinted at the bloodstained skin, but couldn't see a wound. It must have been his other hand. But that one wasn't spurting, either. Nimri's arm had healed miraculously, too. Larwin turned his attention to the channel in the rock and tried not to show his confusion. "Sorry about your wall. I thought wood's density would be similar to plastoid."

Larwin frowned. Wood and yellowish rock were obviously very

deficient products. Larwin lowered the laser-cutter's setting. He leveled up the other ends of the two logs, and trimmed them. Then, Thunder helped him roll one beam off and heft another onto the thick wedges. Thunder's expression was thoughtful as he watched Larwin calculate his next cut.

"When we merged our auras, I discovered that Nimri's anxiety over your safety helped her overcome some of Rolf's mind blocks."

Though Thunder's tone was conversational, terms like aura and Rolf confused Larwin. Not that he'd let Thunder know that. He didn't need an interpreter to understand the concept of a man and woman merging, though. Thunder didn't need to remind him how intimate the two of them were. Larwin's jaw still ached from holding back a curse, when he'd seen the woman he wanted above all others hanging onto Thunder's hand, as if letting go meant death.

Larwin clamped his lips together and vowed not to get baited into a fight over Nimri. At least not until after their alliance had defeated the dragon and then a med-tech verified that she was safe to touch. After that, she'd be worth fighting for. Right now, it was a fight for his life and future.

Thunder absentmindedly stroked his injured hand.

"GEA-4 could stitch your wound for you." Thunder grinned and shook his head. Fine, let the man suffer. Perhaps his smile covered anticipation of how Nimri would fuss over him. Bitterness curled through Larwin's stomach. He turned back to the beam. "Do you believe this catapult will work?"

"If we believe it will, then it will be so." Thunder patted the wood with the same hand he'd touched the wall with, but it didn't leave a bloody mark.

Larwin blinked. Radzuk, but their body chemistry was different. No wonder Nimri burned him. It would be great to have a body that could go from pulsing blood to completely healed within ten minutes.

Of course, half the joy of having their alien DNA would be the ability to touch the woman he loved instead of being forced to watch her smile at another man. Not that they flaunted their relationship, but anyone with eyes could tell there was a deep bond between them.

Acid indigestion gnawed his insides. Larwin gritted his teeth and picked up his laser-cutter.

Thunder shrugged. "If belief fails and the alkali doesn't slow or distract the beast or I am unable to control the weather-" He stopped in mid-sentence and frowned. "Why do you avoid speaking of Nimri?"

"This is your world." Larwin knew his voice sounded strained. "You two obviously have something going. I'm not a threat to that. I'm in this because I don't want this planet's resources ruined." Larwin turned his back to Thunder. At least for now. He sliced the beam.

Eventually, when he didn't turn back, Thunder returned to his workbench and proceeded to manufacture the delicate components. As the day passed, the pile of rough wood took on the shape of an archaic catapult.

Outside, there was another thump. This time, Larwin investigated. A large pile of dusty white cloth bags had materialized. Larwin looked around the area and saw one of Thunder's hairy beasts shambling down the path he'd followed Kazza up; its dark shaggy fur was dusted with white.

Hunkering down, he touched the bag's powdery coating, then sniffed his finger. Sweet. Lime.

The arsenal that Nimri and the creatures were building was as pitiful as the plan.

Still, as long as Nimri insisted on combating the beast, instead of seeking the safety of the mist, Larwin knew he'd fight by her side. The idea of choosing to go into battle and picking his strategy was a novel concept; almost as insane as risking his life for a woman he couldn't touch.

How many of Guerreterre's battles were as senseless as fighting for love? Larwin sat back on his heels. He studied the sun-baked rocks, then looked up at the impossibly blue sky. How many battles would he have participated in if he'd had a choice?

All of them. At first, he would have been afraid that if he didn't fight, he'd be viewed as a coward. Later, it had become a way of life and a matter of pride over being in the best fighting unit. At least when he'd fought for Guerreterre, the odds had been in his favor.

Was he deranged for choosing a battle destined to fail? For going against a fearsome foe with nothing more than a clumsy, primitive weapon, a twisted walking stick, and an unreasonably optimistic sense of destiny?

Almost certainly.

~0~

The next morning, Nimri's shoulder scraped against the rough wood back of the heavy catapult as she threw her weight against it. She ignored the stabbing pain and kept pushing the unwieldy thing, but the rear wheel was firmly stuck in the rut filled path and all she got for her efforts was more blood on the timber.

She would never have believed that pushing the contraption over the ridge behind Thunder's home could be so tiring. Especially since the Yetis and GEA-4 were pulling the forward ropes. But the clumsy wooden wheels seemed to catch on every pebble and get sucked down into every soft spot.

Larwin's face was masked in determination. He groaned as he heaved the right rear wheel out of the furrow.

Suddenly it didn't matter if getting the wretched machine up to the higher cliff mattered. What mattered was that for the first time since he'd returned, Larwin wasn't glaring at her with a mixture of indifference and hatred. Her throat tightened. Nimri closed her eyes against the threatening tears of relief. No way would she let the guardian see her mortal frailty or how his coldness hurt her.

The three of them hoisted the heavy cart over another rock. Again, Larwin groaned. The pain-laced sound mirrored her feelings.

She must focus on saving her people and their world. Personal loss was minor. Nimri wondered if she would have been so quick to agree with Thunder's terms if he hadn't reminded her of Larwin or if she'd known Larwin would return so quickly. She glanced to her left. Thunder's mouth was set in a thin white line, which made it easy to remember Thunder Cartwright was the enemy.

An enemy who held her future in his hand.

An enemy who could confuse her with a smile.

An enemy who seemed to know more about her than she knew about herself.

The cart came to a jarring halt. Nimri gasped as pain ripped through her shoulder.

Thunder grunted. "Rock on my side. Let it roll back a bit." Nimri slacked the force she was exerting. The catapult lunged back. She nearly lost her balance. "Stop," Thunder said. "Got it." With a solid thunk, a melon-sized rock rolled downhill.

"One, two, three, heave," Larwin said through gritted teeth.

The catapult's thick wooden wheels inched forward and upward, then a rope broke with a resounding crack and whipped back across the apparatus. The cart rolled backwards.

The frayed flax cord lashed toward her. Nimri ducked.

Larwin rammed the staff of protection beneath the wheel.

"Can you hold it?" Thunder asked.

Larwin grunted.

Thunder darted forward with the rope. Just as quickly, Thunder was back, shoulder to the beam. "We're almost there." She hoped he was telling the truth.

"One, two, three, heave," Larwin said.

The ungainly contraption lurched forward, jounced, then it surged forward faster than she'd thought possible.

Caught off guard, Nimri lost her hold and fell to her knees. She looked under the belly of the ungainly weapon. The front wheels had reached the level plateau.

They'd made it.

Tears of relief brimmed in her eyes. She blinked them away. If GEA-4's prediction was true, they barely had enough time to set up their defenses before the dragon broke through. Now they had to deal with the real hard part; fighting the planet-destroying dragon.

Nimri scrambled to her feet, ignored her strained muscles and bleeding flesh and threw her weight against the rear of the catapult. It shot forward.

A Yeti squealed.

Again, Nimri fell to her knees. The catapult's heavy wooden wheels rolled majestically to a stop atop the flat precipice.

Thunder looked triumphant as he straightened, put his hands to the small of his back and swayed from side to side. Nimri studied his handsome features. Who was he? Her enemy? Her mentor? Despite her dreams of Larwin, would Thunder become her cherished partner?

Feeling a blush creep up her neck, Nimri lowered her gaze. There was fresh blood on Thunder's palms. Her heart lurched. If someone was injured, no matter how they confused her, it was her responsibility to heal the injury.

Or at least try to.

Ignoring her own aches, Nimri moved toward Thunder and placed her hands on top of his. He jerked, but she held his hands tight. She closed her eyes and thought of his aches receding, his flesh mending.

Thunder shook free, then turned and clasped her shoulders. "You need to save your power." His gentle tone bespoke deep tenderness. He held up his hands, which indeed looked better. Her shoulder felt better, too.

Lightness fluttered within her like a thousand butterflies. She'd done it just like he'd shown her.

She could do anything, except figure out how to love two men. Lucky for her that Larwin wasn't a real man with real needs. Lucky for her that Thunder had made her choice for her. Lucky for her that she'd probably die saving their world and would never need to resolve the dilemma.

Something warm and loving sparkled in Thunder's gaze. How could someone feel so familiar, yet the thought of being with him seem so wrong? Even if he'd been a Chosen, she didn't think she'd have chosen him for her cherished partner. Nimri winced. She'd given away her right to choose.

Nimri wet her lips. "You need your hands," she said. "Besides, you taught me to use my gift, you deserve thanks." She bent and kissed a fading bruise on his knuckle. "There, you should feel better, now."

Thunder kissed her forehead then flexed his hands. "Your control is getting better. Faster, as well."

"I hope you're right."

"I am." Thunder tickled her under the chin, then stepped away. Suddenly, she was face to face with Larwin. She had a brief glimpse of his stormy expression, then he, too, turned away.

Confused by the undercurrent of emotions, Nimri watched them join GEA-4 and the Yetis, who were unloading the sacks of lime near the precipice that overlooked Thunder's home and the sprawling valley.

Despite her suspicion that Guardians didn't strain their muscles or tear their flesh, Larwin had groaned mightily the last few times he'd dislodged his side. Nimri went to him and touched his back. He jerked away from her.

"Be still. Please.

"I don't need your help," Larwin said.

"Yes, you do," Nimri said. "You won't be able to function if your body knots up any more. Either you stand still, or I'll ask Thunder to hold you."

"It'd take more than him to hold me."

"I've seen you fight, but I'll wager he could manage if Gunda and Carn helped."

Larwin's gaze flickered to the Yetis. "Fine. Do what you think you have to."

Nimri closed her eyes and gently touched his joints. Some held the heat of injury, but none seemed to have the intense burning of damage serious enough to warrant tension in his joints.

The moment she broke contact, Larwin stomped away. Nimri stared at him long after he began examining the catapult's wheels.

Thunder tossed the last bag of lime on top of the heap. Nimri turned to him. "You always seem to know—things. Can you read minds?"

"It doesn't take a Diviner to know we're all worried about the Dragon." Thunder looked toward Sacred Mountain's summit. "I hope we succeed. If we don't, I hope I die before I have to witness the destruction of our world."

Nimri nodded in agreement.

GEA-4 moved to the edge of the bluff and stared at Sacred Mountain with the same concentration she gave the sun. Gooseflesh rippled over Nimri's arms.

"And if we win, you'll hold me to my promise." Nimri whispered the words and felt a different type of tingle. Which would be worse—death or whatever Thunder wanted? He was acting friendly—too friendly—now --- but she'd seen Rolf go from serene to seething in the blink of an eye, so there was no telling how quickly he could change.

And Rolf's worst rages happened when someone mentioned Thunder's name.

Nimri gazed across the valley. The river looked like a wide silvery ribbon. By now, she would have been missed and banished. She could never go home, again. Maybe it was good that Thunder meant for her to stay with him.

"We might all be a team now, but we may still have to fight each other." Thunder 's soft statement sent a shock wave from heel to head. Nimri gave him a sharp look. Though he was speaking to her, his attention was centered on Larwin. Why would he even consider fighting with a Guardian? "At least you and I will be in accord."

GEA-4 abruptly turned to Larwin and said something indecipherable. He blanched. Nimri gulped, afraid that she understood the message, even if she didn't speak the immortal language.

Larwin grabbed the strange horse-shoe-shaped device he kept hooked to his belt and clipped it over his eyes. His stiff posture bespoke the worst. Nimri looked at Sacred Mountain's summit and saw a small flash.

"Hurry! It's breaking through!" Larwin shouted.

Nimri jumped.

Suddenly, Larwin was next to her, his hands on her upper arms. "Please reconsider and let GEA-4 be the bait."

"She can't. Like it or not, ready or not, I'm the Keeper of the Peace."

His fingers kneaded her taunt muscles. For a moment, she thought he'd turn and leave. Instead, he asked, "What did you mean about a promise?" He glanced at Thunder.

So he knew about her pledge. Nimri sighed and wet her lips. "I needed help to save our people. To save our world. It was the only way to gain Thunder's cooperation."

Nimri saw the hurt in his eyes as he bent and kissed her

forehead. "That was for luck." He went back to the catapult and redoubled his efforts at breaking the wheel free.

Eyes hazy with unshed tears, Nimri watched him.

Kazza butted her thigh and purred when she took a step toward Larwin. She stroked his back. "So you turned up." Again, he nudged her toward Larwin. Silly cat didn't know how confusing relationships could be.

"The dragon comes," GEA-4 said.

Thunder, GEA-4, the Yetis and Larwin increased their efforts at removing the wheels and stabilizing the catapult. Nimri patted Kazza's head. "I must become the bait." Not wanting Kazza to get in the way, she herded him toward a scraggly clump of mountain laurel at the edge of the plateau.

Nimri didn't look back until she sat down beneath the dark glossy leaves. GEA-4 was holding up the corner of the cart while Larwin and Thunder strained to remove the last wheel. The Yetis moved around making random, nervous gestures.

"Eighteen point five minutes," GEA-4 said.

Heart thumping, Nimri settled into the hatha position, closed her eyes and began humming the proper note. Kazza sprawled next to her. His whiskers tickled her arm. The seclusion of the shrubbery seemed to envelop her in a warm, protective embrace. Kazza's purr rumbled. Nimri imagined that the note was taking her upward. Soon, she actually hovered over the laurel patch. It seemed odd to look down and see herself and Kazza.

She wished she felt as peaceful as her body looked.

Raising her arms, Nimri plunged upward into the sky. Out of the corner of her eye, she saw Kazza match her pace.

A glance at Sacred Mountain revealed an undulating golden speck, which seemed to get larger and longer with every breath.

The dragon had broken through.

A glance at the bluff told her that the catapult still wasn't ready to fire. She glared around the cloudless sky, then back at Thunder, who was still trying to help GEA-4 and Larwin with the wheel. Start your trance! Instead, he continued to force the wheel to break free, so they could level the weapon.

Nimri looked back at the mountain. The dragon was closer, but moved as if it might be injured. That had to be a good thing. She stared at the beast and yearned for something more constructive than baiting it into an unprepared trap. Yearned to go back in time, so she would never follow Larwin to his dismal home or lure the dragon to her own. Yearned for this battle to be over, so that she didn't have to face a future confrontation with the horrid beast. Better that it was over and the outcome was assured, even if it meant her death.

The dragon's haphazard movements solidified into an undulating pattern that would take it to the village. "No, oh, no, don't go there!" Nimri had to do something. Unlike the Lost, who lived in isolated homes, all across their side of the river, almost all the Chosen lived in the village. Even those who farmed didn't have a house where they raised their crops and livestock.

Kazza growled, swished his tail and snarled at the distant speck.

Kazza at her side, and with no weapon, except sheer guts, Nimri moved to cut off the dragon.

Chapter Eighteen

Larwin's fingers were slippery with blood as he fought to dislodge the last wheel. When brute force wouldn't budge it, he rammed the twisted black stick between cart and wheel, hoping the flimsy-looking thing would act as a lever and at least shift the jam before it broke. He heaved against the makeshift lever. The wheel shot off as if it was greased. Unprepared for the response, Larwin lost his balance and fell forward. The wheel's weight hit him square in the solar plexus. It bounced, then tipped over and landed on his lungs with a numbing thud.

Thunder pulled it off of him. "Are you hurt?" Larwin grunted.

Larwin wondered if any primitive civilizations he'd previously attacked had gone to similar futile lengths to protect themselves from his squadron. Still, he couldn't simply sit still and do nothing.

Thunder looked at him, concern in his expression. "Are you hurt?" he repeated.

His lungs burned with each breath and despite years of mind control, panic welled. Larwin didn't know which was worse, the physical pain of cracked ribs or the knowledge of how his actions and superior power had affected his past victims. "I'm fine. Go. Do whatever it is that you must do for your part of the plan." Thunder looked as if he would have preferred to stay or touch his aching ribs, but despite it feeling as if his insides were tearing apart, Larwin sat up and shooed him away.

But the stubborn man wouldn't move.

Larwin struggled to stand, but found he needed to use the stick as a crutch. Thunder gave him a penetrating look, as if seeing his inferiority.

"Go. I'm fine." Each word tasted like blood.

This time, Thunder whistled for his two hairy creatures and moved toward a large boulder. As soon as Thunder wasn't looking, Larwin carefully inhaled than exhaled a hard-won breath. As always, broken ribs hurt like Vilecom. In the Academy, cracked ribs, contusions and cuts had been a way of life. So, why didn't he feel like a kid, again?

"Seventeen point one minutes," GEA-4 said.

Larwin turned his attention to his part of the plan and ignored Thunder. After a moment's hesitation, Thunder sat down in a patch of purple wildflowers next to a gold-toned boulder— presumably to brew up a storm. Though Larwin doubted any mortal could control the weather, these aliens had such unusual biochemistry it could be true.

"Seventeen point two. Seventeen point three."

"Great time to malfunction." Larwin clenched his teeth and ignored the pain.

"Nimri is luring the beast away," Thunder called across the clearing.

Larwin twisted so fast that it felt like he'd pierced his lung. "Mind meld with her," he shouted to Thunder, "or whatever it is you share. Tell her to bring it on." Ignoring the intense pain, Larwin hoisted a bag of lime into the catapult's seat. Teeth clenched, he adjusted the spring's tension.

"By the time I—never mind," Thunder said from close behind

him. Larwin slowly turned to face Thunder. "It's too complicated to explain."

What was so complex? Presumably, instead of napping in the clearing with Kazza, Nimri was facing the beast alone and she needed help. "Get back to your flowers."

"You're hurt. I must help you, then I can-"

Larwin gave Thunder a look, guaranteed to shrivel green recruits. "Now listen to me and listen well. If that madrox kills Nimri because she's following your damned plan, I'll make sure you have the slowest, most painful death possible. Understand?" Thunder raised a brow. "Now get back there and do your part."

Thunder's smile lit his eyes and the feathers fluttered as if they were dancing with delight. "You aren't the only one who cares for her."

He didn't need that reminder or the friendly smile. "Go brew your damned storm."

Thunder nodded and motioned to the Yetis. They gamboled across the plateau, and settled in the patch of purple flowers.

Larwin finished setting up the machine, then detached the viewer from his belt, and watched the madrox's strange flashing oscillations. This was the stupidest strategy anyone in the history of warfare had ever planned.

Paired wings beating in dissonance, the beast looked more like a bizarre crippled bird than burning death.

The mouth opened wide enough to swallow a sequoia and the monster bellowed.

Larwin dropped the viewer and held his ears as throbbing pain constricted around his eardrums. Sweat bathed his brow and though he saw GEA-4's mouth moving as she counted off the seconds to battle, for once, he couldn't hear her.

"Come back here." Larwin knew he'd shouted, but he couldn't hear himself. "You don't need a thousand auras, come get mine!"

Larwin keyed off the audio, then put his viewer back on. The damned beast was heading toward the village. What good was building the machine and nearly killing himself to haul it up here or worrying about Nimri being the bait, if she and Thunder couldn't fulfill their part of the cockamamie plan? How was he expected to protect an entire planet, when he had to wait for the beast to come to him, instead of go after it? Larwin clutched the twisted black wood while he watched the madrox continue toward the village.

He closed his eyes and petitioned the War God. "Kues, these are good, decent people. Take me and allow Nimri to survive. Thunder, too, since she obviously loves him."

"Fifteen minutes," GEA-4 said.

The sudden return of hearing was as unnerving as the rejection he'd seen in Nimri's eyes. "What?"

"It altered course."

Yes! Larwin raised his fist and shouted, "Come on you ugly swine!"

~0~

The dragon was so close Nimri could see how its scales interlocked. So close that she could see that its ginger-toned body looked like iridescent gold because of the heat waves which distorted the air around it. So close that it smelled like a million eggs rotting in rancid sauerkraut. So close that the heat from its body felt hotter than when Quark opened the door to his largest kiln. So close that she realized each of its claws were larger than she was.

Kazza's hair stood on end, his tail lashed. His eyes gleamed as he tilted his head back and roared.

Nimri jumped, startled by the unprecedented hostility in his tone, she looked at her cuddly pet, but saw a ferocious stranger.

The dragon's tongue crackled toward her, but stopped far short of her position. Wings beating, and red eyes, glaring, it moved ever closer. The sight of the thing transfixed her.

Murderous intent in his expression, Kazza flexed his claws.

The hair at Nimri's nape stood on end.

Kazza emitted a roar so terrible that it chilled her to the bone. Nimri was glad Kazza was on her side, even if he appeared as insignificant as a bee when compared to their enemy.

Bees could do some damage, particularly if the person was sensitive to their poison. Nimri wondered if dragons had allergies to people or felines.

Nimri vowed she would do her best to save her people.

To save her world.

To save Larwin and Thunder.

Or die...it might be easier if she died trying.

She wished the trap were ready.

How could she fight a beast such as this barehanded?

Beat by beat of its golden gossamer wings, the monster flew closer. She stood still. As the lightening-like tongue licked toward her, she saw herself and Kazza reflected in one of its murderous, crimson eyes. With every bone and sinew, Nimri wanted to turn and flee, as she had in the tunnel. She forced herself to remain stationary.

Stroke by stroke, she watched her image in its eye grow until she and Kazza had the beast's undivided attention. The Ghilly's jaw opened to reveal teeth larger and more menacing than the Star Bridge's stalactites.

Its roar was mind numbing.

As the blue-lightening tongue shot forward, Nimri stood immobilized, waiting for the inevitable. Its tongue flashed at her, only stopping a pace away.

White light crackled and hissed around her.

Kazza roared and slashed at the tongue, his claws missing by a hands-breadth.

I must move before it sends forth its tongue, again.

Nimri thought she heard the dragon's stomach rumble. It might have been Kazza growling.

With a shriek, the dragon lunged. A wave of scorching air engulfed her. That plus the stench almost knocked her out.

The mouth opened wide as her home. When the tongue flickered, Nimri propelled herself upward to the right. Kazza moved as if he was her shadow. The beast's lips and gaping mouth surged beneath. Bellows of fury made coherent thought impossible. The creature was twice as large as she'd thought and she was still in the path of its demonic eye.

She hurdled through the thick, suffocating air, praying to ascend out of its way, without touching it. But it didn't look like she was going to make it.

Worse, Kazza was no longer with her.

She looked back and saw him hovering motionless in the air, the claws of all four paws extended toward the fast-approaching eye. Nimri screamed for him to move, but her warning was lost in the tumult of noise, heat and stench. She cried in frustration, the tears evaporating as fast as they appeared. Her eyes burned from the horrid vapors and the steam.

Kazza connected with the eye. A heartbeat later, something hot hit her head. Blackness threatened. Blindly, she grabbed for whatever had struck her.

The broiling mass undulated up and down, but she held on, afraid to let go until her vision cleared. A tremor went through the thick mass in her hands.

The dragon roared. The sound shook Nimri to her core.

She clawed for purchase and dug in with her knees. Blinking hard, Nimri confirmed that she was hanging onto the bony edge of one of the first pair of wings.

The dragon's bellows increased in tempo and fury.

Surely her meager weight on a wing wouldn't be noticeable. The brute was probably either irritated because she'd gotten away or because Kazza was like a gnat in its eye.

Nimri twisted to secure her grip and maneuvered so that she could calculate a way to get the creature back on course and into catapult range.

Movement caught her attention. Kazza was clinging to the beast's eyelid. As she watched, he raked his claws against the tomato-red iris.

The dragon wailed and its body shook worse than the earthquake had shaken the balata. Nimri slipped downward.

Kazza's body language indicated that he was having the time of his life as he repeated his attack.

The dragon blinked.

She fought for a hold on the erratic wing when she felt a gap between the scales. She dug her fingers into it for support.

Kazza rode the lid up and down, his claws raking claw-deep trenches with each blink.

Magenta streaks appeared on the fiery eyeball. When the dragon rolled, Kazza leaped to the other eyelid, where he leaned over and resumed his assault.

He's trying to blind it.

Does it need sight to follow me near the catapult?

Despite the dragon's overpowering stench, a new pungent fetidness engulfed Nimri. This new smell went beyond awful. She looked for the source and noticed a purplish stain oozing up from the crack. She raised one hand. Her fingers were covered with the awful slime. Halfway to her nose, the stench became overpowering. Knowing a weak spot when she found one, Nimri rammed her fingers back into the break. The beast shuddered. She secured her grip in the crevasse and pulled at the thick membrane. The dragon shrieked and undulated.

Kazza's claws kept slashing. Both eyeballs were now crisscrossed with thin magenta lines.

Nimri risked a glance to see where they were. The dragon was circling over the plain just west of Thunder's bluff. GEA-4 stood near the precipice, presumably watching. Larwin appeared thumb-size but ready. The dragon rolled before she could spot Thunder and the Yetis.

Despite not seeing any rain clouds, she needed to begin her part of the plan, instead of engage in this petty harassment.

With a mighty heave, Nimri yanked at the fractured scale and dislodged a dishpan-sized slab of membrane.

The dragon flipped into a backward summersault.

Kazza lost his grip and spun away into a wispy line of white clouds hovering over the river.

Nimri dropped the repulsive thick membrane. At the same time, she lost her hold on the beast and barely managed to jump clear of the second set of beating wings.

As the beast passed beneath her, she tried to judge its path and decide where she needed to be if she wanted to lure the dragon into the trap. She looked at the sky. Either Thunder wasn't having any luck or his attempt was puny.

The dragon bellowed and whirled in a loop, like a mad dog chasing its tail, but climbing ever higher.

Despite distance, Nimri still smelled the revolting reek. Looking down, she saw that she'd been showered with putrid purple pus.

She couldn't see Kazza and hoped he hadn't been injured.

A whistling sound from above heralded the dragon's return. She looked up, into the sun and was hit with the wall of heat and immobilizing lassitude. The horrid cerulean tongue flickered toward her. Before she could jump, the ghastly, boa-like tongue wrapped around her waist and yanked her toward its cavernous mouth.

The harder she fought, the tighter the tongue became.

Stalagmites of shimmering semi-opaque opal flashed past. A silvery stalactite grazed her leg.

Abruptly, the light changed to shades of orange and the tongue changed to deep magenta.

She looked back at the closed mouth.

She'd been eaten!

She'd failed.

Chatterre was doomed.

Chapter Nineteen

"What's wrong with that cursed madrox?" Larwin demanded, as he clung to the twisted black stick for support.

"I'm picking up energy patterns similar to the ones I monitored at the cave. The madrox appears to be chasing one," GEA-4 said.

His heart lurched when he realized the beast was going out of range. "Nimri, follow the plan!" As if in answer to his command, the beast changed course.

"It will be within catapult range in approximately one minute," GEA-4 said.

It was the longest minute of his life. Larwin adjusted the sights and trajectory. "Let it get close enough to guarantee the shot hits."

"That would be too close to assure your survival."

"Do it anyway." If he believed in magic and spirit travel, which he must, since GEA-4 was picking up the readings, Nimri was facing the creature one-on-one; he had to help her. Or die trying.

An intense wave of heat rolled over him. In ever widening

ripples, the plateau's grass turned brown. A moment later, all vegetation was blown away as if it never existed; all but the circle of green beneath his feet.

His skin felt hot, but not dehydrated.

The dragon was almost on top of their position. Larwin held the twisted stick in his right hand and the catapult trigger in the other. The madrox opened its mouth wide enough to swallow the hill.

"Get ready," GEA-4 said. "Set...Fire!"

Larwin threw the lever.

The bag of alkali rocketed away, leaving a trail of iridescent dust, which seemed to fall around him in a protective golden cone.

GEA-4 locked the seat into position and loaded another bag while Larwin modified the aim. As the first bag impacted against the dragon's forehead in an insignificant puff of white dust, Larwin launched the second.

The second bag disappeared into the beast's gaping mouth. GEA-4 loaded a third. He fired. Before he could see where this bag landed, the beast's tail slammed into the cliff face below his position. The impact threw him facedown, onto the hard, twisted stick. Overcome by pain and heat, his last thought was that there wouldn't be time for another shot before he died.

The dragon's strangled roar shook the entire mountain.

Larwin heard the catapult fire.

Good for GEA-4.

The last thing Larwin saw was the beast twist away and its spiked tail heading toward him and the catapult.

As blackness overcame him, he felt the ground give way beneath his feet. The land fell, taking everything with it. After that, there was only blackness.

Chapter Twenty

Nimri wouldn't have believed the heat and stench could get worse, but as the beast swallowed her aura, it did.

She'd always imaged food went down quickly, but the dragon's throat was a series of bony ridges between huge cylinders of soft tissue, which contracted and expanded in sequence, pushing her past the unbending cartilage. Nimri slipped slowly down the throat bouncing off protruding ridges. Limbs paralyzed, consciousness close to blackout, she chanted, "Must fi-ght…M-ust fight…" She moved a finger. "Must fight…" Her wrists moved. Then her elbows. Control of her legs came joint by agonizing joint.

Perhaps the horrible descent would last long enough for her to do something to help her people. Gauging her slide, she focused on the next slope and jammed her heels into the yielding flesh beneath the inflexible crest. She stopped moving.

The flesh contracted around her, as if trying to swallow, but she was too small to be affected. Nimri scrambled onto the firm shelf then dug her fingers and heels into the springy pulsating pulp.

Something sharp bit her throat. Nimri waited until the dragon's movement paused, then felt for the new problem. Her fingers found the strap of her amulet bag. She touched the beaded leather; spines pricked her finger.

What sacrilege had attacked her talisman?

A new muscle convulsion nearly unseated her. She dug in her knees, so she could free her hands to take off the amulet.

Sharp silvery spikes appeared to have burst from inside. Gingerly, she opened the lacing.

Her location turned upside down, as if the beast was rolling. Nimri lost her purchase and somersaulted forward. Her sacred bag was almost wrenched from her hand when she seized another ridge.

Once secure, she dug both heels and knees into the tender flesh and gingerly opened the bag. Still, a spine scratched her. She squinted into her special bits. The sequoia bud, which she'd believed part of a dream, had transformed into a lethal-looking silver porcupine sort of thing. She blinked, confused at the transformation; concerned about how she'd ever get it out of the bag, which it appeared to have grown into and become permanently part of. She raised her arm to drop it.

'When the cone is mature, your power will be too and you will know how best to use it.' She lowered her hand and took another look at the amulet. The prophecy seemed twisted. How could she use the cone when it had become embedded in the supple leather? Unless she was meant to throw her entire amulet into the beast's throat. While the spikes were certainly sharp enough to prick the creature, they'd be much more useful if she could thrust them into the tender flesh.

Carefully, Nimri reached into the bag with two fingers. To her astonishment, it came out easily. Once in her palm, the strange pinecone began growing.

She tightened her heels and knees on the sinew and warily tried to pinch one of the barbs, which was now as long as her forearm, but it wouldn't break. She thought how effective it would be embedded in the dragon. It separated from the thing with little effort. Nimri slightly altered her grip. After a moment's hesitation, she rammed it into the tender flesh.

The dragon bellowed and rolled. This time, she held on tight. Then, breaking off more of the growing barbs, she forced them into the soft tissue between the huge, circular rings.

The dragon's bellows intensified into a frenzy and the throat became a nightmare of twisting rage.

Nimri kept thrusting increasingly long points into whatever tender flesh she could reach. She climbed past the closest cartilage ridge, broke off another section and rammed it into the soft tissue, then held onto it as the beast gyrated. The more it thrashed, the more invigorated she felt.

By the time the cone was gone, thin purplish-red stains surrounded each silvery barb she had embedded. Aside from the jostling, nose and stench, somehow the sight reminded her of the white spots in the nighttime sky. But it was impossible to ignore where she was, even the worst of storms had never howled this loud. By comparison, the earthquakes she'd experienced were mild. Not knowing what else to do, she put her amulet bag around her neck and tucked it into her tunic.

She dared not think of the smell.

As if the environment surrounded Nimri hadn't gone mad enough, the beast dove. She lost her hold and tumbled into its mouth. The tongue was coated with a white powdery film. Alkali! Larwin had done his part! She hoped that Thunder had managed to conjure more than the puny clouds she'd seen.

The dragon opened its mouth and bellowed in anguish. She slid forward. Her world looked the size of a melon. No! She grabbed one of the monstrous teeth and willed her fingers to grip the slick surface. They slipped. "Hold," she breathed.

~0~

Larwin's body felt as if it had been broken into a thousand places, all of them critical. He knew he was dying. Knew he'd been buried up to his chest in dirt, rock, uprooted plants and the broken catapult. But if Nimri had survived, his death meant something. He stared up at the dark sky and wondered why he wasn't already dead.

He hoped Thunder would succeed where he'd failed. Hoped whatever his rival could do would be enough to save Nimri.

A mediocre lightening bolt illuminated the blackness. The dragon soared above the oncoming storm and continued going straight up as fast as its wings could carry it. If it went to another planet or galaxy, Nimri would never be safe from fear.

The second bolt of lightening was stronger, but the storm no longer mattered because the beast was gone.

GEA-4 knelt next to him. Filthy as she looked, she must have been buried in debris from the landslide, too. "You have several fractured bones.'' She hesitated. "One punctured a lung." He had suspected as much.

He knew she'd only grazed the list of his injuries, and didn't understand why he was still alive or how he could breathe with such pressure against his lungs. "Nimri."

"Do not attempt to speak." GEA-4 looked to his left.

Painfully, he turned his head. Nimri and Kazza's bodies lay motionless atop the landslide. If he hadn't been half buried in rock, he would have gone to her, despite the pain. As if sensing that her efforts to treat him would be futile, GEA-4 arose, picked up Nimri and carried her to Larwin. The way she held her made Nimri look like a corpse. He tried to touch her face one last time, but his left arm was trapped and his right was too badly broken.

GEA-4 positioned Nimri's limp hand so her cold palm touched his cheek, then, she left. Larwin was certain that Nimri was truly dead. Perhaps this was better.

GEA-4 returned with Kazza's limp body and arranged the great cat on his other side. Tears blurred his vision as she hefted a large rock off his arm. With no tools available, she began to dig him out with her hands. When he was lying flat on his back with Kazza and Nimri arranged next to him, she set some of the bones; finally, she laid the odd twisted stick along his right side and bound his fractured limbs to it.

Dead, all dead, except for him, who should have died at least twice already and GEA-4, who could live without everything but solar energy.

If his mother was correct about there being an afterlife, he'd be with Nimri and Kazza in spirit. If only he could die.

Chapter Twenty-One

Nimri propelled herself out of the dragon's mouth, but slammed against the bridge of the beast's spear-like snout. Immobilized by fear, she hung on for dear life.

Never had she imagined such speed. She twisted, trying to see where she was. The dragon dove toward a bluish ball. Or perhaps the ball was being hurled at them. As it neared, it gained character and definition. Memories of the mind-meld with GEA-4 brought the word planet to her mind. The world appeared to be equally divided between land and water. Perhaps the huge fern-shaped blue they were heading for was the ocean, which Thunder had spoken of. As if sensing the presence of the water, the dragon veered to its left. Nimri watched the panorama increase in size and detail, more interested in this view of her world, then afraid. Fingers of land jutted into the water. The term atoll came unbidden into her mind. Some landmasses were larger than others. Some were flat; others were rugged. Thunder hadn't said anything about their ocean having islands. She tried to determine if they were heading back to her world or if this was another one. Nothing looked familiar. A moment later, the dragon soared high above the clouds, which looked soft as whipped egg white. What should she do if the beast had taken her into the stars and they were near a different world? Could she wake without Thunder from so far away?

Light flashed off to the right. She recognized Sacred Mountain. Relief washed over her. This was her home world. Perhaps Thunder had brewed the storm. The valley certainly looked black enough. My job is to get this beast into the trap. She gritted her teeth and slid to the right. The dragon didn't change direction. She waved her fist at the creature's injured eye. It rolled sideways, toward her. Nimri held on. The dragon slowed, as if looking for her. She glanced over her shoulder, trying to gauge where she needed to lure the beast. They were heading directly at a thick white cloud-mass. Beyond it was a dark cloud. The beast stopped and began to turn. She scrambled onto its snout, and began to dance.

The dragon roared in fury and surged forward. Darkness abruptly fell. There was a terrible boom. White light bloomed over the dragon and Nimri. It screamed. Scalding humidity wrapped around her. Thunder had done it! Despite the pain, happiness thrilled through her.

More lightening flashed. The heavens rumbled. Each stronger, louder, closer. Sheets of water fell; each drop got a fraction closer and cooler before it disappeared, then the dragon altered course and headed upward.

Not again. Nimri danced down the massive nose until she saw her face reflected in both of the monster's crimson eyes.

"Focus on me. Come get me!" She stuck out her tongue. When that didn't distract the beast from the rain, she punched its eye. "Come on! Get me!" The dragon's gyrations became frenzied. "That's it." She moved to her left. It turned to chase her. She imagined that it didn't realize that it couldn't catch her by pursuit. She divided her awareness between making certain how fast the storm was approaching and keeping the dragon's attention focused on her.

Suddenly they were back in the dark cloud. A fraction of a

moment later, she realized they were diving straight at the ground. Nimri leaped clear.

A moment later, the beast plunged head first into the land. Vegetation and dirt shot upward in a wild whirlwind. The turbulence caught Nimri and she was sent tumbling through the vortex.

She somersaulted through the eruption. Her foot snagged on a tree branch. A shaft of lightening showed the dragon's body standing straight as a sequoia on the edge of the river's bank; legs extended as if reaching for the distant trees and wings flapping over the fast-disappearing water. By the time the light faded, its head had embedded up to the first set of wings. Debris and rain swirled around the rigid body.

For a moment, the only sound was the water sizzling into vapor.

By the next flash, Nimri had regained her balance, and was trying to decide what to do next. She was in a thick cloud of mist and so close to the beast that its smell turned her stomach. A moment before darkness returned, Nimri thought she saw its body move toward her.

The next bolt showed its spiny back falling directly toward her and gaining momentum. Kazza shot out of the mist, tackled her and knocked her into thick mud. She should have been in the middle of the river, but all the water was gone and the mud she'd landed on had already begun drying and cracking. A wingtip was headed straight for her heart.

"Wake from the trance…Now!" Thunder's alarmed disembodied voice shouted.

Suddenly, she was freezing wet instead of scalded. Her body lay on painful rock, but her right hand touched skin and blood. She knew it was Larwin, but when she opened her eyes, she didn't recognize the crushed form as anything mortal.

Still, she felt a faint pulse of life beneath the torn flesh and knew that somehow, he lived.

"Eight ribs have been shattered," GEA-4 said. "A lung is pierced. His skull is fractured. His legs and spine have been pulverized."

She'd only listed the most obvious damage. Nimri looked within his battered body, marveling that anyone could survive such mutilation.

"I can not restore him," GEA-4 concluded.

Could she?

She had to try.

Kazza sat on the other side of Larwin's shattered body, his paw on what should have been Larwin's chest, and stared at her as if waiting. Nimri sat up and placed both hands on either side of his paw. She closed her eyes and concentrated. Several bones had been smashed to dust. Larwin took a ragged breath. She began by willing the rib in his lung back into position, then getting the blood out of the lung and myst-mended the puncture.

Slowly, carefully, Nimri worked. When Larwin was breathing better, she started on the other broken ribs. Then, she treated the fractured skull and reduced the cranial pressure.

It seemed to take forever to repair the crushed bones in his lower extremities.

When the last particle of bone was realigned, she proceeded to repair the torn tissue, starting with his face. He took a ragged breath, then stopped breathing.

"Larwin!" She opened her eyes, but he looked dead. Felt dead. Nimri felt a hand on her shoulder.

"He doesn't want to live," Thunder said.

"No! He has to." Grief blurred her vision.

"Unless the person wishes to live, you can not help."

She couldn't stop the tears. Thunder lifted her and hugged her to his chest. "Remember our bargain?"

A sob caught in her throat. Forehead against his tunic, she stiffened while she nodded.

"Remember our bargain," he said again. "I told you that you'd know what I wanted in your heart."

Not now.

Not when she'd just lost Larwin.

How could he?

No wonder the Lost seemed so cold and emotionless.

"Remember our bargain," he repeated. "Focus on something you can achieve. Your pledge." Thunder's voice was soft but insistent.

Nimri looked at Larwin and saw lost dreams.

Thunder's arms tightened around her and his fingers caressed her back. "I want what my parents wanted. I'd hoped you'd remember. I can see you haven't. Think back...Remember your mother."

Not now.

Nimri struggled to kneel by Larwin.

Thunder's grip was too strong.

"Concentrate!"

She buried her face against his chest and bawled like a newborn baby. He cradled her as if she was one. "Wh-at d-did your p-p-parents want?"

"Think back. Remember your mother."

Despite her misery, Nimri smelled roses and saw a dark haired woman humming as she picked coreopsis.

"That's it," he said. "Concentrate."

But she couldn't. All she could do was blink away tears and stare at her lost future.

Thunder stopped rubbing her back. His hands clamped the sides of her head, much as GEA-4 had done when she imparted understanding for the words. This time, she saw herself at two years old. She sat on the floor and played with Kazza, who was a roly-poly kitten.

Nimri blinked, but the image remained steady.

Thunder was making her see this. Why?

The scene changed to a dinner table. For the first time in twenty years, Nimri saw her mother's face clearly. For the first time in her life, Nimri realized she looked like her mother.

Thunder came into the room and tickled her under the chin. Except he wasn't Thunder, he was her father. She was Thunder! She was…

Nimri yanked away Thunder's hands and stared at him. "Why didn't you tell me earlier?"

"I hoped you'd remember on your own." He shrugged. "Besides, we had a dragon to fight."

"Rolf made me forget, didn't he?" Thunder nodded. She remembered a vow he'd given her. "Why didn't you come for me? You promised you'd always protect me."

Her hands fisted and she wanted to hit him for the broken pledge.

"At first, I didn't know you survived." His eyes clouded. "Even if I'd known, I was only six."

Why was she blaming him? He'd only been a boy, unable to defend himself, let alone her.

"Rolf did things because he liked having the power and control."

Nimri swallowed her anger. "We're together, now. We can accomplish what they died for."

He looked past her, into the distance. "Perhaps we already have." Thunder's attention turned back to her. He took her hand the same way he had the day he taught her to walk; the same way he had two days before when he'd taught her to use her power.

Hands fisted, Nimri felt angrier at her great-grandfather than she'd ever been in her entire life and irate at the way she'd allowed herself to be used by him. "I hope you're right." She blinked back tears, ashamed of having forgotten ever having a brother.

A pain-laced groan made Nimri jump. She looked down and saw that one of Larwin's eyelids was twitching. "Larwin!" He was alive!

"N-im-ri." Larwin's tone was laced with regret.

Kazza's tail smacked Larwin's leg with a resounding whack.

"Glad to see you changed your mind and decided to live," Thunder said. "I'm sure my sister is relieved."

Larwin blinked then frowned. "Sis-ter?" Except for the pain-laced word, he still looked like death.

"Our great-grandfather, Rolf, wanted to have an enemy so his position as Keeper of the Peace would be important." Nimri knelt next to him and touched Larwin's cheek to make certain his life force really beat and it hadn't been her imagination. A faint, but steady rhythm assured her. "Our parents found out great-grandfather's plans and decided to move across the river to assure peace." She swallowed the lump in her throat. "But great-grandfather found out and murdered our parents with the flood. Thunder and I were separated when the boat capsized."

She couldn't go on. Couldn't remember the horror, yet.

"For years, I thought I was the only survivor. I didn't think Nimri knew how to swim," Thunder said.

"I didn't. Kazza swam for both of us." She hugged her dear friend. "For years, water terrified me." Nimri looked past Kazza's tufted ear and addressed her brother. "Now, I know why. And I understand why great-grandfather was so angry when I got over my fear of water; he felt his control over my mind was slipping."

Kazza purred.

"An elderly Lost couple gave me a home and their name," Thunder said. Thunder hunkered down and held out his hand to Larwin, who struggled to sit up. After a moment's hesitation, while he felt his body for injuries, Larwin clasped Thunder's hand with his left hand, gripped the Staff of Protection with his right and stood up.

Larwin fingered the dark wood. "How could your parents crossing the river bring peace?"

"There's a millennium old law, which probably began as a petty threat during an argument," Thunder said. "As a result, my tribe crossed the river and vowed never to return. Except they didn't have the skills to make pottery or any laying ducks for eggs, so they decided to return. When they came back, the Chosen enacted laws that stated those who had crossed the river could only return to trade on Market Day and had to be gone by dusk. If a Chosen ever crossed the river to come here, he or she automatically became traitor, and were forced to live as a Lost from that day forward."

"Most people don't want to venture into the unknown when there is no return," Nimri said. "So, you can understand why our parents were the only ones to ever try to challenge the law."

"If they couldn't break the law outright. Our parents knew that once Rolf died, the Chosen would be forced to cancel the law."

"Why?" Larwin asked.

"Keeper of the Peace is hereditary."

"And she or he needed to live with the tribe," Nimri added.

Larwin frowned at her. "Does this mean you can't return to your home?"

Nimri nodded. "Until they change the law. By now, someone has missed me, and I refuse to sneak back in the middle of night." She blushed, as she admitted how desperate she'd been for help. "The only other alternative is to walk over water.

Since the river never freezes, I'll be here forever. Or until the law is changed." She smiled at her brother. "But becoming a Lost has its benefits, since I'm now in the position my parents decided was their last chance to right a wrong." Of course, if Zurgon didn't want her back, the elders would probably vote with him.

She sighed. She'd miss her home and garden, but maybe it was for the best.

"There's a law against building bridges," Thunder said. "I want to change it."

"Guerreterre doesn't have bridges, because my planet has no water other than what circulates in the reclamation system." Larwin rubbed his temple. "But I've seen them on other worlds. Some arch high over the water, others float directly on the surface. If I can help, I will."

"The madrox will require a week to cool. After that, it could be employed as a bridge," GEA-4 said.

It took a moment for GEA-4's meaning to sink in.

Nimri looked from the odd little woman to the mist-shroud. Initially, she only saw torn earth and devastation circling a mountain of mist, then as a gust displaced the fog. It arched, legs straight up as if warding off the clouds and wings splayed over the parched ground, but there was no water. The vapor surged back in to cover the desolate ground.

Gooseflesh tingled over her. "Is it really over the river?" she asked.

"For now, it spans a wide stretch of dried mud," GEA-4 said. "But the water will return to normal as the carcass cools."

Nimri squinted upstream, well away from the beast, the riverbed still held water. She breathed a sigh of relief.

"GEA-4 is correct," Larwin said. "A madrox's body resembles lava more than animal flesh. Once cured, it should withstand anything."

Nimri remembered the overpowering stench and wrinkled her nose. "I don't think too many people will want to use something that stinks worse than rotten eggs."

Larwin laughed. "Once it has cooled the disgusting odor will leave." He looked at Thunder. "There's no law against adding earthen ramps and guardrails to madrox carcasses is there?"

"No…" Thunder frowned. "But I'd hoped to mine it for minerals."

"There are easier ways to mine silica and carbon," GEA-4 said. "Of course, for proper water flow, the wings should be removed. You could have those."

Thunder grinned at the cloaked dragon.

"It will probably take centuries to crumble," Larwin said. "That should give us plenty of time to change the bridge building law."

He'd said "us." Happiness bubbled within Nimri. "Will you stay that long?"

When Larwin didn't immediately answer, Thunder turned to him. "Do you want my sister for your cherished partner?"

Larwin looked at Nimri. "How does one ask someone to form one of these partnerships?"

"I guess one would ask the other to share their life and future." Her neck felt as hot as it had in the dragon's throat. "To raise a family in harmony, should they be so blessed." Her face felt as fiery as the dragon's eyes "To stand by each other as they grow old," she said.

"To be willing to face death for the other?" Larwin asked. She nodded. He smiled. "I accept."

While Nimri wondered what had just happened, Kazza reared up, gently put his paw on Larwin's chest and stared at him.

Larwin smiled and tousled Kazza's ears. "No kidding. We'll have a baby?" Nimri had never felt so confused. He grinned at her over Kazza's shoulder. "This cat of yours is always right. You have no idea how relieved I am to know we're physically compatible," Larwin said.

"It would be illogical if you were not," GEA-4 said. "Guerreterre and Chatterre were both colonized when Solterre's sun went nova." When everyone stared at her, she added, "It's all in the journals."

Nimri massaged her temple. "You're not a magical guardian?"

"Absolutely not." As if to prove it, he gave her a tender kiss. "Kazza might be, though." Dazed, Nimri stared first at Kazza then at Larwin.

"I'd always wondered what happened to the scientists," Thunder said. Thunder tickled her under the chin. "Kazza has been your partner and protector since you were born. His ancestors opened this side of the Star Bridge and bequeathed us this valley." He tilted his head as he looked at her. "Didn't you realize mystics need two or more for proper control of their power?"

"Is that why great-grandfather's temper brought lightening out of a clear blue sky?"

"Probably." Her brother shrugged. "Before she died, great-aunt Violet partnered with him."

"After she died his control did seem more erratic." Several odd memories fell into place. "That's why he tolerated her, even though I never thought he liked her." She frowned. "Did great-aunt Violet help him kill our parents?"

"I don't think so. From what I remember, the storm seemed more like a violent rage."

Thunder turned to Larwin and made a sweeping gesture, which encompassed the land. "Life on Chatterre is simple. Are you sure this is what you want?"

Nimri held her breath and waited for his answer. It took so long coming, she felt faint. Was it her imagination or was he caressing the Staff of Protection? Was it actually glowing?

"It has everything I ever dreamed of and a peace I never hoped for." Larwin gave her a smile hotter than a madrox.

Kazza's tail slapped Larwin across the shin.

"So that is why you sneaked over here in the dead of night." They all looked over their shoulders at the speaker.

Nimri narrowed her eyes, at the bedraggled man who was limping toward her. If it hadn't been for the fringe on his jacket, she'd never have recognized Chase. "You didn't run away, after all."

"I only needed to run faster than you, and you didn't run." He tilted his head. "I couldn't be letting you out of our agreement, now, could I?"

"What agreement?" Larwin asked, as he looked the dirty, torn and soggy man up and down.

"She knows," Chase said.

Nimri studied his face, wondering if he'd eaten since he'd left her on the trail. Wondered if he knew how unlikely his story sounded. Wondered how far he would go if she agreed to fulfill this one last pledge. "Are you certain that's what you want?"

He nodded emphatically.

She sighed, knowing that he must believe that Tansy loved him. Knowing how humiliating it would be for him to learn otherwise. "Fine. There's no better time than the present." Chase seemed surprised by her quick agreement. She gestured to the vapor cloud. "The heat is drying the river downstream, but it won't last for more than a few days."

He started jogging toward the debris-littered shore.

Larwin's fingers entwined with hers. "Do you think he will need your help?" He frowned. "Our help?"

"It wouldn't hurt." She paused and looked back at her brother. "Would you like to come, too?"

Thunder motioned toward the bluff. "I must find Gunda and Carn and see how badly the landslide damaged my home." He grimaced. "Later?"

Nimri nodded. "I'm going to hold you to that promise." Not wanting to leave him looking so alone, she jogged back and hugged him. "Be safe and if you ever need anything – even if you don't."

"I'll become such a pesky visitor you'll grow tired of me." He kissed her forehead.

"To peace," Larwin said. He stretched out his hand.

Thunder nodded. "To peace." Thunder placed his palm on top of Larwin's.

Nimri added her hand. Kazza placed his paw on top. To peace, she thought as she stared at the mist cloud shrouding the dragon.

At that moment, the dark clouds parted and a shaft of sunlight bathed them. The beam reflected across the river and painted the mist in rainbow hues as if promising lasting harmony.

The End

Other books by Jeanne Foguth

Sci-Fantasy - Kazza's Chatterre Trilogy

Star Bridge

Nimri, an herbal healer and Chatterer's new Keeper of the Peace, must safeguard her tribe from their bitter rivals. To do this, she must find her 'magic core'.

Many light years away, Colonel Larwin Atano, an elite Guerreterre Shadow Warrior, fights to save his intergalactic star-fighter. Despite all efforts, he crashes.

Larwin perceives Chatterre's resources as a means to gain power and prestige and views the planet's inhabitants as a minor inconvenience.

Nimri believes Larwin is a supernatural Guardian, who will protect her tribe from their rivals.

Who will survive the coming conflict?

Thunder Moon

Thunder Cartwright dreams that madrox will invade Chatterre and destroy his world unless the Star Bridge is closed.

Raine, a Kalamaran Dragon Shepard, must catch a rogue mooncalf and return it to the herd or face possible death.

Who will win and who will die?

Fire Island

Tem-aki Atano fell through a rift when the Star Bridge was destroyed and now must find a way to survive on an island which worships Fire Dragons.

Cameron must figure out a way to keep the dragons, which are hatching near an extinct volcano at his island's core, dormant, so that they do not destroy things, yet keep the faith alive.

But the beasts are hatching... will they destroy the island and everyone living on it?

Fantasy - Xander's Sea Purrtection Files

Latitudes & Cattitudes

~ a short & free prequel to The Sea Purrtector Files ~

Xander de Hunter is a rising star on Catamondo's kick-boxing circuit and dreams of becoming a Purrtector. After a match in Seattle, he is asked to help find Cha-Cha, a white Norwegian beauty, who is missing.

With Merlin's assistance, they follow Cha-Cha's trail into the Puget Sound where Xander must face his biggest fear – water.

The Red Claw

Dame Esmeralda, the Purrsident's littermate, has been catnapped. Xander de Hunter, Catamondo's Sea Purrtector hurries to Jamaica to help rescue her, even though Jamaica is one of Dogdom's strongholds.

Could this be a trap?

Purr-a-noia

Catamondo and Dogdom's peace treaty is in jeopardy. In Haiti, witchcraft and voodoo seem to be involved in a plot to hex the Purrsident.

Will Xander be able to restore the peace?

The Vi-Purrs (coming in 2016)

The Daily Mews reports continued violence in the Dominican Republic Purrtectorate.

Xander discovers that the Moreau situation is still affecting the ability of Catamondo to purrtect cats. Worse, the office of the Purrtectorate seems to be involved.

Will Xander be able to save the integrity of the Purrtectorate and restore peace?

Contemporary Suspense/Romance

Deadly Rumors

Kelsey MacLennan and Devlin Doran both want to make the world better.

Doran believes the rumors about the MacLennans dealing drugs, so his goal is to bring them down.

Will they be able to separate fact from fiction or will the rumors be deadly to them?

Fatal Attractions

Ariel and Tempest Danner have escaped Tempest's homicidal father for the sixth time in five years. Armed with new identities and disguises, they are determined that Fairbanks, Alaska will be a sanctuary where they can live in peace.

Stone O'Banyon, their new landlord, has been divorced for three years. All his energy is focused on his job and Dolly, who would never hurt him.

The last thing Ariel needs or wants is the attraction she feels for another tall, dark man, who seems hard as the granite he is named for, but the fascination will not go away. Stone isn't any happier with his obsessive thoughts concerning Ariel.

Things seem calm, then Ariel and Tempest catch sight of the man they had hoped they would never encounter and things turn fatal...again.

Passion's Fire

Prior to the blaze that killed her husband, Jacqueline Cardew believed her husband wrote the "fiery messages' she received. Now she finds a new note inside her locked house. Jacqueline suspects her faceless stalker murdered Adam and she is next. She flees north, where she joins Link Gavallan's group on a two week long Alaskan wilderness canoe trip. As they float down the desolate river, she receives another message...

Instead of finding a sanctuary, has she made it easier for the unknown person to trap her?

Connect with Jeanne Foguth

Visit her website:
> http://www.jeannefoguth.com

Subscribe to her blog for pet tips and humor:
> https://foguth.wordpress.com

Follow her on Twitter:
> http://twitter.com/jeannefoguth

Friend her on Facebook:
> https://www.facebook.com/jeannefoguth

www.ingramcontent.com/pod-product-compliance
Lightning Source LLC
Chambersburg PA
CBHW062110170626
46813CB00002B/384